Blue Moon Bay

Books by Lisa Wingate

MOSES LAKE

Larkspur Cove
Blue Moon Bay

DAILY, TEXAS

Talk of the Town
Word Gets Around
Never Say Never

TENDING ROSES

Tending Roses
Good Hope Road
The Language of Sycamores
Drenched in Light
A Thousand Voices

BLUE SKY HILL

A Month of Summer
The Summer Kitchen
Beyond Summer
Dandelion Summer

Blue Moon Bay

a novel

LISA WINGATE

BETHANY HOUSE PUBLISHERS

a division of Baker Publishing Group
Minneapolis, Minnesota

Published by Bethany House Publishers
11400 Hampshire Avenue South
Bloomington, Minnesota 55438
www.bethanyhouse.com

Bethany House Publishers is a division of
Baker Publishing Group, Grand Rapids, Michigan

Printed in the United States of America

Library of Congress Cataloging-in-Publication Data
Wingate, Lisa.
    Blue moon bay / Lisa Wingate.
        p.   cm.
    ISBN 978-0-7642-0822-5 (pbk.)
    1. Texas—Fiction. I. Title.
    PS3573.I53165B57 2012
    813'.54—dc23   2011040770

Unless otherwise indicated, Scripture quotations are from the King James Version of
the Bible.

Scripture quotation at the beginning of chapter 20 is from the Holy Bible, New International Version®. NIV®. Copyright © 1973, 1978, 1984, 2011 by Biblica, Inc.™ Used
by permission of Zondervan. All rights reserved worldwide. www.zondervan.com

The internet addresses, email addresses, and phone numbers in this book are accurate
at the time of publication. They are provided as a resource. Baker Publishing Group
does not endorse them or vouch for their content or permanence.

Cover design by Andrea Gjeldum

Author is represented by Sterling Lord Literistic

12   13   14   15   16   17   18   7   6   5   4   3   2   1

For Mary and Emily
And their awesome grandparents,
The Douglases

The future is a blank page, but not a mystery.

—*Tinker's riddle*
(Written on the wall of wisdom, Waterbird Bait
and Grocery, Moses Lake, Texas)

Chapter 1

Is it possible for nine months and three days of your life to haunt you forever? Can memories become like restless spirits—their long, thin fingers always reaching, and tugging, and grabbing? Their fingernails, in my case, would be some variation of floral pink and nicely manicured. Perfectly matched to a shade of lipstick and possibly a purse or some other accessory. Undoubtedly, this is not the norm for personal demons, but try telling them that. They won't listen, I promise.

There is no escape from those graceful Moses Lake ladies, with their embroidery-adorned pantsuits and their languid Southern drawls. When they whispered in my mind, their sentences rose and fell and rose again, filled with long vowels, padded and powdered with cheerfulness they couldn't possibly be feeling all the time. They became the stuff of my darkest recurrent nightmares—the kind that reprised the most awkward teenage years and found me wandering the halls of Moses Lake High School with no idea where I was supposed to go, suddenly aware that I'd arrived in my Pooh

Bear pajamas. Or even worse, I'd forgotten the pajamas altogether. Yet, somehow, I was just then noticing. . . .

Even from thousands of miles away, after the passage of season after season, the high school dream lingered, along with the feeling that somewhere in the tiny town of Moses Lake, Texas, the ladies were still talking about me. *Such an odd little thing,* they were saying, a purposeful twang morphing the last word into *tha-ang.* *All that eyeliner and that tacky, tacky purple lip gloss. Why, those black T-shirts didn't help her figure one little bit, I'm tellin' ye-ew. But how much can you expect, considerin' what happened?*

I wondered if their conversations turned darker, then—if the women whispered behind their hands about things I was never allowed to know. Did they debate theories or did they discuss facts as they sat at Lakeshore Community Church, making greeting cards or knitting scarves for orphans or boxing cans for the food pantry? Did they *know* what happened?

In my dreams, sometimes I was running toward a door. I heard the ladies on the other side, whispering amongst themselves. I recognized the door—large, white, with intricate molding. A double door. It was made to open inward, to allow the crowds to funnel through.

Then the door grew smaller, and it was a cellar door. It was plain and brown. There was a spider on a web in the corner. I reached for the handle.

I'd awaken in a sweat at that point, still hearing the echoes of the ladies chattering in the dusty corners of my mind.

Their voices found ways to carry into the daylight, sometimes. Occasionally, I heard them talking *to* me, those Moses Lake ladies. *Suga', now, sit up straight,* they'd admonish as I hunched over the table in some meeting, bleary-eyed while watching a computer render a building in 3-D from an electronic blueprint I'd been tweaking all night. *Oh, Heather, hon, put that foot down. A lady never crosses her legs at the knee. Darlin', don't swing your toe like that. Some boy might think you're a hussy. Mercy! Didn't your mama teach you any-thang?*

How, I wondered, is it possible for such a small part of your childhood to linger so persistently? Do we choose the ghosts that haunt us, or do they choose us? And if we choose them, shouldn't we be able to banish them?

The questions were scrolling through my head again as I sat in a meeting room, watching Mel generate a virtual walkthrough of a big-box retail store. He was explaining how customer traffic would flow, how the layout allowed for excellent point-of-sale potential. He laughed and said, "It's about capturing those impulse buys."

Leaning across the table, he inclined his head toward the Japanese contingent on the client side, as if he were sharing valuable trade secrets with them. "Of course, we all know that sixty-six percent of buying decisions are made in the store, and of those, fifty-three percent are pure impulse buys. Our research shows that with this layout, your percentages could increase to . . ." He paused, looked down at his notes, tapped the tabletop with his pencil.

I was only vaguely aware of the glitch in his presentation. I'd had the Moses Lake dream again last night. The past was floating in front of me like a cellophane overlay, scenes dripping and blending with the reflections from the conference room windows. It was raining outside again, typical for Seattle. Not the best weather for a critical presentation that could mean millions.

I'd dreamed all the way to putting my hand on the cellar doorknob last night. I'd curled up on a yoga mat behind my desk to catch a couple hours' sleep before the office came to life, and suddenly there were the doors. The white ones, then the brown one.

It had been a while since I'd seen the door. Maybe a year or more since I'd awakened with a start and moved through the day wondering what really happened at the bottom of those cellar steps.

"Heather, did you pull together the rest of that research?" Mel glanced my way expectantly, as if he hadn't already been given the numbers. My boss was slipping. Seven years ago, when I'd started at CTI, Mel was a lion.

"Sure. Of course." I flipped through the paperwork to save face for Mel. In reality, the numbers and I were on intimate terms. "The consumer research indicates a potential seventeen percent increase in impulse purchases, as compared with your existing stores. Considering that we're discussing stores that are already running at a brisk average of three hundred and fifty dollars in gross sales per square foot, that increase would be . . ." Mel caught my eye and gave me a look that warned me not to start running calculations in my head and spouting figures. This was *his* meeting. Letting the papers settle back into place, I finished with, "Significant, of course."

Mel took over again, but two of the principals were clearly more interested in hard facts than Mel's sales talk about *Environments that perform* and *brand iconography*. Mel was pushing hard, borderline desperate, but after seven years of paddling in the man's wake, I understood his nuances. It was hard to know how to feel, sitting there watching him struggle to revive the old magic. On the one hand, he had plucked me off the bottom rung of the ladder. On the other hand, every time I tried to climb the ladder, Mel's foot was squarely on my head. I wanted to move up, to eventually achieve what he had achieved—project leader, junior partner, partner. I'd never get there with Mel in the way.

My cell phone vibrated in my pocket. I slid it out and glanced while everyone was watching virtual customers move through checkout lanes. The customers started at a normal pace, then gradually sped up, buzzing by like bumblebees exiting a hive, having sacrificed nectar for shopping carts filled with fifty-three-plus-percent impulse buys. They were moving so fast, they never even knew what hit them.

The text message was from Richard. *Problem. Call me ASAP.*

The phone vibrated with an incoming call as I was tucking it away. Surely that wasn't Richard. He knew how long these meetings could take. One advantage of dating a guy who was in the real estate business was that he understood. When clients come to town, the clients come first.

I took a peek at the screen. I didn't recognize the number, but I knew the area code. 510. California. My mother, undoubtedly. Suddenly Richard's text message made sense.

My foot vibrated under the table as the meeting worked toward a close. When it was over, I gathered my files and politely excused myself from the room. Somehow, Mel and I ended up on the elevator together anyway.

"They left quickly." He leaned into the corner, his head falling against the wall as if he couldn't hold it up one more second.

"It was a long meeting." But we both knew what a quick exit usually meant. "They won't find a more comprehensive proposal than ours, though."

"Let's hope." His eyes slowly closed, like he was already trying to figure out how he'd survive if we didn't get this Itega contract.

The doors opened. Watching him there, crumpled against the wall, I felt the need to say something more. I held the doors open with the button, so as not to be ferried to the executive suites along with Mel.

"It's a good proposal," I offered. "We've got a slick design. Perfect fundamentals."

He didn't react.

Like a puppy, I stood there pathetically waiting for a pat on the head, for some acknowledgement of the countless hours I'd put into the proposal, of the devotion I'd given to managing all aspects of the design package. Finally, there wasn't much choice but to step through the door onto my floor. The one nicely above the designers in their Spartan cubicles and squarely below the posh executive level.

"What's going on with that thing in Texas?" Mel's question followed me.

I turned and pushed the button to open the doors again. "What?"

"The thing in Texas. The processing plant . . . Proxica Foods. What's happening with that?" Mel cracked an eye open. "*Your* project." Was it my imagination, or did the emphasis on *your* come with an underlay of resentment—an insinuation that I was overstepping my bounds by insisting that, if I could bring this project in, I would be the project leader.

"Everything seems to be right on target. The principals at Proxica are happy with the design concept. The property deals are in the final stages. They're looking at a state-of-the-art processing plant and eight corporately-owned production farms—six for poultry and two for grain crops." The phone message from Richard crossed my mind, and an uncomfortable sensation settled underneath my favorite blue blazer. The biggest event in my career, and I was banking on something that involved my mother. . . .

Mel's lips pursed, smacking slightly, as if he were tasting the potential of the deal. Maybe now that the Itega bid had soured a bit, Mel was looking to take over my Texas project. Would he really do that?

"Keep me apprised," he said, rubbing his chest as I exited the elevator.

"Aye-aye, Cap'n." The words were a thin attempt at lightness.

The second the elevator doors closed, I raced toward my office, muttering to myself and thinking of the Texas deal and my mother.

A pair of interns, chatting as they ferried mailing tubes, stopped talking and sidled to the wall as I passed, clutching the tubes like Roman shields. I had the momentary pang of regret that comes from knowing someone finds you humorless and slightly frightening, but it quickly passed. Interns rotated through the firm constantly. If they were here to learn architecture and design in the real world, they might as well see how things really were. No point filling them with the warm fuzzies. It was a long, hard climb before you got to take on a project of your own. Those fresh-faced college kids were better off seeing the truth now and then deciding how badly they wanted it.

I dialed Richard's number while rounding the corner into my office. "Hey, what's up?" I asked, an odd little singsong in my voice. Maybe I just felt the need to be girly and cute, so as not to send him scurrying, like the interns. In the dating world, intimidation is not considered a desirable quality. Normal men tended to see me as slightly work-obsessed and hyperfocused. Or, as my friend and former roommate, Trish, liked to put it, *married to my iPhone.*

But Richard was as normal as they came. Normal and successful, and he liked me. He didn't have a string of failed marriages behind him, and he was with a respectable law firm. An especially rare find among the over-thirty set, where pickings became slim.

He sighed, and I knew the news was not good. I loved him for hesitating a minute, as if he felt the need to break it to me gently. In general, Richard hated conflict, which was probably why he was in real estate law and not prosecuting murder cases. "Well, I know you said she was unpredictable, but . . ."

I didn't even wait for him to drag through the rest of the sentence.

"What happened? Did she sign the offer?" Poor Richard. I should never have brought him into this. My mother was probably lighting incense in his office, hanging crystals, or reciting dark, dramatic, obscure poetry by some writer only English professors had heard of.

"She's not here. Not coming . . . Well, not today, anyway."

"What?" My voice echoed into the corridor, and I closed the office door, keeping the conversation inside. No one knew about the Texas project except Mel, Richard, and the commercial broker who was quietly shopping for land he would then resell to Proxica for their new facilities. Proxica had insisted that their expansion plans be kept confidential. Strange things happen when communities find out that a company with deep pockets is sniffing around.

"You've *got* to be kidding."

"I wish I were." Richard sounded frustrated, tired, and uncharacteristically irritable. He'd put in countless extra hours on this real estate deal and managed to get my family an offer of more than the property was worth. He'd sorted out the convoluted deeds for the land that had been in my father's family since just after the Civil War. Once the property was in Proxica's possession and the feasibility studies were finished, my part of the project came in—designing Proxica's new flagship facility, where big pieces of raw meat would become little pieces of cooked meat, neatly sliced and packaged in deli bags for people like me, who don't like to think about where meat actually comes from.

"Where is she?" *Within reach,* I wished. If my mother were within reach, I would . . . I would . . . What? What, exactly, would I do? Talking to my mother was like talking to one of those gauzy, diaphanous scarves the street vendors sell in India. Anything I said would go right through, my breath barely creating a ripple in the fabric.

"In Texas, apparently." I could hear Richard typing on his computer as he replied.

14

"In *Texas*? Why?" My mother hated Texas—especially Moses Lake and the portion of the family farm that had passed into her hands after my father's death. "Is Uncle Herbert all right? Uncle Charley?" A mental scenario materialized in which my dad's uncles had driven to the family farm, fifteen miles outside Moses Lake, and were holed up with shotguns in hand. Even though they both now lived at Uncle Herbert's place in town, they had grown up on the farm and were still sentimental about it.

"As far as I know, your uncles are fine. Your mother is down there with them, apparently. She said they are 'talking about some things.'"

"What things?" Inside my brain, I heard the high-pitched whistling sound of a pressure cooker about to blow. No wonder Richard was irritated. He'd worked so hard to convince the broker to take not only the farm property, but to make a package bid for my uncles' other properties, as well. Altogether, they owned four plots of land and two businesses. Uncle Herbert ran the Harmony Shores Funeral Home in town, and Uncle Charley was famous for the fried catfish at his floating restaurant, Catfish Charley's.

Now that both of my great uncles were in their eighties, the family farmland and businesses had to go. That was all there was to it. Uncle Herbert and Uncle Charley had made plans to relocate to Oklahoma to be near Uncle Herbert's son Donny and his progeny. Selling the property all at once would allow them to leave Moses Lake behind in one clean sweep.

Why had my mom suddenly decided to swirl her big toe in the pool, muddying the waters? She couldn't possibly have gotten wind of Proxica's plans to acquire the farm property, and quite frankly, I couldn't imagine why she would care. She'd hated Moses Lake even before we lived there, and she never wanted to see it again after we left. If my father's portion of the family farm hadn't been

15

squarely landlocked between Uncle Herbert's portion and Uncle Charley's, it would have been gone shortly after my dad's passing sixteen years ago. Now the old dairy farm would be quietly recommissioned as a Proxica location, I would get my first design project, and the town of Moses Lake would see sorely needed new jobs. It was a win-win, if you didn't count the fact that everything hinged on my mother's cooperation.

"I'll call and talk to her about it," I said, and then apologized profusely to Richard, privately admiring his composure. He was accustomed to issues like this. I'd met him while testifying as an expert witness in a case. He was a lawyer for the opposition. My side won. He didn't hold it against me, fortunately.

"I'll take care of it. I'll have her here tomorrow." My words brought on that feeling you get on your first ski trip when you realize you've accidentally turned onto a double black diamond slope.

"The drop-dead date is eight days away. The broker offer expires February fifteenth."

February fifteenth. February fifteenth . . .

The day after Valentine's Day. Valentine's Day was a week away, and Richard and I hadn't even talked about it? That was odd, considering that Richard was a planner, and in Seattle, restaurant reservations on Valentine's Day were a must. Maybe this little silence wasn't purely accidental. Maybe Richard had something special in mind, a surprise.

Could there be a certain little trinket attached to the hush-hush Valentine's Day . . . maybe something that comes in a little ring-sized box? We'd been dating six months. Having turned thirty-four last month, alone in my apartment with a cat that wasn't even my own, I was feeling the nudge. Richard was six years older than me, ready to find someone and settle down. He'd said so sometime early in our relationship. It was one of the things I liked about him. Neither of us had time to play the games that went with dating.

I found myself staring out the window, idly picturing an upscale apartment, two kids. . . . Would they have dark hair like Richard's, or auburn hair like mine? My caramel-brown eyes, or Richard's gray ones? Short and stocky, like Richard's family, or lanky like mine? Wavy hair like mine, or straight hair like Richard's? They'd be good at math. Both Richard and I were good with numbers. . . .

I realized he was waiting for me to reply on the broker issue. "So the offer expires the day after Valentine's Day, then, right?" *Hint, hint.*

He didn't pick up on the nuance, unfortunately. "Yes. Right. February fifteenth."

"Got it." First things first. Right now both of us were focused on the property deal. Between all the confusion about easements, ancient surveys, and my mother's failure to update the deed after my father's death, we'd come way too close to letting the offer expire.

I took a deep breath, then exhaled. "Don't worry." Which, of course, is what people say when they are worried. "If I have to go down there and drag my mother back here myself, I'll do it." The words held the false bravado of a schoolyard bully who's really afraid to fight. The last, last, last part of my life I ever planned to revisit was that terrible high-school year in Moses Lake. I'd shaken off the Texas dust sixteen years ago, and nothing short of the apocalypse would ever drag me back there again.

Truths are first clouds; then rain, then harvest and food.

—Henry Ward Beecher
*(Left on the wall of wisdom by Andrea Henderson, new Moses
Lake resident, and Mart McClendon, local game warden)*

Chapter 2

Famous last words—nothing like planning a last-minute trip to Texas to make you eat them. One should never underestimate the power of twisted family ties and well-meaning church ladies bearing casseroles. Apparently, the Moses Lake ladies had discovered my mother at Uncle Herbert's place, and they'd pulled out the frozen funeral casseroles and the slice-and-bake cookies. They had shown up at Harmony Shores armed with food, ostensibly because widowed men like my uncles shouldn't be trying to cook for company. In reality, of course, they were there to figure out what, exactly, was going on at the former funeral home, and in what way it involved the town's ex-pariah, my mother.

The story, as my mother related it on the phone, grew more bizarre from there. Apparently she'd flown in on a whim, after arranging for a graduate assistant to cover her classes. It sounded like she'd been in Moses Lake overnight with the *uncs* (suddenly she was using the family pet name for my great uncles, to whom she had never given the time of day before). I wanted to ask her what she was thinking, taking off for Texas the day before she was supposed to be in Seattle. But trying to understand her thought processes was like contemplating infinity. It tied your brain in small, painful knots. Her actions were typically based on vague feelings, a sense of karma, or the advice of some spiritual advisor she'd met on the Internet.

When I called, she was walking along the lakeshore, " . . . just thinking," she said, as I rummaged around my office, stacking the Itega files all in one place, just in case I had to fly out of town to round up my mother. "Uncle Herbert found some boxes in his basement that were ours. Apparently, they've been stored here all this time. I wanted a few days to check it out, and then there's the estate sale issue. It's not easy for the uncs, having so many memories tied to the place. . . ."

She trailed off, and I thought we had a dropped connection, but then she started talking to someone who was there with her. I gathered that the pastor from Lakeshore Community Church had just dropped by to say hello and to pass along the phone number of a mortician who might want to buy the surplus caskets, casket stands, skirts, and various other funeral equipment in Uncle Herbert's basement.

"But . . . I thought all of that had been cleaned out. Uncle Herbert and Uncle Charley are supposed to be moving this week." *Right after the papers are signed.* It was a sad fact of this entire process that Uncle Herbert and Uncle Charley had to relocate closer to younger members of the family. They seemed to be handling it well enough, though, and as people age, difficult decisions have to be made. I needed to get my mother out of there before Uncle Herbert's son Donny found out she was meddling and a family war ensued. Donny and my mother had practically come to blows over the Moses Lake property numerous times in the past.

"Listen, Mother, the plans have already been made. You said you didn't want to handle your portion of the paperwork via fax, so Richard made arrangements for you to do it here, in person. He waited all morning for you to show. I don't understand why you're holding things up. You know that Uncle Herbert and Uncle Charley need the money, and you know they can't stay in Moses Lake by themselves any longer. You're just making things harder for everyone."

"Oh, they're fine. We played Chicken Foot last night." As usual, Mother was floating around somewhere in the fluffy cumulus nimbi. She sounded alarmingly relaxed. Not at all like someone about to head for the airport. "They're enjoying the casseroles. We've been writing down a few of the family stories, even."

"You're doing *what*?" The last thing we needed was everyone hanging around the funeral home, waxing nostalgic about the good ol' days. "What do you mean, you're playing dominoes? There's supposed to be almost nothing left in the house, and . . ."

I was momentarily at a loss for words. I imagined my mother camped out with my uncles in the massive Greek Revival house, where back in the day, you could turn a blind corner and unwittingly bump into coffin stands and body boards. My mother hated Uncle Herbert's place on Harmony Cove as much as she hated everything else about Moses Lake, which was why she'd fought like a banshee when my father had been offered the opportunity to supervise the construction and implementation of the Proxica plant upriver from Moses Lake, near the little Mennonite town of Gnadenfeld.

Mom had finally given in and let my dad accept the transfer—but only because my grandmother was in a nursing home, in the final weeks of her life, and my grandfather had been diagnosed with congestive heart failure. My dad was needed in Moses Lake, and so we picked up our lives and went. For me, a math-and-art-class-loving chick accustomed to a big-city high school in Philadelphia, it seemed like the end of the world. I'd long since lost interest in going with my father on his cross-country trips to visit his family in Texas, and all of a sudden I was being told I'd have to spend my senior year of high school and graduate from tiny, podunk Moses Lake High. I hated my father for subjecting me to such a hideous reality. I made sure to communicate that in every selfish, immature way I could.

Sometimes, life turns upside down, and you never get the chance to say you're sorry.

"Listen, the offer on the property expires next week." I pointed out.

"I know," Mom answered, and I wondered at the strange, melancholy rhythm of her voice. Was Moses Lake wrapping its watery veil around her again, dragging her down the way it had in the months after my father's death? "So there's not any rush, really."

"Except that Richard did a ton of the work on the deeds as a favor to me, and he was expecting you today."

Mom exhaled. "Oh, Heather, men are always doing you favors. They love to do favors for you. It makes them feel like they might have a chance of cracking that shell."

"Richard is different." I refused to slide into yet another relationship conversation with my mother. I really did. She was the one with men bobbing in and out of her life like horses on a carousel. She was always holding court—discussing art, or literature, or theater with men from grad-student age on up to those with full professorships. She'd been in and out of love more times than I could count, the only constant being instability.

Just as she was working up what, undoubtedly, would have been some critical analysis of Richard, formed during their limited phone and email conversations over the real estate deal, I heard laughter in the background. A man's laugh. A familiar laugh.

"Mom, who's there with you?" My mind raced through the connections. My mother wasn't in Moses Lake alone. "Is Clay there? Is that Clay?"

Mom didn't have to answer. Suddenly the trip to Moses Lake made some sense.

Clay was there. He'd found out about the sale of the property and seen fit to involve himself, and now he was in Moses Lake, hanging out and giving Mom advice. My stomach clenched at the thought. Clay's involvement in the deal could be a game changer, and not in any good way. My little brother had been floating idly through college and law school for a decade, while taking occasional breaks to climb Mount Hood, or get his scuba-diving certification, or spend a semester in some tiny South American country, working with an earthquake relief team. So far, Clay seemed perfectly happy to move at his own aimless, relaxed pace, while Mother contributed financial support from the nest egg left behind by our dad's life insurance policy. At twenty-seven, Clay didn't seem in any rush to take care of himself.

"I'm coming down there," I said, but the show of bravado was intended only to make my mother snap to her senses. Surely she knew that Moses Lake, in terms of emotional stability, wasn't the best place for her to spend time. "Really, Mother. It isn't good for you to be there. What could you possibly be hoping to accomplish?"

"Maybe putting some ghosts to rest." Suddenly the lightness was gone from her tone. She sounded gravely serious. "They don't just go away on their own, you know."

A sick feeling leeched from the pit of my stomach, darkness spreading over me like a splash of ink. How was it that she could still do this to me? It was as if she knew where the painful spots were, and she could probe them whenever she wanted. "I'll be there tomorrow. I'll help you ship whatever boxes you want to ship, and then we're coming back here and doing the deal as planned."

A long pause left me hearing my own pulse thrumming, and then she finally answered, "Well, if you must know, there's another offer we want to look at, Heather. There's really nothing you can do here. I'll call you in a day or two."

My insides were rolling now, my mind whirling ahead. "What offer? An offer from whom?" There was no way that could be true. No one else was going to come along and pay the price the broker was offering.

"I really can't explain it all. . . ."

"I'll be there in the morning." Rubbing the ache in my forehead, I tried to think through the details. It was Wednesday. I could tell Mel I needed a couple personal days to see to the family matters related to the land sale. Mel wouldn't be happy about it, as *personal* wasn't really in his vocabulary, but I had enough unused vacation stacked up to last me until spring.

I mentally fast-forwarded through the Mel confrontation, then considered the practicalities. I'd have to book a flight, arrange for a rental car, look at a map, and figure out the route from the airport to Moses Lake. It would probably be easier to fly to Dallas and drive from there, rather than taking a commuter flight to Waco. . . .

"You're not bringing Richard along, are you?" Mother's question collided with my thoughts like an asteroid, leaving a fiery trail. Why would she care whether Richard was coming along? Unless . . . Unless she'd already made up her mind to bug out on the land sale, and she was afraid I might use Richard to try to strong-arm her into it. Maybe my brother was giving her some sort of amateur legal advice. Exactly how far had Clay gotten in law school before his last side trip on the highway of life?

The question nagged and nipped as I reiterated that I was coming down there to straighten things out, then said good-bye.

Within an hour and a half, I'd cleared my impending absence with Mel, booked a flight, returned to my apartment, and thrown together a carry-on bag.

I ran into Trish as I was lugging my carryon and laptop case down the stairs. She was ferrying a pizza box to the three-bedroom unit she'd moved into after she fell in love with the guy down the hall and got married. Now she was on the fast track to family life, having had three kids in four years. Since she'd given up ergonomic building design for mommyhood, we had most of our conversations in the stairwell at odd hours.

"Whoa, where are you headed?" she asked, holding the pizza like a platter.

"Texas," I grumbled, feeling pathetic and like I needed someone to feel sorry for me. I would never have let anyone see that but Trish. We'd met while working long hours at our first jobs out of college. She'd ridden the merry-go-round of family issues with me before.

Leaning against the stairway railing, she rested the pizza on the banister. "Your mom didn't show, huh?"

"Of course not." I gripped my forehead. I already had a headache, and my mother was still hundreds of miles away.

"I don't know when you're going to learn not to expect anything from her." She punctuated the sentence with a disgusted smack. "Can I do anything for you while you're gone? Want me to water your plant?"

"I've already killed the plant. I watered it. Really. I mean . . . I think I watered it."

Trish rolled her eyes and opened the pizza box. "Here, take a slice of pizza, so you don't end up like the plant."

I thanked her, we hugged good-bye, and I transported myself to a flight bound for Texas, by way of several irritating layovers. Oddly enough, I didn't even think of calling Richard until I was high in the skies over Idaho. I dialed his number during a layover in Denver. He took the news well, which actually disappointed me a little. I was tired, frustrated, and irritated, and I suppose I wanted him to get manly and protective, maybe tell me it was brave of me to try to deal with this alone but he was hopping the next flight out.

Then again, why would he? Richard had no idea of the history that lay in Moses Lake because I'd never told him. No one in Seattle knew, except Trish. The best thing about living halfway across the country from the past you'd like to forget is that you're not obligated to reveal it to anyone. You really can leave it all behind. As far as Richard knew, Moses Lake was just an ancestral family place to which I had little attachment, sentimental or otherwise.

"I have a boatload of work to catch up on this weekend, anyway." Richard's words brought another unexpected letdown—as if I were dangling over a cliff, sinking a little lower and a little lower as he let out the rope. Maybe it was the whole Texas thing, but I was feeling uncharacteristically needy. The sensation was foreign and unwelcome.

I cradled the phone on my shoulder, juggling my laptop, purse, and carryon as I took a seat at the gate for my next flight. Outside the window, a Colorado moon shone on new-fallen snow. I wanted to walk out the door, catch a cab, and head for the mountains—lose myself in their cottony peaks and have a vacation. "I know. I'm sorry my mom wasted your time today. It's her world, and we're just living in it."

Richard chuckled, and I fell into the warm sound of it. He had such a nice laugh. "I like your mother. She's . . . artsy. A free spirit."

I was momentarily silenced. *I like your mother?* Traitor. "Thanks for being so nice about it." He wouldn't like her if he knew her better, would he?

"It's fine, really. I can understand her attachment to the family home."

He could? Richard understood my mother? "It isn't even her hometown. It was my father's. She never wanted to spend time there when I was a kid. She and my grandmother hated each other." I sounded like a harpy, like one of those bitter family members on Dr. Phil.

"Well, you know, the older people get, the more sentimental they feel about things. They have that sense of time slipping away."

I blinked, watching snowflakes swirl in the pocket of protected space near the Jetway. This didn't sound like Richard at all. "Are you okay?" I leaned away as a guy in a rumpled business suit took a seat next to me.

"Yeah, it's the birthday thing, I think."

Birthday . . . Oh, smack, I'd forgotten all about Richard's birthday. Friday. The day after tomorrow. Forty. Six years older than me. We'd talked about it, like, a month ago while watching the waiters at Chili's bring out a birthday cake and sing to an embarrassed customer. Richard made me promise I wouldn't take him anyplace with singing waiters on his birthday.

"Ohhh, your birthday. I'm sorry. I should be there. If I didn't have to get to Texas and straighten out this family thing, I'd turn around and fly right back." Forty had to be hard. I was glad I was a long way from forty.

"It's all right."

"No it's not." In all the talk back and forth about the land deal this week, I hadn't even mentioned his birthday. Because I hadn't thought about it. "I'm a really bad girlfriend." A flight attendant moved to the microphone behind the service desk, and a line began to form in anticipation of boarding. I stood up, grabbing my things.

"You're just you, Heather." There was a flat quality to his voice, a matter-of-factness, like *The grass is green* or *The air is invisible*.

It stopped me where I was.

The flight attendant announced that due to wind sheers associated with a storm moving over the mountains, all flights had been delayed.

I sank down in my chair. *Is that me? The girl who forgets people's birthdays and kills houseplants, and it doesn't even surprise anyone? They just expect it?*

26

Plans flashed through my mind—a tidy little suitcase of them that I'd been unpacking during these past months with Richard. Richard and I had a lot in common. We got along well. We were both nearing that age where it seemed like it was time to . . . well . . . fish or cut bait, as the uncs in Moses Lake would have said. Not having settled down hadn't bothered me in my twenties, but at thirty-four, you feel the fork in the road coming on. . . .

Some of our conversations had clued me into the fact Richard felt the same way. Maybe that was the reason for the melancholy sound in his voice when he mentioned the birthday. I wanted to believe it was, but really, I was afraid that I was the cause. Who wants to be dating the girl who takes off for another state right before your birthday and doesn't even realize it?

"Well, listen, I'd better let you go," he said, and I felt myself sinking lower.

Don't, I wanted to say, *Don't let me go*. But the words felt too vulnerable, too raw. I'd never been good at hanging my heart on my sleeve. But this was where so many relationships ended—with the old, *You're an amazing person, but we just want different things* conversation. Sometimes I was on the delivering end of that line, sometimes on the receiving end.

"Hey, Valentine's Day is next week." As soon as I said it, I felt pathetic, like I was pushing—fishing to see if he had something planned. The ring box I'd been contemplating earlier suddenly seemed miles away. "We could do dinner at the Waterfront Grill, take a walk through the sculpture park if the weather's all right."

"Let's talk about it when you get home. I haven't really thought that far ahead."

Let's talk about it when you get home? That wasn't the response I wanted, not at all what I expected.

Or was it? Maybe I'd been feeling the cooling air around us for a while—like evening setting in, but when you're busy, you don't notice. Then you look up, and suddenly it's almost dark. Chilly. Was that why I was trying to superimpose visions of a Valentine's surprise—because I was afraid yet another relationship was dying for lack of regular watering and feeding? "Oh . . . okay. We can figure it out when I get back."

"Have a good trip, Heather."

"Richard, are we okay?" As soon as the words were out, I wanted to stuff them back in. What was wrong with me tonight?

His hesitation was an answer, even if it wasn't. "Let's talk when you get home."

A wound, raw and deep, cracked open. On an architectural rendering, it would have been on Layer 1—the layer upon which everything else is built. "I'm sorry I asked." The words were bitter, hard-edged. "But you could have just told me . . . if there was a problem with you and me. You didn't have to pretend."

He sighed. I pictured him leaning forward, his short, thick fingers wrapped over his forehead, rubbing, trying to drum up the right words, trying to avoid a confrontation. "Listen, I know you've had a lot going on with all the family and the property sale. I didn't want to add any more . . . stress."

"I'm fine," I said. "It's fine." But, really, my head was ringing like I'd just had a hard right cross to the jaw. The fact that he was trying to be kind about it only made it worse. Is a gentle smack in the head better than the abrupt kind? It's still a smack in the head. "It's not like we were engaged or anything, Richard. We were just dating, right? It's not like there was any commitment."

He didn't answer at first. Clearly, I'd shocked him by being so blunt, but it was like a knee-jerk reaction, impossible to control. It's so much easier to reject than to be rejected.

28

LISA WINGATE

"Sure," he said, and he sounded like I'd disappointed him in some way.

"I'd better go, okay? It's time to board my flight." It wasn't, but the rip inside me was widening. The only thing to do now was pull it back together before anyone saw.

We said good night, leaving things strangely open-ended, and I dropped the phone into my purse. Beside me, the guy in the business suit ventured a sympathetic glance. He'd heard the relationship drama, of course. He looked like he might be conversational, and there was a dangly fish-shaped luggage tag—the Christian kind—on his carry-on bag, so I grabbed my things, headed for the bathroom across the hall, and locked myself in a stall. The last thing I wanted at that moment was well-intentioned counseling— spiritual or any other sort. I just needed . . . a few minutes alone.

To figure out why.

I could never get.

This one thing.

Right.

After twenty minutes of standing with my back to the stall door and my eyes closed, I still didn't have the answer—what's the likelihood of a profound personal discovery happening in an airport restroom, anyway—but I had pulled myself together. After all, Richard hadn't exactly said we were breaking up. He'd just said we needed to talk, and then he hadn't argued with what I'd said.

I went back to the waiting area by my gate and took a seat along the windows, away from the man with the Jesus tag on his luggage. He looked my way a couple times, but I just leaned my head back against the metal frame and closed my eyes, letting the cold of the Denver night seep through my body as the stewardess announced an indefinite delay.

Be not forgetful to entertain strangers;
For thereby some have entertained angels unaware.
—Hebrews 13:2
(Left by Ruth, who's seen the proof)

Chapter 3

Greyhound isn't so bad . . . until you've been on one for sixteen hours, driving through the plains of West Texas in blinding snow. What idiotic notion had possessed me to climb into a taxi with the Jesus-tag man—Gary from Fort Worth, dentist, two kids, married twenty-nine years—to head to the Greyhound station, I couldn't say. He'd awakened me when all flights were canceled, an extremely kind thing to do.

"Hated to just walk off and leave you here sleeping." The slow Southern cadence of his words had comingled strangely with the fact that I was on my way to Texas, creating the feeling that I'd arrived there already. "Heard you say you had to get to Texas. No more flights going out tonight, and who knows what the backlog'll look like tomorrow? By morning, they could be socked in here for days." He'd smiled, his round face friendly, welcoming, sympathetic. "Greyhound's still moving, if you want to take a chance on it. I'm headed to the station. Tomorrow's my thirtieth anniversary, and I'm gonna be there if I have to walk in on snowshoes."

There's something irresistible about a guy who would combine snowshoes with a business suit and walk through an impending blizzard to get home for his anniversary. I grabbed my stuff, and within minutes Gary from Fort Worth and I were partners on a journey of a thousand miles—the kind that binds you together like two tourists clinging to the same tree as a tsunami washes through.

By the time we reached Fort Worth, I knew all about Gary. Fortunately, he was a talker, so I didn't have to be. He owned a chain of family dental clinics that was expanding through Texas and the Deep South. He was interested in learning about how ergonomic design might make his clinics more efficient. I gave him my card, even though, honestly, his project didn't require a fully-integrated solutions firm like ours. Any licensed architect with an office in the back of a mini-mall could handle it. He asked where I was going; I told him. He knew about Moses Lake. He'd been there for a conference at the resort just past the dam. Small world. Amazing coincidence, if you believe in coincidences.

Gary's wife and teenage daughters were there to greet him when we reached the Greyhound station in downtown Dallas. Seeming completely oblivious to the cast of strange characters that typically inhabit a downtown bus station, Gary introduced me, and all three of his best gals hugged me. Theirs was probably the warmest welcome I'd get in Texas. Things would not go so well for me in Moses Lake, I felt certain. I found myself taking in Gary's family reunion like Scrooge watching the Cratchit family Christmas through the window.

Finally, I stepped back and blinked the bus station into focus, trying to ignore the creepy sensation that it was not the safest place to be on my own. The sooner I was out of there, the better. I'd have to find my way to a cab and then a rental car place, but really, I wanted to be where Gary was, turning the details and the luggage over to take-charge family members.

I leaned close to one of his daughters. "Tell your dad thanks for the help, all right? Tell him he's got my card, if he wants to get in touch about the dental clinics."

"Sure," the girl, Kylee, looked up from texting on her cell phone, and smiled. "Have a nice vacation."

"Thanks." Juggling my stuff, I went to get a cab. In short order, I was loaded up and ready to go—until the cab rolled away from the curb, and I reached for my purse to see how I was fixed for cash, and there was no purse on the seat. I picked up my coat, my laptop bag. Nothing. Panic swirled through my tired brain, lighting up circuits that had been lazily flickering a moment before.

My purse! My purse! Where was my purse?

"Wait!" I screamed. Where? When had I seen it last? I remembered looking at my cell phone as we pulled into Dallas, wishing there would be a text from Richard. . . .

The bus! It's on the bus! While I was gathering my belongings with Gary, sharing the euphoria of having survived our trip, I'd left the efficient-but-fashionable little Dolce purse tucked between my seat and the wall.

My money, my iPhone, ID, credit cards, everything. . . .

"Take me back to the bus station," I gasped. And as soon as we'd made it to the curb out front, I threw open the cab door, abandoned my stuff, and ran down the sidewalk. One peek around the corner confirmed that the bus was gone. My identity was headed to Texarkana . . . or possibly to some shady computer lab in Russia or Nigeria by now.

My mind whirled as I ran back around the corner to the cab, begged the driver to wait with my things for a moment, then burst into the lobby and scanned the crowd for Gary and family. But they'd moved on. Outside, the cabbie was unloading my stuff on the curb, and a couple of bystanders in soiled overcoats were already checking out the spoils. I hurried out and laid claim before anything else could disappear, and then headed back inside, trailing two homeless guys, one of whom told me I was a dead ringer for Julia Roberts.

Despite assurances that I wasn't Julia, he called me Julia and insisted on aiding me in finding my way to an official bus station employee, who could help me. He and his friend stood guard while the counter clerk called the bus, now en route to east Texas. My purse was nowhere to be found.

A desperate search of my pockets failed to turn up any folding money for phone calls, but who would I call anyway? All of my numbers were stored in my iPhone, which was who-knew-where at that moment. My fingers settled on something cardboard, and I knew what it was before I pulled it out. Gary's card.

Oh, thank God. The thought came with an echo of surprise. I'd long since given up attributing much in my life to divine intervention, but right now, the fact that I'd stuck the card in my pocket instead of my purse seemed like a miracle.

The clerk had pity on me and let me use her cell phone, and in short order, my new friends, Harley and Doyle, were walking me to the curb and helping to load my suitcases into Gary's wife's Lexus. Gary thanked them and gave them each five bucks to go buy some lunch. Noticing that Doyle's teeth were in bad shape, Gary dug through the door pocket of the car and produced a brochure for a mobile cost-free dental program, which Gary's clinics helped to support. Doyle stuck the brochure in his ragged coat, shook Gary's hand, offered a blessing my way, and pronounced this to be an example of the mysterious workings of the Lord.

I left the Dallas bus station, sandwiched in the backseat with Gary's daughters, Kylee and Grace, all three of us waving good-bye to Harley and Doyle. There was an odd, tender feeling in the pit of my stomach, and Doyle's broken smile lingered in my mind as we rolled out of downtown. Despite my lack of confidence in divine intervention, I couldn't help thinking that if not for a snowstorm, a bus ride, a lost purse, an impatient cabbie, and a business card haphazardly tucked in my pocket, Doyle might never have found out where to get new teeth. Occasionally, luck and coincidence doesn't explain things as well as you'd like.

After a short conversation, during which I was unable to come up with any good option as to where Gary and his family could drop me off, they made it clear that, no matter what I suggested—the mall, a hotel, a bank location where I could attempt to gain access to my accounts—they were not about to abandon me in a strange town with no money, no phone, and no ID. They would be driving me all the way to Moses Lake. Everyone was surprisingly cheerful about it, and I determined this to be the kind of thing that happened often. Perhaps it was the kindly look of Gary and his family, or the skill that dentists develop for carrying on one-way conversations with unhappy clients, but they were like the Griswolds of mercy meet-ups.

I borrowed Grace's cell phone and called Trish—one of the few numbers lodged in my memory—so she could take the emergency file from my apartment and call my credit card companies and my bank. I didn't even bother to tell her the whole story. I was too tired to repeat it, and Trish's kids were screaming in the background. "Sorry it's such a disaster so far. Just call me if you need anything else," she said, and we hung up.

As we rolled southward under a cloudless Texas sky, sharing takeout food on the way, Gary's family entertained me with stories of past family vacations buffeted off course—or *blessed,* as they put it—by strangers in need. The day outside was clear and perfect, the sky painted with the long white strokes of winter clouds. I found myself oddly taken in as the countryside slowly changed

LISA WINGATE

from rolling plains to hills dotted with live oaks, their green boughs stretching heavy and thick over amber tufts of last year's grass. Here and there, we passed fields where cattle grazed happily on expanses of winter wheat, the lively green pastures and frolicking calves seeming to promise that the startling color bursts of a Texas spring were right around the corner.

I leaned against the window, my mind traveling back in time. I was curled up in the backseat of my father's car, gazing out as wildflowers drifted by like spatters of paint on a bright green canvas—the deep azure of bluebonnets, the bright red-orange of Indian paintbrush, the purple of wild phlox, the yellow and crimson pinwheels of Indian blankets, the pale pink and white of primrose. Beside me, my little brother was asleep. Up front, Dad was driving and Mom was popping a new cassette tape into the player.

We were headed off on one of the trips Dad lovingly called Sunday-ventures. Those trips always occurred after church, which we attended only when my father was not away on business. Generally, following the service, we would pick up my mother at home, and then there was no telling where we'd end up. Sometimes Dad was checking on a Proxica facility, or doing an inspection on a locker storage plant, or taking a look at one of Proxica's massive farms, where rural families raised turkeys, chickens, hogs, and various produce to fulfill Proxica contracts.

Many of those trips took us far into the country, where Dad spied tractors or cattle in the field and told us stories of his childhood on the family farm in Moses Lake. Along the way, Mom would talk him into stopping so she could climb rocks, hike off down a state-park trail, photograph buildings in some derelict small town, or sit in a stranger's cow pasture, writing in one of her ever-present journals. I never worried about how long she would be gone when she disappeared into the woods. I knew that my father would be

35

there taking care of us, making a game of her flighty, unpredictable nature.

Of all the things I remembered about him, that one was foremost in my mind. He was a really great dad.

My eyes fell closed as I drifted between a dream and reality, between Gary's car and my father's. Finally, all of it faded away, and the long Greyhound bus ride caught up with me.

"We're here! Wake up, Heather!" My father's voice probed the darkness, and pulled me away. I snapped upright, smelled water and cedar and the chalky scent of wet limestone.

Outside the window, a sign was passing by. It was old, made of earthy, weathered wood suspended between rock pillars. The etched letters had been newly-tinted with gold paint, seeming incongruous against the burnt umber background.

Welcome to Moses Lake
If you're lucky enough to be at the lake, you're lucky enough!

"Hear that, kids?" My father's voice echoed through the interior of the car. "We just hit it lucky. Anybody bring a swimsuit?"

He laughed, and my mind stumbled into the present. It wasn't my father's laugh, not my father in the front seat, but Gary from Fort Worth. The kindly dentist. My rescuer, without whom I'd still be at the Denver airport.

Next to me, Gary's daughters tucked away their cell phones and stretched in their seats as we rolled into the sleepy little burg of Moses Lake, Texas.

It was just the way I remembered it: a convenience store selling bait and gas at either end of the strip, and in between, a row of brick and limestone buildings with high false fronts. A few new antique stores had gone in, but everything else seemed to have been frozen in time—the Variety and Dollar, the pharmacy with the soda fountain in it, the Wash Barrel Laundry, the chamber of commerce, the little rural medical clinic that was only open a few days a week, the community center, the little brown stone church with the white steeple, a squatty brick building that belonged to the Corps of Engineers.

Not much had changed. Moses Lake was still the same, right down to the little Moses Lake Hardware store at the end of the strip, near the church. Same wooden barrels out front, filled with fishing poles, shovels, and on-clearance tackle. In the summer, blown-up beach balls, air rafts, kites, giant squirt guns, and old tractor inner tubes converted for floatable fun would be stacked there, as well. Tourism in the winter was scant, of course, the place only appealing to fishermen and bird watchers hoping to catch a glimpse of the bald eagles.

Uncle Herbert's place, Harmony Shores Funeral Home, was only a few blocks farther, just past the post office and the Ranch House Bank.

"Let me off here, okay?" I said, suddenly not ready to face my family.

Gary glanced over his shoulder. "Here? At the hardware store?"

His wife swiveled in her seat, giving me a quizzical look. "We can drive you all the way."

"It's all right. My uncle's place isn't far." Somehow, I couldn't imagine pulling in with Gary and family in tow. Harmony Shores was a stately old estate, a classic example of nineteenth century Greek Revival architecture, but strangers tended to find the idea of a combined residence and funeral home rather odd.

When Mom, Clay, and I had moved into the gardener's cottage out back following my father's death, there'd been no end to the whispers. Couple that with the dark, drab, chain-laden and somewhat vampirish style of dress I'd adopted as a protest when my father had moved us to Moses Lake, and I'd looked way too much like I might be sleeping in one of the coffins myself. Kids can be merciless, and when your mother is the reason the prodigal son left town in the first place, so can adults.

Gazing at the hardware store now, I remembered passing by on my way to the pharmacy and wishing Blaine Underhill would come out to help some customer with an inner tube or a fishing pole. In my teenage imagination, Blaine would look my way, and against all social mores and at risk to his reputation, discover his undeniable attraction to the skinny girl in the dark clothes and ridiculous goth makeup job.

It was an insane fantasy with which I both entertained and tortured myself throughout my senior year of high school. It kept me tromping back to chemistry class, day after day, and it broke my heart night after night. I wanted Blaine Underhill to love me; he didn't even know who I was.

Such are the twisted dreams of teenage girls.

It didn't occur to me until I was actually on the hardware store sidewalk, hugging Gary and family good-bye, that Blaine Underhill's family might still own the hardware store. The Underhills had been in Moses Lake since long before the Corps of Engineers ousted a settlement of Mennonites from the farms in the valley, then dammed the river and created the lake.

Blaine had been a prince in this small town; his stepmother was the queen and his dad the banker. When I could get away from home long enough, I used to stand in the convenience store, catty-corner from the hardware store, peeking out the window while I pretended to peruse the magazines. I'd watch Blaine there in his football jersey, his dark brown hair curling on his suntanned neck as he sorted through the inner tubes for kids in swimsuits, or carried bags for little old ladies, or flirted with girls in bikinis. If there'd been a pin-up poster of Blaine Underhill in *Teen Time* magazine, I would have bought it and tacked it on my wall in some secret place.

" . . . that okay?"

I realized that Gary was talking to me, and I hadn't heard a thing.

"Sorry," I answered, noticing that he'd unloaded my suitcase and laptop on the sidewalk. I whirled a hand by my ear, rolling my eyes apologetically. "Had my head in the past there for a minute. This town hasn't changed at all."

"There's something comforting about a place that doesn't change." Gary couldn't have known how wrong he was about that. My sweet memories of childhood visits to Moses Lake had been permanently painted over by the blackness of that senior year in high school. I'd spent the first three months of our stay trying to punish my father for marooning us on the family farm outside town, and the other six months living in the tiny gardener's cottage behind Uncle Herbert's funeral home, mired in the grief and guilt that followed my father's death.

Standing in the middle of town now, I sensed that those emotions could be as potent as ever if I let them, so I concentrated on expressing gratitude to the Good Samaritans who'd spent their anniversary saving me from disaster. "I really don't even know how to thank you. If there's ever anything I can do to pay you back—advice on the clinic designs, anything, really—please let me know. When I get back to Seattle, I'll send money for the gas."

Smiling pleasantly, Gary lifted a hand. "No money needed. It's a blessing to be a blessing. That's what my mother always said. Just pass it on to someone else when you get the chance. Can we pray for you before we go?"

Gary's wife smiled expectantly, and his daughters extended their hands, ready to form a prayer circle on my behalf.

I felt the momentary culture shock of having been asked that question, of being back below the Mason-Dixon line, where such an inquiry was considered perfectly natural. Nine years in the city—and not that I hadn't met plenty of passionate churchgoers—but I'd couldn't recall anyone coming right out and asking me that. Typically, I didn't run in those sorts of circles.

"Sure." I could hardly say no after all they had done for me. Slipping in somewhat awkwardly between Gary's daughters, I closed my eyes and bowed my head, and for some reason, thought of Trish. She was actually quite spiritual herself, in the broader sense of the word. She thought it was ridiculous when I told her that I'd grown up in church with my father and didn't have issues with it, but I just didn't want to go anymore. *That's like saying you believe fatty foods cause heart attacks and then eating fried chicken all day,* she pointed out. *I mean, if what you do and what you believe are two different things, it's a guilt trap, right?*

Trish would have loved the sight of me standing on the sidewalk, hand in hand with the dentist's family as they prayed for my journey.

When the prayers ended, I did feel better, in a strange way—as if perhaps some special blessing had been called down and might ease my return to Moses Lake. Nearby, the white wooden steeple of Lakeshore Community Church glistened in the late-afternoon sunlight, as if in punctuation.

Gary's wife looked up at it and said, "It's a gorgeous day. Let's take a drive around the lake before we head back home. We can do the anniversary dinner tomorrow night."

Gary agreed, and even the girls looked toward the lake, placid in its deep blue winter coat.

"What a pretty little town," Gary's wife remarked, and I was startled by the chasm between their perspectives and mine. To me, this place would never again be beautiful.

Even so, I took a moment to describe some of the sights they might see on their drive—the cliffs above Eagle Eye bridge; the historic marker that told the legend of the Wailing Woman, whose voice could be heard moaning through the cliffs; the spire-like rock formations north of the dam, where tourists pulled off at the scenic turnout to watch bald eagles nesting. I finished by telling them about Catfish Charley's, my great-uncle's floating fried food Mecca, where they could eat batter-crisp fish while being watched by Charley, the hundred-pound primordial catfish who'd been greeting diners from his tank for as long as I could remember.

"I think they're only open on weekends in the winter, come to think of it, but if you want some dinner before you head back, the food is good at the Waterbird, over by the dam," I added, and then I realized that the Waterbird might not even be there anymore. It's funny how the mind believes that the places of your childhood will always be waiting for you to come back to them. "I mean, I guess it's still around. Anyway, the view of the lake is beautiful there, and it's sort of a tradition—people go in and sign the back wall of the store, sometimes leave a favorite quote. The legend is that if you sign the wall of wisdom with someone, you'll return to Moses Lake together again."

A lump rose in my throat. My father and I had signed the wall together when I was a girl. Every time we visited after that, we went by the Waterbird to look at our handiwork, touching the quote like a talisman. When we moved to Moses Lake that final year, I'd refused to visit the wall with Dad. I'd broken the chain. . . .

As I told Gary's family good-bye and watched them drive off, the blessing they'd pronounced over me seemed to fly away with them, rolling down the main street of Moses Lake, growing smaller, and smaller, until it drifted out of sight, and I was once again all alone, with no ID, no phone, and no money, in the last place I ever thought I'd find myself.

The man who troubles the water

might soon enough drown in it.

—*Fisherman's proverb*
(*via Catfish Charley, feeding lakesiders since 1946*)

Chapter 4

I'd barely been in Moses Lake ten minutes, and I could already feel the place winding around me, quietly and efficiently, a spider twisting silken threads about an errant moth before it can break loose and fly away.

The bells on the hardware store door jingled, and my mind tripped over itself. "May I help ye-ew?" The question traversed the parking lot in a long, sticky-sweet Southern drawl, and for an instant, I was like an astronaut being pulled into a black hole, lost in time and space. I turned to find Blaine Underhill's stepmother, a ghost from yesteryear, standing in the hardware store doorway, wearing a peach-colored pantsuit, her puffy hair still the same brassy shade of blond, pulled back in a pearl-toned headband. "Do you need directions to someplace, hon?"

The word *hon* took me by surprise. Even though some of the Moses Lake ladies had attempted to adopt me as a somewhat lost cause after my father's death, I was never *hon* to Mrs. Underhill. She couldn't quite forgive me for being the product of the unwelcome

union of my father and the freewheeling out-of-towner who stole
him away.

Clearly, she didn't recognize me now. I hadn't considered the
possibility that, while the people of Moses Lake still loomed large
in my mind, they might not even remember me. It was strangely
pathetic to think that I'd been reacting all these years to people
for whom I was just a temporary blip on the radar.

"No, I'm fine," I answered, and then started walking, conscious
of Mrs. Underhill staring after me, no doubt wondering why I was
dragging luggage along the side of the highway. She was probably
thinking, *What an odd little thing. . . .*

I headed out of town, past Lakeshore Community Church, its
brown stone walls warming in the winter sunlight beneath a patina
of dust and moss. The doors to the squatty low-ceilinged fellowship hall were open, a half-dozen cars parked out front. An elderly
woman in a red coat was trying to wrestle a wheelchair from the
trunk of her car. After glancing back and forth between her and the
door a couple times, wishing someone would come out and help
her before she hurt herself, I parked my suitcase near the road and
jogged across the gravel parking lot. The suede boots that had set
me back a week's salary squished in a layer of creamy, limestone-
colored goo as I skirted puddles left behind by a winter rain.

"Here, let me help you," I said, and unfortunately startled her
off-balance. She caught herself against the car, with a bug-eyed
look. Such was usually the way with my awkward attempts at
random acts of kindness. I wasn't meant to be folksy and friendly,
but I had promised Gary that I would pay it forward. If not for an
act of kindness, I'd still be standing at the bus station, or worse
yet, sleeping in an airport chair in Denver.

"Oh!" the woman gasped, catching her breath and squinting
at me through glasses thick enough to make me wonder if she'd

driven herself here. Something about her was familiar, but I couldn't decide what. "Oh, well, all right. Aren't you sweet?" She pulled and stretched the words, adding extra syllables on *ri-ight* and *swe-eet*. Scanning the parking lot, she tried to figure out where I'd come from.

She motioned to the sidewalk in front of the fellowship hall. "Just set it up there, hon. It's my cousin's. I was tryin' to make room back here for the casseroles."

Casseroles. Why did it not surprise me that the casserole ladies were on the move again today?

A blue piece of cardboard tangled in the spokes of the wheelchair as I pulled it out, and I rested the chair against the trunk rim for a moment, wiggling the paper loose and dropping it into the trunk. It flipped over and slid partway under a folded navy-and-gold Moses Lake High stadium blanket. I found myself cocking my head to read, from the bottom up, the bold, white letters on the royal blue sign. *Precinct 4. County Commission. Underhill. Blaine. Vote for.*

Huh . . . Looked like Blaine Underhill hadn't strayed far from the hometown. "You shouldn't be lifting this thing on your own," I said, noticing that there was a rather large stack of Blaine Underhill signs wedged against the side of the trunk.

The woman noticed that I was staring. "That's my grandson." Reaching into her oversized purse, she whipped out a flyer printed on red paper. "Are you a resident of the county?" A brow lifted with a hopeful look, and I gathered that my vote was about to be solicited.

"Just visiting." Now I knew why she looked familiar. This was the infamous Mama B. When I used to walk by the football stadium on my way home from school, she was always perched on the bleachers next to Blaine Underhill's father, the two of them watching practice, making sure their golden boy was getting the kind of treatment he deserved. If she wasn't telling the coaches what to do, Mama B was checking up on the teachers, shuffling through the school halls with a pug-nosed pocket pooch in her handbag, pointing out girls whose hemlines were too short and boys who had hair over their collars.

More than once, she'd cornered me and let me know that my oversized black T-shirts were "unbecoming on a young lady," and that if I'd drop by the variety store, she'd be happy to help me look for something more appropriate. Perhaps in a nice shade of blue or mauve. She felt sure there was a cute figure underneath my misguided wardrobe, and she wondered if I'd ever thought about entering the Miss Moses Lake contest.

Thank goodness she didn't recognize me now. I didn't bother to introduce myself as I carried the wheelchair to the sidewalk and set it against the front of the church.

"Thank ya, sweetie." She held out the Vote for Blaine flyer. "Here. Pass this along to someone while you're here. Tell them Blaine Underhill's their man. It's about time we cleaned up that county commission."

I felt obliged to take the pamphlet, and then I quickly backed away, folding it and stuffing it into my jacket pocket.

I could feel Mama B's curious stare following me across the parking lot. "Where'd you say you were stayin'?" she called. A propane delivery truck passed by in a *whoosh*, and I pretended not to hear. Swirls of asphalt-scented air skittered across the parking lot in the truck's wake, and I made a hasty exit, my suitcase bumping along behind me. Mama B hollered at the propane driver, informing him that the speed limit through town was thirty-five.

Dry winter grass crackled under my feet as I left the pavement and moved into the ditch alongside the rural highway, traversing the short distance to the tall limestone pillars and rusting iron gate that marked the entrance to Uncle Herbert's driveway. The sign hanging in the shade of lofty magnolias still read *Harmony Shores Funeral Home and Chapel*, even though the place had been closed since Uncle Herbert's health problems had forced him to shut down the business. It was a beautiful old place, if you didn't find sleeping in the bedrooms above the funeral chapel strangely morbid. Unfortunately, I did, and the usual chill accompanied me through the gate and followed me up the long, tree-lined drive. A shudder gripped me like a fist, squeezing the air from my lungs. A voice in my head was urging, *Run, just run.*

Pulling in a fortifying breath, I veered off across the grass toward the memory gardens, my suitcase bumping over twigs and pecan shucks. Dampness from the soil seeped through my suede boots, making them soggy and chilly by the time I reached a stone path, where holly bushes and magnolias provided secluded alcoves in which grieving families could reflect privately.

Pausing, I gazed at the treetops and did a poor imitation of the yoga breathing I'd learned from a fitness-guru-slash-boyfriend who'd tried to convince me that meditation would help my tension problems. At the time I'd laughed flippantly and told him I couldn't imagine what he was talking about. Me, tense?

Now I wished I'd paid more attention. The muscles in my back were as twisted and knotted as a string of used rubber bands in the corner of a junk drawer. I jerked at the sound of cars coming up the drive, and a charley horse kicked up its heels near my spine.

That odd temptation to bolt for the woods stirred me again. Instead, I did the mature thing and ducked behind the holly bushes, peeking through the limbs as three cars rolled past. I recognized the one in the lead, and I knew whose little gray head that was peering over the steering wheel. Mama B. That would be the church ladies behind her. Apparently, they had arrived on another reconnaissance mission, with food in hand, of course. The fact that the casserole ladies were so interested in what was going on at Harmony Shores was not a good sign.

The third car pulled in, and I peered through the leaves, undercover-agent style. The silver Cadillac rolled to a stop behind the first two vehicles, and doors opened on both sides. The puffy blond hair and peach pantsuit were unmistakable. The venerable Mrs. Underhill, whose stepson I was supposed to help elect to the county commission. She came bearing a foil-wrapped plate, and she had someone with her.

The holly bushes combed my hair as I leaned closer. Who was that with her? Someone young, svelte, and blond in a perky above-the-knee skirt and high heels. Blaine Underhill had a couple of half-sisters, as I recalled, but they didn't look like that. The Underhill girls had the misfortune of having the same figure as their father. They were stocky, muscular, and athletic. When we graduated from high school, they were entering middle school, and Mrs. Underhill was still cramming them into ruffled gowns and making them stroll the catwalk at beauty pageants, and attend cotillion classes. The kids at school used to tease Blaine about it, and ask him if his stepmother expected him to make a bid for Cotton Queen one of these days, too.

The girl with Mrs. Underhill today was definitely not one of Blaine's half-sisters.

She trotted up the steps, the dress swaying back and forth across her knees. My brother, of all people, answered the door, his dishwater blond hair sporting a bad case of bed head. I noted, in the split second before the newest visitors reached the porch, that Clay didn't seem to have changed much. Same rumpled look—khaki shorts, washed-out T-shirt, flip-flops. Mom's soft, slightly curly hair and hazel eyes, a green tone where mine were brown. His face had matured a little in the . . . how long had it been since I'd seen him, other than on his Facebook posts from the far parts of the universe?

Three-and-a-half years. He'd called on the Fourth of July. Just called me out of the blue. He was a hundred miles from Seattle on a bicycle tour—not the organized kind with other people, but a solitary, unplanned journey of his own making. He'd been rained on for three days, was running a fever, and wanted to know if I'd like to come get him. He wasn't complaining about the conditions, really. It was more like he was offering me the opportunity, and he was fine, either way. Maybe the choice between biking in the rain with a fever and visiting with me was pretty much a toss-up. He probably knew I'd ask why he was out of college for the summer and not working anywhere.

The girl in the cute dress tackled Clay with an exuberant hug. I watched in fascination, my mouth dropping open. What in the world was going on? Who was the girl, and why was my brother . . . slipping an arm around her waist and lifting her off her feet?

The casserole ladies twittered, giggled, and seemed delighted—*even* Mrs. Underhill. They politely pretended to be commenting on the condition of the memory gardens, as Clay gave the girl a peck and then set her down again.

Suddenly the ladies were looking in my direction, pointing, and I was cognizant of the idiotic position I'd put myself in, hiding in the bushes, spying on the funeral home. Another thought followed—something petty, and immature, and born of sibling rivalry. It wasn't fair that I was hiding in the bushes while Clay was getting hugs and cookie plates. Moses Lake had always loved Clay. The year we lived here, he was a cute, gap-toothed fourth grader—goofy, precocious, innocent, a little charmer who was easy to like. After my father's death, Clay had slipped neatly under the sheltering wings of not only his school teacher, but his Sunday school teachers and a half-dozen adopted grannies around town, including Mama B. They loved him then, and apparently still loved him now.

"There's someone over there," one of the ladies observed. "In the bushes . . . Look!"

"Where?" That was Mrs. Underhill's voice, the sound shrill, all traces of sugar-and-honey sweetness gone. That was the voice I remembered—the one that sent chills through me, back when there were secrets to hide. Mrs. Underhill loved nothing better than to ferret out people's secrets and spread them around. In particular, she wanted to find out what was *really* going on in the little cottage behind the funeral home. She was certain that, in some way or another, the authorities needed to be involved. She would've liked nothing better than for child welfare services to swoop in and take us away from my mother. It would have proven her right about everything and proven that my father should have married *her* years ago, instead of my mother.

"Yeah . . . you know . . . you're right, I think," Clay concurred, and then added, "Hey, Roger, come'ere. Come'ere, boy. What's out there, huh? You see somebody out there?" Of all things, Clay still had the goofball mutt-slash-golden retriever that was riding with him on the ill-fated bike trip. Roger traveled in a pull-behind bike trailer, the kind made for babies. He'd been an inconveniently manic houseguest in my no-dogs-allowed apartment building for a week, while Clay recovered from pneumonia. I'd come within a whisker, literally, of getting kicked out of the complex, and my Persian rug has never been the same since.

"It's just me. It's just me." Squeezing from the bushes with one hand in the air, I surrendered without a fight. "Everybody calm down." My suitcase wobbled over clumps of grass and loose twigs, threatening to tip over as I started toward the driveway. The

49

casserole ladies squinted, and Mrs. Underhill took a couple of steps my way. Detaching himself from the blonde, Clay trotted down the stairs as his dog sprinted across the lawn, heading in my direction.

"Roger, hey! Roger, wait!" Clay called, and of course Roger didn't listen. He tackled me with the momentum of a linebacker, and we did a clumsy backward waltz as I tried to avoid falling over the suitcase. Roger swiped his long, lolling tongue across my mouth before I could get my balance and push him away. By the time I did, Clay had caught up.

"Heather's here," Clay announced, in case anyone was still confused. One hand caught the dog, and one gave me a shoulder-hug, but I got the distinct impression that my brother wasn't thrilled to see me. "Hey, Sis," he said.

The casserole ladies regarded us with curious, somewhat uncertain expressions, as we walked to the porch. A few uncomfortable greetings passed back and forth, and I was actually relieved when Mrs. Hall shoved a casserole into my hands. It was still warm on the bottom, which felt good. I remembered Mrs. Hall from the pharmacy where, after Dad's death, I'd picked up the prescriptions that were supposed to *fix* my mother, but didn't. Mrs. Hall was always nice about it. In truth, she probably wasn't supposed to be handing that stuff off to a minor, but she let me take it, always with the kind admonition that they'd be happy to deliver next time.

I set the casserole on one of the porch tables and wiped my mouth, still contemplating the gross-out factor of having been kissed by Clay's dog.

Mrs. Underhill gave me a suspicious look, then stated the obvious, "Well, Heather, my goodness, you're a wreck. Was that you outside the hardware store earlier? You didn't walk here all the way from Seattle, surely?" She batted a hand, peppering the artificially sweetened question with a sharp-edged giggle.

I did. You know, I'm on a new exercise kick, and I thought walking from Seattle would be a great way to start, was on the tip of my tongue. Heaven help me, but Mrs. Underhill obviously still held the strings to the broken, bitter, smart-mouthed teenager I thought I'd buried years ago. Even that was disconcerting—as if she had control of me, rather than me having control of myself. "It's a long story," I replied, instead. "Weather problems." Let her ponder that and draw her own conclusions as to how that equated to appearing in town on foot.

She was right about one thing, though. I was a wreck. No wonder the girl who'd just put the smooch on my brother was eyeing me uncertainly. She butted Clay in the shoulder, as in, *Introduce me, already. Who's this Heather person?* Apparently she didn't know anything about me. Strange, considering how familiar they'd looked a few minutes ago.

Another vehicle rattled up just as Clay was about to begin the introductions. The hearse was a dead giveaway, even from the end of the drive. As it passed through the tunnel of live oaks, I recognized three people in the front seat—two tall, one short. Two gray heads, one sandy brown with the hair loosely pulled back, fly-away strands swirling around her face.

My mother, Uncle Herbert, and Uncle Charley. Clay waved enthusiastically, in a way that said, *Hail, hail, the gang's all here!*

The hearse had barely skidded to a stop before my great uncles were grunting and creaking their way out of the car, then heading for the porch in stiff-legged shuffles. Mother, sliding over from the middle, was one step behind them.

"Well, praise the Lord and phone the saints. There she is!" Uncle Charley made a beeline toward me, outdistancing Uncle Herbert, who had to hold on to the handrail to make his way up the eight steps to the porch.

Uncle Charley pushed past the casserole ladies and swept me into a meaty hug. "We just been to the sheriff's department, finding out how to report you for a missing person."

The ladies gasped.

"Huh . . . wha . . . oof!" I stammered and grunted as Uncle Herbert moved in from behind and I was momentarily the filling in an uncle sandwich. The scents of Borax, axle grease, and musty leather flicked at my senses, pulling threads. Memories were tied to those smells—childhood visits to the old family farm with my father, where Uncle Charley gave me pony rides. The dark days after my father's death. My high school graduation, when all I cared about was getting away from here. I didn't want the memories that were tethered to these two old men. I wanted to leave this place and everything attached to it.

Now I felt it all pulling at me again, leaving me confused and lost.

"Heather, where in the world have you been?" My mother's admonition came from somewhere outside the circle of scents and memories. "We had a call from a man in Dallas who discovered your purse in the trash that was cleaned off of a bus, but you were nowhere to be found. We were scared to death. He said he'd FedEx the purse, by the way."

The casserole ladies gasped and twittered and asked questions as I rushed to share the odd saga of my trip to Texas and the lost purse. No telling how big that story would get by the time it circled town a few times.

Uncle Charley brushed a sandy-sounding something off my jacket. "Looks like Roger got the besta you. Clay, you gotta teach that dog not to mug the comp'ny. He almost knocked Reverend Hay in the drink when we were takin' the lights off the restaurant after Christmas, and the UPS man is afraid to even come by here. He's been catching us at the Waterbird when we go for coffee in the mornin'."

Uncle Charley took my shoulders and held me away from him. "Let me get a look at ya." He pulled me into a patch of sunlight and announced to the crowd, "My cow, look at our little Heather! She growed up to be a pretty thang!"

I was too confused to be embarrassed. Clay and his dog had been in town long enough to frighten off the UPS man and help take down Christmas lights? What in the world?

Mrs. Underhill wasn't the least bit interested in admiring my growth or my natural beauty. She regarded me with the fisheye, as if some frightening life-form had invaded the casserole circle. "My word, you got on the bus with a . . . a *man* you met on the *plane*? It's a wonder he wasn't after more than your purse."

I blurted out the first thing that came to mind. "He was a *dentist*." As if that explained everything. "Anyway, I was never in any danger. I just forgot my purse."

"What sort of purse?" one of the ladies asked. "Nothing expensive, I hope?"

"Land sakes, what's that matter?" Mama B snapped, then turned and hobbled toward the car. "Let's leave these folks to their reunitin'. We got more deliveries to make."

Even the members of the Moses Lake human telegraph knew better than to refuse a direct order from Mama B. Reluctantly, they backed away, having ferreted out enough details to successfully add their own and come up with an account of my arrival in town. In closing, they offered a few sympathetic, but pointed, comments about the burden of my two widowed uncles being forced to provide for *all this company*. Then they handed over more food before following Mama B. Clay's apparent girlfriend kissed him on the cheek and whispered, "We gotta drop off a meal for a funeral." Adding a meaningful look, she told Clay she'd see him later.

An uncomfortable silence descended on us as the crowd departed.

I was conscious of everyone surreptitiously watching me and maintaining their positions, in the way members of the bomb squad might gather around a suspicious package.

My mother broke the stalemate by peeking under the foil on the CorningWare pan. "Still hot," she said, her tone overly light and falsely cheerful. "Let's go around back and eat on the sun porch. Clay, maybe you can give Heather a ride over to Catfish Cabins after that."

"The cabins?" I glanced at the house. Despite the presence of the funeral office, parlors, and workrooms, as well as the chapel in what had once been a grand ballroom, Harmony House was still quite large, the entire second floor and both ends of the main floor remaining in use as personal residence space. There was also the small gardener's cottage out back, which meant there was plenty of space for me to stay here. So why was Mom trying to ship me off to the rental cabins, halfway around the lake by Uncle Charley's restaurant? With no car to drive, I'd be stranded there.

Maybe that was their plan. Maybe I was being given the bum's rush—while they were happy not to have to report me as a missing person, they didn't want me around, either. "I thought I'd stay here."

"Oh . . . Well, it's sort of . . . crowded. . . ." Mom hedged as furtive glances darted between the relatives. "Uncle Charley has been living here for a while now, since Uncle Herb shouldn't be alone. It's somewhat crowded with Clay and me in the house, too, and now the mess of getting ready for the estate sale. The place really is a disas—"

"I can bunk out back in the gardener's cottage." I didn't wait for her to finish. I wasn't about to let them warehouse me off-site while they continued with whatever they were doing. I'd never seen a group of people looking so culpable. I was going to be on them *like fleas on a back-porch hound*, as Uncle Herb's Mennonite housekeeper, Ruth, used to say.

Glancing at the house momentarily, I wondered what had happened to Ruth. During those terrible months of my senior year, she was the one who'd saved me. She hadn't tried to convince me to snap out of it, or stop skulking around in black T-shirts and too much makeup, or keep a stiff upper lip, like Uncle Herb and Aunt Esther had. Nor had she echoed the geriatric pastor of Lakeshore Community Church, telling me how much God still loved me. Ruth just baked cookies, washed laundry, and occasionally laid a comforting hand on my shoulder as she passed by in her old-fashioned-looking dresses and sweaters, and a hair covering, as was typical of many of the Mennonite residents upriver in Gnadenfeld.

Uncle Herb rubbed the back of his neck, glancing toward the backyard and then toward my mother, his brows lifting in a way that seemed to say, *Uh-oh . . . Now what do we do?*

"Well . . . but . . . Blaine Underhill has things stored out there," Mother shrugged, dismissing my suggestion. "Signs and whatnot. He's running for county commissioner."

There was that name again. *Blaine Underhill.* Why was my family suddenly so tight with the Underhills? I'd never before in my life seen my mother speak the Underhill name without sneering.

"I don't mind," I pressed, calling their bluff, but there was also a painful little pinprick inside me. Nobody was happy to have me here. "All I need is a bed and enough space to put my suitcase, and maybe a plate of casserole. Why is the benevolence committee bringing food by here, anyway?"

Mom shrugged, her lip curling slightly, flashing an eyetooth. "Oh, you know those women. They're always looking for an excuse to take a casserole somewhere and stick their noses in."

"Stick their nose into what?" The attention of the church ladies was never completely for naught. They believed in Christian charity, with a purpose.

Mom flipped a hand through the air. "Who knows? Heather, don't you think you'd be more comfortable at the Catfish Cabins? The gardener's cottage is a mess."

The sting of rejection put me back in my high-school shoes, when no one other than Ruth seemed to want me around. *I will not let them get to me. I will not.* "No. I'll be fine here. I don't plan to stay long. As soon as we get the hitch in this real estate deal taken care of, I'm gone." *And never coming back. Ever. You won't see me darkening your doorstep anymore.* "In fact, since we're all here, why don't we go on inside and hash it out? What's this malarkey about a competing offer on the properties? When did this come up and who made the offer?" *As if there really is one.*

Mother rolled her eyes. "Really, Heather. You've barely arrived, and all you can talk about is business? Let's have something to eat on the sun porch. The man who found your purse said he'd try to get it to FedEx today. You're stuck here until it arrives, anyway. You can't fly without identification. I think you're safe taking a little time for family niceties."

Irritation crawled over me on sharp little legs, digging in claws. A snappy retort was on the tip of my tongue, *Who are you to lecture me about family anything?* Squeezing my lips tightly over my teeth, I fought to keep the venom at bay.

Uncle Charley, looking embarrassed, nudged Uncle Herbert and started toward the front walk. "Well, I'm starved. Let's head around the back way. No sense traipsing through the house."

I was conscious of more covert glances and a collective holding of breath, but I'd also caught the scent of casserole, and I was hungry, weary, and lost. Every muscle in my body seemed to be liquefying. The afternoon had started to cool, and I just wanted to sit down someplace warm, so I followed the uncs and the casseroles off the porch. Clay grabbed my suitcase and walked along behind me as Uncle Charley talked over his shoulder, pointing out the growth in various trees, a new rose bush on the corner, an old lamppost that had been removed after it became too unstable, and other things he thought might have changed since I'd last seen the place.

By the time we reached the sun porch, it was all just a buzz. I couldn't concentrate on the words. The cold had pressed through my jacket, and my suede dress boots were wet all the way to my socks. On the sun porch, at the urging of Uncle Herb, I took a seat on the faded floral fainting couch that was nearest the old wall-hung propane heater. Mom and Clay headed to the kitchen to get some plates and glasses, and to make a pitcher of iced tea.

"You look plumb wore out," Uncle Charley observed as he turned up the heater. "I'm gonna go put on a pot of good hot coffee."

Despite my insistence that he didn't need to make coffee on my account, he speedily quit the room and was followed by Uncle Herb. I heard the whisper of voices in the kitchen. The last thing I remembered was letting my head fall against the sofa pillows, then catching Blaine Underhill's name again and thinking that I should tiptoe in there and see what they were whispering about.

A life all turbulence and noise may seem
To him that leads it wise and to be praised;
But wisdom is a pearl with most success
Sought in still water . . .
—*William Cowper*
(Left by Ben Murray, retired—no longer in a hurry.)

Chapter 5

Family arguments should not be postponed until first thing in the morning, particularly on a gorgeous February day, when the winter sun slips over the water in a hush, biding its time before filtering through the canopy of live oaks into the rocky nooks and misty valley floors. *No rush today*, a morning like that says. *It's the off season, remember?*

I woke to the sound of ducks landing on the water and a cardinal chirping in the winter-bare climbing rose outside the window. My heart was pounding and I couldn't catch my breath. I'd just had the dream about the door. I'd gone farther than usual, this time. The knob had started to turn in my hand, but then the spider dropped from its web in the doorframe and landed on my fingers. I screamed, jerked back, awakened bolt upright in the bed. . . .

Now I sat clinging to my knees, my mind slowly settling into the fact that I was in the gardener's cottage behind Uncle Herbert's place. Frigid morning air chilled the heat from the dream as I gazed out the window at the cardinal, a bewitching splash of red, like a drop of blood among thorns. Beautiful, yet out of place . . . Somewhat noisy and demanding, as if determined to steal my attention.

The perspiration on my skin quickly turned to ice, and I grabbed the coat I'd thrown over my feet last night after piling the bed with dusty quilts. The collar of the coat was cold against my neck, and even the insides of the pockets were stiff and chilly. Something crisp bumped against my fingers, and I pulled it out, then vaguely remembered Mama B handing me the flyer from her suitcase-sized purse.

I unfolded it now, blinking the sleep from my eyes in morbid fascination, trying to bring the first few lines into focus.

Elect Blaine Underhill

County Commissioner

Precinct 4.

The man was everywhere.

Below the name was a list of bullet points, espousing Blaine Underhill's worthiness for the job of county commissioner.

Lifelong county resident

Experienced leader

Proven businessman—not a politician

Avid fisherman and outdoor enthusiast (now there was an important qualification for office)

Sixth-generation Texan (I sort of admired that one. Being estranged from my mother's family and perpetually conflicted during visits to my dad's hometown because of the in-law wars, I felt an absence of the ties that bind. Occasionally, it bothered me.)

A unifier, who would strive to work across party lines (These days, you had to wonder if anyone could make that claim. Maybe the county surrounding Moses Lake was an island unto itself, where people with differing opinions actually found ways to discuss things like rational, civil adults. Despite the fact that he had ignored me in chemistry class, I liked Blaine Underhill better already.)

A man called to serve, with the county's best interests at heart (Well, he was cute in high school, but I remembered him as kind of a goof-off who got by largely on football talent and an A-list family name.)

A half-dozen endorsements followed. Everyone from the county farm co-op to the local labor union, mostly comprised of employees of the Proxica plant and Proxica poultry farms in and around Gnadenfeld, were squarely in favor of Blaine Underhill's candidacy. Why wouldn't they be? He was an Underhill, and besides, if they didn't support him, his stepmother would borrow a broom from the barrel out front of the hardware store, fly over their houses, and zap them with one of her evil hexes.

It was hard to imagine the goofy, somewhat intractable boy—who'd once kidnapped a neighboring school's mascot costume—now being qualified to make decisions that affected the entire county. A guy who would show up at a pep rally wearing a contraband buffalo costume along with a pink tutu and ballet shoes couldn't really change that much, could he?

I turned the paper over, compelled to read whatever was on the back side, which, as it turned out, was actually the front. There were live-and-in-person photos of Blaine Underhill—one of him coaching a pee-wee baseball team, one of him visiting with a young family in front of their home, one of him holding a rather large fish, and one smiling for the camera.

My first thought was, *Whoa* . . .

The ring of metal striking metal outside tugged my attention away. The noise traveled at light speed through the synapses of my brain, quickly pulling data from dust-covered files. It sounded like someone was moving Uncle Charley's rental canoes, which in the off-season were stored in an old cotton barn at Harmony Shores.

Why would anyone be down by the lake with the canoes on a frosty February morning?

Sliding from the bed, I pressed my face to the glass while shivering and shifting between freezing sock-feet. The corner of the cottage and a bare crape myrtle blocked all but a glimpse of the weathered board-and-batten barn that had seen its heyday when the valley was a fertile river basin.

Uncle Herbert's wife, Aunt Esther, occasionally talked about the days when Harmony House was the toast of Central Texas. Aunt Esther herself had been Cotton Queen of 1942, and she didn't let anyone forget it. Harmony House had been her inheritance, and she never really appreciated the fact that Uncle Herbert had moved his funeral business there in order to help support the expenses of the massive house. Aunt Esther liked to pretend she'd allowed the funeral business into Harmony House as a service to the community, not because her family had spent all the money allotted to them when the Corps of Engineers took their farmland through eminent domain and built the lake.

My teeth started chattering, the cold forcing me away from the air seepage around the wooden windowpanes. I'd forgotten how chilly the place could get at night, even with the heater running on the window air unit. I should have started a fire in the wood stove before going to sleep.

Stiff-limbed and chattering, I did the Frankenstein run to the bathroom and considered the tiny turn-of-the-century propane heater on the wall. A faded box of Diamond Strike-Anywhere matches sat atop, and surprisingly, I could recall exactly how to light the heater. Leaning close, I blew the dust off, then entertained the fleeting question, *How long since this thing's been lit?* A vision of myself and the cottage going up in a small mushroom cloud convinced me to forgo the heater. Instead, I hopped and shivered my way through pulling on some sweats, my coat again, and the cute little suede boots that were somewhat bedraggled and still damp after yesterday's adventure.

The metallic noises stopped as I headed out the door and rounded the cottage, gaining a view of the other side of the barn, where the canoes were stacked under the shed roof on the end nearest the lakeshore. I could just see their brightly-painted tips sticking out—yellow, green, blue, red. Maybe someone was looking them over, deciding how much to pay for the lot at the estate sale.

A nippy February breeze wafted off the lake—not frigid but just cold enough to make the idea of hanging out by the water seem less than pleasant. Even so, I wandered closer, tempted to take a walk along the shore to clear my head before going up to the house. On this morning's agenda was the family meeting that had been derailed last night after I fell asleep in the chair on the sun porch. Conveniently, no one had awakened me until it was time for bed, and the lights in the main house were already off. Mom had given me some coffee and muffins in a ziplock bag, and said that Clay had readied the cottage for me while I was dozing on the sun porch. I'd headed down the hill, too tired and foggy-brained to protest.

This morning, I had to get down to business and dispel this craziness about a competing offer on the property. Someone was trying to throw a monkey wrench into the plans here, and I had to find out who and why. Surely Uncle Herb's son didn't know about this. If my iPhone wasn't somewhere in a FedEx box, I would have called him already. If Donny was aware of this situation, he'd be having a fit.

Wouldn't he?

I knew there had been some hard feelings between Uncle Herbert and his kids in the past, but now that plans for the move had been made, things seemed to be reasonably civil. Donny obviously cared for his father's well-being, and Uncle Charley's, as well.

Water splashed behind the barn, and I moved a few more steps, catching a glimpse of Roger-the-dog frolicking along the water's edge, his tongue lolling and ears flopping as he ran. Someone was on the water in a kayak. . . .

Clay? He was paddling out from the shore with long, even strokes, his orange parka and the royal blue kayak making for a pretty picture. His paddle touched the surface of the lake in perfect rhythm, *left, right, left, right*, bending and shaping the water into swirls pink-tinged with morning light, drawing the froth upward with each stroke, suspending it in air temporarily before it ran down in glistening streams.

For a moment, I could only watch in awe, breathing in the serenity of the single kayak slicing soundlessly through the waters of Moses Lake. Clay looked perfectly at home there, perfectly at peace, despite the chill of the morning and the solitude on the lake. Looking at him I thought, *That's my baby brother, all grown up.* I remembered teaching him to swim during those months we lived at the lake. He was almost ten, and all he could do was dog paddle. Some little girl in his class was planning a swim party for her birthday, and a couple boys had made fun of Clay because, being Clay, he had come right out and admitted that he didn't know how to swim underwater.

I'd found him on the playground after school, crying his eyes out because the kids made fun of him. I wanted to find the little snots and beat them up, but Clay already had enough to deal with. He was small for his age, sort of a gump, way too honest, his dad was dead, his mom wouldn't get out of bed, his sister was the town weirdo, and he couldn't sign up for baseball or soccer because we couldn't afford it. My father's life insurance company was too busy investigating the death to care whether we could put food on the table while we waited for them to pay off. The last thing Clay needed was snotty little rednecks picking on him.

Instead of finding the boys and doing them bodily harm, I took Clay to the water and taught him to hold his breath and go under.

It was late April, and the lake was still cold, but we did it anyway. By the time we were done, we were laughing and shivering. The next weekend, I walked Clay to that little girl's birthday party and ended up having to stand at the corner of the patio like a dork, because once we got to the house, all the parents were there and Clay was embarrassed to go in by himself.

Now I watched him alone on Harmony Cove, and I couldn't believe he was ever the clueless, wimpy little boy who was afraid of the water, the dark, snakes, and (oddly enough) big dogs.

What was that little girl's name? Clay had such a crush on her. He'd cried when, at the end of the summer, Mom decided to get out of bed—she had to, since I was leaving home for college—and announced that she was going back to college herself. She'd contacted a friend, a grad student at Berkeley, and she and Clay were moving there to share an apartment with the friend. Fortunately, my father's insurance policy had paid off shortly after that, and Mom had a way to finance her portion of the apartment and her higher education.

A flash of movement caught the corner of my eye, shattering my reverie. I'd been spotted by Roger, and he was headed my way in a dead run, droplets of water spewing from his coat, catching the light, and giving him a wet, glistening halo.

"Roger! Roger, no!" I scolded, trying to abort another mugging. "Stop! Heel! Stay back!" I hurried to a nearby fig bush, putting it between myself and the galloping water sprinkler. I'd only brought two outfits and a pair of sweats in my carryon. This was one of my few clothing options.

Unfortunately, Roger was not the least bit intimidated by fig trees. He went right through the narrow V in the middle and landed on me anyway. I ended up flat on my rear in the wet, dewy grass.

"Oh, my gosh!" someone screamed—a woman's voice, young with a soft Texas drawl.

64

By the time I tossed Roger off, Clay's friend from yesterday was looking down at me, her hands over her mouth. "Oh, my word," she gasped between her fingers. "Are you all right?" She had a very nice manicure—pink, with little yellow smiley faces on the thumbs. "Roger, no!" she scolded, grabbing the dog's fur in two big handfuls and holding him away from me as I climbed to my feet. "I've never seen him do that to anybody before. He's usually a perfect lil' gentleman."

I blinked at her in disbelief. Gentleman? The dog who'd eaten my sofa, a Formica countertop, and the six-hundred-dollar Gianmarco Lorenzi shoes I'd splurged on during a business trip to Sicily—all in one week at my apartment? Roger was no gentleman, but what I really wanted to know was why this girl seemed to be so well-acquainted with Clay's dog. And why was she at Uncle Herb's at seven fifteen in the morning, all dressed for work?

"Are you oka-ay?" she asked again, her drawl stretching and softening the end of the word. She watched me with the sort of expression you might have when an elderly person slips on a spill in the grocery store. Once I'd righted myself, she let go of Roger and stuck a hand out to shake mine. "We didn't really get to meet one on one yesterday. You probably don't remember me. Amy Underhill? I was just little when y'all lived here."

I suddenly felt old and rather frumpy, standing there in my sweats. Amy Underhill? Blaine Underhill's toddler cousin? The one who attended day care across the street from the school? She used to bolt across the playground when Blaine passed by with the football boys on the way to fourth-period athletics. I'd watched them any number of times from algebra class as he jumped over the day-care fence and she tackled him with hugs. He'd pick her up, swing her onto his shoulder, featherlight, then open the gate and jog off while she laughed and squealed and the daycare-ladies playfully admonished him.

She was all grown up now—nineteen, maybe twenty years old, I guessed. Workin' it in a small-town sort of way: cute skirt, high heels, white faux leather jacket.

"Great to see you," I said, self-consciously smoothing fly-away reddish-brown hairs into my ponytail. "Where's Clay going?" I pointed toward the water, where Clay was almost to the end of the cove. A black boat with a glittery silver rim had just stopped out there, and Clay was paddling toward it. I couldn't imagine why anyone would want to be on the water in the morning chill. It also wasn't normal for Clay to be up before nine, at least as far as I remembered. "Is he meeting someone out there?"

Amy swiveled, watching as Clay glided to the boat and the driver threw out a rope, with which Clay proceeded to tie up his kayak. When Amy turned back to me, she shrugged innocently but averted her eyes and looked at the house. "Oh, that's my cousin. Do you remember Blaine? He was in your class, I think. Anyhow, they go out and fish sometimes."

Tires screeched in my mind as my thoughts did a quick one-eighty. Blaine Underhill? My brother and Blaine Underhill had become fishing buddies? Since when had Clay started cultivating connections in Moses Lake—girlfriends and now fishing pals? Why hadn't my mother mentioned any of this during our talks about the real estate sale? It was as if my brother had a secret life, and no clues to it had ever filtered to me.

You shouldn't be surprised, the voice of conscience admonished. *It's not like you keep in touch.*

But I had been in touch lately, quite a bit with my mother and some with Uncle Herbert, Uncle Charley, and Donny. Why all the cloak-and-dagger stuff? Why was Clay's personal life such a big secret?

"I didn't realize they knew each other," I muttered, and Amy gave me a nervous look, her gaze shifting to the ground, searching the frost-tipped grass for a good answer.

"Oh, well, they got to be friends after they started talking so much. Blaine runs the bank now for his folks. He does business with a lot of people. . . ." She let the sentence drift, then quickly pulled her lips to one side.

"My brother's doing business at the bank?" I squeezed my arms around myself, trying to ward off the cold and the idea at the same time. I was afraid to know where this was leading. "What kind of business?"

Amy took the opportunity to glance at her watch. "Oh, mercy, look at the time. I better head for work." She sidestepped me and was off like a rabbit, headed toward the driveway. "It was really great seeing you, though. You have a good visit with your family, okay?"

I didn't answer because there wasn't time. Amy was out of there as fast as her size-five heels would carry her. I watched my brother exit the kayak and climb into Blaine Underhill's boat, then motor out of the bay with the red kayak trailing forlornly behind like a leftover Christmas decoration.

When they were out of sight I went back to the cottage, got dressed, and headed for the main house, my mind finally fresh and alert, and my determination renewed. Time to unravel the tangled web of family secrets and sort out the sudden appearance of a supposed competing offer. I needed to get my mother to Seattle as soon as possible to sign the papers that would complete the sale of the family properties. Considering what I'd just seen and heard, maybe the competing offer wasn't so sudden, after all. Maybe Clay had been planning this hijacking for a while.

When I entered the house, Mother was in the kitchen, sipping coffee at the breakfast table. The uncs were nowhere to be seen. That was fortunate for me, because the person I really needed was Mom. Alone.

"The delivery man usually comes around three," she offered, just as pleasantly as if we sat down to coffee every morning. "It's a good thing today is Friday. They deliver on Fridays."

"What?" As usual, we were on two different astral planes. Opening the cabinet to search for a coffee cup, I noted that all the dishes were still in place. In fact, everything in the kitchen was more or less where it had been sixteen years ago. There was no sign of an estate auction having taken place or the packing up of any personal items.

"Your purse," Mom answered pleasantly. "I'm sure you're missing your cell phone and all those gadgets."

I poured a cup of coffee and sat down. "I just hope some guy in Hackensack isn't stealing my identity."

Looking out the window, Mom sighed, as if my presence were a black cloud over her morning. "Terrible, to be in your twenties and be such a cynic. Have a little faith in people, Heather. He was a very kind man. A good spirit. I could tell it when he called on the phone." Her eyes, a soft, mossy color in the morning light, turned my way, filled with disappointment.

"I just wish you'd told him to take my purse to the nearest police station, or the bus company. Someone official." Maybe I was being cynical, but losing your ID, your money, and your iPhone a thousand miles from home was about the most vulnerable feeling in the world. I didn't do vulnerable well, especially not in Moses Lake. "And I'm *thirty-four*, Mom. Clay is the one in his twenties."

She lowered her head into her hand, groaning. "Ugh, don't remind me. Where does the time go, anyway?" Pausing, she looked at me as if I were a stranger she was trying to cipher. "Thirty-four . . ." Her brows drew together.

In some families, I suppose it might have seemed strange, even offensive, for your mother to not know how old you were, but it felt normal enough for us. Mother could have discussed any writer from Aristotle to Maya Angelou ad nauseam, but she couldn't tell you how old her daughter was.

"Seems like yesterday we were here." She breathed the words softly, turning to the window again. There was a melancholy tone to her voice that drilled deep into me and lit a fuse I feared had the power to reach the bedrock of my soul and blow things apart. "The four of us," she added.

I felt sick, then angry. All the emotions from that year came back—every day of watching her slowly fade after my father's death, of wondering whether she would disappear completely, pass through the bed sheets by osmosis, and be gone. Every long night of listening to her moan in her tranquilizer-induced stupor and call my father's name, until my baby brother, frightened and distraught, came into my room and crawled into bed with me.

I felt the heat of teenage anger, long dormant, volcanic, rising to the surface, hot and fluid. I hated my mother all over again. "Why are you here?" The words were sharp. "I want the truth."

She swirled her coffee in the cup. "I just . . . needed to be. Here."

"Why is Clay here?" The absolute worst thing for Clay was to be offered one more distraction from finishing law school and beginning a stable, self-supporting life. Didn't Mom ever get tired of paying his way? Didn't she get tired of rescuing him from his mishaps—wrecked cars, tuition payments that came up short because of impromptu ski trips he couldn't afford, the time he missed taking his finals because campus police found rolling papers and a Baggie of marijuana in his dorm room. . . . He claimed those things were left there by a friend, but still. He wouldn't ever grow up if Mom didn't stop treating him like a kid.

She smiled, even laughed a little, staring down at her coffee, reading the blobs of creamer like an oracle. "Oh, Clay loves to come here. He comes all the time."

"What do you *mean* he comes all the time?" Clay and I might not have kept in touch particularly well, but I did have some idea of where he was and when. He'd never mentioned spending time in Moses Lake.

"Roger lives here some of the time," Mom said simply.

I studied her—took in the loose-fitting plaid shirt, the khaki pants that were just as likely to have come from Goodwill as L.L.Bean, the carelessly plaited brown hair, tinseled with strands of gray. She was dressed in her usual garb for rambling around the English department, discussing quatrains, iambic pentameter, and Haiku as an expression of self. Her appearance was normal enough this morning, but maybe she really was having some sort of a breakdown. "Roger the *dog*?"

"Do you know another Roger?"

I bit my lower lip. If I'd had my money, ID, iPhone, and car keys, I would have walked out the door right then. Even the prospect of being project manager on the Proxica facility design wasn't worth losing my mind. I was starting to rue the day that Mother had contacted me to ask if I could remember where the deeds to my father's portion of the family farm had been stored after his death. She was practically gleeful at the news that Uncle Herbert and Uncle Charley were finally ready to sell out. Shortly after that conversation, I'd happened upon an article in the Proxica shareholders' magazine that said the company was planning major expansions in Texas. I'd asked Richard to quietly make some inquiries, and that had started the ball rolling. I should have known it would swerve badly off course and compact me into the soil before the deal was done.

The insanity of this sudden shift, combined with the ghosts in this town, was too much to bear. I couldn't stand it. I couldn't sit in this house, talking about Roger the dog over coffee. "I want. To know. What. Is going on. There isn't any competing offer for the real estate, is there? No one in their right minds would pay the price Richard got for us—not with the economy the way it is. Even if we hang on to the property until the economy improves, we'd never get that kind of money."

Her eyelids held calmly at half-mast, regarding me with a measure of coolness that hurts coming from your mother. "Which would make you wonder why this broker is offering such a sum, wouldn't it? Presumably he has to then resell the property for an even higher price. Who, exactly, would he sell it to, if the price we're getting is so astronomically out of line?"

"Why do you care?" I threw up my hands, let them slap to the tabletop, and affected the look of being completely and thoroughly offended. But an inconvenient smidge of conscience landed on my shoulders, squawking in my ear like a magpie. I had been keeping secrets, too. But that was part of the deal with the broker. I wasn't at liberty to divulge any information. "When we started this process, you couldn't wait to be out from under the place. You were tired of having to keep up with the accounting on the farmland and figure out how to divide up the property-tax payments with Uncle Herb and Uncle Charley. You said you wanted to be able to give Clay and me the money from the land, because it was our inheritance. You said that Clay needed the money to pay off some loans. What, exactly, about that has changed?"

Pausing to take a bite of her English muffin, she tipped her chin up and chewed slowly. "We've rethought it, simply enough. Uncle Herbert and Uncle Charley have owned the farm all their lives, for one thing. They and your grandfather grew up there." Her gaze met mine in a way that seemed intended to stab. "And so did your father."

Emotion balled in my throat and dripped downward, burning like acid, threatening to eat away the steely coating of anger and morph it into something raw and unpredictable. *My father died there*, I thought. There were two houses on the farm—the two-story white clapboard that had been built by my grandparents in the forties, and the modest stone house beside it. The basement of that little stone house was the scene of the accidental shooting that had changed all our lives. Among other memories, the question of whether the word *accidental* really applied haunted that house. It haunted me.

Even now, sitting here at Harmony Shores, I could feel the proximity of that place, fifteen miles down the rural highway. I could feel the house where my father's life had ended, where my nightmares took me again and again. I'd never set foot on the farm after the week my father died, and I didn't want to now. I just wanted that place to be gone. Maybe then the nightmares would stop.

Stay focused. Don't let her get to you. Don't let any of this get to you. "Uncle Charley and Uncle Herbert aren't the problem here, Mom, and you know it. Both of them realize that they have to move closer to Donny. This is about you and Clay, and as much work as I've put in on this deal, I deserve the truth."

She sent a narrow look my way, her lips tightening. I'd finally broken through the layer of serenity, found a nerve. "It's always about work for you, isn't it? Your whole life is about work." She frowned as if she simultaneously pitied me and wondered how I could possibly be her offspring. "You'll have to talk to your brother about it. Clay can explain everything more clearly than I can. He has a better business understanding."

Business understanding? My brother? Clay couldn't even be counted upon not to end up stuck out in the middle of nowhere on a bicycle, with pneumonia. "What business?" Maybe Clay thought he was going to somehow arrange a competing offer on the property—something on which he could turn a dime, perhaps. But as textbook brilliant as my brother was, he was out of his league in this situation. There was no better deal out there to be had. "I don't want to ask Clay. I'm asking you."

Mom stood up, took her coffee cup to the sink, calmly rinsed it out, and squirted a little dish soap into it. "Simply put, we're considering our options, just as I told you on the phone. I know you thought that by coming here you could change things, Heather, but you can't."

"What *options*? What?" I threw up my hands, shook them in the air like a crazy woman. I have never in my life, personal or professional, met anyone else who could bring out that side of me.

"Well, if you must know, your brother thinks we should keep the place in the family." She smiled as if I should be happy to hear of Clay's epiphany. "He's interested in living at the old farm. The renter who was staying in the two-story house has moved out. The place is empty and available. Clay adores the old tractors and the feeling of being close to the land. It suits him. I've never seen him so happy."

"What in the world is Clay going to do to support himself financially, living on what's left of a dairy farm, fifteen miles outside in the country?" A sarcastic laugh tailed the question. I couldn't help it. The idea of any of us living on that farm again made me sick. The little stone house had been locked up since my father's death, and the two-story clapboard next door had been occupied by a series of renters over the years.

Mother shrugged, her shoulders stiff. She hated being challenged. She was accustomed to reigning supreme over underlings and dewy-eyed graduate students. "He is looking into taking over the restaurant and the canoe business. It worked well enough for Uncle Charley all these years. He made enough of a living, and . . ."

My head spun as Mom went on, the insanity growing

exponentially, like the 3-D virtual image of a skyscraper, building layer upon layer from the electronic blueprint, the windows and doors filling in, the walls extruding and becoming real. But this entire building was leaning off-kilter. My mother was supposedly considering moving to Moses Lake, too.

"I'm ready for a change," she asserted. "I've been looking for an opportunity to step off the carousel of teaching and lecturing. I could pursue my writing, maybe teach some classes online. These days there are opportunities, and with my credentials . . . Well, it's perfect, really. Uncle Herb doesn't want to leave his house, and this way he wouldn't have to. I could live here in Harmony House with the uncs, and Clay could live out at the farm. It's crossed my mind that Harmony House would make a lovely bed-and-breakfast. It's already licensed for public occupancy."

"Public . . . what . . ." I stammered. "You have got to be kidding." Bracing my palms on the table, I stood up. There are times when, despite all attempts at keeping things at a rational level with my mother, the fact is that if we stay in the same room any longer, a Jerry Springer moment will erupt. Chairs will fly, claws will come out, and hair will be pulled.

I was conscious of some sort of emotional fault line giving way within me, the tectonic plates sliding and making the ground shake. One more nugget of craziness on my mother's side of the divide, and things would break wide open, allowing ugliness of epic proportion to spew forth. The only thing to do in a moment like that is walk away before chaos breaks out, and keep walking for however long it takes.

There is indeed, perhaps, no better way to hold
communion with the sea than sitting in the sun
on the veranda of a fisherman's cafe.

—Joseph W. Beach
(via Pop Dorsey, proprietor, Waterbird Bait and Grocery)

Chapter 6

The entire conversation had repeated twice in my head by the time I found myself at the picnic grounds behind Lakeshore Community Church. Doves fluttered from branch to branch overhead, their voices incongruously sweet, waves lapped at the shore, and squirrels dashed about gathering leftover pecans as I paced between the picnic tables, muttering and hissing like an alley cat caught in a box.

The situation with my mother and my brother was crazy, even for them. Mom was hardly suited to running a bed-and-breakfast in the country. Who would want to stay in a former funeral home anyway? And Clay had no way of getting the money together to buy Uncle Charley's restaurant and the canoe-rental business.

Unless . . . unless Mom was bankrolling it with whatever was left of the nest egg that had come from my father's life insurance. She'd hated it when Clay left with the disaster relief team. She was scared to death something would happen to him. Now that he was back, was this her way of trying to make sure he didn't wander off to the far parts of the globe again? Was she going to tie him down with fried catfish and canoes? All the money he'd borrowed and not paid back, all his starts and stops in law school were forgotten, and Mom was ready to take care of him, just like always?

Why was it always so easy for him? Why could Clay do whatever he wanted—consume her funds, consume her energy, wander aimlessly through his life—yet remain the object of her adoration? Why didn't I ever get that kind of consideration? Why did she criticize my life while approving of his, no matter what he did? It had always been this way. From the beginning, I was Dad's and Clay was hers. But Dad was gone, and I was on the outside looking in, while Mom and Clay flitted through life, two birds of a feather.

Tears came out of nowhere, and I sank onto one of the picnic benches. Trish was right—I'd be better off if I could stop expecting things from my mother. But no matter how old you get, no matter how hard you try, you can't give up wanting your mother to love you. Somehow, though, I had to find a way to let go of that hope, that expectation. It was hollowing me out little by little, like water dripping on stone.

Taking a breath, I swallowed hard and pushed the tears away. Our family relationships were complicated, confused, upside-down— and they always would be. I had to learn to work from that basis of knowledge. Given a little time, Mother would come down to earth and see that Clay running the restaurant and her turning the funeral home into a bed-and-breakfast was a pipe dream. Surely, I could find ways to help open her eyes and get her to Seattle before the broker offer on the property expired. I could still salvage this thing and save the uncs from certain disaster. . . .

"A little brisk out here for a picnic." A voice from behind startled me, and I jerked upright, feeling like I'd been caught someplace I shouldn't be. But I knew why I was there. I felt close to my father in this place. One of the last things we'd done together was go to Sunday morning service. I was cranky about it, of course. The pastor was boring and the music old-fashioned. There were no projection screens. There was no five-piece band rocking out modern worship music, like we had in our church back home. In tiny Lakeshore Community Church, there was only the pastor droning on while babies made noise, the casserole ladies gave me disapproving looks, and Mama B sang off-key, her voice crackling high above the rest.

I glanced over my shoulder, expecting the pastor I remembered, the one who'd tried to placate me with the usual platitudes as I struggled to comprehend the loss of my father. Instead, a thirty-something man, tall and lanky, with a thin, hawkish face, was headed down the hill.

"Want to come inside?" he asked, thumbing over his shoulder with an amiable smile.

I stood up, the back of my legs now fully chilled from sitting on the frosty stone bench. "No, I'm fine. I just . . ." His gaze met mine, and for an instant I had the weirdest urge to tell him everything. He seemed like the sort who would listen. I wondered if he knew my brother and my mother. Maybe I could gain some information about how long Clay had been hanging around town. I wiped my eyes and introduced myself. "Heather Hampton. I used to live here. I was just taking a walk around town, remembering."

His face brightened, and he held my hand captive between both of his for a moment. "Reverend Hay. Good to meet you. Any relation to the Harmony Shores Hamptons—Charley and Herbert?" I noted that he didn't mention my mother or my brother.

"My great uncles," I answered.

"We're sure going to miss them around here. Moses Lake won't be the same without the Hampton brothers. Tell your uncles I'll get by to see them before they go. I'm a little behind. Been gone three weeks on a mission trip with my fiancée's church."

He flashed a quick smile that was somewhere between giddy and bashful, and I decided two things: I liked him despite the preacher suit, and he knew absolutely nothing about what was going on with my family. As far as he was aware, the uncs were packing up and leaving. So . . . all of Clay's Moses Lake connections and his plan to live here permanently had developed in the last three weeks?

A horn honked up the hill by the road, and both of us turned to look. Uncle Charley's Ford pickup, Old Blue, was rolling along the shoulder. The window cranked down, and he waved us closer. "Hey, there you are!" he called, and Reverend Hay and I started up the hill. "Been lookin' for you, Heather. Your mom said you went out for a walk. C'mon, I'll take you to breakfast. You, too, if you want, Hay."

"Got a building committee meeting in twenty minutes," the reverend answered as we walked toward the road. "Promised Bonnie I'd pick her up at the office in Cleburne and take her to lunch, so I'd better stay here and get everything set for the committee, try to keep things moving along. When lunch hour hits, Bonnie's ready to get out of that counseling office and go somewhere else for a while."

Uncle Charley smacked his lips and shook his head as we traversed the ditch. "Well, sorry I can't be on the buildin' committee. They get things set with Blaine Underhill about the loan for the new addition?"

New addition. Glancing over my shoulder, I winced. I hoped they found someone who could design the add-on space in a way that would preserve the historic character of the building. So often, these little jobs out in the middle of nowhere were poorly done architectural eyesores.

I noted that Blaine Underhill was involved here, too.

"For the most part," Reverend Hay answered. "Blaine can't make the meeting. Said he'd be back in the bank about eleven, so I'll take everything by there for him before I head for Cleburne. He's gone to an appointment this morning."

Appointment? A sardonic scoff passed my lips as I circled the truck to get in on the passenger side. Blaine Underhill was out on the lake with my brother. Fishing. On a workday morning. I couldn't imagine taking off fishing while the rest of the world was at work.

Actually, that brought up the question of why, if my brother was in such a hurry to relocate to Moses Lake and take over Catfish Charley's, he was out fishing. Shouldn't he be at the restaurant, learning the ropes from the manager there, and getting the place ready to open for lunch? A little greasy spoon like Charley's wasn't exactly the kind of high-profit place where the owner didn't have to put in hours. Until his health had declined, Uncle Charley had worked from morning through lunch, taken care of his cattle at the family farm for a few hours in the afternoon, then returned for the supper rush. His wife, Aunt Fea, had worked every day at the restaurant until shortly before her death. They'd lived on a houseboat docked behind Catfish Charley's, and between the restaurant, the canoe business, and the cabins, they were always busy.

Yet Clay had time to spend the morning fishing with Blaine Underhill?

Then again, maybe there was more to the fishing friendship than just dropping a line in the water. What had Amy said earlier? Something about my brother and Blaine becoming friends after talking so much at the bank.

Hmmm . . . How does a guy with no life plan and no money take over ownership of a restaurant? He makes friends with the banker. When Clay was on fire about his latest plan—whatever it happened to be—he could be incredibly alluring. He didn't even have to work at it because his beliefs were genuine. The problem was that Clay's focus was like a butterfly—bright, intense, beautiful to look at, unbelievably compelling . . . but likely to flit off at any moment. Blaine Underhill had no idea what he was being sucked into. Someone needed to clue him in, and it looked like that someone would be me. As much as I loved my brother, I couldn't let him create a situation that could leave a financial mess behind in Moses Lake.

Uncle Charley and Reverend Hay continued their conversation as I climbed into the truck. Uncle Charley suggested that the church should hire me to design the new fellowship hall, since I *drew up buildings and such*. Rather than telling them that this project was too small for our firm, I wrote my email address on a feed-store receipt from the mound of dashboard clutter and handed it out the window. Maybe I could do the job pro bono—a gift to my father's hometown. It would be worth it to see the church building, with its European lines and the decorative stone masonry of the original German pioneers, properly preserved.

Uncle Charley and I discussed the new fellowship hall as we wound our way around the lake, headed, I surmised by the direction we were driving, to the Waterbird Bait and Grocery. The local crowd of fishermen and retirees had been gathering there to sip coffee and solve the world's problems since shortly after the lake went in. I found myself picturing the Waterbird now, remembering my father taking me there when I was little. We bought lemon drops, cartons of squirmy worms, and dips of ice cream. Scoops of ice cream and scoops of worm-filled dirt came in the same white waxed-cardboard containers, so when you reached into the sack, you had to be careful which one you grabbed.

A laugh tickled my throat as I remembered squealing and tossing dirt all over the car once when I opened the wrong container. I was twelve or thirteen then, a sophisticated city girl, convinced that worms were not for me, but the lure of an afternoon alone with my dad was irresistible. We were visiting my grandparents for some holiday—Easter, maybe. The bluebonnets were out, the roadsides everywhere awash with sprays of vibrant azure that rivaled the water in the lake. My brother must have stayed home, because it was just Dad and me.

"Somethin' funny?" Uncle Charley asked as we rounded the corner and I saw the Waterbird's tin roof peeking through the cluster of overhanging live oaks ahead. For an instant, I heard my dad.

"I was just thinking about coming here with Dad," I answered, and I was surprised that, for once, the mention of him didn't trail dark threads behind it.

Uncle Charley chuckled. "Your dad liked this old store. Used to be when he was little, if I ever passed by here with him in the truck, he'd beg me to stop, so he could get at the penny candy counter. That boy did like his sweets.

"Wasn't too many years after that, he would've hung around here all day long, if he could've. It was where the young folks went to look at each other, and all them girls liked your daddy. Back when your granddaddy was farmin' cotton at the old place, if we ever had a tractor or a truck break down and we made the mistake of sending your dad to town, it'd be an hour later, and we'd say, 'Where in the world is Neal?' Sure enough, we'd call up to the Waterbird, and he'd be there—stopped in for a Coke and ended up flirtin' with some girl."

"Really?" I said, trying to imagine that side of my dad. He'd always been the responsible one when I was growing up. He had to be.

"Oh, sure." Uncle Charley chuckled as we drifted off the shoulder into the gravel parking lot. "Your dad was a corker. Gave his mama and daddy more than a few gray hairs. I ever tell you about the time he and some other boys found a little ol' possum curled up in a dead tree during the cold weather? They put it in the choir closet at church on Sunday mornin', thinking they were gonna get it later and use it to play a joke on somebody. That thing got all warmed up durin' service and went to growlin' and thumpin' around in there, and you never seen a bunch of boys sitting so straight in the pew, trying to look like they didn't hear a thing. Ended up, those boys had to work the rest of the winter to pay for a new set of Christmas choir robes."

Uncle Charley and I laughed as we exited the car to go into the Waterbird. Suddenly I was glad I'd come. I'd never heard that story about my father, never known that side of him. When we'd come to Moses Lake to visit my grandparents during my childhood years, my mother had poured on the guilt long-distance, until we felt bad for enjoying anything.

As we entered the Waterbird, old men gathered in the red vinyl booths on the left wall waved and called out greetings worthy of an episode of *Cheers*. They observed that I was much more attractive than Charley's usual traveling companion, Uncle Herb. Already positioned in a seat along the wall with a cup of coffee, Uncle Herb pretended to take offense.

The Waterbird was exactly as I remembered it: the café, deli, and cash counter along the right side of the room; the booths and a pay phone on the wall at the far left; three aisles of indiscriminately mixed groceries, fishing tackle, doughnut cases, and candy in the middle. Beside me, the minnow tanks burbled in strangely close proximity to the drink machine and the freezer case. Along the far wall, a bank of tall windows afforded a view of the lake below, complete with docks, boathouses, and a waterside gas pump for boats.

As Uncle Charley ordered coffee for the two of us, I moved across the room to look at the wall of wisdom. I wondered if Gary and his family had signed it while they were in town. It wouldn't be easy to find their entry, if they had indeed made one, among the countless signatures and bits of Sharpie-pen lore that stretched from the front counter, circled the windows, and went all the way back to the bathroom. Without even intending to, I followed a rhythm of

82

remembered steps, moving toward a place I hoped would still be there, just to the left of the windows. And then I was in front of it, reading the quote my father and I had jotted on the wall together.

You are braver than you believe, stronger than you seem, and smarter than you think. –Winnie the Pooh.

We'd signed our names after the quote—Neal Hampton, Heather Hampton—and then the year. I was nine, my father still a young man. We'd read the Winnie the Pooh books together so many times we could recite them by heart. It had never occurred to me that this place, Moses Lake, was my father's Hundred Acre Wood, and he wanted me to love it as much as he did. Maybe he'd had a premonition when we wrote that quote on the wall. Even now, I knew the rest of the quote—the part we'd left out, so as to save space. Touching a hand to words, I heard my father and me reciting the last part together, giving each other a high five after adding our entry: *But the most important thing is, even if we're apart, I'll always be with you.*

My father hadn't chosen our place on the wall at random. He'd picked a spot directly underneath a wooden plaque left behind by a German tinker who passed through Moses Lake back in the days when tinkers drove from town to town, sharpening knives and sheep shears, and fixing leaky kettles. The tinker's riddle had been the beginning of the wall of wisdom. Looking at it now, I remembered standing with my father as I read it. *The future is a blank page, but not a mystery.* The riddle had eluded me then. I'd complained to Dad that it didn't make any sense; I didn't see how it could be his favorite. He'd only laughed, scrubbed a big, brawny hand over my hair, and said *No sense trying to cheat a riddle. You have to figure it out for yourself, or it's no fun. Keep thinking on it. It'll be clear one of these days.*

Unfortunately, the tinker's riddle was no more logical to me now than it had been then. A page is either blank, or it's not. If it is blank, the possibilities are endless, the end result a mystery.

"Better come fix this cup the way you like it, darlin'," Uncle Charley called from the coffee counter.

I turned away from the wall and crossed the room, feeling unburdened, rather than weighed down, by the memory of that day with my father. The quote we'd written seemed almost a message from him, a promise that even though I hadn't been the person I'd wanted to be during our last turbulent months together, he realized that inside the melodramatic teenager there was still the little girl who loved him in the Winnie-the-Pooh sort of way—always and no matter what. The same way he'd loved me.

One of Uncle Herbert's fishing buddies vacated a seat for me as I finished preparing my coffee and walked to the table. A round of greetings came my way, along with some comments about how I couldn't really be related to Charley and Herb, because I was too pretty. I laughed and blushed at the banter circling the table, a few anecdotes about my father livening up the mix. A warm feeling washed over me as Uncle Herb reached for my coat and threw it into an empty booth like we owned the place. I had the sense of being right at home.

Two of the men sharing space with us looked familiar, although it took a minute for my memory banks to dredge up the information. They'd aged since my time here, but I knew who they were—Nester Grimland, who'd kept the Moses Lake school busses running, and Burt Lacey, the high-school principal, apparently retired now, since he was sitting in the Waterbird midmorning on a Friday.

"Hey, Missy, I ever tell you that your dad worked for me one summer milkin' cows?" Nester Grimland offered, wiping coffee off his thick gray moustache and directing a wink my way. He looked like one of those skinny cowboy statues you'd find for sale in a roadside tourist trap.

"Really?" I asked. "Dad never talked much about his dairy work." Actually, my dad had said that growing up on a dairy made him want to get a college education.

Burt Lacey frowned sideways, squinting through glasses that had gotten thicker since his days as a principal. "What are you talking about, Nester? You never had milk cows." I remembered them arguing just this way any number of times when I'd passed by the bus barn after school.

"I sure did," Nester insisted, seeming offended. "Neal Hampton worked milkin' cows for me." Adjusting his cowboy hat, he flashed a covert glance my way, a brow lifting conspiratorially. "Bet your daddy told 'ya about workin' for me, didn't he?"

I felt compelled to play along. "You know, I think he did say something about that . . . uhhh . . . once or twice." Both of the uncs swiveled toward me, cocking their heads, confused.

"See there," Nester held up a weathered hand, serving me up as proof. "Her daddy milked for me. Only problem was, every time a pretty girl drove by on the highway, that boy would come all unfocused. Ruined a whole batch of milk one time. He ever tell you that story?" Nester aimed a quick head-twitch at me.

"Ummm . . . yes. Yes, I think he . . . did."

Burt Lacey rolled his eyes. "Well, let us have it, Nester. You're not gonna hush up until we've heard the whole thing. How'd the batch of milk get ruined?"

Reclining comfortably now that he had the conversational floor, Nester hooked an elbow over the back of his seat. "Well, see, it was like this. One day, that there boy was a-milkin', and he had him a good rhythm goin' along—playin' a little tune in the bucket. 'America the Beautiful,' I think it was. Must've been close to the Fourth of July." Pausing, he stroked his chin, pretending to think.

Burt Lacey snorted, Uncle Charley added sugar to his coffee, and Uncle Herb scratched his bald head, quiet as usual.

"Anyhoo, so there's young Neal Hampton, milkin' along, and a load of cheerleaders drives by, and he ain't payin' no attention at all to what he's doing. Right about then, a big ol' horse fly comes along and starts circling that milk cow . . . just buzzin' around and buzzin' around. Which ain't really a problem, since there's always flies in a cow barn, but that boy didn't even notice when that fly went right in that old milk cow's ear. The kid just kept watchin' them cheerleaders and milkin' along, tryin' to finish, so he could chase after them purdy girls. He didn't hear that fly buzzin' round and round inside that milk cow, looking for a way out. Didn't notice a thing. Finally, that kid was milkin' so fast it created a vacuum inside the whole cow and sucked that horsefly right out the udder. Landed smack in the milk bucket and ruined the whole batch."

Uncle Charley groaned and pulled his hat low over his eyes, and Uncle Herb shook his head. Burt Lacey slapped the tabletop, air whistling through his teeth. "Nester, that's not one bit possible. Even she knows that."

I shrugged and, quite wisely, kept quiet, not being an expert on milk cows.

Nester drew back against the wall. "She don't know any such thing, do ya, young lady?"

I shook my head again, and Nester took a sip of his coffee, then swilled it while all eyes remained focused on him. "Just goes to show, that boy took after the rest of the Hampton men. Why, you ask any of their wives and they'll tell you that it ain't the first time someone in that family's—" he paused for dramatic effect, the corners of his moustache twitching as he finished with—"let somethin' go in one ear and out the udder."

A chorus of laughter followed, and from his wheelchair behind the counter, Pop Dorsey joined in. I laughed along, having the fleeting thought that it felt good to be here, just sitting and watching the world go by on a Friday morning, taking a little time for coffee and conversation. When was the last time I'd done that?

Ever?

Gazing out at the water glistening in the morning sunlight below, I had the weird thought that I might miss Moses Lake after all of this was over.

The conversation turned to spinner baits and fat bass, and Burt Lacey went to the coffee counter and commandeered the pot to refresh everyone's coffee. As he was returning the pot to its resting spot, a little dark-haired girl wandered from behind the deli counter and walked down the center aisle between loaves of bread, bags of charcoal, and a smattering of plumbing supplies. Studying the shelves, she picked up imaginary items and put them in a miniature shopping basket. The attention of every "grandpa" in the room quickly gravitated to her.

"Hey, Birdie, you gonna come serve us up some tea?" Uncle Charley motioned her over.

The little girl smiled shyly, her wide blue eyes twinkling.

Uncle Charley leaned back in his chair. "I'm tellin' ya, I'm just about dry as a baked horned toad on a six-lane stretch of blacktop. Sure could use me some tea."

Her smile widened, and she skipped on over to us, standing on her toes, so that she could look into his cup. Her lips twisted to one side, and she braced a hand on her hip. "It ain't empty."

I had the fleeting thought that it was a shame Uncle Charley and his wife hadn't been able to have kids. He'd been one of my favorite Moses Lake attractions when I was little. Every kid in town loved him. "Aw, that's just that old black coffee," he complained, giving the cup a disdainful look. "I need me some of that good ol' magic tea. You got any of that in yer basket?"

As Birdie fished around in her basket of random toys and produced a little plastic teapot, I felt a twinge of remorse at the thought of the kids I didn't have never meeting the great-uncle I wouldn't see again after this weekend.

Watching Birdie serve pretend tea, I wished life were different than it was.

The banter started again after Birdie had filled all the cups and then scampered off. A buzzer above the back door interrupted the conversation, and Uncle Charley stood up, peeking out the back window. "Looks like you need to turn on the gas pump down there, Pop. Put it on the Underhill's bill. I'll tell you what, that's a nice fishin' rig Blaine's got. He could win some votes with that thing, sure enough."

Before I'd even given it any thought, I was excusing myself, slipping from my seat, and grabbing my coat. I headed out the back door to discern— from the source—what business was going on between my brother and the local banker.

A brisk February wind whipped over the water and raced up the hill. Swinging the coat over my shoulders, I stuck my arms in the sleeves and quickly realized that I'd grabbed someone else's outerwear from the pile on the empty booth. This one was large enough for me and my two best friends, and it was a camo color with roadstripe-orange western detailing. I pulled it on anyway, the bottom falling halfway to my knees, surrounding me like a puffy tent as I strode down the rock steps toward the lakeshore and the dock, where Blaine Underhill was nonchalantly gassing up his boat, one foot braced on the dock railing, the collar of a khaki-colored barn jacket turned upright against his neck, hiding his face. There was no sign of my brother or the red kayak. Apparently this morning's fishing trip was over.

A strange tangle of past and present swirled in my thoughts, a fruitless attempt to mesh the memory of the boy from high school with the banker of today, my brother's new best friend. If Blaine

Underhill was the moneyman behind Clay's plans, did he have any idea what a mistake he was making? Did he know that, sooner or later, their plan would result in disaster for the uncs and leave Clay responsible for not only financial obligations, but most likely the reality of once again going from hero to zero in the eyes of the family? With Clay's history of chaotic life shifts, there was no telling where things might lead. Clay might join some mission trip to Bora-Bora and never come back. In the meantime, the property that had belonged to Uncle Herbert, Uncle Charley, and my family for generations would end up in foreclosure, in the hands of . . . the bank?

Potential motivations began taking shape in my mind, even though I didn't want to entertain them. Would Blaine Underhill finance my brother's flight of fancy, knowing that Clay would fail and the bank would end up with the property and whatever down payment my mother was putting into this unholy partnership? I tried to imagine the object of my chemistry-class crush, now playing the part of the heartless, shifty-eyed banker—the sort with the handlebar moustache and the evil laugh. The kind who would toss widows, orphans, and helpless old men out in the snow. Could he have changed so much from the prankster who had the ability to answer teachers' questions but typically chose to go for a laugh instead?

Of course he could have changed. Haven't you? After sixteen years, who could say what kind of person Blaine Underhill was? In truth, the Blaine I remembered was a schoolgirl fantasy. Even back then, I had no idea who he really was behind the high-school mask.

It didn't matter now. If he had any intentions of taking advantage of my family, he had another think coming.

Every ounce of nostalgic sentiment evaporated from my thoughts, and I welcomed the empowering rush of righteous indignation. It was easier to handle than leftover puppy love and mushy gushy thoughts of an unrequited adoration. Blaine Underhill was about to find out that the wimpy, quiet, messed-up girl who let everyone push her around in high school had grown up and gotten a backbone.

He hooked the nozzle back on the gas pump as I hit the dock, the wooden heels on my suede boots making a hollow *ping-tap-ping* on the half-frozen wood. I took note of the cracks between the boards. The boots didn't have high heels, but they did have heels, and those cracks were wide enough to create a misstep that would entirely ruin my entrance and put a kink in the strictly-business and slightly dragonlike persona that had served me so well in a male-dominated career field. The banker was about to see that not everyone in the Hampton family was filled with impractical dreams.

Wiping his hands on a rag, he looked up, blinked, and cocked his head to one side, as if a woman in dress boots, skinny jeans, and a giant camouflage coat weren't an everyday sight on the dock.

Employing a strategy I'd long ago learned from Mel while dealing with difficult clients, I opened the dialog and got right to the point. "I'd like to know what, exactly, is going on between you and my brother."

His expression went completely blank, and he backed away a step as I made it to the platform near the gas pumps. The decking rocked slightly in the current, causing me to spread my feet like a gunfighter about to draw down at the O.K. Corral.

"Ma'am?" A dark brow lifted, and his chin drew inward a bit, the little cleft there growing more pronounced. I'd forgotten about that cleft in his chin. . . .

I admonished myself to remain focused. It was harder than I'd thought it would be. His appreciative look, and the lanky southern cadence of his words lured me in some way I didn't want to contemplate. "Please don't insult my intelligence. He may be falling for this, but I'm not. Let's be honest, shall we?"

Blaine finished wiping his hands and set the rag aside. "All right." His eyes narrowed, black lashes fanning over the brown centers.

His dark hair was shorter than it used to be, windblown right now, curling just a bit over his ears and on his collar.

I took a breath, paused a moment to get my thoughts in order, and remembered watching those lashes drift toward his cheeks as he rested his chin on his hand in chemistry class. "Have you checked my brother's credit rating, looked into his background, investigated his history?"

Crossing his arms over his chest, Blaine leaned against the railing, the barest hint of amusement playing on his lips. I realized I was looking at his lips. I quit looking and focused on his forehead.

"That's not really the way I like to do things. I don't see the point."

"Don't see the *point*?" I threw my hands up, and the ends of the oversized leaf-print sleeves flopped like tree branches in the wind. "Are you serious?" Maybe Blaine Underhill really was still the goof-off he'd been in high school. Maybe his parents, aging and unable to figure out what else to do with him, were letting him use the bank as his personal play toy. Maybe he was more like my brother than I'd thought. Weren't there federal regulators who prevented bankers from doing stupid things with other people's money? "What kind of sense does that make?"

He shrugged nonchalantly, his response annoyingly calm. "I think it makes perfect sense. Some things just aren't right to do." He had the same drawl as Clay's new girlfriend, Amy, though Blaine's was less pronounced.

"What?" My tree-branch sleeves flopped up and down once, twice. Talking with my hands was one of those nervous habits I had yet to overcome. "*Some things aren't right to do*. Give me a break. How can you possibly operate like that?" This innocent country-boy act had to be a way of toying with me, trying to throw me off track. Maybe I should report him to some kind of . . . I wasn't sure who . . . the FDIC, or the board of banking, or someone.

"A man's background is his own business." He brushed a scrap of what looked like hay off his sleeve, and I noted that for a guy who'd just been out fishing, he was strangely neat and clean—pressed jeans, fairly new cowboy boots, and a white collar peeking around the top button of his coat. He looked like he was dressed for a barn dance or a night at the rodeo, rather than an early-morning fishing trip.

I rolled my eyes, irritated with the runaround. He needed to be upstairs telling milk-cow stories with Nester Grimland and Burt Lacey. No bank—not even a little redneck bank like the one across the street from the Moses Lake post office—loaned out money without checking the applicant's background. "Pah-lease. Do I look stupid to you?"

"No, ma'am," he answered, his eyes twinkling. "A little fashion-challenged, maybe, but not stupid." His lips spread into a grin that went right to the pit of my stomach and did something strange there.

"This is *not* a joke." And how dare he think that I'd be weak enough to fall for the class-clown act. I wasn't used to people blowing me off, not taking me seriously. I hadn't gotten to the position of senior manager with a major firm by being the simpering little wimpkin I was in high school. "I guess maybe it's a joke to you, or just business, or whatever, but as much as my brother drives me insane, I do care about his future. A lot. I don't want him to end up falling flat on his face and taking the rest of the family with him. As brilliant as he is, he's like a big . . . teenager, basically. He has never managed to stick with anything in his life, and he won't stick with this. He'll be into it just long enough to dig a great big hole, and then something else will catch his eye." My arms, lost within the voluminous sleeves, beseeched him to look at Clay objectively.

"I hadn't heard that about him, but it's good to know."

I had the sense that I might be getting somewhere. Maybe I could sway him and end this whole thing. Clay wouldn't be happy with me, but he'd tack in a new direction soon enough, and then he'd be glad he hadn't entangled himself in Moses Lake. So would my mother, actually, and the uncs would be rid of the burden of properties they could no longer take care of. I would continue on to be the project manager, and Moses Lake would have over three-hundred badly needed new jobs. Everyone would be better off.

"So, you can see that the best thing to do is just . . . not help him."

Uncrossing his legs and then crossing them the other way, the banker blinked, cocking his head back a bit, as if he were trying to make sense of me. "I'm not trying to help him. I plan to come out a winner in this thing."

My mouth dropped open, and I felt like one of those cartoon characters slowly turning red-hot from the chest, upward. Any minute now, my ears would go off like a steam whistle. He was actually admitting that he planned to take advantage of my brother and my entire family? *How dare he!* "You're going to stand right here and tell me that? You're not even trying to hide it?" *The nerve of this guy! The arrogance.*

Did he have reason to be so confident? How involved were he and Clay? Was this situation already beyond salvaging?

"It's no secret," he said, and I felt sick. "I don't play to lose."

A lump rose in my throat, and for a mortifying instant, I had that I'm-not-going-to-cry feeling. I swallowed it and rode another wave of anger, instead. "You know what? You have to be the biggest jerk I've ever met. If you think you're going to just . . . take everything my family has worked for . . . for generations, and use my brother to do it, you'd better think again. That'll happen over my dead body."

His lips tugged at the corners. "That'd be a shame." He watched me with a look that could only have been described as *hot*. And, sue me, but for a moment, I liked it. The mini-grin morphed into a full-fledged smile, and he shook his head, chuckling under his breath.

"What in the world are you laughing at?" An insistent foot-stomp confirmed that my toes were prickly cold. The suede boots were cute, but dysfunctional in this environment, unfortunately.

Lifting his chin, he uncrossed his legs and pushed away from the post. "I think I just figured out that we're chattin' out two different sides of the barn here. I don't have any idea who you are or what you're talking about."

I felt my mouth dropping open again, my chin just hanging there against the flame-orange collar, my mind running like a hamster on a wheel, around and around in circles. Perpetual motion but no forward progress. "Wha . . . but . . . you . . ."

I could see it in his face. There was not one hint of recognition in his eyes. "You don't . . ."

"I wish I did." He delivered another smoldering smile, then wiped it away. "You're not related to that idiot who's running against me for county commission, are you?"

"County comish . . . What?" All I could think was, *Blaine Underhill has no idea who I am. He's looking right at me, and he has no idea who he's looking at.*

I wasn't certain whether to feel wounded or pleased. How should a girl feel when confirming her belief that the object of her high-school crush never even gave her a second thought?

He was thinking about me now, though. That much was obvious enough, and even though I didn't want to, I felt my ego purring like a kitten. Right now, he was clearly waiting for me to melt under the heat of that smile. I was tempted to, but of course that was a juvenile impulse. Somebody in my family had to act like an adult, to get down to business before it was too late. "I don't know what *you're* talking about, but I'm talking about my brother, Clay Hampton. I know he and my mother have some wild idea about getting the financing to buy Catfish Charley's, the funeral home at Harmony Shores, and the thirds of the family farm that belong to Uncle Charley and Uncle Herb. They've been talking to you about it, haven't they?"

He didn't answer at first. He was staring at me, his expression one of pure, unmitigated shock. "You're . . . Heather Hampton?"

Once again, I wasn't sure how to feel. I had, at least, managed to completely eradicate my high school self, as well as to wipe that smug look off his face. While I had him off-balance, I decided to go in for the kill. "Yes. And I don't want you doing business with my brother—bankrolling him or in any other way encouraging him or my mother in this idiotic fantasy they've hatched. I don't know what's going on with them, because the last time I checked, neither one of them wanted anything to do with Moses Lake. But this needs to end now. I can promise you that any business they open in Moses Lake would be a bad investment. My brother has a history of starting things and not finishing them, and my mother is . . . Well, let's just say she's no different than she's always been."

Blaine Underhill shook his head, trying to clear the fog, apparently. "You're Heather Hampton." An eyebrow squeezed low over one brown eye.

"Yes." Enough already. This was getting a little irritating, really. "And I suppose you see my point . . . about the bank loans."

He scratched the back of his neck, looking down at the dock. "Ma'am, I can't discuss someone else's financial business with you."

"This is my *family* we're talking about." Why did he have to be so obtuse? "I have a right to know what's happening."

"You'll have to talk to your family about that." He lifted his palms in a way that said, *Hands off, sorry.*

I clenched and unclenched my fingers inside my sleeves, a half-dozen broken fingernails from yesterday's adventure pressing jagged teeth into my skin. "You're the one behind this supposed *competing offer*, aren't you? You're helping my brother."

"Your brother and I are friends," he answered cautiously.

"You know what? A *friend* doesn't help you do something stupid. A friend doesn't set you up for a fall, so the *friend* can make a profit."

He drew back as if I'd offended him. "That's what you think I'm doing?"

My thin thread of patience was unwinding at a frightening pace. My feet were ice cubes, the cold had penetrated my jeans, and the damp wind off the lake had changed directions, striking me head on and slipping inside the collar of my oversized jacket. "I don't know *what* you're doing. That's why I asked." Pinpricks stabbed my left foot and traveled up my leg. An unsteady backward step sent a bootheel sinking between the icy boards, and the next thing I knew, I was staggering off balance, my hands flying in the air, the floppy sleeves flailing, slapping me, then swatting the railing, then some other solid object, which I realized was Blaine, because suddenly the jacket was tighter on one side. He used it to pull me upright and stop me from landing on the deck.

Once I was safely on my feet, he pulled his hands away as if he feared that keeping them there any longer might result in the loss of a finger or two. We stood for a moment at a stalemate. I felt my cold cheeks going hot.

"Look, all I can tell you is that you need to talk to your brother," he said finally.

Humiliated, angry, and realizing that I'd accomplished nothing other than tipping my hand and refreshing his memory of the uncoordinated, awkward girl he hadn't thought about since high school, I did the best thing I could think of.

I just turned around and walked away, taking care to avoid the gaps in the dock.

The water downstream ain't clear,
if the water upstream is muddy.
—Len Barnes, veteran, proud grandpa, and Moses Lake resident

Chapter 7

After having tried to reason with my mother, confronting the highly-irritating banker on the Waterbird dock, and finally attempting to get some straight answers from the uncs during our drive back to Harmony Shores, I decided to attack the problem at its source: my brother. Clay was at the center of this debacle and obviously had been for a while. The frustrating thing was that he would waste time involving himself in Moses Lake at all. Clay was brilliant, talented, personable—amazing, really. He was three times as book-smart as I could ever hope to be. He would be a great lawyer, if he would just buckle down and get through school.

I found my brother by the lakeshore, unstacking the canoes and setting them upside down on the lawn, apparently checking for condition. I remembered the uncs doing that in the past. My dad and I had helped a time or two when I was little. The uncs had engaged in heated discussions as to which canoes needed to be scrapped and which could go another season.

It was fairly cold to be working down by the shore. I'd zipped up my coat all the way to the neck, but Clay had on shorts and a rugby shirt, the sleeves pushed up over his elbows. Daubs of paint dotted his skin, and there were stencils lying on a long, skinny shipping crate that had probably held a casket at one time. Roger was sitting in a nearby canoe that was right side up, his tail brushing back and forth across the aluminum seat, as if he were anticipating an adventure. I was careful not to make eye contact, lest he decide to launch himself at me again.

"So what's all this?" I asked, stopping in front of Clay.

He glanced at me without standing up, his mouth quirking to one side. "I'm . . . painting . . . canoes?" He answered slowly, as in *Duh, what does it look like?* "And checking them out."

"I can see that. Why are you painting and checking the canoes?"

"Because they . . . need it?" He stated the obvious in the same intentionally clueless tone. Long curls of straw-colored hair, bleached on the ends by the sun, fell over his neck as he turned his attention to the boat again and began sanding some sort of patching material he'd applied over a hole.

After my three previous unsuccessful talks today, I willed myself not to tumble into an emotional exchange. I would remain calm this time, logical. Logic was on my side, after all. "You know what I'm asking, Clay. Why are you here, hanging around Moses Lake, getting Uncle Herb and Uncle Charley all stirred up?"

"They don't look like they're all stirred up." He shrugged toward the house, where the uncs were crossing a shady veranda that had served as an overflow location for many a funeral gathering over the years.

"Stop toying with me, Clay. This isn't a joke." My voice rose slightly, and I willed it back down. "You know what I'm asking, and you know why I came here."

In the canoe, Roger stopped wagging his tail, dropped his ears, and cast a worried look from me to Clay and back.

Clay continued with his work. "I figured you came to see us—have a little visit with the ol' fam."

I heard myself snort, an ugly, cynical sound I instantly felt guilty about, but Clay knew that we never got together just to visit anymore. Actually putting that into words seemed sad, though. "Come on, Clay, be realistic," I pleaded.

Clay chuckled and shook his head. "You know me better than that, Hessie."

The pet name, *Hessie*, pushed past my crossed arms and heavy coat, and plucked a heartstring. He'd given me that name, a combination of *Heather* and *sissie*, when he was still toddling around in diapers. He thought his big sister hung the moon back then.

Looking up from the canoe, he smiled that precocious, frustrating, boyish smile that had always accompanied excuses about lost homework, forgotten chores, and times when he neglected to let us know where he was going before he wandered off to play. The difficult thing about Clay was that he was always so darned cute and he earnestly never meant to do any harm. He never intended for me to end up staying awake until midnight, doing grade-school homework he'd forgotten about, or to leave me running up and down the lakeshore, scared to death that he'd drowned. It just happened, because he was such a dingbat. A sweet, hapless, adorable dingbat with a huge heart that got him into trouble time, after time, after time.

Despite all of that, I fought the urge to smile back at him. "Don't even try to get cute with me."

"I don't really have to try." He grinned again and went back to sanding the canoe. "Cute just oozes out of me. Can't help it." He lifted his green-tinted hands, helplessly.

I wondered if the adorable little country girl he was now courting—Blaine Underhill's cousin—had any idea that she was stepping into a mess way deeper than her cowboy boots. Clay's history with women wasn't any better than his history with college degrees or jobs. Some poor female, usually the older and more mature sort, was always taking him under her wing, and they sailed along blissfully for a little while—Clay was one of the most fun people I knew—until the wind changed and blew him onto another new path. He'd left a trail of broken hearts behind him over the years, but never intentionally.

"Can you please just cut it out? You know, when you go off on these kinds of schemes, other people end up getting hurt. People who can't just go flit off to work at some ski resort or run away with an earthquake relief team. The contracts for the land sale have to go through before the broker offer runs out *next week*. Uncle Herb and Uncle Charley need this money. It's not like either one of them has a pension plan. Everything they have is tied up in property. They don't have time to waste."

"Why?" Clay sat back on his heels, finally listening. He set the sandpaper on the boat and rested his green elbows on his hairy knees. "What's the rush? Don't you even want to take a little time to look around the old place before you throw everything on the auction block?"

His eyes met mine, his gaze a soft, sensitive green, the color so like Mom's. He looked at me the way she always did, seeming somehow disappointed in who I was. In truth, I guess, we were perpetually disappointed with one another, all of us. "Not at someone else's expense. Not if it causes problems for the rest of the family, Clay."

I *didn't* want to look around the place, though. I didn't want it to grow on me or speak to me, or call me back to the past. I wasn't seeking any reason to miss it when it was gone from my life. Perhaps that was an advantage I had over Clay. I wanted to be rid of all ties to Moses Lake and the things that happened here. How could he not feel the same way? How could he look at this place and not think of what happened to Dad? "The broker won't wait forever. That's the way brokers are. If one deal doesn't work out, they just invest elsewhere."

Roger sidled out of the canoe and moved timidly to Clay's side, his large, brown eyes rolling upward as he nudged under Clay's arm. The two of them seemed remarkably, painfully alike—two lost puppies, looking for something they never could quite find.

I didn't wait for my brother to come up with an answer, but pressed on instead, driving the point home. "I know it's hard for Uncle Herbert and Uncle Charley to let go. I know it's hard for them to move. But it's reality, Clay. It's what has to happen. There's no one here to take care of them."

"There can be." Clay tipped his chin up defensively, and I had the sense that he meant well. As usual, he wanted to come to the rescue, but he hadn't thought things through.

"Clay, come on. What about law school? How many times have you applied for an extension on your thesis? You're just lucky the school has been willing to work with you. And they did that because you're so incredibly, amazingly smart that they couldn't stand to see you drop out. But this is the real world. People's lives are involved. Mom doesn't need to be here, either. You know what a mess she was when we lived here. What if that happens again? What if she gets all . . . wrapped up in the past, and she starts to act the way she used to? This sale needs to go through."

"So they can take the land and . . . what . . . develop it or something?" His hand, which had been running through Roger's fur, paused, and for an instant we were locked like a pair of players in a chess match. "Stick some golf course or resort on it?"

"What gave you that idea?" I asked carefully.

"Amy works at the Proxica plant in Gnadenfeld. That place is a gossip mill. She hears things."

"Well, what exactly did she hear?" Disquiet crept up my spine, clingy and stealthy, like a tick looking for a place to burrow in. Amy worked for Proxica? What were the odds that Clay would just *happen* to be dating a girl with ties to Proxica?

Clay nodded, oblivious to the connections spinning forth in my mind. "She heard that the broker guy's been all over the county, looking at land. Why does he want our place so bad? What's he going to do with it?"

I couldn't come right out and lie to my brother, but the confidentiality agreement wouldn't allow me to reveal the truth, either. "You know what, Clay, why does it matter? What matters is doing what's best for our family."

"Forget what's best for the town, I guess, huh?" He stood up, a paintbrush still dangling from one hand. "What's best for the area."

I took a step back, dumbstruck as much by the out-in-left-field remark as by the gravity in Clay's voice. "How do you know what's best for the area? You don't live here, Clay. And if you're looking at this as one of your save-the-world social causes, how about taking a glance at the poverty rate on the other side of the lake, up in Chinquapin Peaks? A broker thinking about development would be a good thing. Look at Gnadenfeld. Look at how much it's grown in the past sixteen years. There are real stores, restaurants, new housing. I checked out their Internet site the other day. The school has a great big gorgeous performing arts center and a new multi-sport stadium."

Clay squinted into the distance, toward Chinquapin Peaks and the river channel. "Yeah, look at Gnadenfeld." His voice held an undertone that I couldn't read. Maybe my brother was on some kind of back-to-nature kick, ready to throw himself in front of the bulldozers to keep anything from changing around Moses Lake.

"You know what, Clay, if there's something you want to say to me, just say it." I squeezed my arms over my chest, shivering.

He seemed to think about that momentarily, and I had the sense that we were finally about to excavate some nuggets of truth.

The sound of a car rattling up to the house caught Clay's attention just as he was about to speak. Casting a curious glance toward the driveway, he moved his paintbrush to a coffee can and started up the hill. I followed, frustrated by the diversion. My irritation sharpened and took on shape when I recognized the dark head, tan barn jacket, and cowboy boots visible above and below the truck door as the driver exited the vehicle. *What is* he *doing here?*

By the time we made it to the driveway, with Roger cavorting happily back and forth in our path, Blaine Underhill was headed up the front walk. The uncs had come around to meet him, and my mother was poking her head out the front door, looking curious.

Everyone greeted Blaine warmly, as if he were a long lost friend rather than a potentially greedy, unprincipled robber-baron wannabe bent on ruining my family. Roger ran across his path and nearly sent him sprawling into the flower bed. Good for Roger. Blaine shook a finger at the dog playfully. "Yeah, I know where you've been, buddy," he said, and Roger stopped frolicking, then sat down and cocked his head, his ears drooping and his tail scrubbing the ground tentatively.

"Anybody here expecting a FedEx?" Blaine asked, and from behind, I could just see the corner of a FedEx box between his sleeve and the side of his coat.

"Me," I answered. Blaine turned around on the path, seeming to realize for the first time that Clay and I were there. Cradled in his arm, he had the FedEx box—the one that would bring me my credit card, my ID, my iPhone, and my favorite red leather purse. Oh happy day! At least something was going right.

What was Blaine Underhill doing with my FedEx, anyway? "Thank goodness," I breathed. "I've been waiting for this all day." I reached for the box, and, oddly, Blaine pinched one corner between two fingers and lifted it from his arm, as if it weighed nothing. The box stretched accordion-style, slowly unfolding, until it was one long string of mangled red, white, and blue cardboard, dangling from his thumb and index finger.

"What in the . . ." I muttered, as family members moved in from all sides, the group of us gathering around the remnants of the box like monkeys in a zoo.

"Uh-oh," Clay muttered.

"Roger!" Mom gasped.

"I told ya that dog chews things," Uncle Charley added.

Uncle Herbert nodded in agreement. "I dig stuff up in the flower beds for months every time Roger comes here for a visit. Probably got that box right off the porch," he added in his dry, unassuming way.

"The delivery people aren't supposed to just leave packages on the porch, are they?" Clay retorted, by way of defending Roger's honor. "Isn't somebody supposed to sign for it?"

"Depends on how you send it," Uncle Herbert answered. "I've had whole boxes of supplies left out here, sometimes."

"I found it tangled in your gate out front," Blaine offered, studying Roger's free-form artwork. "Probably blew out to the road after the dog got done with it."

I just kept staring, unable at first to accept the magnitude of the disaster represented by the pile of cardboard. "The dog *ate* my FedEx?" I questioned numbly, touching the box, then pulling my hand away. It was slimy, covered with teeth marks and dog hair. "Where's my . . . my stuff?"

"He buries things," Uncle Herbert repeated.

From the corner of my eye, I saw Roger slinking away, disappearing behind a holly bush. "My checkbook and my wallet . . . my credit card . . . my iPhone . . . that was a Dolce & Gabbana purse. A seven hundred dollar . . ." I'd treated myself to the Dolce last year, after Mel and I closed a design deal for a high-end sporting goods store. Granted, I'd bought the bag online at a discount, but still . . . I turned to my brother, vaguely aware that my eyes were flaring and my lip was curling. "Your dog ate my Dolce & Gabbana and my iPhone."

There was a rustling in the bushes, and a quick flash of blond fur between the holly leaves as Roger, quite wisely, exited the area.

My shock swirled into full-blown panic, picking up speed, sweeping away my orderly existence, breaking it into pieces of tornadic debris. "My life is in that iPhone."

Clay lifted his hands, indicating that this was hardly his fault. "Who knew the delivery guy was just gonna leave it on the porch?" He gave the front door a disgusted look. "He could've put it up high, at least. How's Roger supposed to know not to mess with it?"

Something primal and sibling-related happened to me at that point. With no prior warning and no way to control it, I reverted to being a thirteen-year-old, stuck in the backseat with my little brother while he sang Sesame Street songs over and over and over, just because he knew it would drive me crazy. "How's Roger supposed to . . . Are you *serious*?"

"All right, all right!" Mom stepped in. "For heaven's sake, Heather, don't be melodramatic. Obviously, Clay didn't mean for the dog to chew up the box. Let's just get busy and find your things. Roger can't have taken them too far."

"I'll grab some garden tools," Uncle Charley offered enthusiastically.

"I'll get some gloves," Uncle Herbert added.

The rest of the day was like a family Easter egg hunt. We even had help. Blaine brought over a metal detector from the hardware store, and Amy showed up after work. We combed the gardens, the roadside ditch, and the lawn. In the front flower bed, thanks to the metal detector, we unearthed a lipstick tube and my key ring. The uncs even broke out flashlights as dusk set in, but it was getting colder by the minute, and everyone was shivering. Mom started coughing and sniffling, and Amy's hands turned blue despite the fact that Uncle Herb brought out coats and hats for all of us. The only one who wasn't cold was Roger. He was having a grand time running from person to person and acting as if he had no idea why we were pointing at the ground and trying to get him to show us where the bodies were buried.

Finally, we called off the search. Mom thought everyone should come in for cocoa, and Uncle Herb wanted to feed us and stoke up the fireplace. "We got plenty of casseroles," he pointed out. "And pie, too."

I hung back, leaning against a porch post and mourning my iPhone, as the group filed into the house. I'd been here a whole day and accomplished absolutely nothing. I was no closer to getting the papers signed for the property deal than I'd been when I left Seattle. Meanwhile, back at the office, Mel probably wondered what was going on. Work-related calls and emails were undoubtedly stacking up in my inbox. By now, maybe Richard had called. I wouldn't even know it. I was stuck in a communications black hole, living the primitive life. No cell phone. No wireless Internet. Outsmarted by a golden retriever.

How much worse could the day possibly get?

I wanted to tell someone about it, to describe the family digging, and raking, and hoeing, the uncs shuffling around wearing baseball caps with built-in flashlights, searching underneath holly bushes, cheering each time they spotted something shiny buried in the leaves. We'd found several soda cans and a Rhode Island license plate from 1955, but nothing else that belonged to me. Roger had hidden his bounty well.

Even if I had found my phone, I didn't have anyone to share the story with, I realized as I stood staring at the yard. Trish would be busy getting her kids fed, bathed, and ready for bed. And Richard . . . Well, Richard probably hadn't called, to be honest. I could call Mel, but he would just want the work-related update, short and sweet.

Sighing, I let my head fall against the porch post and tried to move my frozen toes inside my soggy boots. A cold, lonely, miserable feeling crept over me. I wanted to be someplace else, but I didn't know where. Not home, necessarily. At work, maybe, with my head in a project, hyperfocused to the point that time passed without my even noticing, without my wishing that things were different. That I was different.

"Food's in here." The voice startled me, and I realized that Blaine was in the doorway.

Swallowing the prickly, teary lump, I blinked the moisture from my eyes. I was being foolish, standing here feeling sorry for myself, feeling as if my life somehow didn't measure up. I had everything I'd ever wanted: a good job, a cool place to live, enough money for all the stuff I wanted—a Dolce & Gabbana handbag . . . Well, not anymore, but I could buy myself another one. "I'm waiting for my iPhone to ring," I said, without turning to look at him. "I'll track it down by the sound."

"The battery's dead by now." The hinges let out a long, loud complaint, and the door clicked shut. Blaine's footsteps crossed the porch, then stopped.

"Maybe not," I countered, but we'd trekked all over the yard using Clay's phone to call mine, to no avail. "My iPhone loves me. It'll find its way home."

Blaine chuckled, the sound warm and nice, his breath forming a cloud of vapor, so that I knew he was close behind me. He took a few more steps and stood at the top of the stairs, gazing out into the night. "You ever read any of those self-help books about people who are obsessed with their gadgets?" He glanced sideways, the hazy glow from the gaslights illuminating a grin.

"I don't have the Kindle app on my phone," I said blandly. "I'll have to look into that. Maybe then I can read the books."

He laughed again, rubbing a finger alongside his nose. "I think that would defeat the purpose."

"You could loan me your phone," I suggested. Clay, I noticed, had been careful to take his phone away from me after the yard search. No doubt, he was afraid I'd call Uncle Herbert's son. "I could check in at work and leave a message for my boss, at least."

"It's Friday," Blaine pointed out. "Tomorrow's the weekend."

"He works on the weekends, believe me." I felt Blaine's gaze on me. I had a feeling I knew what he was thinking—that I looked like the type who spent the weekends chained to a desk.

"Anyway, I don't have one with me." His comment seemed to come out of the blue.

"One what?"

"A cell phone."

An indignant cough pressed from my throat, and I gaped at him. Surely he was kidding, making an excuse not to provide me with a communications device. Maybe he really did spend his days out fishing. How could anyone do business without a cell phone, these days? "What kind of a banker doesn't carry a cell phone?"

"This kind." He leaned forward slightly to catch a glimpse of the moon. "When I'm off work, I'm all the way off. The mobile phone stays in the office."

I studied his profile, trying to decide whether he was putting one over on me. "That doesn't drive you crazy?" The few times I'd ever forgotten my phone while I was out on a date, it made me insane. All I could think about was the backlog that was probably building and the fact that if Mel called, wanting to set a meeting or to ask for some numbers, he wouldn't be happy I was out of touch.

"Having that stupid phone going off all the time would drive me crazy," Blaine countered. "If you don't have it with you, you don't have to answer it." He turned my way, his features hidden in shadow, except for the chin with the cute little cleft in it. "You oughta try it sometime."

"I shudder at your ridiculous logic," I countered, and he snort-laughed. I bit back a chuckle, reminding myself that no matter how much fun he might be to trade quips with, Blaine Underhill was not my friend.

"There's a time to work and a time to play." He coated the words with a melodramatic tone that coaxed another laugh into my mouth. I coughed to cover it up.

"My iPhone is out there, cold and alone, and you give me plati-tudes."

"I know it's hard to continue on, considering what you've been through." He patted my shoulder, and instead of sympathy, I felt electricity. "But you have to remain strong for your iPhone."

I couldn't help it, I chuckled in spite of myself. "That's so not funny."

"You laughed."

"It was a courtesy laugh."

Letting his head fall forward, he grinned, the light catching his face. "How about some casserole? You need your strength."

I pushed off the porch post and took a step farther away from him, my mind clearing a bit. I couldn't help but wonder why he was on the porch buttering me up. Come to think of it, why had he spent his whole afternoon tromping around the lawn with my crazy family, searching for Roger's buried treasure? Surely a guy who looked like Blaine Underhill had better things to do, or perhaps a wife and kids out there, waiting for him to come home? Back in high school, there'd been no shortage of local girls looking to fill that role.

But as we started in the door, he followed amiably along, whistling under his breath, the sound filling the vestibule and the front hall, where in the past crowds of mourners had gathered, exchanging greetings in hushed tones as they filed into the chapel for final rites. Blaine's song echoed off the paneled walls as we passed through the commercial area, where a casket stand still stood under the bay windows in Uncle Herbert's office, and into the private quarters, which on this side of the house included a ladies' parlor, a dining room, a den for watching television, the sun porch, and the kitchen.

All of a sudden, I recognized Blaine's tune as a medley of common cell phone ring tones.

"Stop that," I snapped, glancing over my shoulder at him.

He only winked, then changed to another tune. Behind me, I heard his bootheels on the wooden floors, accompanied by the haunting melody of taps.

He that will learn to pray, let him go to sea.

—George Herbert
(Left by Bradley Breal, ministry student headed for the mission field)

Chapter 8

In the morning I slept late, and by the time I woke, everyone—including Roger—had vacated the premises. On the kitchen counter of the main house, I found a vague note from my mother saying that she and the uncs had gone to Waco to pick up restaurant supplies for Catfish Charley's and they wouldn't be back until sometime later in the day. There was no explanation as to where Clay and Roger were, but after a sweep of the personal quarters, I pretty much concluded that I was on my own. No doubt the family had decided to avoid me as a way of putting off further conversation about signing the real-estate papers.

The note in the kitchen had been weighted down with the old milk-glass canister that had always served as Uncle Herbert's repository for loose change and an occasional crumpled dollar bill. When we'd moved into the gardener's cottage after my father's death and money was tight, five- and ten-dollar bills had started appearing there—Uncle Herbert's way of quietly making sure Clay and I had what we needed for lunches and groceries. Aunt Esther would've had a fit if she'd known he was funneling funds to us.

She felt that my mother needed to get out of bed and get a job, or at least work cleaning Harmony House and cooking meals along with the housekeeper.

Looking at the milk-glass canister now, I remembered Ruth quietly taking money from the jar and tucking it into my palm. Sometimes I suspected that she put cash from her housekeeping salary in there, too. Mostly, I liked Ruth because no matter how angry, depressed, uncommunicative, or withdrawn I was when I came home from school, she had oatmeal-chocolate-chip cookies, or Mennonite specialties like zwieback double buns, waiting. Ruth repaired a lot of damage that way, all while washing dishes and barely raising an eyebrow. She was exactly what I needed: someone who did not feel the need to turn me into a perfect Southern lady. She quietly shook her head when I was forced to sit in with Aunt Esther's bridge-club crowd—the theory being that social engagements and a change of wardrobe would cure whatever was wrong with me.

No matter how critical the ladies were in the parlor, or how much Aunt Esther didn't appreciate my lack of cooperation, Ruth extended grace to me. She was willing to love the little mess that I was, rather than trying to instruct, guide, and fix me. Whenever I was finally able to escape from the parlor, I knew I'd find her in the kitchen, a baker's apron protecting her modest flowered dress, her hair neatly plaited beneath a scarf-like head covering, her hands busy at work.

I wished Uncle Herbert were home, so I could ask him whatever happened to Ruth. She'd sent notes and care packages for a while after I'd headed off to college, but I'd moved after my freshman year in the dorm and probably never sent her the new address. Moses Lake had seemed a million miles away by then, and I wanted it to be. As much as I adored Ruth, it was easier to just leave the past behind.

Now I felt the past closing in on me again, voices whispering in the house, boards creaking and settling, a branch scratching the windows on the sun porch, a groaning noise from the vicinity of the front parlor and Uncle Herbert's office, as if someone were leaning back in his old leather office chair. A bird twittered outside, and the sharp, uneven sound reminded me of the ladies in Aunt Esther's gossip circle. I had a sense of not being alone in the house.

A shiver ran across my shoulders, convincing me that the prudent thing to do would be to borrow a few dollars from the canister, grab my laptop from the cottage, and head to the one place I'd seen in town that advertised an Internet hot spot—the combination convenience store, pizzeria, and Chinese food hut on the edge of town. It was a nice enough day for a walk, and considering that I hadn't officially checked in at the office since I left, Mel was undoubtedly not a happy camper. Getting in contact via email and offering a few details about the lost phone would be a good way to buffer things a bit. I could spend some time taking care of whatever I could handle long-distance and lighten next week's backlog of work.

It seemed like a good plan . . . until I actually got to the Chinese convenience store and opened my email. Backlog didn't even begin to describe what I found. Mel was in a tailspin because Itega wanted some tweaks to the design and corresponding cost analyses, and they wanted them now. If it weren't for the fact that it would have taken all day for me to fly home from Moses Lake, Mel would have insisted I come back right then. He wasn't interested in hearing about lost cell phones or anything else happening in Texas. He'd called our project crew in to work, even though it was Saturday.

I spent the rest of the day talking with various team members via Skype, working like a madwoman on my laptop, transferring spreadsheets and AutoCAD files back and forth, downing egg drop soup and crab rangoons, and breaking open fortune cookies. Meanwhile, the owners of the convenience store tried to corral the gaggle of kids who were obviously accustomed to playing in the restaurant when no one was around. On some level, I knew I was imposing, but I was in work mode. The world and everyone in it was outside the bubble.

By the time we put the design changes to bed, I was exhausted both mentally and physically, my eyes were blurry and grainy, and the poor people who owned the convenience store were sweeping floors and washing pans, glancing my way and hoping I would get the hint. I thanked them profusely and made a mental note to drop by with a huge tip when I had funds of my own again. The purchase of a pack of super migraine-killing headache powders seemed like the best way to spend the rest of my canister money, for now. A massive tension headache was pounding in my brain, and all I wanted to do was find someplace quiet to lie down. I didn't even bother to see who was at the house when I returned to Harmony Shores; I just staggered to the gardener's cottage, took my headache medicine, fell across the bed, and closed my eyes.

Sometime after dark I snuggled under the quilt, and on Sunday morning, I woke early, with my mind squarely back in Moses Lake. Lying in bed, I made plans to dig up gardens until I'd either razed the property or unearthed my cell phone and wallet. I'd been at Harmony Shores for two days now, and I had accomplished exactly nothing—and in the meantime, I'd almost been AWOL during an important crunch time at the office. Somehow, I had to bring the Moses Lake issue to a satisfying conclusion and get back to my real life.

I'd tried applying logic and reason with Mother, Clay, the uncs, and the banker responsible for encouraging my brother's flight of fancy. Blaine Underhill actually seemed like kind of a decent guy.

He and my family were clearly on friendly terms, but how could he, as a financial professional and president of his father's bank, possibly condone my brother's plan, or my mother's? Was Blaine such a nice guy that he just didn't have the heart to point out the truth to my family?

Or was he a heartless small-town shyster?

The question chased away the morning drowsiness. This good ol' hometown boy, help-a-buddy-out thing of Blaine's had to be a façade, didn't it? You couldn't run a bank, even a little country bank, and be a pushover. Blaine was out to make money—out to win. He was, after all, the guy who'd mowed over players twice his size on the football field and given himself several concussions, because he had to win. What were the odds that he'd suddenly turned into a teddy bear? Not very good.

At the same time, another image swirled just overhead—tantalizing, like the sweet aroma of an apple-pie-scented candle. I remembered the guy who made me laugh on the porch as I mourned my iPhone, his smile flashing in the dim light, his eyes a deep, dark liquid. His laughter brushed across my ear, sending a prickle over my skin.

"All right, that's it." Tossing the covers aside, I swung my legs around and hit the ground running—literally. The floorboards were like ice again. If I stayed in the cottage any longer, I'd have to bring some firewood down from the woodpile at the main house. My teeth were chattering by the time I got to the bathroom, where I turned on the hot water and hopped from one foot to the other until finally the small space fogged up. My morning routine was rushed and uncomfortable, with little slices of February air sifting through the floorboards and pressing past the gaps around the narrow wood-paned window. My last pair of jeans and a blue sweater helped to cut the chill, and toasting myself with the hairdryer felt like heaven. While I was basking, I plugged the gaps around the window with crispy tissues from an ancient, yellowed box.

I finger-brushed wavy auburn curls and proceeded to the door, where my coat and my dirty, bedraggled, perpetually damp suede boots were like blocks of ice. I pulled the boots on and curled my toes inside, shivering as I started out the door and hoping that both the coffee and the heat were on up at the big house. A trio of cardinals flitted away, surprised by my passing, and a squirrel darted from the lawn, skittering up the hill ahead of me to climb an ancient live oak tree.

A flash of movement near the shore stopped me halfway across the lawn, and I turned, expecting to see Clay down there again. Instead, a tall, slim figure with dark, curly hair was just disappearing behind the corner of the barn. Blaine Underhill? What was he doing here so early in the morning . . . on Sunday? In fact, what was he doing, prowling around our barn at all?

Pulling my coat tighter around myself, I hurried back across the yard and slipped down the hill, staying close to the tree line on the way to the massive weathered-wood-and-limestone barn. When we'd lived at Harmony Shores, the barn had been my hiding place, my private cathedral. Among the narrow streams of sunlight and shade, I could lie on my back and listen to the coo of doves nesting in the rafters and pretend that the upside-down world outside didn't exist. I felt close to my father there, as if he might suddenly walk through the door, once again a hapless teenager bringing hay to be stored for the winter.

The barn wasn't even in use anymore. When we'd talked about the real-estate deal, Uncle Herbert had pointed out that any new owners would have to make some decisions about either repairing the barn or tearing it down. Why would Blaine Underhill be poking around the place when the morning was still frosty and cool, the winter sun just casting pink light over the hills of Chinquapin Peaks?

A hinge squealed as I reached the corner of the barn and peered through the crust of dirt and paint spatters on a wavy, plate-glass window in what had once been the tack room. Beyond the tack room doorway, Blaine was a backlit shadow in the cavernous barn aisle. Resting his hands on his hips, he looked up at the ceiling, turned in a slow circle, walked out of view.

I moved down the barn wall, peeking through knotholes and cracks in the weathered boards, trying to locate him again. Where was he? What was he doing?

A faint, metallic sound rang out—the ping of gravel bouncing off one of the canoes that Clay had left lying around. I tiptoed to the corner and peered around it but couldn't see anything. Frost-covered grass crunched under my feet once, twice, three times, until I spotted Blaine. Rubbing his chin, he walked around the canoe, tipped it to one side, looked under it. The banker was dressed in sweats this morning—in a horrible orange color, actually—along with a ball cap and running shoes. Apparently, he was out jogging. Jogging, and investigating my uncle's canoes. . . .

Just as I was about to duck behind the barn again, Roger barked from somewhere in the woods. Blaine looked up, and I pretended not to have been hiding there, stalking him. "Oh, I . . . uhhh . . . didn't know anyone was down here."

He seemed unsurprised by my presence and not the least bit worried to have been discovered prowling the property. "Mornin'," he said, and smiled like we were old friends. Apparently, the family phone hunt and casserole feed had convinced Blaine that he and I were on amicable terms. That was probably just as well. Best not to let him know I was trying to figure him out.

"Good morning." I returned the smile. "Kind of early for a walk."

He nodded toward the water, a deep blue-gray in the morning light, and as slick as glass. A flock of mallards had landed near the shore to paddle aimlessly about, oblivious to the icy chill rising off the surface. "I like to get out when it's still quiet, before there's anyone on the water. Kind of nice just to look at it the way God made it."

"It's a man-made lake," I pointed out, and he smirked sideways at me.

"Well, now, that's a cynical observation." He licked his lips, worried one side between his teeth, like he was trying to make sense of me. That made two of us. I was studying him, as well. He seemed to know that but appeared comfortable with it, perhaps because we were on his turf. This was *his* town, after all. It always had been.

"Sorry." The apology was hollow, really. There's no point apologizing for who you are. "It's my nature."

"To be cynical?" He raised a brow.

"Analytical," I rephrased. *Analytical* sounded better. Maybe *practical* was really the right word. "I imagine that bankers are analytical, too." *They probably don't show up at someone's place first thing on a frosty morning for no reason—just happening by.*

He cocked his head to one side, his thick, dark lashes narrowing slightly, casting a shadow over his brown eyes, making them earthy and warm, the kind of eyes that pull you closer. "That's not how I remember you."

A little puff of laughter pushed past my lips—a reflex action, like jerking a hand up to block an incoming object before it hits you. "Please. Like you remember me."

He blinked, appearing surprised. "You're making me feel old. There were only seventy-four in our graduating class, and it hasn't been all that long."

"Since high school? Yes it has." *And thank goodness for that.* "I hardly remember anything about the year here." Such a lie. Does anybody ever really forget high school? People like Blaine probably wanted to remember. He probably stood around at the first football game every year, recounting the glory days. Why wouldn't he? He and his friends were always into some kind of fun—making dates for the school dance, jumping off the rocks at the Scissortail, paddling out to the island beneath Eagle Eye Bridge, or having parties in the secluded park on Blue Moon Bay.

"Huh," he murmured contemplatively. "Well, those were some pretty bad times for your family. Guess it makes sense that it'd all be a blur." His eyes caught mine empathically, and I felt an odd little tug. *Those were some pretty bad times for your family.* What I wouldn't have given for someone, for him, to have said those words, made that observation during the horrible months after my father's death. How many times had I walked the halls dreaming that one of those people who looked right through me would suddenly see me, suddenly smile and offer friendship when I so desperately needed it?

Just like all the rest of them, Blaine never had. It was silly for me to still be dwelling on that all these years later, sort of pathetic, even. Old wounds are the slowest to heal.

"So, how *do* you remember me, then?" The words were out of my mouth before I had time to think about them, and a blush tainted my cheeks. What a stupid thing to ask.

He looked me over, as if he were trying to decide how far toward honesty he should go.

Lie to me, I thought. *I really don't want to know the truth.* Something about this place took me right back to high school, turned me into that insecure, lost little girl again.

He pressed a knuckle to his bottom lip. I watched it stroke back and forth while the suspense inside me built to a ridiculous degree. Somewhere outside the bubble of unfinished high-school business, there was the vague realization that my toes were freezing and the wind was slicing through my jeans as if they were curtain sheers. The smart thing would be to leave him to whatever he was doing and head to the main house for breakfast. Blaine Underhill wasn't going to reveal any of his secrets. Not this easily.

But for some reason, I stood there waiting for his answer, rooted to the spot, like a doofus.

"Artistic. Quiet. Little bit of a temper." He assessed, letting his hand drop and bracing it on the bottom of his hooded sweatshirt. His lips spread slowly into a grin. "Guess things have changed a little. You're not quiet anymore."

I couldn't quite decide how to react. He had been generous enough to leave out *dorky, introverted, generally morose,* and *completely lacking in fashion sense.* "Meaning I'm still artistic, with a bad temper?"

"Well, Clay tells me that you're an architect. Creative stuff." He lifted a hand, waving it over the grounds as if to display them as Exhibit One. "And on the temper front . . . Well, you'll notice that Roger is still in hiding after the other night."

"I didn't *do* anything to Roger," I countered, but the words ended in a protest laugh. I could imagine the picture I'd made, keeping all of the family out in the dark, muttering idle threats against Clay's gooberheaded dog.

"But you wanted to."

"Roger and I have a love-hate thing. He loves to destroy my stuff, and I hate that." I shifted from one foot to the other in an exaggerated display of petulance, and tiny needles stabbed my frozen toes. I sucked in air, then did a full-body shiver, shaking the numb foot in the air. Despite the chill, I didn't excuse myself and head to the house.

"Cold?" Blaine stated the obvious.

"Just my feet." Which wasn't really true. I hadn't ever gotten warm this morning. "I'm staying in the cottage, and that place is polar in the mornings. There's no propane in the propane tank, and no firewood for the wood stove. I keep forgetting to bring some down from the big house during the day, and I'm *not* going out to the woodpile at night." I remembered that duty from our time in the cottage. Mom would let the fire die during the day, and it was freezing when we came home in the afternoons. I'd find her lying in bed, ashen-faced and hollow-eyed under a mound of quilts, oblivious to it all. Clay was afraid to go to the woodpile when dusk was settling over the tree line, so the duty always fell to me.

"Your shoes are wet," Blaine observed, motioning to the soggy suede boots.

"I know."

"Kind of cold for wet shoes." He pointed at the boots again. "Suede isn't too good around the lake. Too damp here in the winter, soaks through."

I curled my toes to warm them. "It's all I have with me. I wasn't planning to be here long."

With a backward step, he shrugged toward the lake. "C'mon."

"Yeah, I don't think swimming will help," I joked, but part of me was oddly in favor of following along with whatever Blaine Underhill had in mind.

A lopsided smirk indicated that, of all things, he found me funny. Go figure. "I'll open Dad's hardware store for you. We can walk over the back way."

I paused to consider the offer. Other than the dollar store, the hardware store was the only place in town that sold shoes. A nice pair of combat boots—something waterproof and fleece lined— would be pretty close to heaven right now. I might even sleep in them. I was so tired of having frozen feet.

Come to think of it, the hardware store sold heaters, too. A little electric heater would go a long way toward remedying the temperature problem in the cottage. At the rate things were going with getting Mom to agree to sign the land paperwork, I might be in town a few more days. Some woodsy garb was definitely needed. But . . . "I don't have any money. I'd write you a check, but the dog ate my checkbook."

"I've heard that excuse before." He laughed again. "You can put it on account. I know where to find you." He started walking backwards toward the old path that led through the woods, past the park behind the church, and across an ancient rope bridge to the back of the hardware store. I remembered that path.

The logical part of my mind conjured up reasons to say no. *You don't want to owe him anything. What are his motives here, anyway? You still don't know why he was skulking around the barn this early in the morning.*

No telling what shape that rope bridge is in by now. . . .

On the flip side, Blaine Underhill was being nice to me. There's something irresistibly charming about having the attention of the guy you dreamed about in high school. Besides, I could imagine how displeased his stepmother would be when she arrived to open the hardware store tomorrow morning and found a big, fat charge with my name on it. I would send her a check as soon as I got back to Seattle, of course, but in the meantime there would be some guilty pleasure in knowing she would hate the idea of Blaine letting me help myself. Whenever I went into the hardware store after my dad died, she'd always stalked me like I might steal something.

"All right. Thanks." Perhaps I could use this opportunity to ferret out a few more of Blaine's secrets. "So why were you down by Uncle Herbert's barn so early?" *Casing the place for future repossession? Counting the canoes, perhaps? Major monetary value there. Not.*

He slowed, waiting for me to waddle up beside him on my

ice-block feet, before we started along the shore. "Crossed my mind that we hadn't looked in the old barn last night, when we were hunting for your stuff. Your uncle's old dog, Sadie, used to steal eggs from the chicken coop across the road and bury them in the center aisle. I stacked hay in that barn one summer when I was fourteen, and, man, we busted some rotten eggs in there."

"*Eeewww.*" I felt like such a cynic. Blaine Underhill had gotten up this morning and walked all the way over here to look for my stuff? The idea was bright and alluring, like a glint of sunlight on water, as we moved from the lakeshore into the murky shadows of live oaks and winter-bare pecans. "I didn't know you'd ever worked for my uncles."

"Oh, sure, off and on," he said, as we walked along the old wagon trail, leaves crunching underfoot, the fog off the lake muting every sound. "I think just about every kid in town did at one time or another. I was in shape for football that fall, I'll tell you."

"Was there ever a fall when you weren't in shape for football?" I joked, then realized it sounded like gushy schoolgirl admiration. "I mean, I always figured you jocks spent all summer waiting for the season to start."

The Underhills practically had stadium parking with their names on it. Mama B's bearcat roar was legendary, and even Blaine's normally dignified stepmother was an insane sports mom. She and my dad had been homecoming king and queen together, back in the day—the couple most likely to marry and produce little football stars.

Blaine reached down to toss a fallen branch off the trail. "Yeah, not so much. Football wasn't really my thing."

"Oh, come on." I rolled a who-do-you-think-you're-kidding look his way. "You were the 'pride of Moses Lake.'" My tone mimicked old Hack, the local volunteer fire chief, who'd doubled as football announcer since back when my dad was in school. My senior year, all the talk was about whether Blaine would get a football scholarship. Shortly after we'd come to town, his stepmother had cornered my father at the church door and prattled on endlessly about Blaine's accomplishments. My father probably felt like an idiot, standing there with his own progeny, me, in a Van Halen T-shirt, my hair dyed stark black with the garish red streak I'd included as a particularly potent protest over the Moses Lake move.

"You get to a point where you figure out some things are more everyone else's idea than your own," Blaine said, his gaze turned upward. A whippoorwill was calling somewhere in the trees.

The conversation lulled as we walked through the picnic grounds behind the church, then slipped into the little ravine beyond it and crossed a new wooden bridge where the old rope structure had been. I found myself watching Blaine, contemplating him, wondering if he could really be so different from the image I'd always held in my mind. "So, why did you quit playing football?"

A shrug indicated that it didn't matter now. "By my second year in college, I knew I wasn't really fast or big enough for pro ball. The funny thing was, I didn't feel all that disappointed about it. I was tired of waking up flat on my back on the football field, not knowing where I was. Like I said, it was never really my thing."

I looked over at him to make sure he really was Blaine Underhill. Not that we'd ever been friends, or anything, but I had known him from afar. He'd certainly given the appearance of eating, living, sleeping, and breathing football. "Why did you play all those years, then?"

A sideways glance flicked my way, catching my gaze. I fell in for a minute, my mind slipping into the past as we climbed the hill to the hardware store. "I thought I needed to," he answered, dismissively. "The trouble with expectations is that you feel like you have to live up to them."

Breaking the link between us, I looked at the ground, picking my footing as we stepped over a retaining wall and reached the stairs at the back of the limestone hardware building. I led, and he followed me up, keys jingling as he fished them from his pocket.

"You know, I always admired that about you," he said, leaning around me to unlock the door. For a moment, I was conscious of his nearness, of his breath ruffling the hair by my ear. "You didn't seem like you cared what anybody thought."

"Me?" A gush of warm air slid over me, pulling me inside the store. I wanted to turn and look at Blaine, to see what sort of expression went along with those words. But I didn't. A flush crept over my cheeks, and I felt the need to deflect his compliment with a joke. "Come on. Admit it. You really didn't even know who I was." I added a sardonic cough, resorting to what Trish would have referred to as a *defense mechanism*, using self-deprecating humor to keep people at a distance.

"I knew who you were." He was close behind me again, the two of us hemmed in by piles of boxes. Against the stillness of the building as the door fell closed, his voice was soft, intimate. I tried to brush aside the ridiculous desire to let down my guard. The temptation was almost overwhelming. *Grow a spine, already, Heather. You're here to do a job*, a voice in my head insisted.

Unzipping my coat, I moved from the back hallway into the main part of the store, where things were less crowded. If it hadn't been for the fact that Blaine's wicked stepmother was always in it, this would have been one of my favorite buildings in town. Two stories, with cavernous ceilings, beautiful oak moldings and fixtures, and an ancient Otis freight elevator that, as far as I knew, still worked, the building whispered of the craftsmanship of early

German settlers. They'd taken the time to create perfect dovetailing on the wall cabinets that held a myriad of tiny drawers filled with nuts, bolts, and plumbing supplies. In the center of the room, the open rotunda glowed with light from the tall, arched windows on the front wall. Moving into the warmth of it, I tipped back my head and gazed upward into the waterfall of light slipping through the ornate banisters.

I remembered standing in this very spot with my father, long before I was old enough to understand why the woman behind the counter always snorted and headed for the stock room when we came in. I was holding my father's hand, watching the shadows play over the well-worn wooden shelves, waiting for Dad to take me on the elevator. I was certain that he would. He knew all of the building's secrets. He'd worked there as a teenager.

I wasn't aware then that, until my mother swept through town one summer, my dad had been engaged to one of the girls he worked with. He was going to marry her as soon as he graduated from college, but my mother stole him away from his hometown sweetheart, Claire Anne, and from the rest of the town. A few years later, my father's jilted fiancée had married Blaine's father, the recently-widowed owner of the hardware store, the bank, and a huge ranch outside town. Mr. Underhill was twelve years Claire Anne's senior, but he had more money than my father could ever hope to accumulate.

"Are the clothes and shoes still upstairs?" Emotion cracked my voice, and I cleared my throat, wiggling out of my coat. I felt Blaine's hand grasping the hood, helping me slip free. His fingers brushed the wispy hair on the back of my neck and sent an electric tingle down my back. I stiffened against it.

The coat swished softly as he tossed it over the long, glass-front counter along the west wall. "Same as always," he said, and I had the sense that he was talking about me, rather than the store. For a moment, I wanted to be *not* the same, not the reserved, walled-off girl he expected. I couldn't do that, of course. I had to remember why I was here. Business. Just business. And a pair of shoes.

I started up the stairs, watching from the corner of my eye as he set his keys on the counter, slipped off his coat and laid it over mine, then followed. Beneath the low, eight-foot ceilings of the upper balcony, the space felt cozy, steeped in languid morning light.

"What'll it be?" He swept a hand toward the floor-to-ceiling shelves, crowded with shoe boxes, some of which looked to have been there since slightly after the turn of the century. "We got your steel toes, your stacked heels, your Mary Janes, flip-flops, wool socks, boat shoes, whites, browns, and blues. What's your pleasure?"

My mind jumped back in time again. I remembered Blaine's grandfather repeating the same singsong sales pitch when my father had brought me in for a pair of pink wading shoes with little cartoon fish on the toes. Looking up at Blaine now, I could see a bit of his grandfather in him. They had the same warm, brown eyes and slightly lopsided smile. What would it be like to have your present and your past so closely interwoven, a tapestry in which threads didn't begin or end but meshed so completely that there was no way to know where one ended and another began? Clay and I never had ties to anyone or anywhere. There were the issues between Dad's family and my mother, and Mom's mother and father were divorced and remarried; the family an odd mishmash.

I was jealous of Blaine. In truth, it wasn't the first time.

He grabbed a box from an upper shelf, blew off the dust, and pulled out a cowboy boot that must have been there since the days of *Hee Haw*. It had a silver eagle emblazoned in the vamp, and a ghastly long, pointed toe. "How 'bout some cricket killers?" He fanned a brow and gave the one-sided grin of a snake-oil salesman. "I can get you a discount. These are closeouts."

"From what year?" A chuckle-snort pressed from me. Very unladylike. I slapped a hand over my nose.

Blaine studied the boot, straight, brown brows drawing together in the center. "Not sure. Give 'em a try. They might grow on you."

"That's what I'm afraid of."

He sighed, indicating that I was difficult to please. I remembered now why every girl in high-school chemistry class had been gaga over him. He was charmingly goofy up close. His attention was like a flame you couldn't help wanting to stare into. "Come on, live a little," he urged, extending the boots my way. "When are you ever gonna get the chance to slip your feet into fine footwear like this again?"

"This side of the Grand Ole Opry, you mean?" Even as I said it, I was reaching for the boots, consumed with the odd notion that if I didn't put them on, I'd be sealing my fate as a mindless gerbil running endlessly on the same, boring wheel—missing some weird, once-in-a-lifetime opportunity: The chance to wear silver cricket-killer cowboy boots on the second story of a hardware store.

Kicking off my bedraggled footwear, I pulled on the garish boots, stood up, and walked the length of the balcony, feeling like Dolly Parton—on the lower half, anyway.

Blaine crossed his arms, rubbing his chin appraisingly. "They've got . . . attitude."

I rolled a look at him, then leaned over to observe the boots.

"You'd be the only one in Seattle with a pair," he urged. "You could start a whole new trend."

"Yeah . . . tempting. But maybe something a little less . . . silver." It occurred to me that he'd mentioned Seattle. How would he know that, unless he and Clay had been talking about me?

128

The thought was strange. I wasn't sure whether to embrace it or be afraid of it.

He pulled out a pair of tall mud boots, the black rubber kind the Mennonites used in the mucky corrals around their dairy farms and in the Proxica poultry barns over in Gnadenfeld. I remembered borrowing similar boots when Clay and I went home with Ruth and visited her family's dairy. We did that occasionally when Aunt Esther was planning social events at Harmony House and didn't want us in the way. "Tempting . . . but . . . no. I remember those things from my short stint as a cow milker."

"You were a milkmaid?" Blaine's look of interest followed me as he leaned against the shelf.

I sat down on the bench to release the silver Dolly boots into the wild again and told him the story of my one and only attempt at helping the Mennonite kids with milking chores. Ruth and her husband lived a few miles away on a Proxica poultry farm, but they maintained an interest in the dairy, and Clay loved to visit there. My ill-fated milking career had ended when I sucked cow parts and my own ponytail into the vacuum end of a milking machine. The cow kicked, I panicked, and things went downhill from there. I was saved by a brawny Mennonite boy who was somehow related to Ruth. It was embarrassing. He was only seven.

Blaine laughed goodnaturedly at the end of the story, and we continued perusing the footwear. Finally, I selected a pair of hiking boots, along with some warm wool socks, two pairs of jeans, and a couple of fleecy Moses Lake sweatshirts from the stack near the counter. The only thing I didn't score was a new electric heater. They were out.

As Blaine wrote up my charges, I caught myself thinking it really was too bad that he was potentially in a position to ruin my family financially. He was kind of likable, otherwise. Fun.

But you don't get to the senior manager stage by being drifty-minded. I knew how to stay focused on a goal, how to tune out distractions like Facebook, office chatter, funny email videos of dogs who could dance the cha-cha while wearing ruffled skirts and sunglasses . . . cute guys who want to lure you in, so you won't wonder why they're cultivating your family's good graces.

He offered to walk me back to the cottage after we finished shopping. I told him I was fine. I knew the trail well enough. I used to walk it all the time, back in the day.

On the way back to Uncle Herbert's, my feet warm inside the new hiking boots, the bedraggled fashion footwear and a sack of new clothing swinging at my side, I tried to keep my mind out of the past. I thought, instead, of the silver boots. Maybe I'd go back and buy them tomorrow—well, not tomorrow, because, come to think of it, the hardware store was always closed on Mondays. Trish would think the boots were a riot. I could keep them in my apartment as a conversation piece. A memento from my unplanned detour to Moses Lake.

Then again, I wouldn't be around when the hardware store opened on Tuesday. I wasn't supposed to be, anyway. Somehow, I had to wrap up this mess and get back to work before Mel went postal and my best chance at leading a design project slipped through my fingers. I couldn't let myself forget everything I had to lose if this project fell apart.

I returned to Uncle Herbert's house with that thought in mind, determined to get the whole family into one room so we could get to the bottom of this mess and hash it out. Surely, with enough injections of reason, everyone would have to wake up to reality. A nice, quiet Sunday morning would be the perfect time to do that.

But the house was anything but quiet when I went in. Mom was in Uncle Herbert's kitchen, cleaning up from breakfast and, oddly enough, wearing a dress, which my mother rarely did. The rest of the family was bustling around upstairs. I heard doors opening and closing, feet moving, pipes rattling. Mom quickly informed me that I'd better hurry up, if I wanted to ride to church with the family.

She made the suggestion without missing a beat, and after I reeled my chin off the floor, I said, "Since when do you get up on Sunday morning and go to church?" That was rude, of course, but I couldn't help feeling that they were all playing some sort of game, with me as the patsy. Maybe they thought that by putting on a show they could confuse me into giving up and going home.

Aside from the fact that my mother getting dressed for church on Sunday morning was about as believable as a hippo in toe shoes, I found it slightly offensive that she would choose this particular means of creating shock value. I'd always prided myself on the fact that my occasional church attendance—holidays mostly, with Trish at a historic downtown church, where the architecture of the building was in equal parts inspiring and distracting—was to some degree better than my mother's flavor-of-the-month spiritual existentialism. At least I knew what I believed, in the official sense. Most of the time, Sunday morning found me heading for the office to either meet Mel and prep for a presentation, or get in a little extra time, shoveling at a workload that piled on as fast as I could dig it out.

Mom had the nerve to give me a *you're crazy* look and say, "Well, both of the uncs are deacons, and now Clay and I are going into business here. How would it look if we sat home on Sunday mornings?"

I was speechless again. Twice in one conversation. The fun, relaxed feeling that had bloomed during my footwear safari quickly faded.

"Besides," she added, and I sensed that she was coming in for the kill—putting my battered and bleeding sanity out of its misery. "I feel close to your father there."

The blood drained from my cheeks, flowing downward through my body, abandoning me to a hollow numbness. My mother had been through more boyfriends and live-ins over the years than I could count. How dare she stand there, acting like she'd been pining for my father all that time, particularly considering what I'd seen her doing right before he died. I opened my mouth to say something venomous, then closed it, opened it again.

Mother took advantage of the conversational lull. "And this afternoon, we're driving over to Gnadenfeld. It's Ruth's birthday, and they're having a little get-together for her at the dairy. She lives with one of her nieces now. You know that her husband passed away several years ago, and she's been diagnosed with cancer, right? She can't live on her own anymore."

My head swirled. I leaned against the door frame, my vision of Ruth shifting. All this time, I'd been imagining her still dividing her time between the Proxica poultry farm she ran with her husband, and the family dairy. I knew she'd quit working for Uncle Herbert shortly after I went away to college. She'd told me about it in one of the letters my freshman year of college. Her husband was experiencing some health problems, and she was needed at home. "Ruth has cancer? Is it bad?"

Mom nodded, the first honest look of the morning passing between us. "Yes, it is. Which is reason enough to go get ready for church, right?"

"I don't have anything to wear." It was a stupid thing to say, but I was still stunned, just babbling out words with no real meaning.

"Oh, anything will do," Mom insisted. "Just go get ready. Ruth will want to see you, especially considering the shape she's in."

I quit the kitchen and left her there. Grabbing my things in the utility room, I went out the back door and walked down the hill. The bracing air pulled tears from my eyes until I found myself inside the cottage, looking at my carry-on bag, my new clothes, my laundry pile. I had the urge to throw everything into the suitcase, force the zipper around it, and leave for the airport, to return to a world that was only big enough for one. A world where nothing else, especially anything that happened in Moses Lake, could affect me.

I dressed for church instead, and we headed off in one of the funeral sedans, Mom driving, Uncle Herbert in the passenger seat, and me sandwiched between Clay and Uncle Charley in the back. Clay and Uncle Charley talked about fishing. I thought about Ruth.

Amy was waiting on the small porch outside the church when we arrived. She walked in with us, and I heard whispers around the room. Blaine Underhill's stepmother stiffened in her seat, pretending not to see us sliding into the row across the aisle. I noticed Blaine at the far end of the Underhill pew. A blonde was whispering in his ear, tapping him on the shoulder. I couldn't decide, from this angle, if I remembered her from high school or not.

Reverend Hay took the pulpit and began the announcements by pointing out his new fiancée, Bonnie, in the front. The congregation twittered approvingly. I was glad to have their attention diverted from us, but it quickly returned in the form of covert looks, whispers, little notes jotted in the corners of bulletins, a nudge here or there.

What are they doing here? The question was like smoke in the room, making it difficult to breathe. Sun streamed through the squares of colored glass in the arched windows, choking the air, stirring the voices of the church ladies in my mind. *Sit up straight, hon. Don't slouch like that, you'll get a hump in your back. . . .*

I thought of my father's funeral. I'd overheard Blaine Underhill's stepmother and my aunt Esther whispering about the fact that my mother hadn't made me wear a dress. Aunt Esther had snorted irritably, then pointed out that my mother was impossible to deal with and if it weren't for the fact that there was no way we could continue to live at the farm with my mother completely dysfunctional in her grief, Aunt Esther would never have allowed us to move into the gardener's cottage at Harmony Shores.

Now, glancing across the room, I saw Blaine's stepmother eyeing me coolly from the Underhill pew.

I wanted to get up and leave before the choir even made it to the choir loft.

You don't drown by falling in the water;

You drown by staying there.

—Edwin Louis Cole
(Left by Jim, teaching grandkids to swim.)

Chapter 9

The sermon wasn't bad, actually. Reverend Hay was a low-key sort of guy, and being newly engaged, he spoke from the heart when he talked about love and the nature of it. "In modern culture, we tend to think of love as something soft, frilly, and lacy, like the edging on a valentine," he said, smiling at his future bride in the front row. "And love is beautiful like that, intricate in the ways it changes you, grows you, makes you want to be more than you were before. Love sees in you the best possible version of yourself, and makes you believe it. . . ." I tuned out for a moment, only vaguely conscious of the sermon continuing. I caught myself looking across the room, watching the blonde watch Blaine. She flashed smiles and eye-commentary at him as the sermon went on.

I studied his responses, cataloging them without really meaning to. He laughed when she made cross-eyes at him during some reference to teenagers bouncing in and out of love at the drop of a hat. He returned a couple of smiles, and she winked at him. I still couldn't decide who she was, but her face was familiar—undoubtedly from high school. She flashed a couple glances my way, thinking the same thing about me, I supposed. Each time, I pretended to be studying the colored glass in the windows behind her head.

Farther down the Underhill pew, Mama B swiveled a narrow glance over her shoulder, and caught the blonde flirting with Blaine. Mama B's silent message to the blonde seemed clear enough. *Mind your business.*

Hmm . . .

The blonde turned her attention to the sermon again, and I did, as well.

" . . . and so much of that is true about love. It's the best feeling in the world. It's glorious, but Hollywood teaches us that love is weak and fickle, that evil doesn't have a very tough time overtaking it. If you watch enough movies, you'll end up believing that sooner or later all love is doomed to fail, that a broken, wicked, sinful, hate-filled world is just more than love can stand up against. That when a marriage fails, we shouldn't be surprised. That when a family falls apart, or a neighbor hates a neighbor, or a kid bullies another kid in school, or a church body divides into factions, we should accept that as part of life, because the world is imperfect—so imperfect, in fact, that it's more than love can combat. But what we don't realize—what the writers of the Bible knew that we've lost track of—is that love is the very essence of God, and God is powerful. In fact, He is all-powerful."

Pausing to let the point sink in, Reverend Hay moved from behind the pulpit, stood at the edge of the steps and held up his long, thin hands. "Brothers and sisters, don't let anyone convince you that love isn't strong enough to combat temptation or hate or prejudice or past hurts or misunderstandings or drugs or alcohol or culture clashes or self-loathing or any other form of evil that may afflict your life or the lives of those around you. Love doesn't need us to protect it from those things. Love *is* our protection. Great, big, crazy, extravagant, confident love, like the love God has for every one of us. Love that accepts us just as we are.

"If we only love people who are exactly like us, why, we're really just loving ourselves, aren't we?" He paused, gathering murmurs from the audience and a disinterested look or two from the casserole ladies. I glanced sideways at my mother and my brother, thought about all the ways I'd been frustrated with them over the years, all the decisions I'd criticized. Was I really just pointing at the mirror and saying, *If you'll be more like me, I'll love you more?*

A thorn poked somewhere inside me as Reverend Hay went on, the audience now hanging on his hook, ready to be reeled in. "But when we put on that great, big, godly love and go out into the world, we're ready to do battle with evil, with prejudice . . . yes, and sometimes even with ourselves. Sometimes the armor of love is heavy. Sometimes it's cumbersome, uncomfortable, and unwieldy. Sometimes it'll make you sweat, or keep you from having the knee-jerk reaction that'd be satisfying in the moment but would leave blood on the battlefield.

"Divine love is the key to churches that cleave together, to marriages that last and families that overcome, to friendships that forgive insult, and hands that reach out to those who are different from us. We've got to love each other more than we love our own reflections in the mirror. When we can do that, love is both a sword and a shield. No matter where we go, or what kind of battle we're facing, it's all the armor we need."

Reverend Hay moved to the head of the aisle then, and the pianist played an invitation song. A man and wife came forward to join the church—retirees, from the look of it. Reverend Hay introduced them to the members.

As the service wound down, my attention moved to a survey of the exits and who was sitting near them. I tried to gauge the quickest path out, the one that would allow me to vacate the premises without being stopped by curious church ladies, trying to ferret out information on our family's plans and my mother's reasons for suddenly taking up residence in Moses Lake. If the ladies' drop-by visit to Uncle Herbert's house the other day hadn't clued me in to the fact that we were the current topic of small-town speculation, the plethora of whispers and glances in church would have.

I felt like I was suffocating on a combination of the curiosity in the air and random memories of my dad. He was everywhere in this building, frozen in time. During our visits to Moses Lake, we'd come to church for Christmas pageants, Easter egg hunts, potluck suppers, a wedding or two. Every time we entered this place, people gathered around my dad as if he were visiting royalty, and I could see how much he missed Moses Lake. I always wondered if he resented my mother for putting him in a tug-of-war between his hometown and her.

Just as Reverend Hay was about to end the service, a little boy popped out of his seat and walked the aisle, loudly declaring that he wanted to be baptized. I thought about my dad. The day I was baptized along with a group of friends in our mega-church back home, he'd told me the story about getting up and walking down the aisle all by himself here in this little church. Now, looking at that little boy, I saw Dad. I wondered if, up in heaven, he was looking down and remembering. My dad, I realized now, showed us the kind of love Reverend Hay was talking about. He accepted people the way they were, even my mother, even when her inconsistencies caused him embarrassment, or inconvenience, or pain. If only I had inherited that trait from him, along with his hair and eye color. I wanted to be less like the casserole ladies and more like my dad; I just didn't know where to start.

When everyone stood up to go forward and hug and congratulate the newest members of the church, I whispered to Uncle Charley that I was going to walk home, and I ducked through an exit door into the parking lot. The air outside was brisk, but it felt good. Moses Lake glistening in the midday sun brought memories of my dad, and the thoughts were good thoughts, not painful spears with which I tormented myself. I felt as if my father were walking the path through the woods beside me, glad to see me in the place that he loved.

How would he feel about the land sale? Would he be pleased to know that something was happening that would provide jobs and much-needed income for Moses Lake, or would he be unhappy that the farmland would be developed? I wished I knew.

The family was already back at Harmony Shores by the time I made it there on foot. As we gathered food to take to Ruth's house, I began mentally preparing to start up a discussion in the car, where I would have a captive audience. While I understood this strange, nostalgic idea of Moses Lake as the idyllic family homeplace, in which Mom and Clay would happily settle while seeing the older generation through their senior years, I still knew it was impractical. Mom would never survive without her university dinners, her meditation classes, and the throng of graduate students, smitten by her knowledge of everything from Chaucer to Pope. And Clay couldn't even look after his poor dog properly. Case in point, I'd found the dog dishes empty on the back deck when I arrived at Harmony House after my walk through the woods. Roger was on his hind legs, trying to claw the lid off a metal trash can filled with dog food. I scooped out a helping and put it in the bowl, and Roger ate as if he hadn't seen kibble in a week. No wonder he'd felt the need to commandeer my FedEx package. If he got hungry enough, at least he could use my iPhone to call for a pizza. A twenty-seven-year-old man who couldn't feed his own dog regularly had no business taking on the care of two old men and a restaurant.

I rehearsed the conversation, making plans as to how I would gently hammer the point home while we were driving to Gnadenfeld. Somehow, I would figure out a way to do it as my dad would have—without being hard-edged and critical. When he gave advice, you knew he meant it for your own good, even if you didn't want to hear it. I would channel Dad's wisdom, be calm, yet determined. Businesslike.

Unfortunately, before I knew what was happening, Mom and the uncs had filled the backseat of the funeral sedan with secondhand casseroles. They took off while I was in the bathroom, leaving Clay and Roger waiting for me on the porch.

"Guess you're in the second wave," Clay informed me, seeming cheerful enough about the idea of making the thirty-minute drive to Gnadenfeld with me riding shotgun.

I squinted down the driveway, my feelings oddly bruised. "They just took off without me?" It's pretty bad when you get ditched by people who don't mind riding to a birthday party in a car with *Funeral Procession* written on it. I had the old high-school feeling for a moment. Was I really that unpleasant to have around, or were they trying to avoid the in-transit conversation I'd been carefully planning? "I can't believe they just took off and left me here alone." *How rude.*

"What are we, chopped liver?" Clay and Roger sent smiles my way in unison—two shaggy blondes seeming completely oblivious to any undercurrents in the day. It really is true that people resemble their dogs—or vice-versa.

"Of course not." *But I can't reason with you, and you know it.*

Clay bounded to his feet on the top step and jumped down the other three in one carefree hop. He hadn't gotten the nickname

Tigger for nothing. He could have earned a college scholarship in pole-vaulting, but he was just as apt to ditch high-school track practice as to show up. "I'll go get our ride." He jogged off toward the back of the house, and Roger scrambled from the porch to follow.

I waited, wondering what cars were left back there. I hoped we weren't taking the hearse. As far as I could tell, Mom didn't even have a rental car, which meant that Clay must have picked her up at the airport. Did Clay even own a car? He'd sold the last one Mom bought him to finance his flight with the earthquake relief project.

I heard a rumbling and chugging out back that didn't sound like the hearse or Uncle Charley's pickup, so Clay did have a ride of some sort. Moving down the steps and along the front walk, I tried to catch a glimpse of whatever was headed my way. It sounded like a cross between a motorcycle and a street sweeper.

A white Toyota pickup with a crooked front fender rolled into view, the blinker cover broken on one side, an orange light bulb bobbing like a loose tooth. Something was letting out a dull squeal with each rotation of the wheels, and the entire truck listed to the left. Roger had taken up residence in the passenger seat, his head hanging jauntily out the window as the vehicle drifted to a stop. A string of doggie drool dripped from his mouth onto the door, sliding downward over some sort of badly-decayed decals that remained in bits and pieces all over the vehicle. Bugs, I decided, on further inspection. The truck was covered with partial decals of red-and-black bugs. Moving closer, I read the shadow of decal letters that had long since disintegrated or been removed under the passenger-side window. *Ladybug Pest Control.*

"This is it!" Clay announced cheerfully, not the least bit embarrassed to be piloting a vehicle that looked like it had driven through a swarm of locust and collected body parts. "Hop in!"

I couldn't help it—I laughed. I knew Clay wouldn't care. One thing about my little brother. His ego was all his own. No one else held sway over it. I envied that about him. I always had.

On the other hand, I wondered at the odds of the ancient Toyota making it twenty-five miles down the road to Gnadenfeld.

"C'mon," Clay said. "She runs better than she looks."

"That's not saying much," I quipped, and my brother smirked at me as I studied the truck. The engine sounded a little like the old crank-start Oliver tractor that Uncle Charley had always lovingly referred to as Betty. Come to think of it, I wondered what had happened to Betty when the family farm was cleaned out for sale. The massive estate auction out there had been scheduled for right after Christmas, as I recalled. Hopefully, Betty had gone to a good home.

Opening the truck door, I stepped back so that Roger could exit.

"C'mon, Rodge, scooch over," Clay ordered, hooking an arm around Roger's neck and pulling him into the small space behind the gearshift.

"We're taking Roger?" Surely Roger was not on the guest list for Ruth's birthday party.

Clay stretched, so that we could converse over Roger's head. "Yeah, if you leave him home, he eats stuff."

"Too bad we didn't think of that before he eviscerated my FedEx."

Clay shrugged in acquiescence. "Yeah, but just look at all the entertainment we would've missed. Family bonding and all."

Shaking my head and trying not to laugh, I climbed into my seat and closed the door so that Roger and I were nicely snuggled in. I had the odd thought that Clay was right about the family treasure hunt. All of us tromping around the yard with flashlights and gardening shovels was a postcard moment, the kind of insane family-visit story you'd tell your friends about when you got back home—great fodder for coffee conversation. But who would I tell? I couldn't picture Mel and me chatting about the homeplace while we prepped for a presentation, Trish was always busy with the kids, and who knew what would happen with Richard?

Strange . . . I'd hardly thought about Richard since arriving in Moses Lake. Too much else on my mind, I guessed. But even that seemed wrong. You shouldn't be fantasizing about making a life with someone one day and forgetting about him the next, should you? If a relationship mattered, it wouldn't be so easy to put it out of mind, would it?

What was wrong with me? Was I so screwed up, so damaged that I'd never be able to make the kinds of connections normal people made? Would I always be living in my own private space—running like a hamster in one of those plastic exercise balls, a see-through shield around me, so I could look at the world but not touch it? Would I always be that person Reverend Hay talked about—standing there looking in the mirror, only feeling safe with my own reflection because it didn't challenge my priorities or my choices?

"You've got to admit our impromptu treasure hunt wasn't *that* bad." Elbowing Roger out of the way, Clay put the truck in gear, and we rumbled up the driveway, the Ladybug singing a cheerful song of squeaks and squeals as it bounced over chugholes. "Kind of nice just to chill with everybody for a little while, right?"

I felt the sting of an open wound, and I closed off the tender place as we rolled along the rural highway to Gnadenfeld. "Sorry to kill the fun, but somebody has to take care of business." Deep inside Clay's happy-go-lucky exterior there was a guy with a perfect ACT test score who had to know that what he was doing was wrong. He didn't want me around because he didn't want to hear it.

He shook his head, then rolled his gaze upward in a way meant to indicate that I was totally off base. "Sometimes it's not all black-and-white, you know. Sometimes there're people involved, and you can't just run it all through some spreadsheet. You're just like Dad. You're just like he was. It's all about whatever makes the most money."

I drew back, stunned that his feelings about Dad were so different from mine. How dare he say that. How dare he even think it. Sure, our dad had worked hard—even overworked a lot of the time—but he kept a roof over our heads. He kept our family together. He took care of us when Mom was too busy doing her thing, and he never complained about it. He held down the fort while she flitted off on every passing whim, leaving us to fend for ourselves while she indulged in self-obsessed ramblings in a spiral notebook.

Dad didn't deserve this from Clay, and neither did I.

I felt Reverend Hay's armor of love crumbling piece by piece, clattering through the floorboards and bouncing noisily in our wake as we drove along.

The vulnerable place inside me opened again, bled a little. I turned away and looked out the window, wishing I were anywhere but trapped in a car with my brother. "You know, Clay, why don't you give me a little credit? I'm trying to do what's best for everyone." A lump rose in my throat, and I swallowed hard, overwhelmed with a tangle of emotions I couldn't identify, much less catalog or control. *Stop here*, I wanted to scream. *Let me out. Now.* But if I said anything more, if I opened my mouth, I knew the dam would break and tears would rush forth, draining a lake that had been filling for sixteen years. There was no way of knowing what would be left afterward.

Silence descended over us, leaving an impasse, a broad, dark chasm between us. I focused outside the window, watching pastures drift by, the winter-brown fields dotted dusky green by live oaks and cedars. Roger wiggled around and lay across my lap, his head on his paws. He licked my hand. Maybe he sensed that I needed it. His fur felt soft beneath my hand as he nuzzled underneath it.

Finally I let out a long breath, took in another, and thought about Trish and all the secondhand advice from her therapist. *Deep breathing slows the heart rate. Think of something beautiful and pleasant to produce beneficial endorphins.* . . .

Why did everything have to be so hard? Why couldn't the property sale be quick, clean, painless? Just a business deal with a side benefit of putting the past squarely in the past, now and forever? Why did everyone have to keep bringing it up, to keep harping on it? My dad was a great guy. He died too early, instantaneously, without suffering. A gunshot victim. We would never know if it was accidental or intentional, or what my father was doing with the old shotgun in the first place. The gun had been my grandfather's, used for hunting. My dad could simply have decided to clean it, having no idea that it was loaded after all these years.

Or, his taking the rifle to the basement could've had something to do with the packed suitcases in the master bedroom, the man I saw my mother sneaking around with, and the change in my father's demeanor during the last week of his life. Clay didn't know about the suitcases and the man, and I wasn't going to tell him. What possible good could come from causing someone pain over events that couldn't be changed? Clay was better off writing his own version in his memory book and turning the page.

I wished everyone else would let me do the same.

The Ladybug chugged and jerked, coughing like a chain smoker as we rolled along the rural highway, now ten or twelve miles out of Moses Lake. I turned to Clay. He was frowning at the console, his lower lip pooched over his top one. He tapped the cracked plastic covering over the gauges. "Aw, shoot."

My anxiety perked up. The calming voice of Trish's therapist vaporized and more pieces of the armor of love flew out the window. "What? What's *Aw, shoot?*"

The truck lurched, and Roger slid forward, his front half landing on the floorboard. He turned and eyed me with a frown, as in, *Well, look at what's happened to me.* I pushed the other half of him onto the floor, so that he was sitting on my feet.

Clay downshifted. "Yeah, we're low on gas."

"We're what?" I pictured being stranded in the cold on the side of the road and missing Ruth's birthday gathering, which I was looking forward to.

"The gauge sticks," Clay said, as if that were an explanation.

I sat up straighter in my seat, gripping the armrest on the door, though I wasn't sure why. A bailout wouldn't help at this point. Roger whined, indicating that he, too, was worried. Perhaps he remembered the bike trip, when Clay stranded them both in the mountains. "Well, if the gauge sticks, don't you keep some kind of track of how many miles you've driven since you filled up?"

Clay shrugged. "I knew we'd be going past the farm. I figured we could pick up some gas there, if we needed it."

The logic of that was dazzling. "But . . . how do you know if you need gas, until you, like, run out?"

"It'll chug a mile or two."

"But what if the chugging *begins*, and we're *more* than a mile or two from the farm? Ever think of that?" That sealed it. My brother would never grow up and start to think like a normal human. He would always be some strange combination of Winnie the Pooh and my mother. *Oh, bother.*

"We're not." He motioned calmly toward the window. "Look."

I surveyed the surrounding territory, and it did look familiar. Some things had changed, but I recognized a few of the landmarks that had always told me we were nearing the family farm. While this was great luck, Clay's sense of planning still stunk.

"Have a little faith, sis," he said, as if he knew what I was thinking. Perhaps he could see my white-knuckled grip on the door handle as we chugged along the shoulder of the road, the vehicle gasping, wheezing, threatening to give up, then catching another burst of fumes and lurching forward. In the driver's seat, my brother was perfectly calm. I was envious of him, in a strange way. What would it be like to be so completely unaffected by fear? When I was with Clay, I couldn't help but feel like I was in a straitjacket, barely breathing, missing some grand adventure because I was afraid to strike out without first studying every inch of the map.

But intangibles like faith just weren't my strong suit, and I guessed they never would be. Faith was a blind journey, a path you couldn't predict or dictate. It was giving yourself over to the control of someone who might or might not necessarily agree with your plans. Faith could just as easily dictate that the chugging and the farm gate *wouldn't* occur at the same time, and that you'd end up standing on the side of the road, at the mercy of strangers. That wasn't something I wanted to experience. Clay, on the other hand, would look at it as an event that was meant to happen, an opportunity for an intended side trip of some kind. He would seek the meaning in it. He had learned that kind of thinking from my mother.

Which was exactly why I rejected it.

If you tried to erect a building based on faith, you'd end up with a mess. That was why you needed to create a blueprint ahead of time and follow it.

We ended up rolling into the farm, crawling and staggering up the dusty, gravel lane just as the gas gave out. The Ladybug came to rest in the center of the farmyard, the tall, hip-roofed barn on the left, and on the right, the two-story clapboard house my grand-parents had built. Next to their house, the smaller stone house, the original dwelling on the farm, squatted silent and shadow-filled. I turned away, so that I wouldn't have to see it. I'd been there a thousand times in my dreams. My father died in that house. No one had lived in it since.

Turning toward the barn, I searched for happier memories as Clay put the pickup in park. I remembered my grandfather, a quiet but gentle man, showing me how to whittle and how to find cat-erpillar cocoons under milkweed leaves. I remembered playing pirate ship with Clay on the horse-drawn hay wagon that was slowly rotting in the sun.

Just looking at the barn made my mouth water for one of the RC colas my grandfather always kept in a refrigerator out there. Uncle Charley's old Ford tractor, Betty, was still sitting in the doorway, seeming to indicate that the refrigerator and the RC colas would still be there, too.

"Oh, hey, there's Betty," I observed, anxious to distract my mind from darker things. Didn't it bother Clay at all, coming here, see-ing the house where Dad had died? "I didn't know Betty was still around."

Clay glanced my way enthusiastically, stopping halfway out the door. "You'd be surprised what's here. Want to take a look?"

"Nah," I said quickly, wrapping my arms around myself. "I'll just wait while you gas up. It's cold out there." The cold wasn't the problem, of course; the memories were. They were an assault of roses and arrows, some sweet, some painful. My father used to take me for rides on Betty during our visits. I loved it when he did that. Sometimes we would drive all the way to the lakeshore, through the wooded hills on the back of the farm. He'd sweep a hand over the water and talk about how the whole valley used to be filled with

148

farm fields—cotton, sorghum, corn. There were even a couple of small towns, now buried under thousands of acres of water.

I remembered looking at the lake and trying to imagine what was underneath.

Strange, I hadn't thought about those tractor rides with my father in years. The memories came back now, fresh, sweet, and fragrant, smelling of grease and diesel smoke, dry grass and caliche mud. I rested my head against the seat and breathed in the memories as Clay fetched gas from the barn, fueled up the Ladybug, did something under the hood, then slid back into the driver's seat.

"Remember when Dad used to take us down to the lake on the tractor?" I asked.

Clay turned the key and pumped the gas pedal. "He did more of that with you than he did with me." The Ladybug roared to life, sending out a cloud of black smoke that sailed past us on the breeze. "You were the one who liked the tractors and stuff."

"Guess I was." Relaxing in my seat, I smiled out the window as we circled the farmyard and left the place behind. "You were always too busy coming up with strange costumes and pretending to be a dinosaur hunter or Batman." Even in childhood, Clay's imagination was amazing. He only lived part-time in the real world.

"I haven't changed much." He echoed the thought I'd been forming.

I felt a rush of tenderness toward my brother as we turned onto the highway and rolled toward Gnadenfeld. Whatever else happened, however imperfect we were at loving each other, Clay and I would always be tied together by memories, a shared past, an understanding that no one else could duplicate. "Maybe change is overrated."

He blinked, then snickered, like he couldn't believe he was hearing that from me. The words did taste a little strange coming out, but they were heartfelt. I did love my brother, despite all his impracticalities.

The rest of the way to Gnadenfeld, we talked about some of the imaginary characters Clay had created as a kid. Off and on, I'd served as a bit player or cameraman during his fantasy productions. We were laughing about his Star Wars obsession as we passed through Gnadenfeld, its pristine antique shops, Mennonite bakeries, quilt stores, and mom-and-pop restaurants speaking of a healthy economy and plenty of tourism. *Guten Tag*, the sign read. *Good day*.

Judging by the look of the town, Gnadenfeld was enjoying good days. When I was little, the place had practically withered away, the Mennonite families moving off, finding it difficult to make a living farming in this hardscrabble country. Now the town spoke of prosperity, a symbiotic economy having developed between residents who worked for Proxica, the Mennonites who'd left the family farms to operate corporately-owned poultry production barns or to work in the processing plant, and those who still farmed and lived the old-fashioned way, selling their wares in roadside stands and the bakeries in town. The Mennonite residents of Gnadenfeld ranged from highly conservative to those who lived fully modern lives. They existed harmoniously, other than some differences in philosophy about mindless entertainment, like television. There seemed to be a place for all of them.

I imagined the economy of Moses Lake booming like this, the town thriving rather than scraping along on tourism dollars and dealing with a school in which half the population lived below poverty level in Chinquapin Peaks. I considered pointing that out to Clay, but I couldn't bring myself to spoil the pleasant mood in the car.

Memories—fresh and powerful, like a summer rainstorm—

surrounded me as we turned into the gateway of Ruth's family dairy. I knew this place. I remembered coming here with Ruth several times over the years. She'd brought us here the night after my father's death. She'd taken Clay and me home with her, and we'd stayed in her sister's house at the dairy, where we were surrounded by kids, animals, activity. Distractions.

Ruth had led us into the big, white two-story house, given us fresh milk and oatmeal cookies. She'd stroked my hair, kissed the top of my head, told me everything would be all right. That night she knelt with me by the bed, and we prayed together. But I was praying for something that couldn't happen. *God, please don't let my dad be gone . . . please . . .*

I'd never thought about the specifics of that night until now. The moments, the days after my father's death were a blur of family, dark clothes, dark thoughts, stark little rooms with police officers asking questions. *Heather, were there any problems between your parents that you knew of? Did you hear any arguments? There were packed suitcases in your parents' room. Do you know why your mother was packing . . . ?*

The questions burned again now, demanded answers I didn't have. I couldn't remember anything after hearing the shot and running to the cellar door. I didn't know what happened next. I didn't know how much I'd seen or what I'd seen. Mom said she'd come into the cellar from the outside door when she heard the gun go off. She told the police she'd caught me on the stairs, turned me away before I made it to the bottom, before I could see anything.

Had she? Was that true?

Did Ruth know what had really happened that day? Did she know more than I knew?

The trip up Ruth's driveway took on a strange sense of urgency, an eerie feeling that chased away the beauty of the dairy farm, where various members of Ruth's family lived in three different houses, generations alternating through as elders passed on and younger members married. Beyond the green fields and tall white-washed stone dairy barns, a collection of toys in the yard—a wooden teeter-totter, a homemade swing set, a carousel of a sort, made by cabling a ring of wooden seats to a tall center pole—testified to the fact that there were children living on the farm now.

The swinging carousel had been there even years ago. I remembered pushing Clay on it the day after my father's death, trying to distract him. The sheriff's deputies came to talk with me, and then they wanted me to go with them. Somehow, I gathered that they'd been questioning my mother all night, and they thought I might know something. Clay and the carousel had slowly grown smaller and smaller in the yard as we drove away.

Closing my eyes, I tried to tame the flood of memories. It was ancient history. The police had ruled my father's death an accident. Our lives went on, but barely—the struggle becoming more and more difficult as my mother sank into darkness, her eyes hollow, distant. Her behavior only helped to fuel the speculation of community members uncertain whether to believe the police reports or the gossip. My mother had never been well liked in Moses Lake, so the gossip was tempting, popular among the ladies in their bridge circles and garden club meetings. The men wondered how someone like my father, who'd grown up around rifles and hunting, could have accidentally shot himself while cleaning a gun. There were whispers, of course. Looks.

But not from Ruth. Ruth had stood by us steadfastly. Perhaps it was easier for her. Being from Gnadenfeld, she didn't have to live in Moses Lake, but she had always been devoted to Uncle Charley, Uncle Herb, and the family. She'd stood by my dad through the funeral of my grandmother and through moving Grandpa

Hampton to a nursing home within two months of our arrival in Moses Lake. When our family faced another funeral, sudden, tragic, unexpected, impossible to understand, she was our rock. I couldn't even begin to count the number of times she had stayed over at Harmony House in the weeks following my father's death, when all of us, including my uncles and aunts, were wandering through life in a fog.

I'd never realized how deep Ruth's connection to my family was, but she'd saved us in those dark months—pulled us up by a string, quilted the tatters together with her silent, even stitches. I'd never properly thanked her for that. As soon as high school graduation was over, I couldn't get out of Moses Lake quickly enough. If nothing else came of this trip, at least I would have the chance to thank Ruth for all she'd done to help Clay and me. It shouldn't have taken me so long to say it.

I prepared the words in my mind as we entered the largest of the three farmhouses and walked through the utilitarian but comfortable interior to the sun porch out back. We found Ruth settled in a chair, entertaining a come-and-go crowd of friends, relatives, and community members. It was an eclectic group—the attire ranging from Old-Order cape dresses and mesh prayer caps to jeans and sweatshirts.

In Gnadenfeld, the Mennonite population had always been in a strange state of flux, many of the younger members of the community gravitating toward the more liberal church on the outside of town, and the older people, like Ruth, tending to fall closer to the practices of the traditional church on Main Street. Even so, there seemed to be no hard-and-fast rules as to styles of dress and head covering. For as long as I could remember, Ruth had usually worn modest, floral print dresses and a small scarf-like covering fastened over her braided and coiled rope of hair. Today, she was just as I remembered her, except that her hair was thinner, fully gray now, and her cheeks, in the past always round and plump, had a hollow quality. Her dress hung loose, as if she'd borrowed it from someone else.

Her smile was as welcoming as it had always been, her eyes still a sparkling blue, her hug exactly as I remembered. When Ruth took you in her arms, you knew she meant it. You felt her hugs through your entire body. She held me away from herself afterward, her hands cupping my cheeks. I hung bent over her chair, unable to rise and move back so that the rest of the family could come closer.

"You've been away too long," she said.

I couldn't help feeling that she was right.

Remember ye not the former things,
neither consider the things of old.

–Isaiah 43:18
(Left by Mildred and Millie Millfast, twin sisters letting go of the past)

Chapter 10

Our visit with Ruth was sweet, and relaxing in a way I couldn't quite explain. Ruth's family and friends were easygoing people who loved to laugh. Other than the work involved in cooking and basic farm chores, they didn't believe in laboring on Sunday, so it was routine for them to spend the day visiting.

I couldn't remember the last time I'd been in a roomful of people who weren't in a hurry to rush off somewhere. Not a single cell phone rang. Nobody pulled out an iPod. Nobody was huddled in a corner, texting away on a Droid. I sat back in a chair and just enjoyed listening as Ruth and my uncles laughed and recounted old times, sharing somewhat off-color funeral stories that delighted Ruth's family and friends.

While we talked, two little red-haired girls in long flowered jumpers, Mary and Emily, sat at Ruth's feet, listening. Mary, whose thick red hair had been carefully plaited and secured with a blue ribbon in the back, couldn't have been more than five years old, and Emily, whose hair escaped her braid in wispy red corkscrews, seemed only slightly younger. They sat with their dresses tucked around their white stockings and tennis shoes, their attention moving from speaker to speaker around the room, as if they weren't the least bit disinterested.

I couldn't help being fascinated, not only by the fact that they were adorable, but by their ability to quietly sit and listen. Trish's twins had just turned three, and we couldn't even carry on a conversation with them in the room. They were cute and sweet, but they moved constantly from one form of entertainment to another, and when they were around, they demanded attention.

Emily, the smaller girl with the cotton-puff hair, finally yawned and crawled into Ruth's lap. Whispering something in her ear, Ruth nestled the girl under her chin, smoothing the flowered jumper around her legs, then gently patting her thigh as Emily relaxed against her. Mary, seeming a little lost on the floor by herself, shimmied into the armchair beside me as if it were the most natural thing in the world. Twisting my way, she smiled, and I moved my arm, so that she could wiggle back in the seat. Her hair tickled my neck as she snuggled in, and I found myself resting my chin on her head, drinking in the soapy, grassy scents of childhood and feeling the tug in my chest that had caused me to imagine a future with Richard when there really wasn't one. As much as I loved my work, some primal part of me wanted this. At moments like these, it stood inside me, screaming, *You're thirty-four! You're thirty-four and you're still alone. Time is running out!*

I hated that voice. I hated it because it made me question everything about my life, and really, I liked my life. I liked the excitement of it, the travel, the sense of accomplishment that came from seeing a project I'd helped design take shape in the real world and become something massive and lasting. The feeling of little Mary in my lap ran in direct contrast to all of that. If I had kids right now, with the demands of my job, a nanny would be raising them. What kind of sense did that make?

Ruth glanced my way, her eyes meeting mine with a knowing look, as if she sensed what was going on inside me, as if she could read me like a book, just as she had in the old days. I was grieving again, whether I wanted to admit it to myself or not. Not grieving the breakup with Richard, but grieving the life I might never find. I wanted the sense of connection I felt among Ruth's family. I'd always wanted it.

I tried to put away my painful self-analysis and focus instead on the ongoing story in the room—something about a fiendish escape of Proxica chickens and a run for freedom down the highway. Uncle Herbert and Uncle Charley were red-faced, laughing as one of Ruth's neighbors described his wife and other Proxica plant employees, trying to round up the chickens. The poultry stories continued from there. Before long I was laughing, too, my problems temporarily whisked away, as if one of the hand-tied brooms on the wall had swept them under the carpet where they couldn't cause trouble.

When it was time for us to leave, Ruth rose slowly from her chair and walked with us through the house to the front door. Her steps were labored as she moved along, her fingers clasped around Uncle Charley's elbow, clinging like the roots of a withered tree. Uncle Herb assured her that she didn't need to walk us to the door, and she insisted that the exercise would do her good. Mary and Emily escorted me to the porch, holding my hands, until finally they released me and bolted after some puppies playing on the lawn.

"You're not to start coddling me." Ruth swatted a backhand at Uncle Herb. "I'm fine. These young people fuss over me too much."

Clay's cell phone rang as he stepped onto the front porch. He moved off to answer it, and I strained an ear in his direction. Call me nosy, but I couldn't help it. The phone call was from Amy, and I was still trying to figure out their relationship. Not that Clay wasn't adorable in his own rebellious way, but a sweet, conservative, hometown girl who was by my estimation barely out of high school wasn't the sort I would have pictured him with. Usually Clay wound up being a project for girlfriends who viewed his scruffy surfer-bum look and aimless nature as evidence that he just needed a good woman to shape him up and mold him into perfect husband material.

Amy, on the other hand, seemed somewhat clueless herself, and in need of Clay to take the lead in their relationship dance. Right now they were on the phone trying to coordinate a date. Listening to them attempt to come up with a meeting place, figure out what to do with her car, and decide between options for Roger—take him on the date, leave him here at Ruth's during the date, lock him in Amy's parents' garage, try to sneak him into the movie theater by pretending he was a seeing-eye dog—was somewhere between funny and painful. Clay practically had smoke coming out his ears from the pressure of it all.

Finally, he looked over and caught my eye, then performed a little pantomime of me taking Roger—who right now was having a grand time with Mary, Emily, the puppies, and various dairy dogs—to the Ladybug. Clay's imitation steering-wheel motions indicated that I was being asked to transport Roger home, presumably while Clay and Amy went on their date in Amy's car.

I rolled my eyes and nodded—don't ask me why. After spending the afternoon laughing, talking, cuddling little Mary, and listening to stories, I guess I couldn't help the continued yearning for family harmony.

Clay gave me the happy thumbs-up, then went on with planning his date. I wondered, as I listened, if Clay might have finally found the perfect woman for him. Maybe, by being unwilling or unable to take the parental role in the relationship, Amy would manage to force him to grow up. . . .

It crossed my mind that I was actually thinking about my brother's love life, straining to hear the rest of the conversation as he trotted down the porch steps. How pathetic. Was it because I had no prospects of my own? Sadly, it probably was.

I felt that lost, somewhat pitiful feeling seep over me again, and I pushed it away, determined not to dip my toe into the blue waters of Lake Oh-Poor-Me, as Ruth used to call it. Funny, I hadn't thought about that saying in years. She had some funny little song about it. I couldn't remember the words now, but it had always made me laugh, even on the worst of days.

One thing I remembered about the Mennonites I'd met around Moses Lake was that they loved to sing. They were musical in all ways, in fact. Ruth said this was because, in the more conservative Mennonite churches, art for art's sake had always been discouraged as a vainglorious pursuit. Things like music and quilting had a purpose, and thus provided an acceptable outlet for artistic expression.

A melancholy overtook me as the uncs finished their good-byes. Today's visit was over. I wanted to get Ruth to tell me the words to the Oh-Poor-Me song, among other things. It struck me then that I might never know the words. Once I headed back to Seattle, I probably wouldn't see Ruth again. Her cancer and her thin, frail, fragile appearance had been the elephant in the room all day. No one wanted to bring it up on such a happy occasion, but we all knew that there wouldn't be another birthday gathering.

I watched her hug Uncle Herbert, her eyes closing as she rested her chin on his shoulder. The two of them hung on to each other, the moment seeming private, intimate enough that it surprised me. In all the months I'd lived at Uncle Herbert's and Ruth had helped to take care of us, I'd never seen Ruth hug either of the uncs. Of course, Aunt Esther was around then, and to her, Ruth was *the help*. Aunt Esther believed in the traditional, formal Southern rules about such things. One did not become overly familiar with the help, which at the time included Ruth, a retired man who tended the gardens, and a young guy named Lars, who did heavy lifting around the funeral home and took care of setup for services. Ruth, Lars, and the gardener ate at the breakfast table in the kitchen, while the family ate in the dining room, even on days when there was no one home except my aunt and uncle. Clay and I tended to be AWOL on purpose during dinners at the big house as often as we could. We preferred to eat in the kitchen while Ruth washed dishes.

She smiled at me as she released Uncle Herb and rested a hand against the doorframe, steadying herself.

"Hey, Ruth, I'm gonna change clothes in the dairy room, 'kay? I'm headed over to see Amy," Clay called from the driveway, and I realized he was shopping for date clothes in the rusted metal toolbox in the bed of his truck. What a romantic.

"There's no heat on in the dairy room!" Ruth's voice crackled like the old phonograph disks she used to let Clay play in Uncle Herbert's parlor, when Aunt Esther was gone to her teas and her meetings at the church.

"Not a problem," Clay answered, waving his clothes over his head as he started toward the largest of the barns, a massive hip-roofed structure that was neatly painted and picturesque.

"You come on in the house!" Ruth leaned out the door, looking concerned. She lost her balance a little, and Uncle Charley caught her elbow.

Clay turned and walked backward, cupping a hand around his ear in a gesture meant to indicate that he couldn't hear her. He grinned as he wheeled around and trotted off to the barn. No doubt he knew that if any of us went back in the house, we'd be here another hour, trying to break away again. Already, Ruth looked exhausted, and the niece who lived in the house, Mary and Emily's mom, had gently suggested that it was time to wrap up the birthday gathering.

Ruth frowned at me and shook her head as my goofball brother disappeared into the frigid dairy barn to get dressed for his date.

"Don't look at *me*," I said. "I can't tell him anything. He doesn't listen." I moved across the porch in her direction, while the uncs and my mother excused themselves and headed toward the funeral sedan.

Ruth's hand settled on my arm, her fingers trembling. "He has always listened to you," she said quietly.

I lost myself in the pale, cloudy blue of her eyes. It was hard to imagine never seeing her again, knowing that she had moved on from this world and *unpacked her suitcase in heaven*, as she had often referred to it when there was a funeral at Harmony House. Ruth not being on this earth was an impossible thought, like trying to contemplate the contents of a black hole in space.

"He reminds me of your grandfather," Ruth said.

"My grandfather? Really?" I'd always thought of Clay as being just like my mom—her spitting image in word, deed, and opinion, if not in looks. I was like Dad, and Clay was like Mom. Together, we were an odd couple, like Oscar and Felix.

"Ohhh . . ." Ruth's eyes rounded. "I could tell you stories."

That's just it, I thought, *you could*. But I wouldn't be around to hear them. I wanted to hear the stories. I wanted to know how Clay was like my grandfather. But in another way, I was afraid. I was afraid to bring up the past. I'd worked so hard to exorcise all the family tragedy from my life, to rid myself of the ties to this place, that time. To leave behind the depressed, withdrawn, frightened girl who had wandered through her last year of high school and her first year of college under a black cloud, desperately trying to find a way out.

Who would I be, if I let the past come to life again, allowed it to put down roots and grow leaves, renew its colors? Would I sink into the shadow that had consumed me after my father's death? Would I be even worse? Somewhere deep inside me, was there the potential to become like my mother had been—practically catatonic, completely dysfunctional?

I didn't want to take that risk, to allow it in. I'd changed my mind about even asking Ruth if she knew more about my father's death. What was the point in revisiting it? I had a good life in Seattle, a satisfying life, a job I'd worked hard for, an existence that was . . . was . . .

"Come on, Heather," Mom called, halfway into the passenger's seat of the funeral sedan. "Aren't you riding home with us?"

"I'm driving Clay's truck home," I answered. "With Roger." Mom gave me a surprised look, then glanced at Roger, rolling on the lawn with Mary, Emily, and a sheepdog. I added hopefully, "Unless you want to take Roger with you." It was worth a try, but Mom was quick to shake her head and slip into the sedan.

I turned to Ruth. "Or unless you want to keep Roger here. It's just like having Clay around, only with four legs and a drooling problem."

Ruth swatted me softly and clucked her tongue. I could almost hear her quoting one of her special proverbs, as she so often had. *The man who speaks ill of others, foremost speaks ill of himself.*

"It's true," I defended playfully, and she swatted me again, then reached up and fixed the hood of my coat, where it was balled inside the neck. Her fingers were like ice against my skin. I slipped my hand over hers, held it. "Go on inside and rest. It's too cold to stand out here. I can wait for Clay by the car."

She nodded wearily. "You come to visit me tomorrow. I have a story to tell you."

"I'd like that." But in the back of my mind, I was thinking, *Tomorrow is Monday.* I needed to be back at work. But so far I hadn't accomplished what I'd come here for. I hadn't convinced Mom to return to Seattle and sign the papers. Now, by agreeing to drive Clay's car home, I'd missed another chance to corral the family. What was Mel going to say when he learned that I wouldn't be in Seattle Monday morning, and I still hadn't settled the business about the land deal? *He'll decide that if I can't even take care of this little detail, then I don't have any business taking the lead on the Proxica project. He'll use it as an excuse. Whatever confidence he has in me will be completely undermined. . . .*

I felt stress heating up inside me, working toward a boil, a strange contrast to the cool touch of Ruth's hand. If I hurried home, I could work on my mother and the uncs while Clay was busy with Amy, try once again to make them see reason. "I'm not sure if I'll be here, though," I said, and Ruth's hand slipped away. I pulled my jacket closer over my shoulders.

"You'll call in the morning, then?" Ruth pressed, which for Ruth was unusual. She was never pushy; only kind, strong, and tolerant.

"Of course I will." I glanced over at her, and in the space of an instant, felt a shift in my thoughts. *What is wrong with you?* The voice in my head demanded. *This woman kept you on your feet during the worst time in your life and now she's dying of cancer, and you're worried about taking an extra day off of work?* "You know what, let's just plan on it," I said as Clay exited the barn in rumpled jeans and a sweatshirt, then stuffed his other clothes in the toolbox. Now that the day was cooling off, he'd finally donned a heavier shirt and long pants. "What time should I come? What's best for you?"

Ruth's lips lifted at the corners, pleating her skin like a puckered quilt. "Come for lunch. We'll sit on the sun porch and watch the cows go out on the winter wheat. They're so happy out there."

"That sounds wonderful." Only a farm wife would consider watching cows graze to be entertainment. "Can I bring anything?"

She mulled the question, then raised a finger, indicating a sudden and pleasing thought. "Bring some of that wonderful bratwurst from the Waterbird store—the ones in the natural casings. Do they sell those any longer? Come at eleven, and we'll bake *bauernbrot* to go with it."

A fond memory danced through my mind—one of Ruth and me in Uncle Herbert's kitchen. She was trying to teach me to make something—some dish with dumplings on top. I didn't want to learn. I wanted to wander off by myself, not talk to anyone, not be around anyone, just hide away and not think of anything. But Ruth insisted that I help her cook. In reality, she knew I would be no help at all—Ruth could handle a kitchen completely on her own—but she wanted me there with her, singing the song about Lake Oh-Poor-Me, rather than hiding in some dark corner, drowning in it.

"How about if I just bring lunch?" I suggested, thinking that she probably didn't need to be cooking and no doubt her niece had plenty to do, taking care of kids and farm chores. "I'll bring enough for everyone and just buy some potato salad and beans from the Waterbird. How many do you usually have here for lunch?" Around the dairy, the numbers were always changing, depending on what combinations of family were living in the various houses and which boys or girls from nearby families were working there.

Ruth patted my hand, her attention turning momentarily to Mary and Emily, who were at present trying to boost Roger into the lowest branch of an oak tree. Oddly enough, he was coop-erating with their efforts. "We'll cook. Mary and Emily will be

164

disappointed if we don't. You can supply the bratwurst. . . . And will you do something for me? I wondered if you might bring something from your uncle's house?"

"Sure." My curiosity piqued, but I was suddenly aware of apprehension nibbling at the edges of my mind like a mouse trying to breach a cereal box. Was I jumping the gun, making plans? What if I called work, and Mel went postal about my taking a few more days off? I had plenty of vacation stored up, but that didn't mean that Mel intended for me to actually take it. "What do you need?"

Ruth glanced toward the lawn again, as if to make sure the girls couldn't hear us. "There may be some things . . . some . . . sketches of mine at Harmony House—tucked away in one of the closets or in the basement, perhaps. Your uncle probably doesn't even remember them. They may have been thrown away years ago, but will you look?"

Curiosity and something else . . . a tender sense that I owed Ruth this much and more pushed aside the looming dread of contacting Mel. I remembered Ruth sitting on Uncle Herbert's back deck with a drawing pad late in the afternoons when she was waiting to carpool home with a couple of ladies who did the cooking at the Waterbird store. Somehow, I'd gathered that Ruth's sketching time was private. She seldom showed me what she was drawing. When I asked her about it, she bought me a drawing pad of my own—a sketchbook and a journal. *It helps to put your troubles on paper,* she'd said in that cheery, simplistic way of hers. *Not to look at over and over again, but just to throw away.* She'd lifted a mixing spoon into the air, and I knew a Scripture was coming. Ruth loved quotations of all sorts, but she'd always stopped what she was doing when a Bible quote was on the way. *"Remember ye not the former things, neither consider the things of old."*

"Of course I'll look for your sketches," I told her now. "I'll ask Uncle Herbert if he knows where they are."

She shook her head quickly, then pulled her shawl closer around her shoulders. A sharp breeze rounded the corner and sliced its way along the porch, and she moved back a step in the doorway. "No, just look for them. Bring them to me if you can, but don't say anything to Herbert." The request had a mysterious quality.

"I will," I agreed, then told her good-bye.

Clay was headed toward the dairy barn with Mary and Emily when I reached the Ladybug. The girls were giggling and hanging from his arms with both hands, jumping and swinging through the air every time he yelled, "Look out! Alligator!" or "Oh no, it's a tarantula!"

"Do you need a ride to Amy's?" I called after him, the truck door squealing in protest as I opened it.

Clay spun around, slinging the girls like fins on a pinwheel, as they curled their feet into their skirts. "Nah, Amy's coming to get me. If she doesn't show up pretty soon, I'll just start walking that way until I run into her."

"Okay," I said, then left him to play with the other kids and climbed into the Ladybug, praying for a chug-free journey. As I wheeled around in the yard and started out the driveway, something bolted into my path, and I hit the brakes, causing them to squeal long and loud. Near the dairy barn, a teenage boy in jeans, a barn coat, and a hat stopped to look at me. He pointed to the front of my vehicle, and I stretched upward, catching sight of ears and a fluffy blond head. I'd almost forgotten Roger. Putting the truck in Park, I opened the door, and Roger scrambled across my lap before I could get out to allow him access.

As we rolled down the driveway, Roger yipped at Clay and the girls, now investigating something underneath the edge of the barn.

Roger smelled like he might have been crawling around under there himself, and I hated to imagine what he'd left behind on the girls' dresses. Rolling down the window on his side to create a vacuum seemed the most prudent decision, so I leaned over and took care of it before we headed for home, me saying silent prayers for the Ladybug's continued health, and Roger happily lolling his tongue in the flow of fresh air before finally settling down for a nap, all worn out from playing with dairy dogs and cute little Mennonite girls.

When we returned to Uncle Herbert's house, the place was empty. There was no note and no explanation as to where everyone had gone. My frustration over being ducked by the family again inched up, but since I'd already decided to stay an extra day to see Ruth, there seemed to be no point in agonizing over it. I decided to take advantage of the quiet time to go down to the cottage, gather my laundry, and throw my things in the washer, so I'd have some clean clothes for tomorrow. The phone in the kitchen reminded me that a call to Mel was an absolute must-do tonight, and sooner was probably better.

I picked up the receiver, put it down, then picked it up again, only to set it back in the cradle. Around me, the house creaked and groaned, as cold and stiff as an old man climbing out of his chair on a winter night. My skin tingled with chills that had nothing to do with the drafts around the window sashes. I'd always hated being alone in this house. From the time I was big enough to understand that Uncle Herbert was in the business of handling final remains, I'd made any excuse I could not to come to Harmony House whenever we'd visited my grandparents out at the family farm. Usually, it was just as well, because Uncle Herbert's house was tied up with the funeral planning sessions, services, and visitations, as well as Aunt Esther's social engagements. Plus, Aunt Esther didn't really seem to like kids. Children running around weren't conducive to the peaceful, somewhat sophisticated atmosphere she was trying to cultivate.

That last year in Moses Lake, Clay had come home from school with countless ghost stories about the place. Legend had it that a young belle had hung herself in the stairway after her beau left her for someone else. Uncle Herbert said no such thing ever happened. I hadn't been upstairs since, and I'd always known what happened in the mortuary rooms in the basement, so I avoided that area, as well. That didn't leave much territory.

Now even the kitchen felt spooky.

I heard Roger outside, and thought about the clothes that Clay had shoved in the back of the truck. Maybe, before making the Mel call, I'd grab those few things from the toolbox along with my laundry, then start a batch and bring Roger into the house to curb the creep factor. Roger could provide moral support while I called Mel.

The thought had barely begun to process before I was in the utility room, turning the heavy glass knob. When I opened the door, Roger was on the veranda, happily gnawing on something that may have been leather at one time, but now had the pockmarked, slimy consistency of a rawhide chew bone. It looked suspiciously like my wallet.

"Give me that!" I squealed and made a lunge. Roger leapt to the right, and we played a rousing game of keep-away on the frozen decking. Finally Roger bolted into the house, where we toured, at high speed, many of the rooms I'd never liked. I was reminded, while hunting for him upstairs, that Harmony House was filled with beautiful architectural details: ornately carved mantels gracing every room and gorgeous pilasters lining the halls. It was a grand house, if you didn't think of it as a funeral home.

By the time I finally cornered Roger in an upstairs bathroom and pried what remained of my wallet from his jowls, some of the creepy feeling had dissipated. If there were any ghosts watching, they were probably either laughing their heads off or feeling sorry for me by now. The exercise had helped me to pull my head together a bit, too. It was silly for me to be scared of a house. I wasn't a child anymore. *It's no different than any other house,* I told myself as I went downstairs with Roger trailing behind me, looking defeated. He sat at my feet, watching the emptying and towel-drying of my wallet and its contents. Miraculously, everything was still inside.

The newfound sense of empowerment from regaining my stuff made me feel almost whole again, except for the hollow spot in the center of my being, where my iPhone should have been. Trying not to think about it, I picked up the kitchen phone and reinstated my credit cards, then made my call to Mel. Fortunately, he didn't answer, so I was able to leave a voice mail explaining that the loss of my purse and some family issues were going to keep me in Moses Lake a couple of days longer. I left the funeral home number in case he needed to call me, and I promised to check in.

Now that I had my wallet with the little card that explained how to dial into my voice mail from another phone, I decided to check. There was a message from Gary the dentist, of all people. He wanted to tell me what a nice time his family had during our visit, following the rescue from the Dallas bus station. He also wanted me to get in touch sometime soon regarding designs for his new clinics. He and his partners were talking about building at least three more in the next year.

I mused on that as I slipped into my coat and went to the cottage in the thickening darkness to get my laundry. Then I headed to Clay's truck to gather the dirty clothes he'd deposited there. Maybe designing dental clinics wouldn't be so bad. It wasn't a state-of-the-art commercial production facility, but it was something.

Maybe Gary really had the kind of money it would take to engage our firm. I could talk to Mel about discounting our fees. The man had saved my life, after all.

The Ladybug's toolbox seemed to be rusted shut when I attempted to open it, but muscle and determination finally won the battle. I pulled out Clay's frayed khaki cargo shorts first and quickly realized that his wallet and cell phone were in there. Apparently Amy was not only driving on the date, but she'd be paying for it, as well. Dropping the pants into the basket with my laundry, I reached into the toolbox again to grab the shirt. Something glass slid out of the pocket and clattered against the bottom, then rolled to one side. Behind me, Roger barked, and I jumped backward, the shifting moon shadows having set my nerves on edge.

"Roger, cut that out."

He answered with a growl that was surprisingly menacing, for Roger, and he homed in on something near the corner of the house. The branches of the bushes moved in the breeze, and for a moment I thought I saw someone there. A man in a dark coat and a fedora hat. Heebie-jeebies crawled over my skin, drawing forth an uncontrollable shudder.

"Stupid dog," I muttered, reaching into the toolbox and fishing around for whatever had dropped out of Clay's shirt. My fingers touched something small and round, roughly the size and shape of a prescription bottle, and a disquieting thought slid through my mind, fluid like the shadows. Why would Clay be carrying medication? Despite his reluctance to wear a coat and his strange eating habits, he was just about the healthiest person I knew. The object rolled in my palm as I lifted my hand and held it in the dim light fanning from the kitchen windows. It wasn't a prescription bottle, but it was a bottle of some kind—small and round, made of glass, with a plastic screw-on lid. There was a residue of something loose and silty inside.

Slipping it into my other hand, I reached in again and searched the floor of the metal toolbox. My fingers slid over a jumble of hammers and screwdrivers, some rusty nails, and a rubbery blob that felt like melted fishing worms. There was something else, but I couldn't quite reach it. . . .

Roger barked again, and nearby in the woods, a coyote howled. Roger took off to give chase, and it quickly became evident that no amount of hollering from me would bring him back. A sense of being watched slid over me again, causing me to give up the toolbox search and hurry inside. On the table in the laundry room, where casket draperies and curtains had always been folded, I laid out Clay's clothes and felt something in the baggy side pocket of his cargo shorts, then pulled out a dirt-encrusted ziplock bag. The plastic felt grainy, like it had sand on it or in it. Laying it on the table, I flattened it and looked closer. The residue inside the bag was powdery and white. A search of the other pants pocket turned up a small glass vial with a lid on it. The bottom of the vial had been charred. I held it to the light, looked inside. Empty.

A cold feeling traveled from my fingertips, through my arm, and into the center of my body. Setting the vial on the table, I pushed it to the corner near Clay's cell phone, raked all the clothes into the washer, dumped in soap, pushed the button, then stood with my hands gripping the corners of the washer, my back to the folding table. I didn't want to turn around. I was afraid to. I'd been living in the big city, in a high-pressure career field long enough to know what ziplock bags of powder and burnt test tubes meant.

What if that incident with Clay, the campus police, and the marijuana paraphernalia wasn't so innocent all those years ago? What if it was actually the beginning of something?

Was Clay into drugs? Was he using? Was that why his behavior was even more unpredictable lately? Could that be the reason he'd

171

come to Moses Lake in the first place? Had he come here looking for an escape, a change of scenery, a chance to detox, far from whatever company he'd been keeping since he'd returned from the earthquake relief in the jungle? Could the problem have worsened there? Drugs were readily available in South America.

If it was true, did Amy know? Did she have any idea? Did Mom? Did the uncs? Did Blaine?

I turned around, looked at the bag and the vial. Clay wouldn't do something like this. He wouldn't. There had to be another explanation.

But the possibility that he had a problem could explain everything—his sudden hairpin life turn, my mother's willingness to support it, the uncs going along with some crazy plan for Clay and my mother to take over the restaurant, the canoeing business, and the house at Harmony Shores. Even Mom's willingness to be here made perfect sense now. She would do anything for Clay. Even pour all of her money into an ill-conceived business venture and a move to Moses Lake, especially if she thought his life depended on it.

I picked up Clay's cell phone, paged down the list of contacts. Blaine was on speed dial. So were Amy and my mother. The phone numbers for Harmony House and Catfish Charley's weren't even in Clay's address book. If you were really planning to take over a business, wouldn't you have the phone number logged into your cell? Wouldn't you be spending time there? A lot of time?

Was it possible that Clay didn't have any intention of following through with this deal? That all of this was some sort of scheme to take the money and run? I couldn't imagine my brother doing a thing like that. Clay had always been the kindest, gentlest person I knew. He never wanted to hurt anyone. I could picture him bringing about the family's downfall accidentally, through lack of planning, inadequate foresight, his usual pie-in-the-sky attitude . . . but on purpose? My brother didn't have that in him.

But people feeding a habit did strange things. Terrible things . . .

I heard the door slam in the foyer, and I jumped, my heart bolting into my throat, my body caught in a moment of indecision. Should I leave the evidence on the table, confront Mom and the uncs about it? Should I wait and ask Clay in private? If I kept it private, would I be helping Clay to hide it, enabling him?

Uncle Charley was turning the corner into the kitchen. Sweeping Clay's things into a towel, I folded it up and tucked it on the top of the dryer behind a laundry basket.

"Well, there you are." Uncle Charley set a Styrofoam container on the counter. "We stopped off at the restaurant for a bite. Didn't have any way to get ahold of you, but we brought you some fried catfish and hush puppies. Good eats." Pausing, he directed his full attention toward me, scratching his head as if I'd confused him in some way. "You all right? You're pale as a Sun-dey shirt."

"I don't feel so well." I caught the scent of fried food either coming from the box, or wafting off Uncle Charley's clothes. My stomach roiled. "I think I'm just going to head down to the cottage and get ready for bed early. I started some laundry, but I can finish it in the morning."

"We could put a movie on while you wait," Uncle Charley suggested. "Sit up a little till you're feelin' better. Your mama's got a whole bunch of them teas she makes. Her and Herbert'll be here in a minute, I reckon. We ran by the church, and I picked up my truck. Must be they got tied up talkin' to somebody. The associational music meetin' was just letting out. I scooted before all them old hens could waylay me. Good-lookin' single fella like me has to be careful."

He winked and smiled, but I could only shake my head and

stumble back a step, my mind on Clay. "I think I'm just tired. It's been a long day."

"A good day, though." Uncle Charley's soft brown eyes, so like my father's, met mine, and for an instant I imagined my father standing there. He would hate seeing our family this way. He'd be worried to death about Clay. "It's good you're here, Heather."

"Thanks." Emotion choked the word. I hugged him, and he held on for a minute, rocking me back and forth. I closed my eyes and imagined I was hugging my dad. What would he do, if he were here right now?

"Good to have family back in Moses Lake." His voice was rough and gravely against my ear, his hands so dry and weathered they scratched over the fabric of my T-shirt like sandpaper. "The older you get, the more you realize that's what matters. I love you, darlin'. You're the spittin' image of your daddy, and I always loved all my brothers' kids, since I couldn't have any of my own. I love you younger ones, too."

I felt sick again. Did Uncle Charley have any idea what was going on with Clay, what was hidden in the towel just a few feet away? "I love you, too, Uncle Charley." I meant it, but all I could think was, *Grab the towel. Don't forget to grab the towel.*

The tender moment ended as quickly as it had begun. Uncle Charley handed me the Styrofoam container and a to-go cup of iced tea, just in case I wanted it later. I slipped the towel with Clay's belongings on top of food, then escaped out the back door and hurried down the hill. Overhead, an owl hooted in the trees and the wind clattered among the branches, sending a shudder across my shoulders. I didn't catch my breath until I'd rounded the corner of the cottage and stepped into the glow of the porch light.

A small stack of freshly-split firewood had been left in the rack by the steps. On top of it was a box. I picked it up and recognized the picture of a woman in a snuggly blanket toasting her feet in front of a brand-new electric heater. A note had been tucked into the edge of the box.

Cold night ahead, it read. There was no signature, but I knew who'd left the heater and the stack of wood there on my porch.

If there is magic on this planet,

it is contained in water.

—Loren Eisely

(left by Kat and Rhee, gal pals on a girlfriend weekend in Cabin 3)

Chapter 11

When I woke in the morning, a solitary loon was singing to the rising sun. In the misty hinterland of sleep-waking, I realized I was baking alive under my pile of quilts, thanks to last night's load of firewood and the new handy-dandy electric heater, which wouldn't have to remain a freebie now that Roger had returned my wallet. Throwing off the covers, I peeled my pajamas away from my sweaty skin. Outside the window, the pile of firewood was just visible, and with it came a warm feeling that had nothing to do with the temperature in the room. It really was nice of Blaine to bring the firewood and dig up an electric heater for me while we were gone to Ruth's . . . thoughtful.

Now, did I want to admit that to him, or not?

I pictured him giving me that wickedly confident smile—overconfident, really—those big, boyish eyes twinkling. How many times, while slaving over the high-school-yearbook layout, had I dreamed of those eyes? I gave Blaine the prime spots on every page—in the feature about the guys who had lettered in more than one sport, in the article cataloging debate team awards, on the page with the homecoming court, and the section about the Fellowship of Christian Athletes. He became the poster child on the page listing football stats. I added him and his Hampshire hog to the feature about the county fair, bumping some other kid and some other pig, who had actually won the blue ribbon.

I wondered if Blaine ever noticed that he was the center of yearbook fame that year, if he knew who was behind it, or if he was even aware that the quiet girl in the dark clothes worked on the yearbook. I was only in the journalism class because I had to be somewhere, and it was a good place to hide out. Journalism was during the athletics period. The room was filled with nerds and misfits who didn't talk to anyone. It was a fairly comfortable way to spend the hour, and I could moon over pictures of all the kids to whom I was invisible. I could fantasize that, because I'd put them in the yearbook, they would suddenly decide to invite me to their secret parties at Blue Moon Bay and ask me to share lab tables in chemistry class.

There was no end to the rock-star status of Blaine Underhill back then. He was always the center of a crowd, cracking jokes and handing out high fives. Too cool for someone like me. Too self-important to even look my way. Could it be that, all that time, he really was a genuinely nice guy, and I was the one with the attitude problem? Had I been largely the cause of my year of Moses Lake High School misery—the big, fat chip on my shoulder and the secrets at home causing me to reject everyone before they could reject me?

Was I still doing it?

Was that why my life was stuck in the same place? Was I really still the girl who lived in the shadows, coming home and locking myself in my room so that I would never again become close to anyone, because people could be gone in a heartbeat? Had I forgotten Richard's birthday, maintained unusually long lag times between our dates, resisted calling him on nights when I actually could have . . . because I was trying to establish a certain separation? Was it all a subconscious effort to keep my distance, even as I fantasized about engagement rings and told myself I wanted a life with him?

Was I really that big of a coward? That much of a mess?

Sighing, I rested my elbows on my knees and combed a mop of tangles from my face. I felt like my hair looked—twisted up, tied in knots. Either the heat in the cottage or this place, Moses Lake, was making me insane.

The towel and yesterday's clothes stacked nearby on a wooden chest caught my eye, breaking the morning reverie. It looked harmless enough, an innocent still life of sloppy housekeeping. But through the white terrycloth, Clay's cell phone flashed lazily, and of course, I knew what else was wrapped in the towel. Evidence. Hints of something terrible.

The reality descended on me, heavy and hard to manage so early in the day, like a death you forget about overnight, and for the first few glorious moments of waking, it doesn't exist. Then your mind engages, and it hits you like a slap, turning life upside down again.

There was no way I could leave Moses Lake now—not considering what I'd found in Clay's pockets last night. I had to get to the bottom of things, make sure my brother received whatever help he needed. I'd have to call Mel and let him know I'd walked into a family crisis. I would need a few more days.

Just a few? What if it took longer? I couldn't imagine hopping a plane and going home without proof that my brother was all right, but part of me wanted to run, to retreat to my own life. Anything could happen with the Itega project next week. Beyond that, the

LISA WINGATE

problems here, this issue with Clay, were far beyond the scope of my experience, far beyond my control.

Back home in Seattle, life was structured, manageable. In Seattle, I didn't wake up freezing, or sweating under a pile of quilts that smelled like old fabric and humidity off the lake. I didn't find strange things in people's pockets. My apartment was a peaceful shrine to furniture designed by some of the masters and procured from eBay. There were no dusty corners or leaky windows plugged with wads of Kleenex, or people doing things that were unpredictable, dangerous, impossible to face.

I loved my life in Seattle. I loved my apartment. I'd always loved that apartment. It was modern, clean, spacious, located in a concept building I'd helped design. There were retail stores on the bottom, then two floors of income-assisted apartments designed to help homeless families get back on their feet. From there on up, the higher you went, the nicer the apartments got. I was about three-quarters of the way to the top. Not bad for a girl only thirty-four years old.

My days in Seattle were mine to manage, mine to control, mine to schedule. Here in Moses Lake, the days tacked back and forth with the whimsy of a poorly-rigged catamaran, buffeted by the winds and the water, propelled by forces I could neither anticipate nor direct. This place, my family, made me crazy. Challenged everything I knew about myself.

Crawling to the edge of the bed, I leaned across and reached for Clay's cell phone. In an hour or so, I could call Mel and try to beg off for a longer stay. Mel was always in a better mood first thing in the morning, before the office came to life. Not a good mood, especially lately, but he was slightly less likely to breathe fire and render me to ashes.

The phone was cool in my hand, chilled by its proximity to the

179

window, where the war of hot and cold air had formed diamond-like patterns of frost on the glass—tiny masterpieces that caught the morning sun in a dazzling array of facets. The surface felt grainy beneath my fingertip, the frost slowly melting, a dewy hole forming.

A memory struck me, old, and misty like the frost. Dad and I were studying the crystals on a windowpane, watching the sun illuminate its intricate designs. I was fascinated by their complexity, their beauty, their geometric structure. That so much detail could be laced into something so small, so insignificant as frost on a windowpane stretched my mind, pulled me toward a belief my father shared that day, in his quiet, unassuming way. The very proof of God's infinite power was in the details of life—those things we often looked past. His work was everywhere. In people. In nature. In the sensations that traveled through human contact, in the pleasantness of a loved one's voice.

We sometimes don't see God because we're so busy looking for something more complicated than frost on glass, my father had told me that day. *If God could put that much effort into something that only lasts a few hours in this world, think about how much He pondered you.*

A sigh pressed my throat. I couldn't remember the last time I'd studied the frost on a windowpane—given it, or God, any real thought. These days, I got up on Easter and Christmas and went to church because it was something I'd always done with my dad. I was afraid he'd be disappointed in me if I didn't, and showing up at church a few times a year was a way of apologizing for the wretch I'd been before he died.

Last Christmas, Richard and I had even gone to midnight mass at one of the historic churches downtown, but that was about as deep as my thoughts went. Most days I had enough on my mind. I was running on too little sleep and too much caffeine. The rush of daily existence didn't leave time for contemplating frost. But sitting here in Moses Lake, I felt the lack of connection in my life, the lack of contemplation of something larger. In the years of working for Mel, of trying to earn my stripes under his tutelage, I'd become like Mel. Mel had no life. His wife had left him. His kids never called. He was living in a big house. Alone.

At the very least, I had to be sure that my family was all right before I left Moses Lake. At the very most, I might find some of what was missing inside me. A connection. But how could I explain that to Mel? Spirituality and emotion meant nothing to him. Family was not a permissible excuse for lack of work performance. A day or two extension of this trip was bad enough, but a potentially open-ended leave to see to the care of a brother who might be struggling with a drug problem? There was no way.

If I wanted to keep my career intact, I had to find a solution to my family issues—and quickly. The real estate papers that had been so important a day ago hardly seemed to matter now. That issue paled in comparison to my little brother's future.

Setting the phone back on the windowsill, I decided to opt for a detailed email later that morning. I exhaled a warm breath to create a fog on the glass, drew a little heart in it with my fingertip. Somehow everything would work out. It had to work out. . . .

Please, God, show me how all of this works out . . .

A movement on the porch pulled me close to the glass again. Barely visible in the bottom corner of the window, a blond tail lay curled over a rubbery black nose.

Roger was sleeping on my doormat?

The chill of morning slipped over my legs as I found my slippers and crossed the cottage to the other side, to look out the kitchen window toward the house. It was awfully cold last night; not very nice of Clay to leave his dog outside.

Rolling my eyes, I went to the front door, opened it, and surprised Roger, causing him to scramble on the icy decking. The tips of his fur were covered with frost, and miniature icicles clung to the ends of his whiskers.

"What are you doing out here?" I whispered.

With a soulful look my way, Roger walked past me into the cottage like he owned the place.

"Oh, for heaven's sake," I muttered as Clay's dog proceeded to investigate the living room, his tail sweeping and swatting various pieces of furniture, stirring up dust moats.

"Where's Clay?"

Roger paused to look at me again, both brows lifting, as in, *Search me?*

Crossing the room to the cabinet filled with free promotional mugs and treasures from estate sales, I took down a '40s-era jelly glass with yellow flowers and a picket fence painted on it. It reminded me of my grandmother. She'd had an entire collection in the house at the farm. I loved to look at the various designs. Grandma was, in general, particular about her things, but she always let me select my own glass, even the ones from her good china. She was trying to build a rapport with me, I understood now, but in general, I resisted her offers to teach me how to crochet or can pickles or bake nut bread. I'd heard countless arguments between my parents about visits to *that house* with *that woman*. I knew I wasn't supposed to like it there.

Filling the jelly glass with water, I poured some in a bowl and put it down for Roger, and he drank like he was dying of thirst. Either his water dish at the house was empty again, or it was frozen over. Poor thing. Maybe even he didn't feel like traversing the frozen mud at the edge of the lake to get a drink. I was tempted to take Roger's water dish, march it into the big house, and put it in bed with Clay. If he was going to be out until all hours of the night, the least he could do was to make sure someone looked out for Roger. . . .

Headlights pressed through the murky fog on the driveway, slowly growing brighter in the mist. I watched as they drifted closer, cutting the fog, disappearing into the low area where the driveway crossed a small watershed, then appearing again. Who would be visiting so early? Grabbing a dish towel, I wiped the condensation from the window and leaned close to gain a view of the parking area beside the house, where the family cars were kept. The approaching vehicle looked like Amy's, but it was hard to tell in the dim light. I watched as the passenger door opened, and Clay climbed out. He stood talking a moment, his hand on the doorframe, then he leaned in one more time, like he was going for a good-bye kiss before closing the door.

A blush traveled down my neck. I felt like a voyeur.

He stood in the driveway watching as the car made the loop and retreated into the fog, then he tiptoed toward the house and, of all things, stole down the cellar stairs like some sort of miscreant. I wanted to go up there, catch him sneaking in, and smack him. Twenty-seven, and he was staying out all night, then slipping through the cellar door? How involved were he and Amy, anyway? Did she have any idea that he had ziplock bags and unmarked vials hidden in his pockets?

Another possibility entered my logic stream, and the data byte was disturbing in a new way. How could she not know, if she and Clay were spending this much time together? What if it was *okay* with her? Surely, whatever he was into, they weren't into together. She didn't seem the type. She had a job, a decent car. For a girl barely out of high school, she seemed fairly stable, living somewhere in that hinterland between childhood and adulthood, still in her parents' house, doing what people from Gnadenfeld did if they weren't headed to college—working for Proxica, where there was decent pay and health insurance. How did Amy's parents feel about her staying out all night with a guy who was eight or nine years older and worldly, in comparison to her?

Theories buzzed in my head, landing just long enough for me to swish them away and dismiss them. It couldn't be true—but there was only one way to know for sure. Clay, and probably my mother, held the answers to these questions, and I needed those answers. I had to know what I was dealing with. If Clay did have a substance-related problem—it was hard to even think those words in conjunction with my brother—I couldn't leave him with my mother. Her friends smoked weed in the name of inspiration, and she seemed to have no problem with that. There were good treatment facilities around Seattle. I could take Clay home with me and work with him to find the right kind of program. If he did need help, Moses Lake, a teenage girlfriend, and my mother weren't the solution.

The issues tumbled in my mind as I showered, dressed in jeans and one of my new Moses Lake sweatshirts, and mentally prepared for a trip up the hill and a conversation about Clay's issues. Roger was scratching and whining in the entryway, ready to be let out as I took one last look at the towel with the vials wrapped inside, then grabbed my coat, tucked Clay's cell phone and wallet into a pocket, and proceeded to the front door.

My wristwatch caught a thread on the coat, hemming me in momentarily as I attempted to knee Roger out of the way and work my arm loose at the same time. "Roger, quit." For whatever reason, he was determined to dig his way out rather than moving, and finally the sacrifice of a few threads or the wristwatch seemed worth it in order to grab the collar and manhandle the dog. "Move out of the . . . Come . . . on . . ."

The moment the gap was wide enough, Roger lurched forward, taking the collar and my fingers with him. We staggered out the door in a tangle, each growling for different reasons, and the door slammed shut behind us. Canine momentum carried us halfway down the porch before I found my feet and brought the situation under control. Roger, intent on something near the corner of the cottage, continued straining as I leaned over, catching a glimpse of the dull, wintery shadow of a crape myrtle tree shifting and the branches snapping against the house, as if someone had just brushed by. Fine hairs rose on my skin, and I felt a prickle that had nothing to do with the cold. Just like last night, I had the feeling that someone was nearby.

"Clay?" I whispered. Maybe he'd seen me in the window and realized I'd noticed him coming home in the early morning hours.

No answer. Roger sniffed the air, his throat rumbling.

"Is someone there?" Pulling Roger along, I crept across the porch and down the steps. I couldn't see anyone in the yard, along the shore, or near the barn. Nothing out there but the quiet morning shadows and the waters of Moses Lake, blue-gray in this light, lapping at a ribbon of ice along the shore. A flock of mallards circled, honking and chattering, in search of a landing place.

Roger stopped growling and turned his attention to the birds, yapping and wagging his tail. The minute I let go of his collar, he was gone, and I wrapped my coat closed, hustling up the hill, my breath coming in quick, smoky bursts. The lights were on in the kitchen, and the scent of coffee bid a cheery hello, dispelling the sense of uneasiness that had come over me at the cottage.

Mom was on the sun porch, wrapped in a quilt, watching the lake and sipping her morning coffee while reading a copy of Charlotte Brontë's *Villette*.

"Oh, you're up," she observed, like she wasn't entirely thrilled about it. "There's coffee in the pot."

"I'll grab some in a minute." Leaning against the doorway, I glanced over my shoulder, making sure no one was sharing space with us. This was probably as good a time as any to feel Mother out about Clay and drugs. I had to be subtle. If I just bluntly asked, she'd jump to his defense and if she did know what was going on with him, she'd feel like she was doing him a service by hiding it from me. Clay had been gone on the earthquake relief mission for weeks before she'd even admitted to me that he'd left, and that was only because I'd gotten an email newsletter, soliciting donations. The notice had Clay's email address on it, and he was pictured with the crew, helping to convert shipping containers into emergency housing. Mom hadn't told me, because she knew that I'd complain about his taking another detour from law school and hocking the last car she bought him.

"Where is everyone this morning?" That seemed like a suitably innocuous opening line.

She shifted the half-moon-shaped reading glasses lower on her nose, so as to get a better look at me. "Haven't seen the uncs, but you know they usually get up and head straight to the Waterbird to drink coffee and do political commentary with the docksiders. They could be gone already. I'm not sure where Clay is—still in bed, I suppose. Guess he and Amy made a late night of it."

So late that he just got home, I thought, but I didn't say it. One issue at a time. "Amy seems sweet."

"Yes, very." Mom took another sip of coffee, eyeing me with obvious reserve. She was wondering where this conversation was headed.

"Is it serious—this thing between Clay and Amy?"

Mom's head tipped to one side. "A little, I think. Why?"

I shrugged and reached across the doorframe to brush a smudge of dirt, but it didn't come off. "I don't know. I just wondered how

Clay could be so close to someone in Moses Lake. I mean, he just got back from South America a couple of months ago."

"They knew each other back when Clay was in school here. Her brother was in Clay's class. Clay remembers going over to their house a few times." She acted as if that explained everything. Of course Clay and Amy could be dating seriously—they were playmates when Clay was in elementary school and Amy was barely out of diapers.

I found myself searching for the path from dating Amy to, *So . . . does my little brother have a drug problem?* Unfortunately, my mother was an astute woman. She understood language. She'd spent a lifetime dissecting it, manipulating it, analyzing the fine points of character motivation. I reminded myself to watch my body language, so as not to tip her off. Thank goodness for those Dale Carnegie classes. "You don't think it seems a little odd . . .?" *That they're out all night, and he's ditching Roger for her?*

She shrugged. "I think it's fine. Your father and I met one month and ran away to get married the next. It wasn't anywhere in my plans or his. It just happened."

And look how that turned out. I drew back at the thought, and she must have seen it, because she stiffened, her lips pursing. She pulled her glasses off and set them in her lap. "People fall in love, Heather. Sometimes at first sight, even."

I blinked hard. I couldn't help it. Now, on top of encouraging Clay to give up law school for frying catfish, Mom was in favor of my little brother falling into a relationship with a girl he barely knew? "So you think it's, like, love at first sight?"

Mom licked her lips, and I could feel a debate coming on. Her eyes brightened and sharpened, like a cat's when it spots a tempting movement in the grass and it's contemplating a little sport. "Don't you believe in love at first sight, Heather?" My mother had the most annoying habit of answering a question with a larger question—broadening a simple, concrete discussion into the sort of nebulous, intellectual debate she and her crowd lived for. This topic was obtuse, even for her.

"What does it matter what I believe? We were talking about Clay."

Mom watched me with a closed-lipped smile that conveyed anything but pleasure. "There's someone for everyone, right? Maybe she's his someone. Isn't that the way it is with you and Richard?"

My stomach dropped through my shoes. I swallowed hard, an uncomfortable, tingly feeling in the back of my nose. Did she know about Richard and me? Had she said that just to land a blow, to shut me up?

"Is Clay all right?" I blurted out.

Mom jerked back, her chin tucking in. For just a flicker of an instant, I saw a crack in the calm façade, a hint that there was more going on here. My mind once again spun the scenario in which Clay, under pressure in college and impulsive by nature, had experimented with drugs, then perhaps broadened a habit in some third-world country where the hard stuff was easy to get. Was that really it? Was she convinced that she could fix the situation by moving to Moses Lake, by letting him take over the restaurant and the canoe and cabin business?

She crossed her arms, the copy of *Villette* sliding off her knee and landing soundlessly in the chair. "I've never seen your brother more centered. It's *you* I worry about, really. You seem so uptight, Heather. So . . . unhappy."

Maybe that's because everything is upside down and backward and nothing makes sense, and no one will tell me the truth. "Does Clay have a drug problem?"

I'd done it. I'd gone too far, spilled the beans.

Her reaction was exactly what I expected. She blinked at me like I was the crazy one, then gave a sardonic little laugh. "Really, Heather. That's going too far. Why would you even say that?"

I bit my tongue, knowing better than to tip my hand again. I'd revealed too much, but something in her reaction told me I'd struck a nerve, scratched close to whatever they were keeping hidden.

She masked any initial shock with a sympathetic, slightly sad look. "I know you have some rivalry issues toward your brother, but honestly, why not just be happy for him? Not everything in life is a competition, Heather. Not everything is a race. There's something to be said for learning to just . . . be."

I swallowed hard, pinched my lips between my teeth, felt my eyes bulging with the pressure of the things I was biting back. *Me? Competitive toward Clay? Puh-lease! In what way, and for what reason?* "I'm worried about him—that's all."

A hand swat dismissed the notion. "Don't be. Your brother is fine. Everything's fine. Just because things aren't happening according to your plan does not mean anything's wrong. Perhaps the rest of us are entitled to want something completely different. Perhaps, Heather, you should leave the ruling of the universe to bigger hands than your own."

I didn't bother to delve into the meaning of that sentence. There was no point. My mother was just spinning words that were, like much of her poetry, intended for shock value. My only choice was to retreat, sufficiently burned, and leave her to Brontë.

Passing through the family rooms, I found my brother sacked out on an antique brocade parlor settee, his head and shoulders askew against a pile of needlepoint pillows Aunt Esther had probably purchased at various church bazaars. A trail of drying mud-and-grass footprints led across the room from the cellar door. The path ended at Clay's feet, which were hanging off the sofa, as if he'd sat down to take off his shoes and simply crashed. I stood over him, watching him breathe. His nose and cheeks were still red from the cold. A piece of a dead oak leaf had tangled near his ear, its brown color slightly darker than the sandy strands around it. His hands were dirty, grime pressed under the fingernails, and the cuffs of his pants hung wet and sloppy over his shoes.

I tried to imagine where he'd been. Maybe he and Amy went parking in the woods? Back in high school, that was what local kids did. They knew all the out-of-the-way spots at the Ice Hole, Seven Springs, and Blue Moon Bay, where they could hang out and party without getting nabbed by the sheriff's department, rangers from the state park, or the local game wardens. Wasn't Clay a little old for that? Then again, he was dating a girl who was not far out of high school.

"Oh, Clay." I sighed, trying to see through him, to understand what was going on. Finally, I leaned over and shook his shoulder, attempted to rouse him, but I knew it was probably an exercise in futility. Once Clay fell asleep, a freight train could speed through the room, and he wouldn't notice. He only moaned and pulled away, his head falling off the pillows. Finally, it seemed hopeless to do anything more than cover him with a lap quilt and move on. Uncle Charley passed through the room just as I was about to walk away.

"Looks like he didn't make it to the bed last night." Uncle Charley jingled a set of keys in his hand.

"Guess not." I didn't have the heart to point out that Clay had come in only a short time ago. Apparently, Uncle Charley hadn't noticed the damp shoes or the tracks on the floor.

"I'm headed down to the Waterbird." He thumbed over his shoulder in the general direction of the driveway. "You could come along and class up the joint."

I was tempted for a minute. Morning banter with the docksiders

190

and a funny story or two seemed like just what I needed. Maybe I'd run into Blaine there. . . .

The thought was appealing in some way I was afraid to analyze, especially first thing in the morning, not yet into an initial cup of coffee. "I'd better not." In terms of what I needed to take care of in Moses Lake, I would accomplish nothing by hanging out at the Waterbird. "I'm supposed to go see Ruth for lunch. By the way, can I borrow one of the cars this afternoon?"

Uncle Charley nodded, patting me on the shoulder. "Sure, help yerself to whatever's out there. The keys are on the pegboard by the washin' machine, where Herb always keeps 'em." He thumbed in the general direction of the kitchen. "I'm glad you're gonna see Ruth. She can use the company. All the young folks are out working the dairy during the day or in school—or runnin' around after the chickens, like little Mary and Emily. As you get old, you sit by yourself too much, seems like."

The words had an unusually somber quality, and I realized something I hadn't before: Uncle Charley was lonely, despite all of his connections to the community in Moses Lake. He had no kids of his own, his wife was gone, and the nieces and nephews he'd helped to raise were living far away now. Clay, my mother, and I weren't much of a substitute. Clay did his own thing, Mom kept her nose in a book, and I was only in town for a few days.

I couldn't come up with the right thing to say, so I changed the subject. "Listen, Ruth asked me to look for some sketches of hers. She didn't want them to end up in the estate sale, I think."

Uncle Charley chuckled. "Oh mercy, if you find any of her pictures around here, don't tell Herb you're takin' them back to her. Ruth used to draw them things and then put them in the trash. Herb would fish 'em out and hide 'em away. You know that Herb can't stand to see anything good thrown out. One of the few fights

I ever saw the two of them have was over those sketches. I don't know why Ruth didn't just take them home to throw away, but Mennonite folk can be kind of funny about pastimes like art. The older, stricter folks don't always approve. Guess maybe that's why she did her sketchin' here, and why she was a little embarrassed about it. Anyway, if there's any of her drawings still around, Herb would've tucked them away someplace where Ruth wouldn't know. You'll just have to look around."

We said good-bye then, and he headed for the Waterbird. I made a cup of coffee for myself and began canvassing the house. Since I didn't want to go into the basement, particularly not first thing in the morning, with the light still dim, I concentrated on closets and bedrooms and did my best to ignore the creaks and moans of the old house. Footsteps passed by in the hall as I searched bedrooms. I assured myself that it was the floor joists creaking as the morning warmed.

In a quilt trunk in the bedroom where my mother was staying, I found a sketch pad. The cover lay crinkled with age and had been snacked on by a mouse, who quite fortunately was no longer present. An odd feeling settled over me as I slipped the pad from its hiding place, closed the lid of the trunk and sat on it, and then ran a finger along the edge of the pages. Only a few remained, just a sheet or two of paper tucked between the covers. If Ruth's sketches were private enough that she wanted to make sure they weren't left in the house, maybe I shouldn't be looking.

But I couldn't help it. I lifted the cover anyway.

The first page was blank, a faint image in charcoal having bled through from the page behind it, the ghost of a stranger, the hint of body.

I lifted the sheet, watched it flip over, saw the face of a young woman. She'd been captured, frozen in a moment in time, her eyes filled with life, her dark hair swirling around her waist in loose waves. She'd turned to look over her shoulder, as if someone had surprised her from behind. A friend or a lover.

Her essence had been preserved in charcoal, in confident strokes of gray.

Her floral print dress and her eyes were blue. Pastel.

I watched her, tried to imagine the moment Ruth had recorded. Who was the woman? Her dress was vintage, perhaps from the forties, but form-fitting and stylish—not Mennonite garb by any means. The barest hint of a smile played on her lips, as if she were toying with someone.

I wondered what secrets she'd been keeping all these years as she lay in the quilt trunk.

In this house, everyone had secrets.

But whosoever drinketh of the water that I shall give him
shall never thirst.

—John 4:14
(Left by Jack, glad to be back, found God on a battlefield in Iraq)

Chapter 12

I finished searching out-of-the-way places upstairs and netted nothing beyond the picture of the woman in the blue floral dress. When I came back down, Clay's cell phone was vibrating in my coat pocket in the utility room. Tucking the drawing pad under my arm, I slipped the phone out and took it to the family parlor, where Clay was still crashed on the settee. The phone buzzing near his head didn't seem to bother him in the least. An incoming text from someone named Tara was on the screen. Tilting my head, I read the first few words. *Hey, babe. I miss u bad . . .*

I blinked, sidestepped, and touched the phone with one finger, swiveling it toward me. This technically amounted to snooping, but I couldn't help myself. Who in the world was Tara?

. . . come home soon, K? Not fair leaving me here alone for Mimi's party, BTW. . . .

The text went on from there, but I resisted the urge to scroll down. The area code was 817—Fort Worth, like Gary the dentist. Clay had a girlfriend in the Metroplex? One who expected him to go

194

to *Mimi's* party with her? Who was Mimi? Who was Tara? She was waiting for him to come home sometime soon? Where was *home*?

He'd left some girl behind and not even told her he planned to move to Moses Lake?

My stomach sank. The cell message lent credence to a theory I still didn't want to entertain—that my brother really was scamming everyone in Moses Lake, and he had no plans to stay. What about poor little Amy? She seemed completely smitten with him. Was he planning to dump her and move on whenever he was done here? Was he two-timing her with another girl? Did Amy have any idea? Could Clay do something like that? He'd never been the kind of person to intentionally hurt someone. Could he possibly have changed that much?

But a drug addiction could change people completely, make them do things they wouldn't normally do. . . .

A floorboard squeaked, and I jerked back. My mother was in the doorway. She looked from the cell phone to me, as if *I* were the one doing something nefarious.

I didn't bother defending myself. We'd played enough verbal chess already. "Who's Tara?"

She blinked, remaining silent for a moment, then shrugged, indicating that she had no idea. "You'd have to ask your brother, I guess." A curious glance angled toward the drawing pad I'd unearthed upstairs.

"Clay's not answering any questions right now." I glared at him in a way that should have fried him on the spot. "He was out all night. With Amy."

Mom only smiled pleasantly, rolling her eyes a little, as in, *Boys will be boys,* then she gave Clay an adoring glance, indicating that he could do no wrong. "He *is* an adult, Heather." Another glance targeted the drawing pad with a hint of suspicion.

I flipped a hand in the air, frustration taking over. Again. "You know what, I've got to get out of here for a while." I wasn't about to show her the sketch of the girl in the floral dress. In a game where everyone seemed to be one step ahead of me, there was a small but perverse nugget of satisfaction in the fact only I knew about Ruth's request. "I'll see you later."

An idea popped into my mind, lightning fast and strangely alluring. Amy was Blaine's cousin. Blaine was probably at work at the bank. How much did he know about Clay and Amy's relationship?

Mom's lips pursed, as if she suspected that I was up to something. "Where are you going?"

What do you care? I wanted to answer, but instead, I just said, "I have some things to do, and then I'm eating lunch at Ruth's." I vacated the room without giving her a chance to formulate any more questions, then moved through Uncle Herbert's office, the kitchen, and the utility room at a good clip. I didn't stop until I'd commandeered a funeral sedan and rolled out the driveway, leaving Mom and Clay to continue their codependent dance without me.

If Mom wasn't willing to be forthcoming about Clay's issues, other sources of information would have to fill in the blanks. A little background about Clay's previous visits to Moses Lake and his relationship with Amy might be helpful. How long *had* they known each other? How often did he visit? What did he do when he came? What was his motivation for visiting?

A sickening possibility nibbled at my mind. Even back when we lived in Moses Lake, Chinquapin Peaks and the remote areas along the river were known drug havens. Far from any paved roads, up in the timber country, marijuana patches grew in secret and meth labs operated in the woods. Maybe Clay was coming to the area for . . .

Stop it. Just stop. That's ridiculous.

I had to quit jumping to conclusions. My sources of information

---

in Moses Lake being few, Blaine was a logical choice. Surely, Blaine wouldn't want his cousin setting herself up for heartbreak. He would want to protect her, wouldn't he?

Aside from the need for information, the idea of seeing Blaine was alluring in a way I didn't want to contemplate. It wasn't until I reached the bank that I realized I had no idea what I was going to say or how I'd broach the subject. I couldn't just walk into Blaine's office and blurt it out. Somehow I had to work my way around to it. Delicately. Tactfully.

Was there a tactful way to say, *My brother is cheating on your cute little cousin, and I found what looks like drug paraphernalia in his pocket, and I'm wondering if she's involved, too?* Blaine would think I was some sort of a paranoid crazy person, obsessed with my brother's life.

I tried to come up with an opening line as I walked through the lobby and tracked down Blaine's office. The blinds were closed over the tall plate-glass windows with his name painted in gold letters, and the blonde who'd been whispering in his ear at church sat poised behind a desk in front of his door. *Marilyn,* the nameplate read.

Marilyn's face narrowed in a way that told me she knew who I was, even if I couldn't place her. Folding her nicely manicured hands on the desk, she gave me an unhappy look when I asked to see Blaine. "He's in a meeting." After tongue-swiping her teeth for lipstick, she flashed a quick, plastic smile, her gaze sliding toward the exit and back, as if to sweep me through the lobby and out into the street like a stray dust bunny. "Do you have an appointment?"

"No, but I'll wait." I moved to one of the maroon-and-gray tweed chairs opposite her desk.

My continued presence rated an eye roll, her irises forming unnaturally blue half moons beneath her lashes, which were un- naturally blue, as well. I remembered the blue mascara and the peeved expression from high school algebra class, and suddenly the name clicked, too. *Marilyn Hill*. When I was at Moses Lake High, she was a second-year senior who'd transferred in from some other state to live with her grandparents. She was finishing up a few credits in order to graduate. She was tall, blond, and well developed, even then. All the boys were fascinated with her, including the algebra teacher. Marilyn didn't like algebra. The teacher cut her a break every chance he got, which I found irksome at the time.

"I'll tell him you stopped by." She wagged a finger in my direction, as if to indicate that she was searching her memory banks for my name. "Uhhh . . . Don't tell me. I know it starts with an H. . . ."

The door opened behind her, and both of us jerked toward the sound. Blaine poked his head out, saw me there, and smiled, seeming not the least bit surprised by my presence in his bank. "Well, hey," he said.

A fluttery feeling flitted around my chest, touching here and there at random, like a cleaning lady with a feather duster. I forgot all about my brother. "Hey, yourself." The words came out sounding throaty, flirtatious. Embarrassingly familiar, actually.

Marilyn drew back in her chair, her chin tucking into her neck, creating an accordion of flesh that looked like it belonged on someone much older. Clearly, she liked me even less now than she had a few minutes ago.

Leaning out the door, Blaine handed her a folder with papers askew inside it. "Make sure Charlotte gets these."

Marilyn's long, red fingernails closed over the file, her fingertips brushing his in a way that indicated . . . well . . . something. "All right." The words came with a scrunchy playful sneer. "But you'll owe me."

"Always do." He was smiling when he said it, but there was a hint of weariness in the undertone, as if he was tired of whatever game she was playing.

Blaine turned his attention my way. "You here to see me?" He blinked, his eyes brightening with curiosity, and for a minute, all I could think about was what gorgeous brown eyes he had. I couldn't even remember why I was there.

Brother. . . . What brother?

"Ummm . . . well . . ." *Yes. Yes, I am. Either that, or I stopped in to see Marilyn, since she likes me so much and all.*

He knew I was there to see him. He just wanted to hear me say it, or else he wanted me to say it in front of Marilyn. Maybe the two of them had a thing going. Were they dating in high school? I couldn't remember for sure.

"I just had a quick question. If you're not busy." I craned to the side slightly, trying to see whether there was someone in his office. He was "in a meeting," after all, or so I'd been told. I could feel Marilyn's gaze making a radar sweep back and forth between Blaine and me, trying to discern any hidden connection between us. Rumors would probably be all over town about two-point-five seconds after I vacated Marilyn's space.

"Nope. Not at all." A push opened the door wider, and a friendly hand motion invited me to enter his office. "Come on in."

Marilyn showed her irritation with a soft, passive-aggressive snort as I circumvented her desk. I pretended not to notice, but trailing along behind me was the feeling that coming to the bank had been a bad idea in more ways than one.

If Blaine was worried about his secretary spreading information around town, he didn't show it. Offering me a chair slightly larger and more cushy than Marilyn's maroon-and-gray tweed ones, he shut the door, then hooked a leg over the corner of the desk. He sat-stood, his arms crossed comfortably over an open blazer with a pink polo shirt underneath. It takes a confident man to wear pink. "So what's on your mind this morning?"

If he only knew. Right now, I was looking at him, propped there in his starched jeans, blazer, and cowboy boots—a strange outfit for a banker, but I had to admit that it really did work—and I was thinking, *Is he trying to flirt with me, or am I imagining that?*

The imagination scenario seemed more likely, but I found myself hoping for the first idea.

"Well, first of all, I wanted to say thanks for the firewood and the heater. That was really thoughtful." *Am I blushing a little or is it just hot in here?*

"Least I can do for a good customer." He winked. "Let me know if you change your mind about those cricket-killers."

"I'm still considering it, but . . ."

The door rattled in its frame just as I was thinking about playfully haggling the price. The movement was probably just caused by pressure equalization when someone came or went through the street entrance, but I pictured Marilyn leaning against the wood with a coffee cup to her ear, or perhaps listening in on an intercom.

"Can she hear us from out there?" I nodded toward the door. The transom over it was open, for one thing.

Blaine blinked, his lips forming a quirky, slightly startled twist, as if he thought I might be suggesting a need for closed doors and privacy. A need of the intimate sort, so to speak.

The flush pushed upward and outward, toward my ears and my forehead. All of a sudden the room felt close, and he seemed way too near. I could smell his cologne—something leathery, musky, slightly woodsy. Nice.

Leaning back in my chair, I tried to clear my thoughts. What in the world was wrong with me? I couldn't remember the last time I'd lost my head and stumbled all over myself around a guy.

Sometime shortly after leaving Moses Lake and the high-school me behind. "I mean, I had something I needed to talk to you about, and I wouldn't want it all over town." *Ooch*. That sounded bad, like I was accusing Marilyn, whom I really didn't even know anymore, of being a gossip. Not too nice of me, considering that she sat right up front in church on Sunday.

Smooth, dark brows knotted in Blaine's forehead, and he traded the relaxed posture for one somewhat confused and slightly suspicious . . . with perhaps a hint of disappointment. Had he been hoping this was purely a social call?

Twisting to swivel the phone around on his desk, he punched the button, said, "Marilyn, can you go ahead and take those loan applications over to Charlotte now?"

I heard what sounded like footsteps and shuffling outside the door, then the squeak of a rolling chair as a backside settled into it. "Charlotte's gone to career day at the school this morning. I won't be able to give them to her until after lunch."

Snapping his fingers, Blaine grimaced playfully, then stood up and grabbed his coat—the canvas western sort that says *I'm all man*. "Let's walk across the street and grab a cup of coffee."

A warm, prickly feeling slid over me, as if I were diving into the coffee rather than talking about getting a cup. "Oh, hey, I don't want to interfere with your day." Why I said that, I wasn't sure. It bothered me a little, Blaine's smoothness, his confidence, the fact that he didn't ask if I wanted to go for coffee; he just assumed. Admittedly, I was probably splitting hairs, but then, splitting hairs was what I did best. Architecture is all about the minute details. And something about the minute details of Blaine Underhill just didn't add up.

Why was this guy, who undoubtedly had smitten-small-town girls fighting to wrap themselves around his little finger, trying so

201

hard to put the moves on me? What could possibly be the purpose, considering that I wasn't his type and he wasn't mine, and we both knew I'd be leaving Moses Lake sooner rather than later to return to someplace where things actually made sense. "But . . . ummm . . . I do need to pick up some bratwurst at the Waterbird." Close door. Open door. What a basket case I was.

"Not a problem. The coffee's good there, too." He circled the L-shaped desk, tapped his computer mouse, and scrolled upward to close the window on the screen. Just before it disappeared, I caught a glimpse of what looked like . . . a video game?

"Ummm . . . you're playing video games?"

He shot a sideways grin, a little boyish, a little devilish. "Investment opportunity. Looking it over."

"Yeah, right."

"Software company." He moved to the door, then opened it and stood back, waiting for me to pass through. "Seriously."

"Like I believe that." I was just bantering, really. It didn't matter whether I believed him or not.

Marilyn glanced up from her computer as we exited the office. She gave the coat on Blaine's arm a wary, somewhat unhappy look. "The guy from the software company called."

Blaine swept me the platter-hand, as in, *See, I told you so.*

"The bank in Moses Lake invests in software companies?" I inquired as we crossed the lobby. Was it my imagination, or were all three tellers sending out the hawkeye?

"We're trying to diversify," Blaine explained. "Trying to convince my dad to grow with the times. In this business, you either get innovative, or you sink."

"How *did* you end up in this business?" As I recalled, Blaine was headed to a midsized college in West Texas to play football and major in . . . coaching, or something. I couldn't quite remember.

His father, a big man with alligator-skin boots and an even bigger cowboy hat, was so puffed up about the scholarship, he'd erected a giant *Congratulations, Blaine Underhill* billboard in front of the hardware store. The family threw a huge graduation soiree at his grandparents' cattle ranch outside town. My mother, Clay, and I were not invited, of course.

Now, considering what Blaine had told me during our walk through the woods yesterday, I wondered how he felt about that scholarship, and the billboard, and carrying the whole town's expectations on his shoulders. He claimed he never even liked football. It was hard to assimilate that information with the got-it-all golden boy I remembered from high school. Amazing how you could be so wrong about someone. He hid his feelings well at the time. Maybe he still did. That was one of the things that both concerned me and drew me in. I wondered who he really was.

"My dad had a heart attack my junior year in college." He slipped his coat on as we left the bank building and proceeded toward his pickup nearby. "I had to come home to help take care of things. I didn't mind it, really. By then, I was a redshirt on the college team with a blown tendon, and I'd had my bell rung a few too many times. I was okay with coming back to Moses Lake for a while. Dad was in bed under doctor's orders, my stepmother was a wreck, my sisters were just starting high school, and Mama B had started showing up at Dad's office, trying to run the place and driving everybody crazy. I just kind of . . . fell into taking over the bank—there wasn't any way my stepmother could handle that, Dad's rehab, the hardware store, and the ranch at the same time. She can't even keep the books straight at the hardware store, really. I went ahead and finished a finance degree by commuting over to Stephenville. The music major didn't seem too practical anymore, at that point."

"You were a *music* major?" I queried, as he started the truck.

He waited until he'd backed out of the parking place to answer. "Yeah, you know, I was gonna head for Nashville and make it big if football didn't work out." A soft laugh seemed to dismiss the idea as comical now. "Funny, the dreams you have at eighteen."

A memory teased the dust moats of my mind. I was sitting in the back row of the school auditorium. Our English teacher had dragged us over there to watch the dress rehearsals of the talent show. I just wanted to go home. The cheerleaders had finished doing some dance in spandex, and then Blaine walked on stage. Just Blaine and his guitar. "I remember you in the talent show rehearsals," I said, drawing a breath. "You were good."

"Well, you know, you grow up and life gets in the way." He paused, seeming to reassess whatever he was about to say. "Sometimes what you've got in mind and what God's got in mind aren't the same thing. They needed me here. I got to help look after my grandpa the last couple years of his life. My stepmother couldn't have done it alone. She had all she could handle with Dad's heart attack, and Mama B was wearing herself out, trying to take care of everything and everyone. I moved in at my grandparents' ranch and kind of fell in love with home all over again, you know? Decided I wanted to stay. Your priorities change. You grow up and leave some things behind."

Main Street rolled by as I contemplated priorities while watching our reflection paint a wavy spill of color against the old plate-glass windows of the hardware store, the dime store, a couple of antique stores, the chamber of commerce. I'd never believe that Moses Lake could be anyone's dream. "Guess that's true. Things happen. You could still do it, though. Strap your guitar on your back and head for the big city."

"Nah, I'd miss my boat too much." A glance toward the lake

seemed to say that he was already fishing in his mind. "It's good here. I can leave the ranch and be at work in ten minutes—fourteen if I get caught behind the school bus. No sitting in traffic for hours on the way to work. You city folks don't know what you're missing."

"No theater, no museums, no five-star restaurants . . ." I retorted, but I was just teasing, really. Blaine seemed so completely at home in Moses Lake, so completely at peace with himself. I envied that.

"We've got Catfish Charley's," he countered.

"No shopping mall . . ."

"Thank goodness," he answered, and both of us laughed. The rest of the way to the Waterbird, we talked about Seattle and my job. He actually seemed somewhat impressed when I mentioned the national and international clients for whom we'd designed commercial buildings. My job had taken me all over the world. I didn't mention that on most trips I'd seen little more than the insides of hotels.

"Sounds exciting," he said as we parked at the Waterbird. Neither of us moved to exit the truck.

"It can be," I admitted. "Mostly, it's a lot of details and a lot of chipping away at a project, but when you see the steel going up, it's like watching something from your imagination come to life on a massive scale. It's an amazing feeling, even with the stress factor. Projects never go exactly the way you plan them."

"I've financed enough construction to know that." He rested an elbow on the window frame, seeming content to sit there talking.

I sensed an open door to opportunity. I needed to bring the conversation around to Clay, Amy, and the issues in Moses Lake. "I imagine you have to be careful about what kinds of investments you take on, being a small bank, I mean."

"Yes we do." His attention veered off as the little dark-haired girl who'd served us pretend tea on my last visit to the Waterbird stepped out of the building. This time an old man was with her, and both of them were carrying fishing poles. They crossed in front of our truck, hand in hand.

Blaine opened his door and waved. "Hey, Birdie, you taking your granddad fishing?"

"Yeah-huh." The little girl smiled enthusiastically. "Gonna get a big bass."

"There a school vacation today?" Blaine leaned farther out the door, and both the old man and the little girl gave him sheepish looks.

"Had to ugg-go to the udd-doctor today," the old man answered, his speech strange and slow. "Purdy udd-day fer fishin'. Udd-don't tell the uhhh . . . school ubb-board."

Blaine chuckled and waved. "I won't say a word. I promise." He watched them disappear across the parking lot. "See, that's the beauty of doing business in a small town. We helped old Len get the money to finish fixing up his house, so he could raise that little granddaughter of his. The man's a military veteran, injured in combat in Vietnam. He ought to have a decent roof over his head. He deserves a road to live on that's passable in the wet weather, so he can get little Birdie to school, too. When it rains, Len has to take her three miles to the bus stop on a mule, or bring her across the lake in a boat, in the rain. That's just not right. People wouldn't put up with it over on this side of the lake, but the folks with money really don't care what happens up in Chinquapin Peaks. That's one of the reasons I put my name in the hat for county commission. Some things just need to be different, you know?"

"That does sound wrong." I found myself trying to jibe the mental image of the guy who was trying to steal my family land with one of this guy, who wanted better treatment for families in

Chinquapin Peaks. Even I knew that the undeveloped side of the lake was like the Land that Time Forgot. That was one of the reasons I felt good about helping to bring in the new Proxica facilities. "The real solution is jobs, though. If people have income, they're not at everyone's mercy."

Blaine turned my way, gave me a long, appraising look, his brown eyes intense. I realized I'd strayed too close to the real reason for my visit here. For an instant, I wondered if he knew, but then his intensity lessened. "You're not thinking of throwing your hat into the commissioner's race, are you? Because I've already printed my signs."

I pretended to consider it. "I think you're safe. I couldn't get elected trash collector in Moses Lake, anyway."

He caught my gaze again. "Don't be too hard on yourself. You're not so bad after a while." He grinned, and a laugh convulsed from my lips.

I liked Blaine Underhill a lot better than I wanted to.

The realization both tempted and worried me as we exited the truck and went into the Waterbird. Uncle Charley, Uncle Herb, Burt Lacy, and Nester Grimland were playing dominoes in one of the back booths. They registered surprise as we walked in, and I quickly realized that coming here probably wasn't the best idea. It would soon be common knowledge that Blaine and I were out for coffee. His stepmother would probably come after me with a wooden stake and a sledgehammer.

Blaine didn't seem the least bit worried. He chatted with the coffee club and the woman behind the counter, Sheila, as we procured coffee and doughnuts, and then took a booth as far as possible from the ongoing domino game. To restart the conversation, I asked how long my brother had been dating his cousin. I tried to make it sound like an innocent question.

"A while, I guess," Blaine replied vaguely.

"Do you think it's serious?"

He scratched his head, brown curls sweeping off his forehead, then falling into place again. "Feeling protective? Amy's a nice girl. I promise."

They just pulled an all-nighter, and then he got a sexy text from Tara, was on the tip of my tongue, but I didn't say it. Ears were straining our way from the domino booth, for one thing. I wasn't sure how much they could hear. I sipped my coffee and tried to decide what else to say.

We made small talk about the wall of wisdom for a few minutes. Blaine's favorite entry was *May the holes in your net be smaller than the fish in it—Irish blessing.* He and his grandfather had written it on the wall in 1985, a bit of homage to the old country.

"My dad and I wrote one together, too," I said, feeling a kinship.

"Well, it's kind of a tradition, bringing your kids here to sign the wall." His cell phone rang in his pocket, and he pulled it out, sneering at the screen. "Now you see why I don't carry one of these things in the evenings." He answered the call, and it was clear from the conversation that he was needed back at work. While he finished talking, I bought a batch of the Waterbird's famous bratwurst and then we returned to the bank.

"Raincheck," he offered, walking backward as we parted ways in the bank parking lot. "How about we finish the conversation over dinner?"

"Sure" was out of my mouth before I even had time to think about it. It made sense, though, considering that I hadn't been able to roll the conversation around to my brother, Amy, bank loans, and substance abuse. How did one smoothly bring up such subjects, anyway? Blaine flashed a smile, and even though I knew that agreeing to have dinner with him might not turn out to be one of my better ideas, I suddenly wasn't sorry.

After watching him disappear into the bank, I picked up my laptop from the gardener's cottage, then went to the Chinese food convenience store and agonized over composing an email explaining my situation to Mel. What I ended up with was a jumble that intimated some sort of impending, but unspecified, family disaster. After promising to check in daily, I pushed Send, released my excuses into the ether, and cracked open a fortune cookie. The fortune was one of those generic types that could apply to many situations. *From unlikely sources come unlikely surprises.*

I glanced toward the bank and thought, *Blaine Underhill just invited me to dinner. Did that really happen?*

I found myself mulling it over, trying to discern his reasons. Was he a nice guy, a sensitive type who wanted to be a musician but grew up amid the pressures of a sports-obsessed family? Or was he a small-town playboy, just looking to score? Why would Blaine be interested in someone like me? We had absolutely nothing in common. Not one thing, other than my brother, and you didn't have to be a genius to know that Blaine started mincing words every time I even tried to lead the conversation around to Clay. Which raised another question. Why would Blaine be keeping Clay's secrets, if he knew them? Because Clay was dating Blaine's cousin? What would happen when Blaine found out that Clay had interests, so to speak, somewhere in Fort Worth?

The whole thing made my head spin to the point that I finally had to just give up thinking about it and leave for Ruth's. I'd always been far too skilled at coming up with *what if*s, at anticipating the worst. Predicting all potential forms of failure and disaster made me a good architect, but not always so winning as a person.

The tension in my shoulders eased as I drove through the rolling hills near Gnadenfeld, passing miles of green winter wheat. Horses, cattle, and sheep grazed happily, and tall, white farmhouses built for large families languished in the winter light. On the seat next to me, the cover of Ruth's sketch pad fluttered in the breeze from the heater. I flipped it up, looked at the drawing of the woman in the blue floral dress. She was beautiful, her long hair floating about her in a swirl, loose and free, her lips parted slightly, smiling, her eyes holding a startled but confident look, as if she'd been caught by surprise but wasn't worried about it.

Who was she? When had Ruth drawn her portrait, and why?

The cows were dozing happily in the pasture when I reached the dairy. In the barn, Ruth's relatives were processing the morning milk. The wind carried a strong whiff of cow barn as I exited the car. That smell, and the complete absence of television on the place, were two things I'd never envied about the lives of the dairy kids. Operating a farm was hard work. The kids woke early and did chores, and then many of them headed off to the public school in Gnadenfeld, where they would get a reception similar to the one I had received daily in Moses Lake.

For the most part, the Mennonite kids in Gnadenfeld had lacked the essential coolness revered in high-school social circles. The fact that there were plenty of them, living various levels of an old-fashioned, conservative life-style, didn't seem to matter. The whole group fell fairly low on the popularity spectrum, which was probably why the dairy kids had liked me. They thought I was cool—a strange dresser—but cool. They taught me some valuable lessons about grace, as well. Despite the ways in which the world was unkind to them, they didn't return what they got. They were taught to give to the world what was right and godly—kindness and tolerance. Sometimes after a visit with Ruth's family, I wore that mantle of grace for a day or two. But it was so much easier to simply hate all the kids who hated me, to hate the church ladies for trying to reform me into a proper little Southern belle, to hate my mother for failing to take care of us, to hate my father for leaving, to hate Moses Lake for being the place where he died. . . .

As I closed the car door, Mary and Emily appeared in the barn doorway, each dangling a puppy under one arm. When they figured out who I was, they bolted across the lawn, the puppies' plump bottoms swinging back and forth against billowing skirts. Both girls stopped a few feet away. Emily cuddled her face against her puppy, eyeing me shyly, while Mary stepped forward and offered to share.

"I got the big one," she informed me, holding the puppy out and trying to peer into my vehicle. "He's just precious."

"I can see that." The loaner puppy groaned as I accepted him into my hands. His eyes rolled upward in a way that said, *When you're done with me, please don't give me back. Hide me somewhere.* He grunted and rooted around as I snuggled him under my chin, taking in the sweet scent of puppy breath. "I think he wants his mom."

Mary's brows drew together as if, perhaps, she'd been told a few times before to let the puppy have a break. Emily chewed her lip and looked over her shoulder toward the barn with a hand-in-the-cookie-jar expression. "The mama's busy," she whispered, her voice disappearing into the puppy's dark fur as she rubbed her cheek back and forth over its head. Her soft red curls brushed the puppy's nose, and it sneezed. Both girls laughed.

"I brought some bratwurst for your Aunt Ruth." I scratched my puppy's tummy, and its little foot paddled wildly. "Want to come in and help us cook lunch? You could put the puppies away for a nap." The puppies would thank me for this, I felt certain. During childhood visits to Moses Lake, I was always in trouble for overhandling whatever baby animals were around the farm at the time. *Now let's stop wartin' the babies,* my grandmother would say gently, and instruct me to release my prisoners.

Emily squeezed her puppy reluctantly, but Mary nodded with enthusiasm, reaching for the one I was holding. As the girls dashed for the barn, I retrieved the bratwurst from the car. Then the three of us proceeded to the house together, Mary carrying the bratwurst, and Emily's little hand in mine, making me feel welcome.

We found Ruth in a kitchen chair kneading bread dough, working alongside Mary and Emily's mother. She was dressed less conventionally than Ruth, in a jumper that was conservative but looked like it might have come off the rack, and tennis shoes. Her hair was pulled into a bun, covered with a scarf much like Ruth's. She fawned over the pile of bratwurst as if I'd brought her gold nuggets. The residents of Gnadenfeld generally loved food, especially high-quality German fare. Mary and Emily followed Ruth to the cutting board to watch her unwrap the package and separate the links.

"I found one of your drawing pads," I said to Ruth. "There was only one page in it, though. Just one drawing. I ransacked the upstairs, and it was all I came up with."

A twist of Ruth's lips formed a dimple in her cheek. "Your uncle hid them away in strange places. If you keep looking, you may find another. You can bring it tomorrow."

I smiled, but didn't say anything. With Ruth, there was always a reason for another visit.

Her eyes sparkled with anticipation as she wiped her hands on her cook's apron, then told the niece that we were going to the sun porch to visit and watch the cows graze. The niece waved us off, saying she would put the bread in and call us when the food was finished cooking. She and the girls were singing in the kitchen as we wandered through the quiet old house with its odd collection of antiques and salvaged items that looked like they'd been rescued from someone's curbside castoffs.

On the sun porch, Ruth lowered herself into a chair and reached for the pad. "Who have you found?" she asked. I didn't answer, but let her turn back the cover and discover the woman for herself.

The blue eyes captivated me again as I sat on the settee and leaned over the end table so that I could see the drawing. Ruth breathed long and deep, studying the sketch.

"I remember her," she whispered, running a finger along the paper, tracing the woman's hair, then looking at the smear of charcoal on her fingertip.

"Who is she?" My chest filled with anticipation. I wanted to know the woman's story.

"I never learned her name, but I knew her." Ruth's eyes softened, going unfocused, as if she were looking beyond the drawing, as if she could see more in it than I could. "She walked with them, with three German officers. She was smiling and laughing as they went along the road from town. She was bold. Can you see that in her? And she was beautiful. So beautiful. She wore a blue flowered dress. As blue as her eyes. She turned to look at us, the poor, huddled mass of us, marching away with the Nazis as they retreated. What did she think of us, I've often wondered. What did she make of the tired, ragged lot of us?" Ruth turned the sketch toward me, as if she wanted me to understand the deeper history of the person pictured there. In my imagination, she began to come to life as Ruth continued her story.

"She was glad to see us leaving Russia, no doubt. Catherine the Great had given the Mennonites land there many, many years before. The Mennonites had a reputation for being good farmers. The intention was that they would improve the land, making it more valuable to Catherine and the country, but the Russians didn't like having foreigners as neighbors. The Communists had taken every-thing from the Mennonites by the time of World War II. They'd left our population sick, and starving, and dying; had sent the young men off to work camps. My father was glad to see the Germans take ground in Russia, and later, when the Russian forces drove the Germans back, those who were left in our community followed the German army in retreat, for fear of what would happen to us when the Russians returned. We were German by heritage, of course."

Looking away from the drawing and then back, she shook her head. "They knew who this woman was, the Germans. They knew that she had reported German troop movements to the Russians. I suppose she thought her beauty would cause her to be spared. I suppose she thought no man could destroy something so lovely, so young. Even going up the hill, she seemed unafraid. She walked to her death without stopping. I have always wondered if she really was unafraid. . . . Or if she was only hiding her fear. I have wondered if she had a faith, if she knew God, or if her beauty was her god." Her eyes moved from the paper, cut slowly toward mine. "It's the difference, you know. Faith. It's the difference between hiding fear and mastering it."

Ruth's gaze settled on me, and even though I felt it, I didn't meet her eyes. I was looking at the woman in the floral dress, studying her face, trying to decide.

Was she smiling because her life meant nothing to her?

Or was she smiling because she knew there was nothing mere men could do to take away the life that mattered most?

Love is the only water that can quench the heart's thirst.

—Anonymous
(left by Agnes and Fred, 70 years together, happily wed)

Chapter 13

Reasons why accepting a dinner invitation from the guy you always dreamed about in high school, while on a trip back home, is a bad idea? Let me count the ways: *One*—you have nothing to wear but the three completely uninteresting outfits in your carry-on bag and sweatshirts from the hardware store. *Two*—you quickly realize there's no way to do this without the entire family knowing about it. *Three*—you can just imagine what the family will say. *Four*—unless you leave town for the date, everyone else will know, but if you do go out of town, it implies something more than just a let's-do-a-little-catching-up get-together. *Five*—you'll feel like you're in high school again and be so nervous you'll spend an hour fixing your hair, then hate it, and change in and out of your three possible outfits a dozen times. *Six*—what's the point anyway, since you live halfway across the country? *Seven*—upon spotting your date on the porch, one of your uncles will invite him in, and the two of you will end up side-by-side on the sofa in the funeral parlor, with your mother looking on and the uncs acting parental and protective, asking where you're going and when you'll be home.

Technically, the last one would only happen to those who have nosy uncles and a funeral parlor in the family, but it's nonetheless mortifying (no play on words intended). Fortunately, Blaine was a good sport, if somewhat evasive in answering their questions. I still didn't know where we were going, but Blaine was laughing as we walked out.

"Looks like I'd better watch my back," he said and grinned, his mirth illuminated by gas-powered yard lamps that gave the driveway the look of a landing strip at twilight.

"I'm sorry." The evening air nipped at the burn on my cheeks. "I should've sneaked through the memory garden and met you at the driveway."

"Now, how much fun would that've been?" Blaine stopped at the T where the front walk met the driveway, but there wasn't a vehicle anywhere in sight. Surely we weren't going to walk to dinner. The only place open winter evenings in downtown Moses Lake was my favorite Chinese convenience store. Surely I hadn't paced the bedroom for an hour and changed clothes countless times so that we could eat Chinese in the convenience store.

Aside from the ambiance issue, there was the fact that, for the sake of fashion, I'd put on the suede boots. Even though it was a surprisingly mild evening for February, the winter chill was already starting to press through the too-thin soles of the boots. If we were walking, I needed to detour to the cottage and change footwear.

"So, where are we going?" I looked around for a vehicle. Maybe he'd parked out back by our cars.

"Good question." He made a show of standing beside me and looking up and down the driveway, as if he didn't know, either.

"No . . . seriously. Should I change shoes or grab an extra coat?"

Cocking his head, he pointed a finger at me. "You know, you worry ahead of yourself a lot."

LISA WINGATE

It almost felt like an accusation. "I like to be prepared. I mean, I don't like surpri . . ." Wow, that sounded bad. *I don't like surprises.* Talk about a euphemism for *I'm no fun.* "Okay, that's not what I meant. I like to anticipate . . . possible contingencies, that's all." *Which makes me great at my job, by the way.* "I mean, that's the business I'm in. You have to think of everything.

"Look at those new Ambrosia Resorts, for instance. The back of the building is concave and it's west-facing. Guess what happens when the afternoon sun hits it? The building acts like a giant magnifying glass. Nicely focused solar energy aimed right at the pool. Can you say, southern-fried tourists?" I realized that I was babbling. I couldn't help it. All of a sudden I was as nervous as . . . well, a schoolgirl on a first date.

Blaine stroked his chin, thinking about the southern-fried tourists perhaps, and then he chuckled, his breath coming out in a little puff of vapor. "You know, I can never quite get a grip on where you're going next with the conversation."

It was impossible to tell from the tone whether that was a good thing or a bad thing, in his view. Probably bad. Things were so much easier with Richard—predictable. We could drone on about business through an entire date, and that was fine. Both of us expected it, in fact. Nobody analyzed anybody else's personality. Which was probably because there was very little personality involved. The idea was a small, silent blow to my already flagging confidence. Maybe I didn't have much personality. The only thing I had to talk about was work, and some people didn't want to hear about that.

I had a sudden sense of panic about the date . . . errr . . . dinner . . . whatever it was. The evening would be a disaster. And what was the likelihood I'd be able to ferret out anything about the situation with Clay, anyway? Blaine had been uncooperative so far.

I needed to find a way out of his dinner invitation. Now.

"I'm sorry. I'm really not fit company tonight. My boss dumped another project on me, and I should probably just go get started on it. I won't be any fun, anyway. I've got such a headache . . . a migraine, really." *Lie, lie. lie.* Lightning would probably strike me any minute. I moved a step toward the cottage, halfway tempted to pull a Cinderella and just bolt from the scene. I pictured myself curled up on the sofa instead of standing in the middle of the lawn freezing and feeling stupid. It sounded good, really. Safe. Maybe Roger would come around, and we could hang out together. . . .

Just me, myself, and I . . . and Clay's stupid dog.

Now there was a pitiful picture.

Blaine caught my hand, as if he knew I was thinking of making a run for it. He leaned close to my ear, his breath warm against my ear. "Come on. You're not going to balk at a little adventure, are you?"

A tingle slid over my skin from head to toe, and suddenly the night was thirty degrees warmer. "Ukh . . . no," I coughed out. "It's not that I'm balking. It's just that . . ." He leaned back and watched me again, and I completely lost my train of thought. "I don't want to fry any tourists." I blinked, covered my mouth. Where had that come from?

Blaine laughed. "I promise you, there will be no fried tourists on this trip."

"Oh, well, then, okay," I said to save face. I'd provided humor, at least. That was charming in its own way, right? Maybe I could work toward making him laugh so hard that, in a fit of hysteria, he would finally reveal whatever he was keeping from me about my family.

His face straightened slightly. "Trust me." His voice was soft and low.

That's just it. I don't . . .

LISA WINGATE

A movement inside the house caught my attention. Checking over my shoulder, I realized there was an audience peeking around the heavy velvet curtains. If I didn't go on the date, they'd be all over me, wanting to know what happened. If I went, I could later quell the family banter with a bland report like, *We went to dinner. It was nice to catch up.* End of story. "At least tell me if we're walking somewhere."

"Not exactly . . . but sort of."

"Do I need my combat boots?" I shifted from one foot to the other. The little cold prickles were already starting. Fashion be hanged, these boots were going in the suitcase until I got back home.

"Probably a good idea" was all Blaine would divulge, so we proceeded toward the cottage, leaving our audience behind.

After a quick change of footwear, we were off. I followed Blaine down to the lake, and from there, he turned left, walking up the shore toward town.

"Where are we going?" I felt like I might explode if I didn't get some details.

"You'll see."

"Well, how *far* are we walking?"

"Not far."

"Because it's cold out here, and . . ."

He turned my way, his face shadowy in the twilight. "You know, just because you haven't been apprised of the plan doesn't mean that a plan doesn't exist." He shrugged toward the horizon. "Beautiful sunset, huh?"

I let my gaze drift across the water to where the hills had all but vanished into dusky hews of purple and lavender. Overhead, the last rays of sunlight outlined the long, wispy winter clouds, drawing bold strokes over the deepening sky. Not five feet from where we were walking, the water lapped rhythmically at the shore. A dove called, its voice floating in the cool mist, low and peaceful. I realized that I hadn't noticed any of it until that moment. I'd missed it all. "It's beautiful out here," I said, but then I couldn't resist adding, "Has anyone ever told you that you're just . . . disgustingly serene, though?" I had to wonder at this point, if anything, including the land deal with my brother, ever rattled Blaine.

He laughed softly, unconcerned. "No. Has anybody ever told you you're really . . . tightly wound?"

"No," I countered. In terms of architecture, where fractions of an inch meant millions of dollars, there was no such thing as being too tightly wound.

"Then we're both learning new things about ourselves, aren't we?" He pointed to a dock, and we steered our trajectory toward it. To our left, the path ran uphill, through the church picnic grounds and into town. Apparently, we weren't headed for the Chinese pizza place.

"Either that, or we bring out the worst in each other," I joked.

He shook his head good-naturedly as we walked to the dock and then along it, his boots making a hollow echo that glided over the water. Blaine's black-and-silver boat was tied to the end. Apparently, wherever we were headed, we were going there via the lake. . . .

We ended up at, of all places, my uncle's restaurant, Catfish Charley's. A warm, homey feeling flowed over me as we pulled into one of the boat stalls there. Several spaces were occupied, and onshore, where a floating walkway led to a gravel parking lot, a couple dozen cars lounged idly as stars twinkled to life overhead. I'd always loved this place because my father had loved it. A visit to Moses Lake never passed without a trip to Catfish Charley's to say hello to my uncle's hundred-pound pet fish, Charley. Dad, Clay, and I would grab an ice cream cone, then sit on the dock to fish, or stay inside and partake of Uncle Charley's famous fried catfish and corn pups.

I'd been afraid to come back because I wasn't sure how I'd feel about it, but it felt good. "Looks like the place is hopping," I observed as we departed the boat and walked along the dock. "I thought Uncle Charley was only keeping it open on the weekends now."

"Friday through Monday," Blaine explained. "Live music on Monday nights—helps bring in a crowd."

"Looks like it's working." Now that he mentioned it, I could hear music wafting from the gaps in the old building, riding the fumes of fry grease and onion rings, like steam from a boiling kettle.

"There's still a lot of life in this little juke joint. It's a landmark, you know—the only thing on Moses Lake that was actually on the river before the lake was built. History like that shouldn't be lost." He patted the weathered railing as we walked by, his action showing obvious affection. "Bringing back the live music was a good thing. That was a big draw here in the forties and fifties. My folks used to talk about it. Your grandfather and your great-uncles had a jazz quartet with my granddad. Entertained the ladies." He fanned an eyebrow at me in the orange light of the dock lamps.

"Really?" It was odd to think that other people in this town knew more about my family than I did. . . . Strange to realize that my father had left those connections behind when he married my mom. What kind of love would cause a man to abandon everything he'd always cared about? What kind of selfishness would it take for a woman to force the man she married to all but sever the ties with his family, with his history? Couldn't my mother have just gotten over herself and gotten along? Why had she felt the need to cause us to hate this place? Why, now, did she feel so differently?

We entered the building, and as we waited to be shown to a

table, it was like old home week. I recognized several of the patrons from my high-school days: the track coach who was married to the English teacher; the cheerleader with the red hair and the high, squeaky voice you could hear all the way across the stadium; the postman; the kid who showed championship swine and always smelled like it; the man who handed out the bulletins at church . . .

My brother and Amy?

They were seated in a booth near an area of raised decking along the back wall, where I recalled that there had once been tables. Now the tables had been cleared, and the decking was a stage built to look like an indoor pier. A four-piece band of middle-aged guys in fishing hats was plucking out a tinny waltz. Behind the stage, a wall of windows looked onto the outdoor deck, where torches and tall propane heaters burned away the winter night. A young couple was dancing under the stars. A waltz. I recognized them in silhouette. Reverend Hay and his fiancée. Her head rested on his chest, tucked safely beneath his chin. There wasn't an inch of space between them.

I found myself watching, imagining the feel of that moment, yearning for something, until finally I pulled my gaze into the room again. At the corner table, Clay and Amy were talking intently, completely oblivious to everyone else in the room. Clay drew something on a piece of paper, pointed to it with his pencil. *Tap, tap, tap.*

I wondered if he was breaking up with her, maybe telling her the truth, finally. The communication there definitely didn't look romantic, but neither did it look adversarial. I wasn't sure what to make of it.

The waitress grabbed menus and motioned for us to follow her to a table. Blaine said hello to my brother before I could get close enough to see what Clay was writing. Quickly flipping the place mat over to the preprinted side, Clay stood to shake Blaine's hand in greeting. Amy tackled Blaine with a hug, and he kissed her on the top of her head. I was weirdly jealous, which seemed almost perverse. Amy hugged me next, and I felt like a heel. I couldn't help thinking about Clay's text message from Tara.

I should tell her, I thought. *Someone really should tell her. . . .*

The opportunity seemed to present itself a short time later. Just after Blaine and I had ordered catfish platters, Amy left Clay's table at the same time that the postmaster came by our booth and pulled Blaine into a conversation about the roads in Chinquapin Peaks, mail delivery, and the upcoming debate in the county commissioner's race.

I excused myself and crossed the dining area to the rest room line, where Amy was standing alone.

"Well, hey," she said, in a way that instantly made me feel guilty for arriving with the intention of bursting her bubble. Maybe I should just let things happen on their own—take Blaine's advice and relinquish control to the powers that be.

Then again, if I were Amy, I'd want to know.

"You and Clay look like you're having a good time." Actually, they didn't. I'd been watching from the corner of my eye for a while, and for the most part, their dinner looked like a business meeting.

"We were talkin' about the restaurant," she said, quickly enough that the response didn't ring true. "He's got big plans." She nodded along with the words, as if to give them substance.

I wasn't sure what to think. "Oh. Seems like what he'd really need to be doing is actually working here. You know, learning how to run the place."

Amy fidgeted. "I guess he does that during the day when I'm at work."

"No. He really doesn't."

Amy blinked, her blue eyes wide, earnest, painfully clueless.

She cut a nervous glance toward the bathroom door. I heard the toilet flushing.

"I imagine he's got it all figured out." Amy shifted a step closer to the rest room. "I love this place. My pop-pop and my nana met here, right after World War II. It was love at first sight. First dance, really. She was the only one he ever met who could follow his lead like that."

An acidic feeling drained from my throat to my stomach. *Please don't tell me you're in love with my brother. He has a girlfriend in Fort Worth. . . .*

I bit down on the words, unable to say them. The bathroom door opened, and the front-desk nurse from the rural medical clinic came out. Her hair was gray now, but her face hadn't changed. Amy bolted for the door like she'd been catapulted from a crossbow.

I returned to my table, where the catfish platters had arrived. Blaine and I chatted as we ate, and I was once again trying to steer the conversation around to the subject of Clay and Amy when the band returned from a break. We paused to clap along with the rest of the crowd, welcoming the band back to the stage. They weren't half bad, the music a combination of country and Cajun, the perfect atmosphere for a floating catfish joint. My gaze drifted to the deck, where couples were dancing again—the pastor and his fiancée, an elderly couple, a guy in a uniform—probably a park ranger or game warden—and a dark-haired woman. Clay and Amy were out there, too. I remembered the story about Amy's grandparents. Love at first dance. What would that be like? How would it feel?

I wanted to know. I was afraid I never would. I was afraid I didn't have it in me.

"Want to dance?" Blaine offered, perhaps misinterpreting my dewy-eyed look as a desire to hit the outdoor dance floor.

"I don't know how." I hated to admit that, but it was the truth.

While kids like Blaine were scooting a boot at the rodeo dance or having parties at backwoods hangouts, I was home cooking supper, taking care of my little brother, washing clothes for school, or helping set up for funerals at Harmony House so that I could earn a little money to keep us from being total freeloaders until the insurance company paid off my father's policy.

"It's just a two-step," Blaine pointed out, finishing the last bite of his coconut cream pie. "It's not that hard. One-two-three, one-two. You're the math genius, remember?"

I studied the deck again, pushing the remains of my dessert away. A part of me, the girl who'd sat home on Saturday evenings dreaming of a moment like this, wanted to be out there under the stars, twirling off into the night. But the woman who practically lived in her office spoke up instead. "No way I'm dancing in front of everyone."

Blaine's gaze tangled with mine, and I felt the two of us toying with the ends of the rope in a playful tug of war. "C'mon . . . where's that sense of adventure? What are you afraid of?"

"Ummm . . . let's see . . ." I sifted for an answer. *Looking like a dork in front of everyone*, was on the tip of my tongue, but I was reaching for something more clever, more . . . charmingly coy.

The man in uniform and his dance partner came in the back door and stopped at our table, and Blaine introduced me. Mart McClendon, the local game warden, and his girlfriend, Andrea. Blaine asked about Andrea's broken wrist, and she held up a pink cast, offering a wry smile and saying she would never again let her son talk her into skateboarding down the driveway. The conversation went on from there, but I lost track of it. I was watching Blaine and marveling at the fact that he seemed to have a rapport with everyone in town. Not only did he have rapport, but he knew about their lives. He asked after their health and well-being. Either he was a natural-born politician, or he genuinely cared. It was no wonder Clay liked him. He was incredibly charismatic.

As he was wrapping up the conversation, I glanced at the takeout counter and spotted someone familiar. My stomach sank, lead-lined all of a sudden. Blaine's stepmother had just finished putting in an order. She was turning around, her gaze slowly sweeping the room from left to right. She offered finger waves here and there. I sank in my seat, working toward invisibility, but the game warden moved away just in time to leave me directly in her line of sight. She stiffened immediately, her chin coming up. In my head, I heard the sound that alley cats make when they meet in the night—an unholy noise between a scream and a growl. One of Mrs. Underhill's eyes narrowed more than the other, squeezing almost closed as if she were sighting down a rifle at me. Good thing she didn't have one in her hands.

Blaine, completely unaware that we had gained an audience, leaned across the table, pat-tapped me on the shoulder, and said, "C'mon, let's go. I've got an idea."

I was fully in agreement with the *Let's go* part, except for the fact that Blaine's wicked stepmother was standing by the door. "Let's head out the back way," I suggested, nodding toward the exit onto the deck.

"Let me get the bill first." Before I could stop him, he started across the room. I vacillated between following and staying put, then finally proceeded to the counter. I wasn't letting that woman put me in a corner anymore. I was no longer some shy, messed-up teenager. I was Heather Hampton. I could travel the world, handle demanding clients, bridge cultural barriers, mediate difficult situations, find solutions, impress the bigwigs, create tall buildings with a single stroke of an electronic tablet. Surely I could handle an aging small-town belle with an attitude.

"Heather." My name appeared to have a bad taste to it at first, then she forced a smile. "I'm surprised to see you here."

Blaine cleared his throat and sent her a warning glance over his shoulder. I had a sense that, in the few moments I'd been deciding whether or not to cross the room, they'd had a conversation about me. Mrs. Underhill pressed her lips together, wrinkles forming around the edges. "I meant to say that I thought you wouldn't be in town for long."

"I don't plan to be." With some luck, I could allay any reason she might find to either give my family trouble or sic the casserole ladies on me. They undoubtedly loved Blaine as much as everyone else did. They wouldn't want to see him out to dinner with me, of all people.

I had the sense of being watched from behind. Perhaps some member of the casserole mafia had called Blaine's stepmother when Blaine and I showed up at Catfish Charley's together, and that was why she was here—doing recon, so to speak. "Just a little longer than I thought," I added lamely.

"Oh." Another pucker-lip punctuated the response. "Well, have a lovely trip home, if I don't see you again."

In other words, *Don't let the door hit you in the backside on the way out.*

A gush of water-laden night air pushed past us, and when I looked up, Mama B was working her way in the door, the hood of her pink sparkly jacket blowing over her face. Pushing it back impatiently, she spied Blaine at the cash register. "Well, hi, darlin'! What're you doin' here?" Without waiting for an answer, she swept him into a hug and rocked him back and forth before letting go.

He actually blushed a little, which was cute. "Just having catfish, Grandma." He glanced my way, and Mama B honed in, her gaze traveling back and forth between Blaine and me. "Well, my lands, are y'all out on a date?"

Blaine's stepmother gasped, horrified at the concept. "Of course they're not. I'm sure Heather just wanted to see the restaurant before she *went home*. To *Seattle*."

Mama B scowled at her. "Oh, for heaven's sake, Claire Anne, mind your business. The boy needs to meet some gals he hasn't known since kindergarten. Maybe he'll get interested."

The wash of color in Blaine's face crept down his neck, giving him the look of a little boy having his cheeks pinched by the old ladies in church. A laugh tickled my throat, and I coughed to cover it up. Was it my imagination, or was Blaine in a remarkable hurry to get his wallet back into his pocket? The teenage checkout girl tried to suck him into a conversation, and for once he didn't respond. He turned back to me and said, "Ready?"

I definitely was. Mama B patted my arm and gave it a little squeeze. "Y'all have a good time this evenin'. Go look at the stars or somethin'." Then I exchanged a lemon-juice good-bye with Blaine's stepmother and hit the door before Blaine could even open it for me. An awkwardness descended over us, and as we climbed into his boat, I couldn't help asking myself what I was even doing. What could I possibly hope to accomplish?

I'd be better off back in the cottage, curled up with Roger. At least a half-dozen times during dinner, I'd tried to bring up the subject of my brother, and Blaine had deflected the conversation every time. Now he turned the boat away from Harmony Shores, rather than toward. "Where are we going?" I bundled my coat tighter and sank down into the furry collar.

"Just across the cove."

I knew what was across the cove—the legendary Blue Moon Bay, a little inlet with an old campground where the teenagers probably still congregated on summer weekends. Not much ever changed in Moses Lake. I'd never been to the Blue Moon, except in a few ridiculous teenage dreams.

"You're taking me to the Blue Moon?" I didn't have to work at it to sound incredulous. The Blue Moon was also known as the place where kids who were fortunate enough to have access to a waterborne vehicle went parking.

"Ever been?" His tone was intimate, slightly suggestive. It flowed over me like warm water, raising goosebumps on my skin.

"Oh, sure, lots of times."

He knew that wasn't true, of course. The trouble with spending time around someone who remembers you from high school is that you can't gloss up the past. In Seattle I had total anonymity. I thought I liked it that way, but now there was something alluring, even freeing, about not having to hide.

I tried not to focus on it too much as we crossed the cove. The night and the location seemed too perfect to be tainted by worry. Overhead, the winter moon hung large and heavy, casting a soft light that reflected off the quaking leaves of the live oaks, making them wink and shine as if each leaf had been freshly washed just for us. The air smelled cold and sweet, and Blue Moon Bay, with its overhanging cliffs and ancient, gnarled trees was, indeed, as beautiful by moonlight as I'd always imagined it would be.

"They have a private dance floor here, you know." Blaine's voice held just enough volume to be audible over the low rumble of the boat, as if he were taking care not to disturb the peace of the night. When he cut the motor, I could hear the twangy rhythms of music drifting over from the dancing deck at Catfish Charley's.

"A private . . . wha . . ." I stammered as we floated up to the wide, flat rock shelf where tiny crystals reflected the moonlight like a sprinkling of sugar. I gathered his meaning as he grabbed a scraggly cedar to tie on. "You realize that would be, like, taking your life in your hands?" I imagined our feet tangling, and the two of us tumbling off into the lake, potential hypothermia only minutes away.

"I'm not worried." He climbed out of the boat in three agile steps—one on the seat, one on the side rail, and one on the rocks. He made it look easy enough.

"You know, I'm seriously not one of those girls who hung out at the rodeo and learned to scoot a boot at the street dance." I kept my seat, but I was only teasing now, really. I knew I would be going over the edge soon enough. There was a private dance floor waiting, after all. The idea was heady, thrilling, exciting in a way I wasn't prepared to defend against. Nothing like this had ever happened to me. I'd wanted it to, but it hadn't.

"That was my mistake," he murmured, and I was hopelessly lost. I stood up, moved toward him, took his hand when he stretched it out. The boat shifted underfoot as I stepped onto the seat, then tried to decide whether to step on the railing or go straight for the rock. Below, I saw a narrow, black slice of water reflecting the glow of the boat's running lights. A chill slid under my coat, a pinprick of fear coming with it. The boat was drifting farther from the rocks now, the watery crevice widening.

I thought of Ruth's story, of the girl in the blue floral dress— bold, certain, unafraid.

I wanted to be the girl in the blue dress.

One jump from the boat suspended me in space, Blaine's hand pulling me in, guiding me until I landed safely on the rocks. Momentum carried me forward, so that I was pressed against his chest, my free hand clutching his coat. I wondered if he could feel my pulse pounding through the tips of my fingers as his face dipped near mine. I looked up and knew he was planning to kiss me. "I thought we were dancing," I said, but the words were an invitation.

"We are," he whispered close to my lips, his arm sliding around my waist, his fingers, cool from the trip across the cove, trailing over the wind-reddened skin of my cheek. "Dancing." The words were barely a hint of sound. His lips found mine, and I felt the dance begin.

By the time the chill of the night forced us to return home, I knew two things. The waltz and the Texas two-step weren't as far beyond my reach as I'd thought, and I'd never gotten over my high-school crush on Blaine Underhill.

I came home feeling buoyant and giddy. Unfortunately, right after Blaine delivered me to the cottage door, I discovered that I had locked myself out during my earlier rush to change footwear.

"Here, let me try," he said, as if somehow locked doors would open for him when they would not open for me.

"It's really locked," I assured him, but he tried it anyway, then bent down and gave the knob a good look, trying to peer through the old keyhole.

"It's locked," he concluded.

I shook my head, chuckling despite the fact that I was stuck out in the cold. "I can get a key from the main house." Both of us looked up the hill. The windows were dark, everyone obviously in bed.

"I'll drive you up," he offered.

"We came in a boat."

"Good point. I'll walk with you." Considering it was after midnight, Blaine was amazingly upbeat. He didn't sound the least bit cold or tired.

"No, it's okay, really." The last thing I wanted was to create a bunch of commotion that would wake everyone so they could take note of what time I'd arrived home and whether I had a telltale flush on my cheeks. I was fairly sure I did, but I was better off keeping that to myself. The evening had already traveled far, far beyond anything I'd planned.

Blaine stood in front of me, blocking the steps, his head tipping to one side, dark curls bunching in his collar. "My grandma raised me better than that. What kind of gentleman would let a lady go tromping around in the dark by herself?"

The kind I usually date. "I don't know. What kind?"

He walked backward down the steps, his lips spreading into a grin as he gave a quick, sideways jerk of his head, motioning toward the big house.

I felt myself wavering. Was there any way this guy could possibly be for real? I mean, it had to be an act, right? Anybody that perfect would be married to a former beauty queen and the father of two-and-a-half kids by now.

"Not this kind, darlin'," he said, his voice throaty, the words hanging in the air in a puff of vapor.

I melted into a little ball of goo right there on the porch. *I give up. I'm putty in your hands,* I thought as I followed him onto the lawn. We walked up the hill toward the house without talking, our feet making trails in the white-tipped grass amid the moon shadows of the winter-bare trees. At the top of the hill, the house towered imposingly, the tall, wood-paned windows unevenly reflecting the glow from outdoor gaslights, creating the haunting appearance of movement.

Blaine tucked his hands into his coat pockets. "Man, I can see why this place was a double-dog dare at night."

Was it my imagination, or was he slowing up a little? "You're not scared, are you?"

He scoffed indignantly, "Uh, no . . . Do I look scared?"

I pretended to check him out as we passed by one of the yard lights. "Well . . . yeah, kind of."

"I just didn't want *you* to be scared." Climbing the steps to the veranda with me, he studied the house.

A chill slid under my collar as I moved carefully across the slick, frost-covered decking. "I used to live here, remember? Anyway, they can smell fear, you know? The ghosts. It wakes them up."

"Thanks a lot." He stood to one side and waited while I reached for the utility room door, which I quickly determined to be locked. "Uh-oh." It was a fairly certain thing that, if this door was locked, all of the doors were locked. Back when the funeral home was in operation, Uncle Herbert had always been somewhat meticulous about that, as combinations of money, personal effects, and trea-sured loved ones could be stored in the house at any time. Old habits died hard, I supposed.

I turned around and started back across the veranda. "We'll have to go in through the cellar door." For those who knew the way around Harmony House, the ground-level doors that led to the basement were easy to jimmy.

"The place with all the old coffins in it?" Blaine wanted to know. "That basement?" His cowboy boots slid on the decking, and he did a fairly agile ice-skating maneuver before grabbing the railing.

"I thought you weren't scared." Despite my show of bravado, a shiver ran over me, making the shadows on the side of the house and the vapor puffing from our mouths seem unusually eerie. I had never liked Harmony Shores at night, but if the alternative was to wake everyone up and have a date discussion—which we would, because Uncle Herbert, having been in the funeral business, was hospitable at any hour of the day or night—I'd take my chances on the basement. I was glad, however, that I didn't have to do it by myself.

"I'm *not* scared," Blaine assured. "I was just worried about you."

"Hey, I did the two-step next to an icy lake. It's all downhill from there." The comment won a chuckle just before we reached the cellar door. I leaned over to grab the handle, and the bite of the frosty metal caused me to jerk my fingers back, pulling them into my sleeve.

"Here." Blaine took a pair of leather gloves from his coat pocket, put them on, and lifted the door.

"I don't suppose you have a flashlight in that pocket, too?" I asked, peering down the steps. The blackness in there was so thick that the cellar seemed bottomless, only small, faint circles of light coming from the wavy glass windows at ground level. I knew exactly where the light switch was—on the other side of the room.

"Actually, yeah." He produced the boat keys with a little pinch light on the end of the chain. The faint glow was just enough to allow him to proceed into the basement. Apparently, he wasn't the kind of gentleman who would let a lady descend into a dark, scary subterranean lair first, either. I didn't argue with him about it. I just grabbed a fistful of his jacket and followed along.

The penlight died when we were halfway across the room, blowing out like a candle and leaving us huddled together in the darkness like Shaggy and Scooby-Doo. "Well, that's not good," Blaine muttered. I felt his coat stretch as he reached ahead, trying to feel his way along. He collided with something, and I collided with him, knocking him forward.

"I think that's a coffin," he observed, jerking back.

"I don't even want to know." I was happy enough to take his word for it as he clumsily circumvented the obstacle, and I followed. In the dim light from the windows, shadows shifted at chest level, painting strange shapes and swirls, leaving the territory below murky and impossibly black.

234

A chill brushed my cheek and slipped over my skin, causing me to do a full-body shudder. A moaning whisper circled the floor joists overhead. I clutched Blaine's coat in two tight fists.

His foot hit something else, sending an unknown bit of cellar flotsam skittering across the floor to a corner, where it collided with a hollow metal object. I heard what sounded like a note of music, and then the faint melody of a woman's singing drifted overhead.

"Do you hear that?" I whispered, thinking of the girl who was rumored to have killed herself in the house, and of all the generations of people who had lived and died there.

"I hear it," Blaine answered in a hush.

I do not believe in ghosts. I do not believe in ghosts. I do not . . .

The singing grew louder, seemed to be coming from everywhere, all around us.

Blaine tripped over something again. It collapsed and clattered to the floor. I squealed, trying to decide whether to stay put or make a run for the door.

Footsteps echoed through the basement. They were coming closer. A door creaked slowly open. I caught a breath.

Light flooded into the room, and a voice hollered, "Hey, down there!"

When I looked up, Uncle Charley was at the top of the interior stairs. "What're ya'll doin' sneaking 'round the cellar way? C'mon up. We got *The Sound of Music* on late-night TV!"

For with thee is the fountain of life;
in thy light shall we see light.

—Psalm 36:9
(left by Ron, still climbing highline poles to keep the power on)

Chapter 14

Mary and Emily were helping their mother to prepare *verenike* and cream gravy when I arrived for my next visit with Ruth. I'd found another of her drawings, not in an art pad this time but just on a piece of paper that had been torn out. I'd discovered it in an antique serving buffet in the vestibule, where prayer cards and pictures of the deceased were traditionally displayed. Ruth's drawing had been tucked into the drawer haphazardly among left-over funeral programs dating from at least three different decades.

The day was blustery and gray when I arrived at the dairy, so Ruth and I sat in the main room of the house next to a crackling fire, Ruth in a simply-made rocking chair that looked well-worn, and me on an aging gold velvet sofa that had probably been rescued from someone's discards. The sofa wasn't in bad shape—just out of style. One thing about Ruth's family, they could squeeze a dime until you could see through it. As a rule, they didn't believe in waste. Fashion not being of high concern either, they found other people's junk to be perfectly useful. During my high-school year at Moses Lake, I'd learned to be careful of hitching a ride with

Ruth when she went out on an errand in one of Uncle Herbert's vehicles. More than once, we had ended up on the side of the road, digging through the castoffs in curbside trash piles. During these unplanned detours, we not only rescued things Ruth wanted, but anything and everything she thought she could give to other people. We cleaned up the treasures—soaped them and polished them—and she presented them to neighbors and friends, either Mennonite or non-Mennonite, depending on the item. Ruth was not above rescuing clothing or toys, and after a washing and mending, she pronounced them good-as-good (not good-as-new, which would have indicated that new stuff was in some way inherently superior to things that were nicely preloved).

Clay adored playing the treasure-dig game with Ruth. It was entirely possible that was why his fashion train still stopped at Goodwill. I, on the other hand, was horrified by the idea of germs, and dead skin cells, and other people's hairs, as well as the possibility of being seen on the side of the highway, should someone from school drive by. I was already weird enough.

I laughed now, stroking the sofa, thinking that some of the best things in life are the ones you're dragged into kicking and screaming. Those treasure hunts with Ruth were good times. She'd probably be pleased to know that much of the décor in my apartment centered on found items from thrift shops and eBay. There were no harvest gold sofas, but I had discovered an egg pod chair and an Oscar Tusquets vintage table that gave the place a serious Jetsons-era look.

Ruth's eyes twinkled as I set her sketch on the sofa beside me, face down. "I found another one," I said, smiling because I knew she would be pleased. "Sort of stumbled upon it, actually. But anyway, here it is." I lifted the paper to hand it to her, but she motioned for me to leave it where it was, upside down on the sofa cushion.

Lacing her fingers in her lap, she indicated no hurry to look at the drawing. Ruth's patience had always been surprising and difficult for me to relate to. "They are probably hidden all over the house. Your uncle was terrible about rescuing them from the trash and hiding them where I wouldn't come across them and throw them away again."

Curiosity nibbled. "Why not keep them? Your drawings are beautiful. It seems like a waste not to frame them." I thought of all the times I'd watched her sitting on the porch with her pad at the end of the day, when she was waiting for her carpool friends to pick her up. The older Mennonites of Gnadenfeld, while not opposed to car ownership like the Amish, still seldom drove anywhere by themselves. To do so would have been less than frugal, and a lack of frugality implied ingratitude for the resources God provided. In a de facto sense, they were green before green was in vogue.

My aunt Esther had a hard-and-fast rule about our bothering Ruth, or any of the help, after working hours were over. We were strictly not allowed, but I often watched Ruth from a distance while she sketched. I never knew her creations were destined for the trash. She must have thrown them away in the funeral parlor, where I never went unless I had to when I was working for Uncle Herbert.

"They weren't for framing. Not for anyone else to see." Ruth's fingers twitched against her floral print skirt.

"But why not?" It occurred to me that Ruth, who in her spare time sold home-canned and baked goods, could have more easily sold her drawings to produce income. "It's okay if you don't want to answer."

"It would have been vainglorious, I think." She shrugged slightly, as if shedding the compliment, but I suspected that the vaingloriousness of artwork was something she didn't quite believe in.

"Besides, I would not have wanted to look at them again. Not all of them, anyway."

I thought about the story of the girl in the floral dress, and Ruth's behavior made sense. Her drawings were like diary entries—some painful, some beautiful. "I understand." I did, really. There were boxes in Uncle Herbert's cellar, according to my mother. Boxes that had been packed away since we left the little stone house at the family farm and moved into the gardener's cottage at Harmony Shores. Neither Mom nor I had brought up the issue of the boxes since the phone call that hastened me back to Moses Lake. I hadn't gone looking for them, and I didn't have a desire to. I would come and go from Moses Lake without seeing them, unless I was forced to sort through them with my mother. I knew exactly what was in those boxes. I'd watched Aunt Esther and her church ladies pack them. They were filled with videotapes, photo albums, the framed pictures that had always hung in the halls of my childhood. Images of life as it once was—soccer practices, Halloween parties, picnics by the ocean, my dad and I in line for Mr. Toad's Wild Ride at Disney World.

I understood why Ruth threw away her drawings. Some things are too painful to revisit.

"What is that one?" She wagged a finger toward the drawing.

"Children playing, and a horse," I said, but I didn't turn it over. "We don't have to talk about them if you don't want to. There was a story you were going to tell me. Something more about my family, maybe? You said you wanted to tell me about my grandfather. We never got to it last time, because we were talking about the girl in the blue dress."

I wasn't sorry to have learned about the girl in the blue dress yesterday, but I did want to hear about my family. Even though Ruth was already assuming that I would be back tomorrow, there was no telling how many more times I would be able to visit before I had to leave Moses Lake—work, family, or the Proxica deal could change my circumstances at any time. I'd checked my email on my way to Ruth's, and even though Mel had grudgingly allowed me to take a few personal days, he was not happy about it. He wanted me to know I was *on notice* and would be called back immediately if anything critical came up.

Right then, sitting by the fire with Ruth, the office seemed a million miles away. I'd never had much interest in family history or stories about the pioneering days in Moses Lake. When my grandmother and grandfather brought up those things during our occasional visits, the information had seemed fairly unimportant. I suppose I'd always felt that there would be time to reconnect if I ever wanted to—maybe someday after I'd found Mr. Right and the two of us had created a couple of surprisingly perfect and multi-talented offspring. Now, with the prospect of selling off the old family places, I felt the need to carry at least a little bit of that history with me. Who could say if I'd ever see the uncs again after they moved to the retirement community in Oklahoma? Their lives would be filled with Donny and the grands and great-grands.

Ruth motioned to the paper, her gaze drifting toward the fire. "Look at it and tell me what you see."

I turned the sheet over and did as she asked, even though I didn't need to. I'd studied the sketch previously. It was a collage of sorts—several children playing in the grass and a teenage girl standing on the back of a farm horse, balancing with her arms out, her legs clad in long, black stockings. Her bonnet had slid back, so that tendrils of hair whisked around her face, swirling like the horse's mane. She'd tucked her chin slightly and rolled her gaze upward in a way that seemed coy and confident. Her lips held a precocious smile, as if she knew she was doing something she shouldn't, something dangerous, but she didn't care. Her eyes were green, the only bit of color on the image, except for the wildflowers beneath the horse's feet.

I described her to Ruth, but I couldn't put into words the expression on her face.

Ruth gave a small, private smile, as if she were imagining it anyway. "That is my sister." Taking in a long breath, she seemed to drink in the scent of the picture, the lingering of graphite and pastel, the fragrance of the wildflowers, bright and alive in a world that was otherwise gray. "She was not afraid of anything, Lydia. Not then. That was before."

"Before what?"

"Oh . . . before . . ." Ruth drifted off momentarily, then turned her head to the sound of the front door opening. A boy, perhaps seventeen or eighteen wearing jeans and a blue chambray shirt, stepped in and dusted his boots on the rug.

"Is that John?" Ruth called without turning around.

"No, it's Hosephat. Gee Hosephat," the boy said, smiling slightly at his joke but remaining reserved. Ruth's family had never known what to make of mine. The Mennonites worked any number of places around the area, but the more conservative they were in their views, the more they tended to socialize amongst themselves. Close connections like the one Ruth had with my uncles weren't all that common.

Ruth shook her head at the boy. "Lunch is almost ready, Mr. Gee Hosephat. I know that must be why you came."

The teenager cast a hungry look down the hall. "I thought I smelled something." He crossed the room to greet both of us before proceeding on to the kitchen.

After he was gone, Ruth shook her head. "John is a grand nephew, Mary and Emily's cousin. One of my sister's grandsons."

"The sister in the picture?" I asked.

"No." Taking a long breath, Ruth let her lashes drift downward until she was gazing into the fire, her eyes unfocused. "John's grandmother went to be with the Lord last year. I miss her. Every day of our lives, we cooked together, did our ironing and mending together, and prayed together. I couldn't have children, you know, but Naomi had seven, so there were plenty to share. Naomi was a good, quiet woman. Obedient to the Lord. Plain in her appearance, as I am plain." Pointing toward the paper, she shook her head. "But this one, Lydia, she was not the same. We were eight, in all; our mother, father, three brothers and three sisters. Most of us were plain and pale, quiet in nature, but Lydia came into the world with her dark hair and her confident ways. She was second in line, behind John, but you would have thought Lydia was the eldest. Then there was Matthew, then Naomi, and I was younger, and finally the baby."

Pausing, she cradled her arms, as if she were holding the baby now. "He was such a fine, fat little one. My grandfather had built a beautiful home in the Ukraine on the land allotted to the family years before. So many of the Mennonites had beautiful farms in the villages between the Black and Caspian seas, but after the revolution, the land and what it could produce belonged to the Communists. They were suspicious of Mennonite people and their low German and Plautdietsch speech. I remember men and boys being sent to work camps, the *gulags*, and never coming home. Of course, you prayed that it wouldn't happen to your family, but they took away my eldest brother, and then Matthew. . . . He was only a child. Just a bit over ten years old. My father sat at the table with his back straight against the chair. He did nothing to stop them. Lydia was angry about it. She was about thirteen, then, I think, but older than that in her mind. She had seen things. I was young, but

I had seen things, too. Always we were afraid that Stalin's secret police would come to the village and put us on a train. Always we were hungry, but if you were caught stealing food or trying to hide what you had produced, terrible things could happen."

Shivering, Ruth pulled her knitted shawl closer around her shoulders. I stood up, took a log from the woodbox, and added it to the fire, then returned to the sofa and waited for Ruth to begin again. Lydia, the girl with long waves of dark hair, the one who was different from everyone else, was coming to life in my mind.

I waited for Ruth to tell more of her story. Finally, she pressed a hand to her lips, laughing privately. "But there was joy, too. Children will always find joy, somehow. Lydia wanted to run away and join the circus before the war. We went sometimes to the Russian villages to beg for food, and once there was a circus. Lydia peeked under the tent. She told us of it in whispers, when she knew my father couldn't hear. She told us she would have those glittering costumes with the crystal beads and the gold threads sewn into them, and she would ride a white horse. I could not imagine such a thing. To entertain the idea, even!"

Pressing three fingers to her lips, Ruth leaned forward to look at the drawing of her sister. "My mother and the baby died when cholera came. My father was weak, especially after the illness. The Second World War had begun by then, and I was just beginning to become a woman. There was even less food than before. The Russians prevented us from travel, so it became more difficult to go begging in the villages. My father admonished us to have faith through all of this. He told us that the Germans were drawing closer and when they came, because of our German heritage, we would fare better."

Leaning forward, Ruth pointed to one of the girls playing in the grass at the horse's feet. "My sister Naomi clung to my father's faith. But Lydia grew tired of it. She was sixteen then, prideful, beautiful in a way that was noticed, that was rewarded by the few men and boys remaining in the villages when we could go begging. There was a bit of extra bread here, a cup of milk there. Lydia turned against my father. She was not modest. She uncovered her hair. She said, if she were not to do it, we would all starve to death. 'Who is going to feed us?' she asked my father as he lay in his bed, too weak to punish her. 'You? Naomi? You only lie there. You only lie there, waiting on the Lord while we go hungry. If this is what the Lord asks of His people, then I do not want it.'"

Ruth turned to look at me then, moving her gaze slowly away from the contrasting images of Naomi and Lydia on the paper. "You may wonder which of my sisters was right—the one who honored my father's instruction, or the one who turned away. Terrible things had happened to us, after all—death, disease, hunger, our family torn asunder, abuses I cannot even speak of. How could a God who loves us allow such things, you might wonder?"

She seemed to be waiting for an answer, but I didn't have one. A log popped in the fireplace, a spit of flame tearing away and floating upward. *I have wondered. I've needed that answer all these years, but there is no answer.*

Ruth shifted in her chair, her breath coming in labored grunts as she tried to reposition the bed pillow tucked behind her back. "I cannot tell you the answer. There is none on this side of heaven, on the dark side of the glass, I think. The Germans came, and there were rewards for those who would help them in their battle. The Mennonites would not agree to fight, of course, but some were forced and some gave information. Some told who in the Russian villages had helped the Russians, who might be helping them still.

"Lydia told what she knew. The Russians were, after all, the very people at whose hands we had suffered. 'It is only justice,' she said. I have wondered if she was aware that those people would be walked up the hill, like the woman in the blue dress, and positioned at the edge, so as to fall into a grave with so many others. I sometimes think Lydia must have been unaware. It is easier to believe that."

My stomach roiled at the thought of mass graves and people being walked up a hill, knowing they were walking into death. Looking at Ruth, it was hard to imagine that she had seen these things, that to her these were not just pieces of history, images from some sad newsreel. This was her past. She'd lived it. "Did Lydia report the woman in the blue dress? Was it your sister who told?"

Ruth answered with a long, sad look. "I have never known. I don't want to. Naomi told me never to ask, and I didn't. But Lydia was not the same after the killings. She lost her laughter. Even when we followed the German army in its retreat from Russian soil, she was hollow and angry. Her revenge had fed her for a day, but it was a meal that emptied her afterward, and there seemed to be nothing that could fill her again. She married a German man as the war was ending, but her life was never happy. Naomi and I came here to America. Naomi had seven children and lived well all the rest of her life until the Lord called her home. But that story is for another day."

"I'd love to hear it," I said, but I could tell Ruth was wearing down, getting tired. She'd sagged against the pillow, her body cocked to one side in a way that looked uncomfortable. Once again, we hadn't gotten to the story about my grandfather.

"You come back again tomorrow." She smiled at me, her withered fingers patting the arm of the sofa as if she were patting my hand.

"I will."

"Which of my sisters did the right thing?" Ruth stared into the fire again, her head drooping forward. "The one who fed our

245

stomachs but was faithless, or the one who kept our faith but let us go hungry?"

"I don't know," I admitted, though I suspected that wasn't the answer she wanted.

"I sometimes think both of my sisters are inside us." Her eyelids were sinking now, silver lashes brushing her cheeks. "I have always thanked God that I was younger. It did not fall on me to make the choice between the two paths."

She sighed, her eyes closing, her breaths lengthening. I tiptoed away quietly, leaving her there to rest. Lunch was ready in the kitchen, and I stayed to share the meal at a long table with Mary, Emily, John, and various members of Ruth's family. The prayers settled over me as grace was offered, and for the first time in a long time, I felt grace. I'd always thought of my life as irreparably marred by tragedy, but now I could see that we all have marks of some kind, scars we'd rather not live with. It's what we do in spite of them that matters.

After the meal, Mary and Emily walked me out, and we visited the puppies in the barn. I watched the girls take them to the barn-yard and try to corral them against the wall.

"You shoulda brought Roger," Mary pointed out, running after a chubby puppy to put it back in the puppy containment area.

"Rod-er likes the puppies," Emily added.

"Yes, he does," I agreed. Watching Mary and Emily, I couldn't help contrasting their lives with those of the children in Ruth's drawing. They were growing up in completely different worlds. "Maybe I'll bring Roger back next time. You two have fun today." I hoped Mary and Emily's world would always be this gentle, this welcoming and sweet.

As I walked to my car, I thought about Ruth's story of the two sisters. Ruth had made the choice, whether she realized it or not. She'd witnessed terrible things, suffered hunger, disease, watched her family be torn apart while God seemed to do nothing to stop it. Yet she still believed in love and mercy.

I wanted to believe. I needed to. There was a hunger in me that couldn't be filled by anything I'd achieved or purchased or invested my time in. I was like Lydia. For everything that was beautiful about her on the outside, there was a piece on the inside that was broken, jagged, dangerous. She curled inward, protectively around herself, until finally she bled herself dry.

I was living Lydia's life, but I wanted Naomi's. I wanted peace. I wanted hope. I wanted the joy of those two little girls playing in the grass.

Low clouds gathered overhead, and the scent of freshly baked bread hung heavy in the air as I left the dairy and drove through Gnadenfeld. My mouth watered, drawing me toward one of the bakeries, my justification being that I'd just take a few things home as a treat . . . for the uncs, of course. A little comfort food.

I needed some comfort at the moment, and even though I fully understood the wisdom of not having Mennonite baked goods around the house—I'd gained ten pounds my senior year in high school and gone from stick-thin to curvy—I went into the remodeled Texaco station, anyway.

The interior smelled like heaven. Behind the counter, a teenage girl in a soft mauve dress with a mesh prayer covering pinned over her bun was working on math homework. She set her pencil down and looked up at me. She had beautiful eyes. I thought of Lydia in the drawing. Lydia as drawn by Ruth probably wasn't any older than this girl, yet she had seen unspeakable things, experienced horrors of a sort I couldn't even imagine.

A lump swelled in my throat and I swallowed hard, then ordered some treats, feeling foolish. The girl behind the counter probably thought I was off in the head.

Leaving the bakery, I stood on the curb a moment, took in a long, slow breath, and smelled the faint scent of emissions from the Proxica plant, held low over the ground by the cloud cover today. Something familiar on the street caught my eye. An old white Toyota pickup. The Ladybug. It turned just past the building across the street and disappeared into an alley. I walked down the curb a few steps to catch sight of it again.

Clay was parked in the alleyway. I started to call to him as he got out of the truck, but something in his movements stopped me. He was looking around, checking over his shoulder to make sure no one was watching. A man came out the back door of the building, handed something to Clay in a brown paper sack. My brother tucked it under his jacket, hurried back to his truck, and was gone.

My stomach rolled as I stood on the sidewalk, watching his taillights disappear around the back of the building. Suddenly the smell of the baked goods in my arms seemed off-putting. Despite everyone's assurances that my brother was fine, the body language of that alley meeting was impossible to misread. I knew what kinds of packages had to be picked up via the alley doors of buildings, in secret.

Siddhartha looked into the river
and saw many pictures in the flowing water.

—Herman Hesse
(Left by an artist, who painted the day away by the shore)

Chapter 15

When I returned to Uncle Herbert's place, Mom and the uncs were down by the old barn, where Clay's collection of partially-repainted canoes still languished on the lawn. Uncle Herbert, Uncle Charley, and Mom were walking around the barn, pointing and talking. Perhaps they were making plans for future hoedowns to entertain the throngs of bed-and-breakfast customers looking to stay in a former funeral home? Whatever was going on, they seemed to be deeply engaged in it, the three of them looking up at the roof while Uncle Herbert pointed and talked, and Uncle Charley shook his head, disagreeing. They didn't notice me driving in, so I closed the car door quietly and went into the house, my mind still on Clay.

Inside, a laptop computer sat idling on the kitchen counter. I bumped it accidentally-on-purpose while setting down my supply of bakery goods, and the screen came on. Two windows popped up side by side, and I paused to look at them. One appeared to be an email containing a series of instructions for a graduate student or fellow professor who was covering Mom's classes. She'd asked him to give her freshman composition students an assignment—the dreaded term paper, a social criticism of *Sonny's Blues* by James Baldwin. Scanning down the page, I read the last line, a final note to her colleague.

> Thank you for your understanding, Andrew. I could be gone on family leave for a couple weeks yet but should return well before finals. Sorry to miss Valentine's Day, but we'll make it up in style—dinner and a theater night, perhaps? You pick . . .

The note stopped there, as if she'd been interrupted before finishing it. In the window beside the email was a drawing—an attachment she'd downloaded, apparently. The sketch was someone's crude attempt to create a 3-D walkthrough of a living room interior, using AutoCAD. Whoever had done it didn't know the software well. The representation was rough, and from the notations, it looked like someone wanted to design a room based on knobby cedar poles, hand-hewn beams that fit together with wooden pegs, and barn wood.

Barn wood . . .

I looked out the window at my mother and the uncs, who were now investigating the framing around the big sliding doors that, when there were farm fields nearby, had been designed to admit wagons mounded with freshly-harvested cotton. Maybe Mom was planning to tear down the barn—sell it off to someone who wanted to use the rustic materials inside a house or cabin. It seemed a shame to do that. The barn was part of the history of this place. Even though it was over a hundred years old and needed some work, it wasn't beyond saving.

Aside from that there was another question, one even more perplexing. Mom had someone back at Berkeley waiting for her to return, planning a belated Valentine's dinner and teaching her classes? *Thank you for understanding . . . gone on family leave for a couple weeks yet . . . Sorry to miss Valentine's Day, but we'll make it up in style . . .*

That was even stranger than Clay's text message from the girl with whom he was apparently two-timing Amy. Why would my mother be stringing along some poor guy in California if she intended to move to Moses Lake for good? Why would she lie to him? She had to be lying to someone—she couldn't move to Moses Lake and return to California at the same time. Had she been lying to the uncs? Did she intend to go back to her teaching position? Why come here and build up the uncs' hopes with talk of settling down in the country? To what purpose?

Would she do that so Clay could secure bank loans? Was Mom pretending to be a future partner in Clay's business ventures so she could set him up in Moses Lake, and then leave? It wouldn't be the first time. When Clay was in his last year of high school, she'd accepted a fellowship in Paris without telling anyone. Out of the blue at Thanksgiving, she'd announced that she'd be boarding a plane four months before Clay's graduation, but there was nothing to worry about, because the rent on the house was good until the end of May. She'd asked the neighbors to help Clay out if he needed anything.

I still remembered the wounded, confused expression on Clay's face. He looked like an abandoned house pet that had just been booted from the car on the side of some lonely highway. Surely she wouldn't do that to him again. Maybe she was lying to the guy back at Berkeley—Andrew, whose name had never come up in conversation before, but with whom she was apparently close.

Was she lying to Clay, or were she and Clay lying to me . . . to everyone?

251

The phone rang just as my thoughts were melting into a slag heap of molten theories too corrosive to handle. A scenario was forming, and I couldn't face thinking about it. The idea clarified and hardened as the phone rang a second time and a third, until finally Uncle Herbert's recorded message echoed from his office. On the message, he was using his funeral voice, smooth, low, and soothing. "Hello, you've reached Harmony Shores Funeral Home. We're no longer offering services, but if you'd like to leave a message . . ."

I listened until the caller began recording a response. "Hi, Dad, this is Donny." I pictured Uncle Herbert's eldest son, Donny. He and his family had come down for my father's funeral. Even though they were only cousins, Donny reminded me so much of my father that it hurt just to be around him. Same laugh, same eyes, same tall frame and broad shoulders, same receding hairline.

I sidestepped toward the kitchen phone, my ear still cocked toward the message. "So, listen, Dad, I just wanted to check in and see how everything's going. The Craigslist guy should be there to move the stuff out of the basement a week from tomorrow. He says he'll just warehouse all of it until it sells, no problem. Who knows, maybe there'll be a rush of vampires looking for places to sleep, and the display coffins will sell off in a hurry. Anyway, be sure you've got the red tags on anything down there that you don't want him to haul off, okay? All of that stuff is going to do better on Craigslist than in an estate sale, and this way you won't have people tromping all through the place. Remember, the furniture stays unless it's something that's got sentimental value. They want the rest of it left where it is. Anyway, I'll call back later and . . ."

I grabbed the kitchen phone and pushed the button for the funeral home line before Donny could hang up. "Hi, Donny, this is Heather. Your dad is down the hill with Uncle Charley and my mom."

Donny hesitated long enough that I thought maybe he'd hung up. "Oh . . . Heather," he said finally. "Well, I didn't know you were down there."

Why am I not surprised? Wait until I tell you what else you didn't know. It occurred to me, then, that Donny didn't seem surprised that my mother was at Harmony Shores. Apparently, he already knew. "I've been in town for a few days. Ummm . . . has anyone told you what is going on here?"

"Going on, as in . . ." Donny's lead-in was strangely cautious, as if he were concerned about where I might be headed.

"With the land sale, the estate sale. Everything. The broker offer expires soon. We were supposed to have signed and executed it last week in Seattle, but my mother didn't show up to do the paperwork, so I came down here. What's weird is that no preparations have been made here. Everything, and I mean everything, is just the way it's always been. It doesn't look to me like Uncle Herbert and Uncle Charley are planning on moving anywhere, and all of a sudden my brother is talking about taking over the catfish place, and my mother thinks she's going to open a bed-and-breakfast in the funeral home." *I know, I know. Go ahead and laugh. It sounds really ludicrous when you say it out loud.*

"Hmmm," Donny muttered. Even for a straight-laced electronics engineer, it was a strangely flat response. He hesitated for a long time afterward. "Well, I'm sure it's fine, Heather. Dad and Uncle Charley just sent their deposit check for the new condo. They're looking forward to living the retirement life with all those hot senior babes. I think most of the furniture stays with the house there at Harmony Shores. Don't worry about it, all right? The moving company will be coming in to pack Dad's personal belongings for him. He's supposed to red tag anything he wants to hang on to. When I took the deposit check to the retirement village last week, I measured his condo, so he could make some more decisions about what furniture to take and what to leave behind."

My mind tripped and stumbled. An actual check had been sent to Donny? My understanding had been that Herbert and Charley needed the money from the broker offer to pay the thirty-thousand-dollar deposit on their retirement condo, which was why the broker offer was such a godsend.

If Uncle Herbert had sent money to Donny, that meant that actual cash had already changed hands between my mother, my brother, and the uncs. But if Uncle Herbert intended to stay in Moses Lake, then why was he making the down payment on a condo in Oklahoma?

"Donny, listen, I think you'd better come here. We need to all sit down in one room"—*lock the doors*—"and get to the bottom of this before it's too late."

"Hang on a minute, Heather." I heard someone talking in the background, and the scratchy sound of Donny putting his hand over the phone.

Donny came back on the line. "Listen, Heather, I'm headed to a meeting. Don't worry about it anymore, all right? Everything's fine. Dad's got it under control. Good talking to you."

"No . . . wait, but . . ."

He hung up. I held the phone away from my face and looked cross-eyed at it, my mouth hanging open. "He hung up on me. . . ." The words were for no one but the ghosts in the house, and they didn't answer. I quickly pushed *69 to dial back Donny's number. He didn't answer. I tried three more times. No luck.

"Ohhh, that is just . . ." I didn't even have words for it. Finally, I smacked the phone into the cradle and paced the kitchen, thinking, *Apparently his meeting matters more than his family, and* . . .

The strangeness of that thought struck me. Talk about the pot and the kettle. Was this not exactly the personality flaw my mother and Clay had accused me of? Their complaint about me? Richard's complaint about me? Even Trish's, when I got right down to it? I was so overburdened with my own issues, I didn't have time for anyone else's.

That's not who I am, I thought. *It's not. That's not me.*

Not this time.

Whether the Proxica deal worked out or fell completely apart, I was going to make sure my family came out of this in one piece, and the basement was as good a place to start as any, whether I wanted to go down there or not. If I could find any evidence of items that had been packed or red tagged for moving, that would at least be proof of something. Proof I could use to confront my mother and force her to tell me the truth.

I was still muttering to myself as I turned the corner to cross through Uncle Herbert's office. The rustling of papers caught me off guard, and I stopped short, slapping a hand to my chest, a breath hitching in my throat.

There was a strange man behind the desk. He was young, maybe in his twenties, dressed in a sport coat and slacks. He seemed to be making calculations, using a graph paper and an antiquated adding machine. Apparently he was unconcerned with my passing.

I had the fleeting thought that he was a ghost. A fully solid ghost whose breath ruffled the adding machine tape, as he peered at the numbers. A ghost who chewed Juicy Fruit. I could smell it.

I stopped just past the desk and turned to look at him. "What are you doing in my uncle's office?"

He glanced up, seeming surprised that I had addressed him, but not alarmed. "I'm with the auction company."

"For the estate sale?"

"Right." He turned back to his work, indicating a lack of interest in engaging me. He punched in a few more numbers, studied them.

"You're getting stuff ready for the estate sale?"

"Right."

"My uncle knows you're here?"

"Right."

The one-word answers fanned the burn in my stomach. With the exception of the visit to Ruth's, it had been another upside-down and backward, down-the-rabbit-hole day, filled with events that, lumped together, made no sense. "The estate sale, which is . . . when, exactly?"

He punched in more numbers, snorted softly, erased something on his graph paper, rewrote in the spaces. "You'd have to talk to Herbert about that, ma'am."

"But I'm asking you." My inner dragon lady, the one who sent interns scurrying against walls, was rapidly coming to the surface. I'd been way too much of a wimp since my bedraggled arrival in Moses Lake.

"I don't have any information. Your uncle would be the one to talk to." He began furiously punching numbers, muttering, "Mmm-hmm . . . mmm-hmm," to himself, as if I were no longer in the room.

"Might I ask what you're doing, exactly?"

"Calculating." The answer was flat, intentionally off-putting, meant to let me know that he wouldn't be divulging anything.

Clenching my teeth over a snippy retort, I continued on toward the basement. The red tags, if they were there, would at least be proof of something. I wasn't exactly sure what, but . . .

Outside, a pickup truck was coming up the driveway. As it popped over the hill, a soft, sweet feeling, like a dusting of powdered sugar, fell over my churning inner self. Blaine. I needed a friendly face at that moment.

But in reality, I had no solid reason to believe Blaine was a friend. However interesting, different . . . all right, even magical last night's dance at Blue Moon Bay had been, Blaine was somehow wrapped up in this business with my mother and my brother, and he wasn't willing to divulge any secrets.

Maybe if I told him what I'd seen today in Gnadenfeld, it would make a difference. Blaine really appeared to be a decent guy. Surely he had just been taken in by Clay's enthusiasm and the high energy of Clay's current manic interest in Moses Lake. All I had to do was make Blaine see the truth.

Grabbing a jacket, I hurried out the front door as his truck tooled into the circle in front of the house—moving rather fast, actually. Gravel flew as he skidded to a stop, and I hung back until the dust died down. Blaine leaned across the front seat to throw open the passenger door. "You up for a little adventure?"

I hesitated at the base of the porch steps, the voice in my head saying, *Who cares about the land deal, the family's financial stability, or the future of your career. Get in the truck with the hunky guy.* "Where are we going?"

"Just trust me. This'll be worth the ride."

"That's what you said last time." I moved a few steps closer.

His smirk broadened into a devil-may-care grin, unabashedly confident. "And was it?"

Heat traveled from my head to my toes. There was only one answer to that question, and we both knew what it was. Call me coy, but I couldn't quite bring myself to admit to it. Grabbing the door, I dragged myself into the passenger seat, trying to appear reserved so as to not make evident my inner voice cheering, *Yee-haw! Let's go, cowboy!*

Moving his foot from the brake to the gas, he grinned, his eyes sliding over me in a way that made my stomach flutter. All thoughts of my brother and my frustrating afternoon flew out the window. I remembered last night's dance and the kiss.

Never in my life had a kiss brought such an onslaught of emotions that I couldn't even think straight while it was happening. That kiss wasn't like any other kiss. I still wasn't sure why. Maybe it was the night, or the magic of Blue Moon Bay.

Or the dance.

Or maybe it was the man.

That prospect bothered me. I reeled my mind in like a Macy's balloon, pulled too high by a stiff wind. If I was going to hang out with Blaine, I had to be smarter this time, more in control.

That thought took wing as Blaine glanced over at me, a little dimple forming in his cheek when he checked for traffic before pulling onto the road, and turning left, away from town. "Don't look so worried. Last night's surprise worked out all right, didn't it?"

I felt hot, despite the relatively cool air wafting through the vents. "Maybe I was just playing along to make you feel good." My cheeks twitched upward, making it tough to keep a straight face.

A knowing smirk answered. "Tell me you're not the kind of girl who would mess with a guy's heart."

Tell me, I thought. *Tell me you're not that kind of guy.* But I felt my little balloon head floating up and up and up. I wanted to lose myself in the moment again, throw caution to the wind, abandon all sense of reason, gamble like a high roller.

"Last night was nice." The admission surprised me. It felt vulnerable and raw. Whatever else happened, I would carry that dancing lesson with me. My chance to finally visit the Blue Moon on a dream date. It had only taken me sixteen years. "Never know when the two-step will come in handy, back in Seattle."

His face straightened, as if the mention of my going home bothered him. Maybe I was just imagining it. Wanting it. It was silly, of course. Leftover high-school emotion, more than anything.

"Hang around awhile. I'll teach you a few more steps."

My heart tumbled, pressing against my chest. I let my eyes close for a moment, tried to collect my thoughts. "I wish I could." The words were just a whisper. I didn't realize I'd said them out loud until I heard them.

"They construct big buildings in Texas, too," he pointed out quietly.

I didn't reply. I didn't know what to say. Everything was so up in the air. Depending on what was going on with Clay, I might be around for a while. If I couldn't convince him to face the problem and go back to Seattle with me to seek some kind of treatment, I'd have to take an extended leave of absence from my job and stay in Moses Lake. What would Mel say? He would have to replace me with a new second in command. Temporarily. But temporary could quickly become permanent. I'd become Mel's second when his last right-hand man had taken off to nurse his wife through cancer. All I'd seen at the time was my opportunity.

There were dozens more just like me, waiting in the wings. Looking for a big break.

If Mel doesn't understand, after all you've done for him, after all you've put in, then forget him. There are other places to work.

Were there? Would I really do something that drastic?

If Clay was willing to consider some kind of treatment here, I could look for a position in Texas—Dallas or Austin—maybe help get myself into a firm by telling them I had a line on designing a group of dental clinics in the area. . . .

I felt the colors bleeding outside the lines, racing in directions I never thought they'd go. Texas? Staying in Texas?

Outside the chaos in my mind, I heard the grinding of the tires on the pavement, a rattle in the air conditioner fan, the keys jingling as we passed over a pothole. I realized how quiet the truck had become. Had Blaine somehow picked up on the crazy track my mind was taking? Could he see it, just by looking? When I glanced over at him, he was focused on a trailer load of new speedboats passing by. Oblivious, thank goodness.

"Blaine, I have to ask you something, and I just . . . really need the truth right now." Breath cramped in my chest, feeling solid and painful.

"All right." His tone was wary. "I'll answer, if I can."

I pulled in air, then let it out with words laced into it. Dangerous words. Words that could change everything. "Do you know what's going on with my brother? Do you know what kind of a . . . a problem he has?"

"Problem?"

There was no choice but to lay it out now. "Drugs, Blaine. I found . . . things in his clothes, paraphernalia. A vial, a ziplock bag that had some kind of powder in it. Then today I saw him sneaking around in some alley over in Gnadenfeld . . . making a transaction of some sort. He knocked on a door, and someone gave him something, and he hid it in his coat."

Blaine didn't look at me but remained focused on the road as he piloted the truck into a scenic turnoff high on a bluff overlooking the lake. "Heather, I don't think . . ."

"Do you *know*, Blaine? Do you know what he's into—what he's using?"

I felt the truck settle into Park, heard the engine die. Blaine's hand slipped over mine, his fingers a warm, reassuring circle. Meeting his gaze, I searched for lies and secrets, but I couldn't see any. There was only the soft brown of understanding, of kindness and concern. "Heather, I can promise you that your brother's not on drugs."

"But how . . . I . . . I found things . . ."

He swiveled toward the front window before I could repeat myself. "There they are." He motioned to draw my attention, and I turned just in time to take in something so beautiful it chased away all other thoughts. Silhouetted against the bluffs, two bald eagles floated on the mingling air currents over the lake. They moved effortlessly, rising and falling, circling one another and cartwheeling through the sky, consumed by the joy of the moment and the freedom of flight.

Blaine exited the truck silently, and I followed, even the soft click of the door seeming too loud. The eagles dipped out of sight, and Blaine moved toward the edge of the overhang.

"C'mon," he whispered, stretching a hand toward me. I slipped my fingers into his, and he led me through a tangle of cedars, the two of us creeping one step at a time, like photographers stalking the perfect shot in some remote Discovery Channel location. Overhead, the eagles' shrill cries sliced the crisp winter air, sending a primal shiver over my skin, the instinctive reaction of predator and prey. They seemed closer now, as if their wings were beating the air just above the cedars. Blaine continued to pull me with him until we were crouched side by side on the edge of a bluff, an arch of thick, green cedar surrounding us.

The eagles swooped past, so close I drew back out of reflex and caught a breath. Blaine glanced at me and winked as the birds dipped near the water, then soared upward in tandem, their massive, powerful wings pumping long, even strokes as they rose against scattered winter clouds.

"That's amazing," I whispered, exhilarated and at the same time feeling a lump in my throat. I'd been all over the world, had helped to design buildings that seemed to defy gravity and meld into the surrounding expanse of sky, but I'd never seen anything so incredible as the eagles in flight over the lake. Nothing man-made, no feat of engineering could even begin to compare to this.

At the apex of flight, the birds circled, then seemed to hesitate, almost suspended in midair.

"Watch." Blaine squeezed my hand, leaning close to me so that he could see around the fringe of cedars. I felt his nearness. The sensation and the spectacle overhead sent electricity surging through me, bringing to life every inch, every fiber of my being, capturing every thought and breath into the moment.

"What are they doing?" I whispered.

"They like each other." Blaine's breath rustled my hair. I felt myself tumbling over the edge of the abyss, floating and swirling. "It's a courtship dance."

I thought of last night, of gliding across the rocks at Blue Moon Bay in Blaine's arms, the two of us moving as one to the tinny strains of music drifting across the water. That moment was like this one—an instant of being completely present, swept into an experience so powerful that nothing else could compete with it.

I'd never been drawn in that way before. It was at once impossibly alluring and frightening.

"There they go." He stretched a hand up, pointed, and in one sudden, powerful collision, the eagles locked talons and spiraled downward, their bodies whirling, the white feathers on their heads glinting like the fins on a windmill, spinning impossibly fast. The velocity increased as they tumbled downward in free fall, spiraling toward the ground. I'd heard of eagles locking talons in a death spiral before, even seen it once on the nature channel, but I'd never expected to witness it in person.

I felt myself spinning along with them, felt the fear and the elation of something so free, so dangerous, so wild. Every muscle in my body tightened. I realized I was holding my breath, clutching Blaine's hand, afraid to watch but unable to stop as the ground raced closer. They surely wouldn't survive the fall. . . .

A burst of air escaped my lips, then a laugh as the eagles released one another within inches of the bluffs and swooped upward. I slapped a hand to my chest, catching my breath. "Oh, wow. I've never seen anything like that in my life. That was . . . was . . ." Emotion stole away the words. Moisture welled in my eyes, pooled and spilled. Some moments are beyond the capacity of words, beyond the measure of any earthly comparison.

I turned to Blaine and saw a reflection of everything I was thinking, a mirror of everything I was feeling. His eyes, his smile seemed to tell me, *You don't need to say anything. I get it.*

I kissed him, or he kissed me. It didn't matter. The feeling of being there with him, of sharing something so profound, carried me away from myself.

When our lips parted, he reached up and gently wiped the trail of moisture from my cheek with the backs of his fingers. Then he let them sink into my hair and trail down my arm until he was holding my hand again. The mat of last year's leaves rustled underneath him as he shifted, resting on one elbow and looking at me. I wondered what he was seeing, what was in his mind. I wanted to know everything. I wanted to tell him everything.

"I used to think about you, you know," he said, then cleared his throat and looked away, as if the words made him too vulnerable.

"What?" I had to know what was behind the revelation. "When?"

"Back in chemistry class." Smirking a little, he picked up an acorn and tossed it over the bluff. "I used to think about you."

"You did not," I teased, but I wanted to believe it was true.

"Second row from the wall, second seat from the back. I remember." A little twist of his head added, *Yeah, take that.*

I tried to recall where I'd sat in chemistry class. He was right, actually. "You never said anything." I couldn't blame him, but I wished he had. It wasn't his responsibility to save me from myself during those dark months, but someone like him could have made such a difference. I needed a friend back then.

"I should have." His chest rose and fell in a sigh, like he was admitting to something he was ashamed of. "I wanted to. I mean, I was little when my mom died. I didn't remember that much about her, but I still knew what it was like to miss her, to wish she were here. Every time I saw you around school, I felt like I should tell you that. I was just . . . embarrassed to say it, I guess. I shouldn't have been. Ever since I was little, Mama B told me stories about how my mother was always headed someplace or other to help someone out with food, or offering to babysit somebody's kids, or staying up at the hospital to look after folks, or starting a prayer chain. I always felt like she'd expect me to do the right thing for people, but to tell you the truth, it was easier just to keep my head down and stay off my stepmother's radar."

My perspective shifted, new depth filling the profile of Blaine Underhill, like one of Ruth's drawings suddenly becoming real, taking on three dimensions from two. I'd never even considered that he and I had something in common—then, or now. I'd never considered that anyone could understand the pain I felt after losing my father, or that maybe, growing up in a blended family, he felt like a bit of an outsider himself. I'd never seen him as someone who might have an empty place inside, just like I did.

"Thanks," I said, toying with his fingers, watching his skin against mine. "But I don't blame you. I didn't exactly try to be approachable. I know I wasn't Miss Congeniality."

"What . . . you?" Both eyebrows shot up into the curls over his forehead.

The deer-in-the-headlights expression pulled a snicker from me. "I wanted to be one of those life-of-the-party girls. I just wasn't." I'd never admitted that to anyone until now.

"Yeah, me neither." His chin dipped downward, his lips curving into a little smirk.

"You can't even say that with a straight face," I pointed out, swatting his arm, almost like one of the fun girls. He made me feel like one of those giddy, silly types. Like Marilyn in algebra class, knowing she had everyone, including the teacher, hanging on her every pout and twist of the pinky finger.

Blaine tossed another acorn into the abyss, then flashed a look at me from beneath thick, dark lashes. "Looks to me like you turned out all right."

A hot flush started in my cheeks and seeped over my body.

The funny thing was, I'd been thinking exactly the same thing about him.

A little water clears us of this deed.

—Shakespeare, Macbeth
(Left by Dustin Henderson, writing an English paper on the run)

Chapter 16

I was walking barefoot along a dock, the day quiet and peaceful, the weathered decking radiating the leftover warmth of a waning afternoon. In the distance, eagles flew against the sun, their shadows sailing over the water, larger than it seemed they should be.

A sundress swished softly around my knees, caught the breeze and flipped upward. I stopped to smooth it. High overhead, the eagles locked talons and spiraled downward, their bodies whirling toward the water.

I stood frozen where I was, holding my breath, watching the spectacle with fear and awe.

The eagles spun faster and faster, bound in their dizzying embrace, the water's surface rushing closer.

"No!" I screamed. "Stop!" But the wind whipped my voice away.

In a fury of movement and sound, the birds disappeared below the edge of the dock, struck the water and plunged in. The surface turned placid and silent. I moved forward slowly, one step, then another, another, trying to gain a view.

Were they there? Were they alive?

Suddenly I was running toward the doors—the white ones that led to the chapel room of the funeral home. The ladies were filing through, crowding the entrance in their dark dresses and matching gloves. I stretched upward to see over the wall of hats and hair and mesh.

"Who is it?" I asked. "Whose funeral?" But the organ was playing so loudly that no one seemed to hear.

"Who?" I yelled louder, reaching for the woman in front of me. My hand was clothed in a black kid-leather glove, a floral pattern of beads at the wrist. I drew it back slightly, surprised, then realized I was looking through a mourner's netted veil. I shook the woman's shoulder, but she only continued moving along with the crowd, her wrist raising her veil slightly as she wiped her eyes. Amy?

"Amy? Amy, whose funeral?" I begged, but the crowd was pulling her away. Her shoulder slipped from my hand, a length of her veil trailing through my fingers. I tried to cling to it, but I couldn't. The ladies were pressing all around me now, squeezing past, pulling me into the chapel room. I didn't want to go. I remembered my father's body in the casket, my mother sitting numbly in the front pew, Clay in a black suit that was a miniature of the ones my father wore to church on Sunday. Clay's blond hair had been carefully combed by Ruth. Tears slowly streaked his sunburned cheeks.

The crowd was forcing me in, lifting me from my feet as I tried to turn and run. Behind me, I saw Ruth's family coming in the door, their heads bowed, the women's faces unveiled, sober beneath their tightly-bound hair, mesh prayer caps, and scarves. They were carrying food—heaping platters filled with *fleischballe* and *apfelsalat*. They stopped in the entry hall, seeming unwilling to enter the chapel area.

"Ruth!" Twisting, I reached for her, but she didn't respond. "Ruth!"

267

I was in the chamber then. The crowd parted and the doors began closing behind me, people fanning into the room, the old oak pews groaning softly as mourners selected seats. I tried for the door, but my body was heavy, filled with stone. The sundress from the dock had turned to thick, black wool, binding my legs so that I could barely move. The latch clicked into place as I grabbed the ornate brass handles and tried in vain to return to the vestibule. Outside, the Mennonite women sang a hymn, silverware clinking and plates rattling.

Inside the chapel there was silence, utter and complete—absent of coughing, sniffling, or the comforting words of a service. I turned slowly and realized the crowd was waiting for me, everyone motionless, expectant. In the front row my mother lifted a hand, palm up, indicating that I should file past the casket. I remembered the day of my father's funeral, when they'd forced me to stand beside his body as the mourners moved through. I'd felt sick. I couldn't look at him in that box, pale and gray, artificially painted with life. It seemed so impossible that he could be gone. Forever. That there was nothing I could do to bring him back.

I was angry with him for leaving us behind. I was angry with my mother for fighting with him, for making him so upset that he walked away from her and headed down to the basement to decompress. I'd heard the fight, but I didn't know what it was about. Was it worth his life?

I felt myself moving toward the casket now, not willingly but as if the floor were shifting under my feet to bring me to the front of the room, past the pulpit, where Reverend Hay stood silent and stoic, scarecrow-thin. His long face turned my way as I moved up the steps to the coffin.

Every eye in the room focused on me, following me to the casket, forcing me to gaze downward at the dark, freshly-polished shoes, the black slacks, the suit coat, the blue tie, the broad, muscular shoulders, and then the face.

"Clay?" I whispered, and in the gallery, a single mourner let out a long, animal-like wail. I collapsed on the floor, my legs suddenly uncooperative, refusing to keep me by Clay's side. I wanted to shake him from his slumber, tell him this wasn't funny. This was a twisted, sick joke.

Uncle Herbert and Uncle Charley, dressed in dark jackets, moved forward, slowly closing the casket. I crawled to the base, reached upward, clawed the wood, tried to scratch my way through. Another mourner put forth a long, loud wail, piercing the silence. . . .

Snapping upright, I took in a gush of air, felt my heart pounding as the chapel room, the mourners, and the image of my Clay in the coffin disappeared like a whiff of smoke. Only the scratching and the keening remained. I realized that Roger was outside the cottage, trying to get in.

For once I was thankful for Clay's hapless dog. Anything that could vanquish such a horrible dream had to be a gift. How could my mind come up with such terrible things—the eagles dead in the lake? Clay in my father's place, in the coffin? What kind of twisted, subconscious conjuring could create that?

Rubbing the sleep from my eyes, I scooted to the edge of the bed. The chill in the cottage slid over my skin, raising gooseflesh. Poor Roger was probably freezing out there. It was colder again tonight, and apparently I'd set the damper on the wood stove too low. My slippers were like ice on my feet. Frigid slices of air pressed through the pine floorboards, knifing at my legs as I moved through the interior of the cottage, dim except for the glow of the moon and the yard light, drifting through the windows. On the kitchen clock, the hour hand ticked into place with an electronic click. Four in the morning? Clay had left his poor dog outside overnight again, apparently.

On the porch, Roger heard me coming. He yipped, then furiously clawed the stoop, trying to dig his way through. The door rattled on its hinges as I reached for the latch. "Hang on, Roger." I pushed, then pulled the door, performing the magic combination that had always caused the latch to release. A blast of frigid night wind slipped through the opening, and I stood back, expecting the dog to barrel through in a flurry of hair and movement, but nothing happened.

"Come on, Roger," I called, impatient with the cold air rushing in. "Roger, *come on!*"

His toenails clattered on the frosty wood outside as he scampered down the steps. Apparently, he didn't want to come in; he wanted to play. At four in the morning.

When I poked my head around the door and looked out, he was standing in the glow of the yard light, watching me expectantly. Leave it to Clay's dog to decide the middle of the night was an opportune time for a game of catch-me-if-you-can.

"Roger, get in here." The sleepy voice had been replaced by the parental voice—the one employed only on rare occasions when I acted as an emergency babysitter for Trish's kids. Unfortunately, it didn't seem to be working on Roger. He stood his ground on the lawn. "All right, then. Stay there, if that's what you want." That always worked with Trish's kids. Once they knew that not all adults will chase you around the house with a peanut butter and jelly sandwich and beg you to eat it, the game was up. I got along really well with Lila, Laura, and little Nat. We had fun, even.

Roger needed to learn the Lila, Laura, and Nat lesson.

"Closing the door now," I warned, then followed through, and just as I'd expected, Roger returned to the porch and repeated the whimpering and scratching. After leaving the door shut long enough to make my point, I opened it again. "See, Aunt Heather really will leave you out there in the cold."

270

Once again, no Roger. I leaned out, poking my face into the chilly air. Roger was back on the lawn, barking and looking excited.

It occurred to me that I was playing mind games with a dog, and losing . . . at four in the morning. Which made it doubly stupid. Clearly, Roger wasn't in danger of freezing to death. He was too busy having fun. "All right, you're on your own." After closing and latching the door, I trundled back across the living room, adjusting the stove damper on the way. With a contented sigh, I was back in my bed, burrowing beneath the quilts by the time Roger clattered onto the porch again. Tomorrow, I'd have to tell Clay in no uncertain terms not to leave his dog outside at night. It was just cruel, irresponsible, and the dog was bothering other . . .

He was scratching at the door again, ready to continue our fun little game.

"Go away, Roger! Bad dog!" I nuzzled in deeper and pulled the covers around my ears. He'd give up in a minute or two. If I could outlast Lila and Laura, I could outlast Roger.

Roger scratched, whined, yipped, then knocked something over on the porch. Something heavy. It clattered down the steps.

"Stop it, Roger!" I yelled.

Another object tumbled off the porch. Firewood. Roger was unstacking my firewood. Ohhh, I was going to have something to say to Clay about this in the morning. In fact, if that dog didn't vacate my porch pretty soon, we weren't even going to make it until morning. I wouldn't be responsible for what happened if I had to go out there again. I really wouldn't.

Even the pillow mashed against my ears was no match for Roger's canine determination. The cottage walls were paper-thin. He might as well have been scratching at my bedpost.

"All right, *that's it!*" The covers flew off and I staggered from the bed, feeling fairly certain that, had anyone gotten in my way,

I could have done the Medusa thing and created a pillar of stone. Stalking to the front door, I clumsily put on my coat, then staggered around while trying to cram my feet into the nearest available footwear—my suede boots. I was going to hunt that dog down, grab him by the collar, take him up to the house, and dump him on Clay's bed. I . . .

For the first time, I noticed that Roger's bark was different somehow—not the playful squeaky yip I'd become accustomed to, but a low, demanding sound. Barking, then silence, then barking again—as if he were pausing to see whether anyone was listening. What if he wasn't playing? What if something was wrong? What if he was actually delivering a warning? Every once in a while, there was a story on the news about some trusted pet awakening a family, saving them from a house fire or carbon monoxide poisoning.

I sniffed the air. No smoky smell . . .

Could you get carbon monoxide poisoning from a wood stove? Probably. Maybe Roger had detected something. I didn't feel sick. Didn't people have headaches or other symptoms if they were breathing carbon monoxide?

Roger barked again, this time from somewhere near the corner of the cottage on the side that faced the main house. Was something wrong up there?

My mind conjured horrible images of Harmony House engulfed in flames, and I hurried to the kitchen window to check. Everything seemed normal, but my heart was fluttering unsteadily in my chest, my nerves on edge—such a far cry from the comfortable, sated feeling I'd had after visiting the eagle's nest and then going to the Waterbird to have a sandwich with Blaine. We'd sat there talking forever—not about anything particular or anything important. We'd talked about high school, my life, his life. I'd tried again to bring up Clay. *Let's not hash over family stuff tonight,* he'd said.

He'd walked me down to the cottage after he brought me home. Smiling, he lamented the fact that he couldn't take me out for another dancing lesson. He had a school board meeting at eight o'clock. He'd invited me to the big Valentine's soiree tomorrow night at the school, then kissed me, and I'd walked inside, floating on air. The lights were off in the big house, so I'd stayed in the cottage reading old copies of *Field and Stream* and watching for Clay to return. In spite of Blaine's vague reassurances, I wanted Clay to explain what I'd seen in Gnadenfeld and what I'd found in the truck. Unfortunately, my brother seemed to be making himself scarce. I'd finally fallen asleep on the sofa. Clay's truck still wasn't in the driveway later, when I moved to my bed.

Maybe that was why I'd had the dream. I was worried about him.

Maybe my dream was a warning. If Clay was mixed up in something, he could be keeping Blaine in the dark, just like all the rest of us. . . .

Stop, I told myself as I stumbled back to the door, my legs clumsy and uncooperative. *Stop letting your imagination get the best of you. Just go make sure everything's okay up at the house. It's probably fine.*

While I was up there, I'd leave a note in my brother's room, tell him we needed to talk before he left in the morning. Period.

An icy, watery wind slipped in the door as I opened it, the sharp sensation slicing away the last remnants of sleep with one quick stroke. Roger was standing between the cottage and the barn. He remained motionless, silent as I walked out.

"Roger?" My voice was hoarse, but the sound rebounded against the buildings and the frost-tipped woods.

Roger glanced my way, growled, then walked toward the center of the yard, out of view. Tugging my coat tighter around myself, I crossed the porch, moved down the steps, and instantly felt the cold ground penetrating my shoes. "Roger?" I called again. "Roger?"

A chill pressed over me, but it had nothing to do with the temperature outside. A branch crackled in the woods, and I had that eerie feeling again—the one that told me someone was nearby, watching. Fine hairs rose on my skin as Roger's barking drew me around the end of the cottage, until I could see the lower half of the yard. Roger was waiting halfway down the hill, near the ring of light from a gas lamp. He looked at me, barked, then turned toward the big house, barking twice more. A gust of wind whipped off the lake, driving me backward a step before I moved into the open, checked the main house, and then began a slow, visual sweep of the yard. Nothing out of the ordinary. Maybe Roger had spotted a possum or a raccoon marauding in the trash cans or . . .

Near the center of the gas lamp's glow, I saw what Roger wanted me to see: Clay's truck was there in the yard, not more than a hundred feet from the lakeshore. It rested at an odd angle, high-centered on the fig tree, the driver's side door hanging slightly ajar, the dome light giving the branches an eerie luminosity. I looked back and forth toward the house, scanned the set of tire tracks in the frost.

No wonder Roger was barking. Apparently Clay's truck had somehow rolled off the edge of the driveway and gone rogue. It seemed to be empty, and there was no sign of activity around it—no tracks other than Roger's. Maybe the impact had caused the door to pop open on its own?

Roger followed me to the truck and around the back of it, stood waiting as I checked the cab, then leaned over to look underneath. The Ladybug was beached like a whale on a sand bar, and it didn't look like it was going any farther without the help of a tow truck or maybe a crane to extricate it from the remains of the scraggly fig tree. Closing the door, I looked up the hill again. The windows in the house were dark, everyone apparently having slept right through the Ladybug's midnight rampage. Really, it was pure luck that it hadn't ended up in the lake.

Catching Roger's collar, I rubbed between his ears, feeling like I owed him an apology. He'd actually had a good reason for rousing me. Nothing could be done about this mess tonight, but it would be quite the source of family conversation in the morning. The uncs would have an exciting tale to share with all their buddies at the Waterbird. "Good boy," I told Roger. "You're a good boy. C'mon, let's go back inside now." Giving the Ladybug one last perplexed glance, I started toward the cottage.

Roger twisted against my grip, pulling backward and shaking his head, trying to wiggle out of the collar.

"Roger, stop!" I dragged him a little farther.

He yipped and fought like an animal possessed, squealing and gagging when the collar twisted tight. The chain pinched my finger, and I let go out of reflex. Roger was gone in an instant, bolting through the dim circle of light and disappearing on the other side of the truck. His insistent barking beckoned me to follow, and as I circumvented the vehicle my mind flashed back to the dream, to the chapel steps, each one bringing me closer to knowing what was inside the coffin, to seeing something I didn't want to see.

In front of the truck, Roger was sniffing the ground, digging at a mound of dirt, or trash, or . . . something . . . No, not trash . . . clothing . . . a coat . . .

I squinted, trying to make out the mass in shadow. Someone was lying face down in the frosty grass. . . .

My heart flipped unevenly. "Clay?" I ran the last few steps. A soft moan stirred the frosty air as I dropped to my knees.

"Clay!" I gasped, rolling him over, supporting his head. My fingers touched something warm and wet . . . blood?

"Clay, what happened?" Leaning closer, I searched for answers, thinking of the day I'd found him on the settee in the parlor, crashed after his all-nighter with Amy. Maybe he wasn't just tired that day, either. Maybe he'd passed out. Had he come home tonight not fully within his faculties, passed out in his truck, and let it roll down the hill? Had he hit his head when the truck crashed, or afterward when he was trying to get out? "Oh, Clay," I whispered. If not for the fig tree, he could have ended up in the lake. He *would* have ended up in the lake. I'd be calling the police right now, watching them pull my brother's body from the frigid water. . . .

"I'll go get help." I moved the hood of his jacket so that I could lay his head on it. His hand flailed clumsily, catching my arm just above the wrist. His fingers were as cold as the frost-tipped grass, barely able to cling.

"Nnn-no," he whispered, his face hidden in the shadow my body cast over him. "Just . . . the cot . . . cot-tage."

"Clay, you need to be looked after. We need to call a doctor. You shouldn't try to get up until someone checks your neck."

His grip tightened, and he shook violently. Rolling to the side, he pulled his knees under himself in an attempt to gain his feet. A violent cough racked his body, and his arms quivered inside his coat as he struggled to brace himself up.

"Unn-no, Hess . . . the cot . . . cot. . . tage. Just help . . . meeee . . ."

I understood his plea, even though I didn't want to. He was desperate to avoid having everyone else see him like this.

I knew it wasn't the best course of action, nor the safest, but I helped him up. Tremors wracked his body, and he swayed against me, leaning hard on my shoulders as we dragged trails in the frost, one unsteady, labored step, then another, across the hillside, the distance seeming an impossible barrier. In our wake, Roger followed quietly.

My lungs were burning by the time we reached the porch and

climbed up. My knees buckled and shook under the strain of lifting Clay's weight up each step and then finally through the door. The night chill followed us inside, clinging to us, and I laid my brother on the couch, then went back and closed the door. Roger trailed me nervously as I opened the damper wide and grabbed the quilts from the bed, piling them on top of Clay. His face and hands were white, icy cold. Turning on the lights, I saw the blood-streaked hair on the side of his head and bent to check it. The cut wasn't that large, but it had bled quite a bit, and the flesh around it had swollen into a nasty lump. Roger sat beside Clay and watched with concern as I made an ice pack and wrapped it in a kitchen towel. Moaning, Clay rolled onto his side and curled into a ball, his body trembling when the towel touched his head.

"Shhh," I soothed, looking under the towel, then carefully placing it back on my brother's hair. This wasn't an unfamiliar position for us. As a kid, Clay was always falling out of trees or having wrecks on his bike and coming home with injuries. "You've got a pretty good bump under there." The blood in his hair was crusty and tipped with ice. How long had he been out there? How much longer would he have made it in the cold, if Roger hadn't come looking for me? Roger might have saved his life.

Clay could be gone right now. We could be one of those families, huddled together in some hospital in the middle of the night, telling a police officer that we didn't know Clay had a substance abuse problem.

Despite what Blaine had told me, what he'd promised, was there any other possible explanation for Clay's behavior, for what had happened tonight? I wanted to come up with one, but I couldn't. How could Clay do this? How could he be so irresponsible? How could my mother have let it go on? Clay could have killed someone on the road. He could have killed himself.

"What happened to you?" I leaned over to him, tried to pry his eyes open, to tell whether his pupils were dilated. "Where were you tonight? What were you doing?"

Groaning softly, he batted my hand out of the way, taking over holding the ice pack. "G-guess . . . I . . . uhhh . . ." His brows squeezed, and his lips drew back, his teeth clenching as he changed positions slightly. "I'm . . . so c-cold." Another round of shivers racked his body.

"Clay, where were you tonight?" I sat on the coffee table, an ache spreading inside me but my voice surprisingly level, my mind still racing. *Should I call 9-1-1? Go wake up Mom and the uncs? Drive him to a hospital?* "What happened?"

His free hand dragged the quilts higher, then investigated the head wound, his fingertips quivering at the hairline, slipping under the ice pack slightly, then pulling back. "I bump . . . g-guess I bumped my head-d-d. . . ." He opened his eyes, then let them fall closed again.

"Clay!" I snapped, in the bossy, impatient big-sister voice from days gone by. "Clay, don't you dare go to sleep. You tell me what happened. Now. How did you end up out there?"

Slowly, he shook his head, the frosty tips of his hair melting into little round pools, some clear, some reddened with blood. Roger climbed onto the opposite end of the sofa and belly-crawled forward, resting his chin on Clay's leg. "Hey, bud-d-dy." Clay reached for the dog, but then just let his hand fall and sighed. "Got home . . . from . . . from Amy's, I th-think. The truck . . . rolled down . . . maybe. What . . . what time is . . . ?"

I glanced at the clock by the stove. "It's four thirty-five in the morning. It's freezing. What were you doing, sitting out there in your car?" Had he come home, parked the car, and passed out, or had he arrived home so messed up that he'd driven right off the end of the driveway? Had he gone out there to maybe take a hit of something where he wouldn't be seen? What? "Clay, what were you doing sitting in your car in the middle of the night? When did you get home? What time?"

Dragging his eyelids upward again, he moved the ice pack away from his head, the white towel now pink with watery blood. "I'm not . . . don't remember . . . coming. Here . . . take this. It's-s-s cold." He set the ice pack on the table and bunched the blankets under his chin. Roger looked at me, brows wrinkling, as if he were doing the same thing I was doing—trying to piece together the evening's events. Clay had been out on a date with Amy, come home and . . .

"You've been outside a long time, Clay. What were you doing in the truck? Why didn't you go in the house when you got home?"

"*Ummmph* . . . don't remem . . . ber," he muttered, turning his head away as if I were disturbing him. "Fell asleep . . . I guess. I was . . . listening . . ." His voice drifted off as he sank deeper into the pillows. " . . . to a song . . . I think."

"So you were listening to a song, and you fell asleep, and the truck rolled down the hill. Is that right?"

"Umm . . . maybe. Yeah-h-h. I g-guess."

He shivered again, his knees curling upward. I wanted to grab him and shake him, yell at him, *You know what, if it weren't for the fig tree, you'd be in the lake right now! If Roger hadn't been outside, you might have frozen to death! What is wrong with you? What are you doing to yourself?* "All right, listen. I'm going to go wake up Mom and the uncs, and we're taking you to the hospital. You need an MRI or something to check for a concussion." *And a toxicology scan, too.* We could kill two birds with one stone, and with a hospital report to back me up, we'd finally be able to face whatever Clay was dealing with. There would be no more room for denial, on anyone's part.

I put my hands on my knees to push to my feet. My legs were stiff and logy, like I'd just run a marathon.

Clay caught my wrist, holding me in place, his eyes opening, suddenly more alert. "No."

"Clay, you need help."

He blinked hard, pushed against the sofa, and lifted himself slightly, as if he intended to get up and stop me from leaving. "I just fell . . . asleep. I'm fine."

I couldn't say why I gave in to the pull, but I sank onto the table again, weary, confused, drawn in by the sudden intensity in my brother's face. "You're not fine, Clay. People who are fine don't fall asleep in the car and almost end up in a frozen lake. People who are *fine* don't carry vials and ziplock bags in their pants pockets. They don't sneak around in alleys, making secret pickups through back doors. You're not *fine*. You're on something, and that's why you passed out in the truck tonight, isn't it?"

"On some . . . thing?" His lip curled, flashing an eyetooth, and he blinked again, seeming alert but genuinely confused.

"Drugs, Clay." Finally, the chance to spell it out, to confront the problem at the source, and with evidence to back me up. "Drugs. How stupid do you think I am? How long have you been doing this? Does Mom know you're using? Do the uncs?" *Does Blaine? He promised me you were fine, that there was nothing to worry about. Was he fooled like everyone else? Would he lie for you?*

I jerked my arm back, but Clay's fingers squeezed tighter. "There's not . . . There's n-nothing to know." He forced a lopsided, wavering smile before a shiver coursed through him. "I'm not on dr-drugs, Hess. I was just . . . tired. Too m-many late nights."

"With Amy? With Amy, whom you're so crazy-serious about that you're texting with some chick from Fort Worth? Tara somebody? What's going on with you, Clay? That's not even like you. You've never been this way with people—lying, cheating, this whole line about taking over the restaurant, but you're never there. You're not exactly working yourself to death learning the business. If all of this is some sort of scam, you have to come clean. Now, Clay. Before things get any worse. You could have died tonight."

Tears pushed into my eyes, blurred my vision of him, spilled over. He met my gaze, and through the sheen of water, I saw the little brother who had been my only reason to keep moving forward through the most violent storm of my life.

The words I hadn't been able to find then came to me now. "I love you, Clay." I realized it had been years since I'd said that to anyone, since I'd allowed myself to feel the raw vulnerability of love. A tomb inside me cracked open, a slumbering spirit rising like Lazarus. I remembered how it felt to really love. "I don't want anything to happen to you."

His fingers slid down my wrist, and he took my hand in his, pulled it toward him, tucked my fingers under his chin like he used to when he was little. Fresh tears filled my eyes. I remembered all the nights I'd sat by his bed, comforted his hurts. All the times we'd walked in the woods together, when I'd played along with his games of Robin Hood and Star Wars.

"I love you, too, Hess," he whispered, his eyes earnest, compelling, tender, seeming completely lucid now. "I just fell asleep . . . and the p-parking brake . . . it's old. That's all. I promise . . . I'm not on dr-drugs, all right?"

"All right," I answered. Then I just sat watching him, trying to decide what should come next.

The river reveals its mysteries in its own time.

—*Anonymous*
(left by Herbert Hampton, undertaker, Moses Lake)

Chapter 17

Valentine's Day dawned bright and sunny. Clay was still sleeping on the cottage sofa when I walked up the hill for breakfast. I'd checked on him several times, and he seemed to be fine, just exhausted and embarrassed about what had happened. His admonitions not to worry Mom and the uncs swam in my head as I crossed the veranda. What possible good could come of my keeping it a secret that, if not for Roger, Clay might have drowned or been found on the lawn this morning, hypothermic or worse?

But in the back of my mind, there was a still, small voice. A memory of the look in Clay's eyes when he begged me not to tell. If I outed him to the family, would he do what he had often done in the past when one of his card castles came tumbling down—simply take off for parts unknown, disappear into the wide, wide world until he decided he was ready to turn up again? What if this time, he disappeared forever?

But did I really have it in me to tell Mom and the uncs what Clay wanted me to tell them—that the Ladybug was marooned on a fig tree because it had rolled down the hill unoccupied? They would never know the difference, of course. Morning sun had caught the lawn. The frost was already melting off in glistening, watery patches, Clay's footprints and mine bleeding together in an indiscriminate slug trail. Slipping through the back door, I took one last look at the truck, listing like a shipwreck as moisture drew streaks in the layer of grime. What was the right thing to do?

Inside the house, Mom and the uncs were gathered on the sun porch. Snatches of an ongoing conversation floated in the morning air, but the flow stopped abruptly when they heard me in the kitchen.

"Is that Heather?" Mom called.

"It's me." I leaned back from the counter to see if she was coming into the kitchen. When she didn't appear, I poured a cup of coffee and headed for the sun porch, glancing into Uncle Herbert's office as I passed. The desk was stacked with carefully-arranged piles of what looked like papers and receipts, and on the overhead shelf, an old mantel clock had been wound, its steady *ticktock* the only noise in the room.

Everyone turned my way in unison when I entered the sun porch. They were gathered around the wood stove, avoiding the winter chill at the edges of the room. The white shutters were closed on the back windows, barring the low-angled morning sun off the lake, which explained why Clay's marooned truck hadn't yet been noticed. I had the distinct feeling that I was interrupting something, though.

"So what's the deal with the guy working in the office?" I asked, stalling for time, trying to decide what to say about Clay. I couldn't just pretend I hadn't seen his vehicle balancing at a forty-five degree angle in the backyard.

Mom's lips curved upward. She was trying to look cucumber-cool this morning, but she wasn't. There was something haggard and haphazard about her appearance. She hadn't combed her hair and plaited it in the usual braid. It hung loose around her shoulders, and mascara circles rimmed her eyes, as if she'd gotten out of bed in a hurry and come straight downstairs. "He's just going over Uncle Herbert's books from the funeral business—you know, getting everything ready for the sale."

"The sale to you and Clay?" I was determined to pin her down. "Why would the books from the funeral home have anything to do with that? I thought you were buying the house so you could open a bed-and-breakfast, not a funeral home." I stressed *bed-and-breakfast*, so as to let her know that I didn't believe any of it. The entire time I'd been at Harmony Shores, I hadn't seen Mom working to refit the house for use as a bed-and-breakfast any more than I'd seen Clay frying catfish.

Mom squirmed in her chair. "We just want to get everything squared away." Scooting forward, she glanced out the side window toward the driveway, where the funeral sedan and the hearse were parked right now. "Have you seen Clay today?"

It was my turn to be uncomfortable. I felt the moment of truth upon me. To tell or not to tell? *Tell*, a voice insisted in my head. *Tell them about last night.*

But I remembered the way Clay looked at me—just the way he used to when the kids at school had picked on him or passed him over for a dodge ball game, or he'd forgotten to do some assignment and received a bad grade. Disappointing everyone and admitting failure, when he finally had to stop pretending and face it, was almost more than he could bear. All his life one big plan after another had come tumbling down upon him, like buildings constructed on sand. "He's down in the cottage, asleep. He locked himself out last night," I heard myself say. Guilt slipped over me, heavy and itchy. "His truck rolled down the hill. It's stuck on the fig tree."

That revelation, of course, was enough to end the morning conversation. Mom and the uncs hurried out to see about the truck. There was some discussion about waking Clay, but as usual, everyone was weirdly sympathetic to the fact that he'd kept himself out all night. They decided it would be just as well to let him rest, since there was really nothing he could do about moving the truck, anyway. In short order the uncs had made a few phone calls, and we were waiting for Blaine to show up with a tractor. He soon arrived wearing a faded barn jacket and jeans that were haphazardly tucked into the tops of muddy cowboy boots. The well-used boots called up a memory that unfurled, full and clear in my mind.

My father and I were at the farm when I was little. The barnyard was muddy, but he carried me over it, his feet sinking into the muck, his jeans tucked into the tops of his boots.

Closing my eyes now, I could smell the fresh scents of hay and Irish Spring soap. Dad set me on the tractor seat, then walked through the mud and opened the gate while I played with the steering wheel and the levers, pretending to drive. Finally, he climbed onto the seat behind me, and I half sat, half stood between his arms, my hands wrapped on the wheel next to his as the tractor chugged out of the barnyard. After we passed through the gate, we turned the wheel, pointing the tractor down the dusty lane that led past scrappy fencerows overgrown with mustang grapes and wild roses. The remaining animals on the farm were old and tired, seemingly unmotivated to challenge the ragtag barriers. My grandfather was known for being frugal to the point of patching the fences together until they were as threadbare as a hobo's pants. Inside the pasture, the grass was short, the cattle shearing it down near the soil.

I pointed to a broken place where only one wire and a cedar tree kept the little herd of Angus cattle from making their way to the lane, where high grass awaited.

"They could get out," I said, gazing back at the pasture. The bull looked massive and mean. I didn't know much about cattle, but my grandmother had warned me many times to stay out of the cow pasture because the bull liked to chase people.

"They won't get out," Dad assured me. "There's always been a fence there."

"But there's not a fence there now. Not really." Even at nine years old, I was inquisitive, prone to questioning—a kid who liked science fairs and wanted electronics kits for Christmas when my mom insisted on buying me sets of watercolors, blank journals, classic novels, musical instruments, and weaving looms, trying to bring out my sadly anorexic whimsical side. The truth was that I wanted to be like my dad, to align myself with him, not with her. My dad's world was measured, secure, reliable, while hers seemed unpredictable, like waves on a stormy sea.

In a weird way, I had a feeling that the very thing I disliked about her was what drew my father in. She ignited a different sort of passion in him, tossed glitter and spatters of bright color over his black-and-white life.

Then again, he was gone on business at least half of the time. He didn't have to deal with the parties she threw to keep herself occupied when he was away. On those nights, there might be strangers in the living room discussing art-for-art's-sake or rehearsing lines for community theater at all hours of the night, seemingly oblivious to the fact that there were children nearby who needed a snack and a bath, or a fresh diaper and a bedtime story. By eight years old, I had assumed responsibility for the practicalities of caring for Clay. Unless my father was there, I took care of baths, baby food, and read *Cat in the Hat* a million times.

That day on the tractor, Dad had rested his hands over mine on the steering wheel, forming a physical connection between us.

"I want you to listen to me, Heather. A lot of people out there are like those cows, and they can go along that way their whole lives. They get comfortable in one place, even when it's small and dirt bare, like that pasture. You know why they do that?"

I shook my head, thinking, *Because cows are stupid?* But I knew he was probably looking for a better answer than that.

"Because they don't use their minds," my father said. "Because they make assumptions. Those people don't change the world, Heather. They just live in it. They're like those cows who'll stand all their lives behind one strand of barbed wire, not because they can't get out, but because they're convinced they can't. You keep your mind sharp, all right? Always look for yourself. Never let other people tell you where the fences are."

"Okay, Dad," I answered. My nine-year-old mind only grasped the fringes of meaning behind his comment, but I understood the thing that mattered most. My father thought I was capable of great things. He believed in me.

When we started down the lane again, he put my hands on the wheel and pulled his own away, resting them on his knees, so that his arms were like steel bars on either side of me, holding me in place. "You drive," he said. "You're big enough."

All of a sudden, I felt ten feet tall.

That was one of the things I missed most about my dad, I realized now. He'd made me feel like I was capable of anything. I wished he were here now. I wanted him to tell me what to do about Clay, to make me believe that I could somehow solve the problem and have everyone in the family come out of it in one piece.

Watching Blaine on the tractor, I tried to conjure up that connection to my dad, to decide what he would be thinking, what advice he would give if he were with me. He loved Moses Lake so much. When we'd moved so he could bring the new Proxica plant online, he was so happy. But the longer we stayed, the more he'd been preoccupied, distant, lost in his own thoughts. Something was very wrong those weeks before he died. Moses Lake was wrapping itself around him, dragging him down in a way I couldn't understand.

Was history repeating itself? Was this place trying to claim my brother, as well?

Blaine glanced my way as he jumped down to unhook the chains from the Ladybug. He did a double take, cocking his head to one side as if he wondered why I was staring grimly into space. "Want me to drive the truck up the hill for you?" he asked Uncle Herbert.

Uncle Herbert shook his head. "Naw, that's all right. We'll get it. Doesn't look like too much damage done, except to my fig tree. Can't imagine how this truck ended up rolling off like that, though. Lucky it didn't make it to the lake."

I shuddered, thinking of my brother plunging into the icy water, sinking below the surface, passed out, unaware, trapped in the car. I remembered the dream that had awakened me last night. I saw Clay's face pale and gray, his body in my father's coffin. Even the warmth of the midmorning sun couldn't keep the chill off my body as the uncs studied the front of the truck like a couple of golfers gauging a putt, and Mom checked the inside of the cab, looking for something. *What?* I wondered, but there seemed to be no point in asking, so I started up the hill toward the house, instead. I needed a cup of coffee and a chance to clear my head.

The tractor passed by me on the way to the house, and Blaine parked on the pavement, then cut the engine. He was waiting when I reached the top of the hill. We went into the house for coffee.

"You all right?" he asked, leaning against the counter, his hands wrapped around the steaming cup. "Where's Clay, anyway? Seems like since he's the one responsible for the truck, he ought to be out there with the rest of us."

"He's still sleeping." I felt myself sneering when I said it. "And no, I'm not . . . all right. I . . ." My voice trembled, the admission cutting close to the core. "I don't know what to do, Blaine. I really just . . ." Tears pressed harder, and I blinked, stuffing down the emotion. Crying wouldn't do any good. What I needed to do was think. Think of a way to solve the mess my family was in. I needed help.

Blaine's hand slid up my arm, into my hair, offering comfort, solace, sympathy of a sort that made me want to fall into his arms and give into the need to lean on someone. "Hey, what's going on?"

I stiffened against the tears—not against his touch, but against the helplessness of the situation. My brother was in trouble, and I couldn't fix things. "That truck didn't roll down the hill on its own, Blaine. Clay was in it. He begged me not to tell anyone. He's lucky he didn't end up in the lake."

Blinking, drawing back a little, Blaine looked out the window. "Did you ask him how it happened?"

"I asked him, and he says there's nothing wrong, that I'm out of my mind for thinking he passed out in the truck because he was stoned or drunk when he came home. He says I'm crazy for wondering if he has a problem. Mom told me the same thing. Everyone just acts like I'm nuts." *Even you.* "But a normal, healthy, sober person doesn't fall asleep in a truck, in the cold, and roll down a hill. He passed out. He must have."

Blaine squinted toward the cottage. "Your brother's an adult, Heather. If he says . . ."

"*Ffff!*" I spat, rolling my eyes. "You don't know Clay very well. He's an overgrown adolescent, and every time he flakes out, my mother comes to his rescue. She makes excuses for him over and over again. That's why he is where he is right now."

"You don't give your brother much credit."

The frayed thread that had been holding my composure in place snapped with a twang, and my emotions rushed forth in all directions. Anger took the lead. "You know what—I'm tired of everyone making me out to be the bad guy! I'm not some kind of harpy with a sibling-rivalry issue, trying to pick on poor Clay. I love my brother. I'm worried about him."

I flailed a hand in the general direction of the path that the vehicle might have followed, if not for the fig tree, and thank God for that. There was no other way to explain the series of events that had saved my brother's life last night. Divine Providence had intervened, sparing Clay and all the rest of us. Watching Blaine move the truck, I'd also become aware that there was a gas lamp to the left of the fig tree and a gas meter to the right. If the truck had run over one of those on its way down the hill, the whole place could have gone up in a fireball. I wasn't even ready to put forth that possibility. "We could be fishing my brother out of the lake right now. Dead. We're just lucky we're not."

The vision from my dream came back, and all of a sudden I couldn't stand there any longer, thinking about what could have happened. "You know what, never mind." I pulled away, hurt that even Blaine didn't seem to be on my side.

"Heather, wait." He stepped toward me, but I moved out of reach, raising a hand to stop him.

"No. I'm tired of waiting for someone to finally tell me the truth around here. Whatever game they're playing, and whatever game you're playing, I'm sick of it. I don't want anything more to do with it. I'm done. I quit." I spun around and headed out the back door, hoping he wouldn't follow and perversely wishing he would.

He didn't, which was undoubtedly for the best.

Roger bounded off the front porch when I turned the corner to the cottage. Taking one look at me, he ducked his head and veered toward the woods, no doubt perceiving that a storm was underway. My anger dulled to a slow boil as I climbed the steps, and exhaustion followed, along with a sense of dread at the idea of talking to Clay again. After last night, I lacked the energy for sorting through more of his excuses. I wanted to curl up in a dark corner somewhere and forget it all. I wanted to get on a plane and go home and leave every bit of it behind.

Something collided with my toe and skittered across the decking—one of Roger's finds, no doubt—a stick or a bone. Opening the door to the cottage, I glanced down, stopping in midstride. In a ball of leaf-covered goo lay a small, square object that looked suspiciously like . . . my cell phone? I extricated it from the leaves and stared at it in awe. It *was* my iPhone, and thanks to the heavy-duty OtterBox case that Richard had given me for Christmas, it appeared to be in remarkably good shape. Awed by its reappearance, I stepped inside with an inordinate sense of relief, as if this were an omen of sorts. The connection to my normal existence had come back at the most opportune of times, reminding me that my mother, my brother, and Moses Lake had done just fine without me for years. Real life—a life I could predict and control, measure and plan—was just the touch of a button away.

In the space of a few minutes, I could book a flight home. I could tell Clay that, whenever he was ready to talk, I was ready to listen, but I couldn't play this cat-and-mouse game anymore. Maybe he would wake up. Maybe he would finally understand how serious his situation was.

But when I turned toward the sofa, it was empty. The shower was running, steam seeping underneath the bathroom door and dancing in the hallway light. Apparently Clay was up. He was doing better than I thought he'd be. Hopefully I could get some more coherent answers while I had him here alone.

Even as I thought it, I was afraid the answers would be the

same today as they had been yesterday. Wherever the truth lay, I was powerless to bring it into the open. Ultimately, you can't help someone who doesn't want to be helped.

I wiped off Roger's latest treasure in the kitchen and then went to the bedroom to unearth my charger and plug it in. When I did, the phone came to life as if nothing had ever happened. The sound of its awakening was music to my ears. Some measure of sanity returned to me as I scanned through the list of missed calls. Scores from Mel and a couple from Trish. Nothing from Richard. Mel had called five times this morning, already. Something must be up. I did a dial-back on the last call and looked out the window while I waited for Mel to answer his cell.

Oddly enough, Mel's newest underling, Rachel, picked up instead. She breathed a sigh of relief instead of saying hello. "Oh, Heather, thank goodness!" Rachel was twenty-nine years old, fresh out of a mini-cubicle in the design department, and hungry. Right now she sounded uncharacteristically frantic.

The tone of her voice made hairs prickle on the back of my neck. "Rachel, what's up? Why are you answering Mel's cell phone?" Typically Mel and his phone were never more than two feet apart. As far as I could tell, he slept with the thing. Even I didn't touch Mel's phone.

"He's been in the hospital, but he got out this morning. He went home to shower and pack some clothes," Rachel rushed out. "Itega wants another meeting, at their headquarters in Tokyo this time. Mel says for you to get your rear on a plane, tonight. He'll leave a package for you at LAX with your passport and anything else you need. I've already checked flights for you. It looks like the nearest airport is in Waco, right? I think I can get you out of there around five o'clock. I'll call you back with a flight number. Mel's leaving as soon as he can get packed. I just emailed everything to you for the Itega meeting. . . . Is there anything else you can think of?"

Is there anything else you can think of? I couldn't think at all. The world outside the window went out of focus. "Mel was in the hospital? What's wrong?"

Rachel snorted impatiently. "Something about blood sugar and ketoacidosis. But anyway, he says if you want to be his second on the Itega project, you better get out of Toad Waller, Texas, and show up in Japan by tomorrow. That's a direct quote, by the way." She breathed the words *second on the Itega project* with obvious awe and a back draft of envy that said *Yeah, I'd jump into your shoes in a heartbeat.*

Tossing my carry-on suitcase on the bed, I started grabbing clothes off the wooden chest and tried to propel my mind out of Moses Lake, to the airport, onto an international flight. "Well, but is it okay for him to travel? All the way to Japan?" I passed by the bathroom door, heard Clay drop something in the shower, felt my concentration veer off.

"Guess so. Must be," Rachel answered blandly, her tone seeming to say, *How is that my problem? There's a project at stake, for heaven's sake.* "Anyway, he didn't say. His mind's on the deal, *of course.*" She stressed the last words, silently pointing out that my mind should be on the deal, too. "Okay, you're confirmed for the flight. I'm texting you the information. What do you need me to send with Mel?"

Rachel's words, her complete lack of interest in anything but the deal, made me stop for an instant. I heard an echo in the words, had a sense of déjà vu. They reminded me of someone. *Was that me? Is that who I've been?*

The shower turned off across the hall as I told Rachel to grab a couple of clean suits and blouses from the stash of I-slept-at-the-office clothes in my closet there. After making a list and promising to send everything with Mel, Rachel reiterated the flight time and hung up. My mind sputtered, refusing to fully kick into gear. A flight to Japan on the red-eye. I'd go to sleep on this side of the world and wake up on the other, thousands of miles from Texas. Maybe that was the best thing. Maybe it was a blessing in disguise. I was driving myself crazy in Moses Lake, getting nowhere, hopelessly outnumbered.

Every muscle in my body tightened, adrenaline streaking through me like an electrical current, making my breath come in fragments and my pulse speed up as if I were preparing for a race. Bracing my hands on the bed frame, I took in moist, cool air that smelled of lake water and damp wooden window frames, the scents pulling me back to the here and now. The flight out of Waco wasn't for hours yet. I could at least try to talk to Clay one more time.

I heard the bathroom door open as I was zipping my suitcase, and a moment later Clay poked his head into the room, his chin dropping when he saw me lowering the carryon to the floor and clipping my laptop case in place. "Listen, Hess," he said. "About last night. It was no big . . ."

I lifted a hand, held it out like a stop sign. "Don't. Okay? You know what, Clay? I love you. I can't even really express how much, but if you won't face the truth, if you're not ready to admit that you've got a problem, there's nothing I can do. You need help, and you need it now. Before something terrible happens."

Combing wet curls from his face, he gave me an earnest, perfectly sober look. He'd washed the blood away, smoothed his hair over the cut to hide it. Everything looked perfectly normal. "It's not like that. I promise. I just fell asleep—burning the candle at both ends too much lately. I'm sorry I scared you. Don't go, all right?"

I closed my eyes, turned away, then grabbed my wallet and stuck

LISA WINGATE

it into the computer case. "I have to go. I'm flying to Japan this evening." My thoughts sped forward through the day, demands and expectations pulling and tugging, at war with emotions and needs. I tried to focus on the practical. "I want to go over and visit Ruth before I leave. I'll cut over to Waco from there and leave the car locked at the airport with the keys under the seat. You and Mom can just bring an extra key and pick it up, okay? That will be easiest." I didn't want some long good-bye. I couldn't handle it.

"Okay, sure, but Hess . . ."

A long breath spilled from me as I looked at my brother and saw all the years and experiences, heartbreaks and changes we had experienced together. Tears welled, and I swallowed the sentiments before they could seep out. "You need help, Clay. When you're ready, call me. I'll do whatever it takes to get you what you need. I'll pay for it. I'll arrange it. I'll help you find the right resources. Anything. I want you to be okay. I need you to be, but I can't do it for you. Please, please, whatever's going on, don't drag the uncs into it. They don't deserve that. They're too old to recover from it. Just think it all through, Clay, all right? I'm only a phone call away. Tell Mom and the uncs I'll be in touch in a day or two. Hopefully we can still figure out something about the property deal."

Even though I told myself I was doing the right thing, guilt burned in every part of me. I pushed it back, hugged my baby brother, held on until it was too painful to cling any longer, and then gathered my things and walked out the door.

Clouds gathered on the horizon as I hurried up the hill to the driveway and loaded my things into the sedan I'd driven the day before. Inside the house, the family was probably having breakfast, but I didn't go in to check. I couldn't handle some emotional scene if they tried to talk me out of leaving. I also had the sense that it would be even worse if they didn't. Suspecting that your family

295

doesn't want you around is much better than actually knowing it for sure.

It's better this way, I told myself as I started the car and rolled down the driveway. *We all know it, really. I don't belong here.*

I'd call later, after I'd left Harmony House behind. *No hard feelings,* I'd say. *A project came through at work. I had to fly to Japan.* . . .

I'd try, long distance, to convince Mom that Clay needed help.

Maybe that would be enough. I couldn't keep beating my head against a brick wall any longer while my life, my career, went down the tubes. It was too painful. Beyond that, it wasn't logical. Sooner or later, when a design isn't going to work, you have to scrap it and start over.

Could you scrap your family, leave behind the places you came from?

I tried to convince myself that it was possible as I passed the Moses Lake sign.

Welcome to Moses Lake.
If you're lucky enough to be at the lake, you're lucky enough.
Come back soon!

I wouldn't be back soon. Or ever. This time it was really good-bye. The thought lay like a lump of stone in my chest.

How about a pair of cricket killers? Blaine's voice whispered through the car, flowing over me like the draft from the heater. *We got your steel toes, your stacked heels, your Mary Janes, flip-flops, wool socks, boat shoes, whites, browns, and blues. What's your pleasure?*

The heavy feeling slid slowly to my stomach, like a swallow of something too warm. My throat swelled and prickled.

I'm not going to cry. This is stupid.

I reached for the iPhone, punched up the text messages. Mel, Mel, Mel, Mel . . . Gary the dentist . . . Mel, Mel . . . Richard. Only one from Richard, in all this time. Judging by the first couple of words, it looked like he was checking in about the real estate contracts. Just business.

I was hurt, but in a strange way, not disappointed. At some point during the last few days, I'd gotten over wishing that Richard was *the one*. And if I really let myself admit it, I knew why. That night with Blaine, dancing beneath the stars at Blue Moon Bay, had made my relationship with Richard seem inconsequential. Richard was absolutely right in wanting the kind of passion that made you remember someone's birthday, that made thinking of that person as natural as breathing, little puffs of memory coming in the course of normal events, life-giving, like oxygen—a smile, a laugh, the color of an eye, the touch of a hand, the sound of a voice.

I couldn't even describe the exact color of Richard's eyes—grayish, I thought.

Blaine's eyes were the color of warm earth. They sparkled like topaz when he laughed.

But Blaine wasn't *the one*. He wasn't the one, but I wanted someone . . . like him. Someone who fit into my life plan. Someone who wasn't helping my brother keep secrets and lying to me about it. . . .

My mind swirled with questions as I wound along the quiet highway, shards of sunlight and thready winter shade slipping soundlessly over my car, dry amber grasses bending and waving in the wakes of other vehicles. When I passed by the gate to the family farm, I looked the other way. I didn't want to reminisce about the place or to admit to myself that I'd let this trip come and go, and I still hadn't faced the cellar door that had haunted my nightmares. I supposed I never would. After this meeting in Japan, I'd go back to my life. The farm would be sold—either by some miraculous resurrection of the broker offer, or through Clay's arrangement, whatever it really was. If Clay managed to pull it off, the property would eventually end up in the hands of the Underhills, perhaps. Blaine's father had become land wealthy over the years, taking on property and buildings when the mortgages were in arrears. . . .

I tried not to think about it the rest of the way to Ruth's. It was too painful to consider. Maybe Clay would come to his senses. Maybe he'd call me and ask for help.

Turning into the dairy, I waited for the quiet peace of that place to slip over me, to soothe away my hesitations, but all I could think was, *This might be the last time I see Ruth. It probably is the last time. . . .*

It would be, of course. I wasn't coming back. Once I got home, I'd be busy with all the normal things, consumed as usual. Maybe I'd try to do a little better job of maintaining connections, in the human sense. I could make more time to get together with Trish, go with her to take the kids to a playground or the zoo. Maybe I'd join a gym, get involved at a church—start going more than a few times a year.

My visit to Moses Lake had brought one realization at least: I wasn't really accomplishing anything by hiding from God and from my past. All these years of being angry hadn't brought my father back or changed what had happened. I'd only succeeded in making the past part of the future, spreading it like oil, a slick, sticky coating over everything. I'd allowed my father's death to claim my life, as well. I was like Ruth's sister, Lydia, bitter and old before my time. I couched it under the guise of being dedicated to my career, but deep inside, I knew the truth.

When I got back to Seattle, I was going to change things. Be more open, have a talk with Mel about his health and the ridiculous hours we were keeping. . . .

The ideas were still cycling in my head when I knocked on the door at Ruth's, and Mary and Emily let me in. Ruth was surprised to find me there much earlier than expected. I explained to her that I had a flight out today; I had to get back to work. She only frowned, as if she were looking through me, seeing all the things I'd kept hidden, even from myself.

She didn't question me, though. Ruth was never confrontational. It wasn't her nature. She only watched me as we moved to the sun porch and sat down, Mary and Emily trailing behind us.

Emily whispered to Mary, and Mary moved to my chair, cupping a hand near my ear to ask where Roger was.

"Oh, Roger couldn't come," I admitted apologetically. "I'm sorry. I couldn't bring him today."

Emily's lip pooched, her jumper bunching on her shoulders as she reached up to smooth escaped corkscrews from her face. "How come?"

"I'm not going back to Moses Lake from here, so Roger wouldn't have a way to get home." I felt like a heel, a fun-killer, a promise-breaker for failing to bring Roger to visit again. Beyond that, there was the tug that seemed to haunt me when I looked at these two little redheaded girls in their starched dresses, their smooth skin like china-doll porcelain. They were adorable and sweet, and they made me feel like the most interesting person in the universe, as if they were certain I had the answers to all the important questions. I loved that feeling. I loved the touch of Emily's hand on mine, the inquisitive look in Mary's bright hazel eyes.

I wanted to be somebody's mom someday, to have a family of my own, to bake bread and talk about puppies and go for long walks along a riverbank somewhere. I wanted first days of school and summer vacations, first cars and graduations. But the possibility seemed so far away.

"Can Roger come next time?" Mary pulled an escaped strand of hair over her nose and twisted it into a rope, her eyes crossing as she watched it.

The questions and Ruth's unwavering regard hemmed me into an uncomfortable position. "Maybe Clay can bring him next time."

In the corner of my vision, Ruth laid a finger alongside her lips, then shoed the girls from the room, so we could talk. "I'm glad you've come by," she said, but there was a melancholy tone in the words. I wasn't accustomed to seeing Ruth like that. Even sick with cancer, she had an upbeat, peaceful quality that I admired . . . craved, really. I wanted to be more like Ruth, more serene, more certain that God was laying the path, watching over my shoulder, guiding each step. Planning to give me what was best for me in the future.

Ruth was good at faith in the way that I was good at my job, I realized. She worked at it. *Nothing worth doing comes easily,* had always been one of her favorite sayings.

"I didn't find any more of your drawings," I told her. "I'm sorry. I never made it down to the basement to look. I'll send Clay a text and ask him to search the rest of the house."

Ruth shook her head. "No matter." She leaned across the arm of her chair—an aging leather recliner with a crocheted afghan over it. "I only wanted them for you to see. You always asked me about them, but I was never ready to tell those stories. Do you remember?"

"I remember." How many times had I secretly watched her as strokes of charcoal became figures, and figures became people? "I used to peek from the window sometimes, when you were out on the porch. I remember watching you draw the circus performers. I guess those were the ones Lydia saw when she decided she wanted to run away."

Ruth smiled and nodded. "I never saw the circus people, but

Lydia told me about them—every detail she could remember. I was
on the hillside when she sneaked down and peeked under their tent.
I stayed there with Naomi and the other girls, because I was too
afraid. Of all of us, Lydia was the only one who saw the circus. She
was the only one who had the courage. After that, we played circus
on the old farm horses, but we had to go on Lydia's say. She was
the one who knew how the circus looked, so she became the master
of us all in the circus game. We did her chores for her, so that she
would let us play circus. It is easy to do that sometimes—let fear
make hostages of us, don't you think?"

"Yes, I guess so." I was uncomfortable again. Ruth was pushing
harder than usual, perhaps because she knew that I was leaving.
She had a point she wanted to get across, but she would never
come right out and say it. In general, the Mennonites I'd met in
Gnadenfeld were unfailingly polite, gentle, and unassuming in a
way that most people are not

"Why do you think we let fear hold us prisoner?" She turned
her attention to the magazine rack on the floor, looking for something. "Our pastor spoke on this last Sunday. I've been pondering
it since then."

I didn't have to consider the answer too deeply. It was on the tip
of my mind already. "It's easier that way—to do what's safe, what
you think you're supposed to do," I admitted.

"I believe that may be right." She nodded solemnly, her lips
forming a downward arc, as if she were acquiescing for the both
of us. "But then you never see the circus."

"True." I let out a laugh-breath to break the tension, and Ruth
smiled.

"You can regret it all your life, not seeing the circus." She wagged
a finger at me. "Your sister might make a slave out of you."

"If there were a circus nearby, I'd take you to it, Ruth."

She checked the doorway before answering, "At this point in my life, I'd go."

We laughed again, together this time, and then Ruth resumed digging through the magazine rack, searching for something among local newspapers saved for fire starters. "Well, I can't find it just now," she admitted, sinking back in her chair, breathing more heavily. The shallow sound of it reminded me of how sick she was. I considered asking about her prognosis, but I didn't want to dampen our last visit.

"I had a drawing for you. I unearthed it upstairs with some of my old things. Perhaps Mary and Emily have run off with it." Frowning, she patted the arm of the chair and craned toward the doorway, as if she were considering calling for the girls. "Well, when I find it, I'll send it to you. You should have it."

"What is it?" Resting my elbows on my knees, I leaned toward her and looked at the magazine rack, hoping to spot a bit of art paper peeking out. Maybe she'd missed it in there. "What is it a drawing of?"

"Soldiers," she answered, and I felt the slightest twinge of disappointment. I was hoping for the one of Lydia, as a reminder, perhaps. I felt a connection to Lydia, but I still wanted to be Naomi.

"Soldiers? I remember seeing you draw soldiers, more than once, actually." I'd seen soldiers, nuns, other children, a priest. I'd always suspected that at least some of the drawings were inspired by Ruth's past. While we worked in my uncle's kitchen, Ruth had told me stories about her arrival in New York, along with a group of orphans permitted to immigrate from Germany after the war. They were housed in a tall, dark building that was drafty, cold, and undersupplied, but the nuns and a priest were kind to them. There was no place to play, but when the weather was nice Father and the nuns took them to the park. Some of the people there gave them harsh looks, because they spoke German, Yiddish, and Plautdietsch, the only languages they knew.

"These were special soldiers," she said. "You would recognize them, I think, if you saw them. Did you know that your uncles and your grandfather saved Naomi and me? In order to come to America after the war, orphans required a sponsor, one who would guarantee that expenses for the child's care would be arranged for, and that the child would not be consuming public funds. Your grandfather was in America at the end of the war. I'm sure you know that he was injured at Normandy and sent home to his parents' farm, while your uncles continued to serve with the occupation forces in Europe. Your uncles arranged for Naomi and me to leave Germany with a group of orphans and come to the United States. Your grandfather was our sponsor here. He knew we were Mennonite girls, of course, and some of his neighbors were Mennonites. He felt that he could find a place for us among those of our own faith, and he made it his business to do so."

"He did?" My father hadn't talked much about his family history, nor had my grandfather, who never fully recovered from his war injuries, emotionally or physically. I always knew that my grandfather was a good man, a good farmer and a hard worker, but he was largely a stranger to me. "No one ever told me any of that."

Ruth didn't seem surprised. She glanced over the edge of the chair again, as if she were wishing for the drawing. "We never talked about it after we came here and were adopted into a Gnadenfeld family. Oh, your uncles looked in on us. They made certain we were faring well, but they never spoke about how they found us. I suppose they wanted to forget the things they saw in that war, and they thought it was better for us to forget. I suppose they believed it best not to remind us."

"Remind you of what?" I probed, carefully.

Ruth seemed to consider whether she should answer, then she relaxed in her chair, her fingers steepled in front of her like knobby hackberry branches growing together. "There was a man in Berlin. He took in children, orphans like us, and gave them shelter. Lydia had married by this time, but her husband was German, just coming home from the war, and he had nothing. He could not even provide for himself and Lydia. He told us he'd heard about a man who took in orphans, and we went there, Naomi and I. The man was Russian. He seemed kind enough. There were beds and food, other young people, parentless like us. We felt that the Lord had delivered us, that our prayers had been answered. We had no way of knowing what he expected in return for our care."

Ruth's gaze lifted slightly, met mine, her blue eyes narrow and intense, drawing me forward in my seat. "We were Mennonite girls from a tiny village. We had never known of such a thing, but after a day or so, we began to hear of it from the other children. We would have to do what the man wanted, they said. Bad things would happen if we didn't, and then we would be left on the street to starve, to suffer in the cold. We were so afraid, Naomi and I. It is a terrible choice between your soul and your stomach. A frightening choice for a child. We sneaked out on the fire escape after all the children were asleep, to pray, or to run away, but the ladder had been taken off. We could only go down so far, and below was concrete."

Pausing, Ruth peered over the arm of her chair, as if she were remembering. I imagined her and Naomi, young teenagers, innocents, trapped and desperate for a way out. "We sat and we prayed, and then we heard voices, American voices. When I opened my eyes, there were men looking at us, American soldiers, four of them. One of them spoke to us in very bad German. 'Are you a little Mennonite girl?' he asked and pointed to our prayer caps. We nodded and told him that we were. 'Come down here,' he told us. 'You don't belong in that place.' We told him we couldn't get down, and he said, 'You jump and we'll catch you in my overcoat.'"

Wagging a finger in the air, Ruth met my gaze. "I have relived that day many times since then, that moment of decision. I think it is appropriate that we were on the fire escape, don't you? God walks with us through the fires of life, all of them. Even this latest one, this cancer. Some good will come of it. It brought you here, for one thing."

Moisture gathered in my eyes, and I blinked hard to keep it from showing. How could Ruth believe that good could come from the disease ravaging her body? How could she say that my visits in any way compensated for what she was going through?

A chuckle broke the silence, and her eyes sparkled with a thought she kept private at first, then revealed. "Your uncle Herbert was the strongest man I ever met, and the most handsome. I fell in love with him that day, when he took us away. A girlish sort of love. I was so young."

I blinked, shocked. I'd never known there was so much history between Ruth and my uncles, and certainly not that sort. "Did you ever tell him?"

She adjusted the scarf covering her hair, looking flustered, as if she'd gotten caught up in the moment and blurted out something she hadn't meant to. "Oh, of course not. I was so young, and I was afraid. I kept those feelings to myself, and he married after he came home, and eventually so did I. I did what was expected and married within the Mennonite faith. The family who adopted Naomi and me had been good to us. I wanted to please them. I wanted to live a life that was humble and plain." She laughed to herself, swatting a hand in the air as if to wave away an alternate past, like smoke.

"You never told him in all these years?" Suddenly I had a greater understanding of Ruth's devotion to my uncles, of the special relationship between the three of them. I understood why Uncle Herbert saved Ruth's drawings, why she went out of her way to bring canned goods to him or to bake the German foods that he loved, even though my aunt hated the smell of vinegar and sauerkraut in the house. Ruth loved him, and in some capacity, that affection was mutual.

Watching her now, I understood the way I'd caught her looking at him on the porch the other day. I'd always thought that his reserved nature, his lack of interest in communication frustrated Ruth, but in reality, the emotion in her eyes had been longing, the regret of an opportunity missed, a desire that would never be fulfilled.

Uncle Herbert had never seemed fully happy in his marriage to Aunt Esther, even though the marriage had provided him with a position in the community and a big house in which to operate his business. Aunt Esther had run his life with an iron fist, fussed about pomp and circumstance and their social standing. Ruth, I suspected, had never been close to her husband, who was considerably older than she. How might their lives have been different, if they'd chosen each other instead?

"Fear can cause you to miss more than just a peek under the circus tent." Ruth pointed at me as if she knew what was in my mind.

Mary and Emily came in the back door then, and the moment was gone. We talked and watched them play for a while before sharing a small lunch with the family. Ruth was tiring when we finished, and I felt the flight time closing in on me, as well.

"I'd better go," I told her. "Thanks for lunch and . . . well, for everything." My throat burned as we walked to the door, Mary and Emily trailing along. Ruth wrapped her arm in mine, leaning on me, her steps unsteady.

We were walking together for the last time, and both of us knew it.

"You are always welcome here anytime," she offered, as if to deny the fact that this was really good-bye, probably forever. "You could put off your flight and stay a few days. Wherever you are headed isn't going anywhere. There's no need to run off."

I wanted to accept her offer. Everything in me yearned to slow down, take some time to think, to call Mel and tell him he needed to go back to the hospital and look after his health—and by the way, I wasn't coming home. I'd decided to become a Mennonite. Take up milking cows and baking zwieback, maybe design a few dental clinics on the side for extra cash. But instead I said, "Oh, I'm not running. I'm just going on this trip for work, and then back home."

"I suppose it depends on your definition of the word." She squeezed my arm, then watched the girls dash onto the lawn to play horsey on a live oak branch that dipped near the ground. "Home."

I patted her hand but didn't answer. What was I supposed to say? *Moses Lake isn't home. I've always hated this place. . . . But there was this one night out at Blue Moon Bay . . . and this trip to the bluffs to watch the eagles fly . . . and this moment in the shoe department of the hardware store. . . .*

We hugged good-bye. She held on to my hand for a moment afterward, as if she meant to lecture me again. I halfway wanted it to work this time.

"Oh . . . I've remembered where the drawing of your grandfather and your uncles disappeared to." She let her head fall back, silently scoffing at herself. "I gave it to your brother yesterday evening. He came by here to borrow a shovel and a few canning jars." Fanning a hand by her head, she rolled her eyes heavenward. "Goodness! My mind these days. I think the medications might be worse than the disease."

I stopped where I was. "Clay borrowed a shovel and jars from

307

you? Last night?" What in the world did that add up to? "Why didn't he just get those things from Uncle Herbert's place?"

Ruth's brow creased. "He was doing something out at your grandparents' old farm, I think. He said there wasn't a shovel out there and it was closer to come here and borrow one. He didn't have time to go back to Moses Lake before dark. I gave the drawing to him, so he could bring it to you. I wasn't feeling well, and I thought I might not be able to visit with you today, but the Lord is good. I woke feeling quite chipper this morning. Your brother hasn't given you the drawing, then?"

"No. Not yet. He got in late." No sense in worrying Ruth about last night's fiasco with the Ladybug. "It's probably still in his truck. I'll ask him to mail it to me."

I turned to leave, then paused again. "Are you sure Clay said he was working out at the farm? There have always been plenty of tools out there. As far as I could tell when Clay and I stopped by there for gas the other day, not a thing has been moved or sold off. . . ." *Leave it be, leave it alone, Heather. Don't get involved. Head for the airport. Don't get sucked in again.*

But even as I thought it, I felt like that little Mennonite girl standing on the hill above the big top, trying to decide whether to play it safe or go take a peek at the circus.

You either think on your feet, or sink on your feet.
—Dale Tazinski, LPC
(Fifty pounds lighter on his feet, after joining Weight Watchers)

Chapter 18

The airport in Waco was quiet and easy to deal with. Short-term parking was free, so leaving the car wouldn't cost a thing. My exit from Texas was growing simpler by the minute, as if heavenly blessings were raining down upon it. There was even a bit of Proxica PR on the airport wall. *Feeding a New Generation,* the lighted sign read.

I found my gate and sat in the waiting area, my thumb rubbing slow circles over the slick plastic iPhone case. The broker offer was set to expire tomorrow. The day after Valentine's Day. I needed to call Richard, see if there was any possibility of having the offer extended a week, or even two. By then Clay would probably have lost interest in Moses Lake. Hopefully if I kept trying, I could convince him to admit that he had a serious problem and needed help.

What if he doesn't? What if something terrible happens, like last night but worse? The question was uncomfortable and confining. Inconvenient.

Maybe I was wrong to be leaving. I could still tell Mel he'd have to handle Japan on his own. Maybe I should stay and keep fighting.

But how? No one in my family would listen. They were all fully determined that I was the one in the wrong, the pariah taking my sibling-rivalry issues out on poor Clay. Even if I told them everything that had happened last night, Clay would counter with his story about having fallen asleep in the car, and they would believe it because it was easier to believe, more pleasant.

I dialed Richard's number, put the phone to my ear and sank in the chair, letting my head fall back against the wall, my eyes closed.

Richard's voice was all business. "Richard Lawson."

"It's me." For an instant I wished I could rekindle the intimacy that had been between us. It was Valentine's Day, after all. How was he planning to spend the evening?

Maybe I didn't want to know.

"Heather?" He sounded as if I'd been gone for a month, and he wasn't sure who *It's me* might be. I waited for him to ask how I was, how things were going. I wanted to pour out the whole story to someone. I wanted someone to be waiting for me at the Seattle airport whenever I finally made it home from Japan. I thought of Gary the dentist and his family. I wanted my return to be like his.

The longing hurt.

"What can I do for you?" Richard's tone conveyed that he was pressed for time.

I swallowed my disappointment and moved right to the heart of the matter. "Any chance of getting the broker to extend the offer on the property—a week, maybe two? I think this thing will work itself out, given a little time." As soon as I had a moment to collect my thoughts, I'd get in touch with Donny and let him know in no uncertain terms that he needed to extricate his father and Uncle Charley from the mess my mother and brother had created.

"I don't see that happening." Richard's answer sent my hopes spiraling downward. "Proxica needs to seal the deal immediately to minimize any chance of information leaks. It's hard to keep things under wraps in a small town. I know that the broker is working an offer on another piece of property nearby. They'll ink that immediately after this offer expires. They're getting nervous, with the AP picking up the Kentucky story."

"The AP . . . What? What Kentucky story?" Not only was I out of sync with my family, but now Richard was speaking in riddles, too.

"The pesticide case. There's a class-action suit against them in Kentucky—the thing about that pesticide, Armidryn. Proxica was using it widely on their farms until about the midnineties, when there were some court cases about a similar pesticide in Europe— they say the chemicals show up in water wells, farm produce, cow's milk, that sort of thing, and cause health problems. That it stays in the soil for years.

"Anyway, at the time, Proxica denied that Armidryn was similar to the European pesticide, and they produced lab results and chemical specs to prove it. They did quietly quit using Armidryn on their farms and around their production facilities, though, and they patented a new formula, Armidryn II, that was supposed to be even safer. But some recent soil and water tests in Kentucky have shown high residual concentrations on some Proxica farms.

"The suspicion is that when Proxica needed to quickly and quietly get rid of their stores of Armidryn I, they may have buried it on some of their farms. There are also some accusations that either they continued shipping Armidryn I but claimed it was Armidryn II, or that Armidryn II isn't as biodegradable and safe as Proxica claimed. None of it has been proven, though. Chances are, it'll be tied up in court for years. Proxica isn't about to just knuckle under. They can't."

He paused, talked to someone on his end of the phone, then came back. "But you can see why they wouldn't want to be trying to close land deals for future expansion after the court-case story goes national. The paranoia over something like that could cause all kinds of protests, problems with zoning, trouble with the locals and so forth."

Trouble with the locals . . .

I sat up, opened my eyes, stared numbly at the windows, where the day was dimming as planes came and went. Everything seemed to stop, growing dark around the edges as I looked down the hall, taking in a skewed view of the illuminated Proxica sign.

Feeding a New Generation . . .

My father was so proud of that slogan, of Proxica's commitment to healthy foods and to providing jobs for rural families. Were the facilities in Kentucky anything like the ones that would be built in Moses Lake? Anything like the ones that were already in Gnadenfeld? Had they been shipping this chemical . . . this Armidryn II to farms in our area? Could some of the original Armidryn stores have been buried here?

"What kind of health problems?" The fluorescent lights behind the sign flickered. A mother and a little girl walked past, pushing an old woman in a wheelchair. I thought of Ruth. She and her husband had lived on a Proxica farm for years, ever since the plant and the farms went in. My father helped Ruth's husband get the job. "What kind of health problems do they think Armidryn causes, Richard?"

"I didn't read up on it too extensively. My paralegal pulled a few things while she was getting the file together for the land deal. I skimmed it. Try Google. The conspiracy theorists are all over it. You'll find what you need." His answer was bland, matter-of-fact, giving no indication that he had any concept of the string of Black Cats exploding inside me. "Listen, Heather, I'm headed into a last-minute mediation. I'm going to have to sign off."

I stood up as if to run after him. My carry-on bag fell over, hitting the floor with a smack. "Wait. Wait a minute! You knew about this? You were aware of this lawsuit, this . . . issue when you were putting the deal together? You never said anything to me?"

"I figured you knew. You usually do your homework, Heather." He was getting impatient now. I wanted to reach through the phone and grab him by that perfectly-pressed collar of his. "Besides, you and Mel both have more connections to Proxica than I do."

I slapped a hand to my throat, swallowing a ball of ashes. "You figured I *knew*? You figured I *knew*, that I just didn't care if a company that's under a class-action lawsuit moved into my father's hometown? On land that's been in my family forever?" What kind of a horrible, disgusting mercenary did he think I was? How could he, the man I was dating, the man I thought I wanted to marry, think that of me?

The answer was clear enough. I hadn't given him any reason not to. He'd only seen me as the person I appeared to be.

Maybe as the person I was?

Ruth had cancer . . . "How could you think I would be okay with that?"

He responded with a harsh, cynical sound, something between a laugh and a hiss. "Oh, come on, Heather. You couldn't wait to get rid of the place. You hated it. You wanted to stick it to your family and the whole town."

I squatted down to pick up my carryon, stayed there with my head resting in my hand. "I would never . . ."

"Mel knew about the Kentucky lawsuit. He wasn't worried about it. By the time anything happens in terms of a court case, the facility in Moses Lake will be a reality, and your firm will be out of the loop. You're going to tell me that Mel never said anything to you? You're going to tell me the Kentucky issue never came up?"

"No, it never came up. Mel didn't mention anything like that.

I would never help some . . . some corporate entity that's hurting people—that's *poisoning* people. Who would, Richard? What kind of a person would do that intentionally?" Was this the sort of life I'd built for myself, a thief among thieves, a person who would do whatever it took to turn a profit?

"Listen, I've got to go," he repeated. "I'm due in the meeting."

"You know what . . . ? Good-bye." This time I meant it with every fiber of my being. I hoped I never saw Richard's face again. Or Mel's. The idea of spending time in the same room with either one of them disgusted me.

The walls of the airport dissolved in a blur of movement as I grabbed my things and hurried toward the door. Passing the Proxica sign, I wanted to pick up my suitcase and smash the plastic, obliterate the innocuous-sounding slogan.

After throwing my belongings into the car, I stopped long enough to text Mel and tell him I wouldn't be making it to Japan—today or anytime. I ended by letting him know exactly how I felt about the class-action lawsuit against Proxica in Kentucky. Before I could change my mind, I took a breath, pushed *Send*, and set down the phone.

My thoughts rushed ahead, forming connections, the events of the past few days coming together like pieces of a puzzle as I pulled out of the parking lot and started toward Moses Lake. Everything that had confused me solidified into a scenario that made perfect sense. Shovels, ziplock bags, vials . . . Clay's hint that he knew the broker offer on the property had something to do with development, the fact that he just happened to be dating a girl who worked at Proxica's Gnadenfeld plant, his sudden interest in Moses Lake . . .

All along, even in the face of overwhelming evidence that seemed to indicate it, I couldn't quite picture my brother succumbing to a drug problem. It just wasn't like Clay to get involved in something like that.

But it was like him to take up a cause.

A cause that may have turned dangerous. . . .

What if, all those times I'd felt like someone was watching us at Harmony House, someone really was? Maybe I hadn't been turning shadows into ghosts but had been seeing people lurking. People who were trying to figure out how much my brother knew, where he was hiding the proof, and who he'd told.

I had to find out the truth, and if I was right about what Clay was doing, I had to stop him before something terrible happened.

When I made it back to Moses Lake, the high-school gym was lit up like a Christmas tree. Western swing music poured from the gaps around the windows of the WPA-era stone building. Under the portico hung stars made of rebar framing and red Christmas lights with the paint partially scraped off, so that portions of the stars twinkled a gaudy combination of red and white. The sight of them brought back memories. They had been a fixture at every high-school dance and community gathering I'd missed out on during my senior year. I'd seen them hanging in the eaves, sitting on the stage, poised in the bleachers, or out front under the portico, as I hurried through the gym from one building to the other. Cheerleaders hauled them back and forth while decorating for pep rallies and socials, giggling and working in pairs to lug the stars around the gym and decide where to position them.

I'd hated those stars. They were one more reason to be angry with my father, to hate what he had done to me by taking the job at the Gnadenfeld plant and moving us to Moses Lake.

After he was gone, the fact that I'd barely spoken to him the last three months of his life, the fact that I'd hated him, was one more reason to hate myself. The stars reminded me of all of that.

Tonight, Reverend Hay was standing under the portico with the high-school principal from back in the day, Burt Lacey, along with Uncle Charley, and Mr. Hall, who'd been president of the school board when I graduated and probably still was. They stopped me before I could get to the door, but I couldn't focus on their greetings. My mind was awash in thoughts and questions, coming in short, rapid fire bursts. *Armidryn, cancer, Proxica. Did Dad know?* I wanted to find my mother, to force her to tell me exactly what was happening that last week before my father died. Did he know what Proxica was doing? Did he suspect that something dangerous had been buried as the facilities were being built? Had he found evidence? Was that why he had been acting so strangely before the accident?

Accident . . . Was there a chance that my father's shooting wasn't an accident or a suicide, but a murder?

"Couldn't get a plane out tonight after all, huh?" Uncle Charley stretched out an arm, pulling me in for a shoulder hug. "We've been having us a little school board meetin', right here during the community Valentine's shindig . . . sorta on the sly, so to speak. There's a bond issue about to pass, and we gotta figure out how to get Moses Lake ready for the twenty-first century without letting Claire Anne Underhill tear down this old place and put up some glass-and-metal crackerbox. Kids shouldn't go to school in something that feels like a hospital. A place oughta have history, and this old building's strong. It'll go another hundred years, if we treat it right."

Lips curving upward contemplatively, he gazed into the eaves, small puffs of steam floating from his nostrils, the stars reflecting off his glasses. "Young boys mustered up to go to war in this old buildin', danced a last dance with their best gals, said good-bye to their folks, stole a kiss from their sweeties behind the bleachers. You can't replace history like that."

I shifted impatiently from one foot to the other, Uncle Charley's arm weighing heavily on my shoulders, his vision clouding my mind. I pictured young men with duffel bags—a change of clothes, clean socks, and their parents' fears packed inside—their dreams on hold. I pictured Ruth and her sister coming to this school, the ladies of the community gathering around them, taking in those frightened, damaged Mennonite girls, telling them they were safe within these walls. I pictured my father and his friends running across the gymnasium during pep rallies, their blue-and-gold Moses Lake football jerseys loose with no shoulder pads underneath as they tore through paper signs reading *Smear the Spartans!* or *Beat the Bulldogs!*

The images haunted me like unwanted ghosts, even as I tried to push them away. I couldn't think about that now. "Uncle Charley, there's a lot involved in rehabbing a building of this age. The existing structure would have to be closely studied and assessed, and plans drawn up to provide for an expansion that would blend with the historic structure. It's not impossible. The right person could do it. When I get back to Seattle, I could help you find—"

"We think you're the right person," Uncle Charley interrupted, squeezing my shoulders and hanging on in a way that insisted I stay there. "We got a majority of the school board standin' right here. A quorum, so to speak. We wanna hire you. You got history here, and family. You know what this old buildin' means. Somebody who's not a Lakesider won't understand that."

I was momentarily stunned silent, my mental dialog flowing in a half-dozen different directions. *Stay longer in Moses Lake? Design the new high school. Armidryn . . . Proxica . . . Did Dad know? Ruth has cancer. . . .*

Inside the door, people passed by, a woman laughing as she tried to loop a chef's apron over the neck of a man carrying a bag of charcoal. He waved her off, ducked and turned, but I didn't have to see his face or hers to know their identities: Blaine and his secretary, Marilyn, having a little fun at the community Valentine's gathering.

I spotted my mother crossing the empty space in the center of the gym. My focus narrowed again. "I . . . I have to catch Mom right now," I murmured, and then twisted out of Uncle Charley's grasp. I couldn't think about anything beyond the moment. I had to find out what Clay was into and figure out how to keep him from putting himself in danger.

Uncle Charley and the rest of them gave me strange looks as I turned and hurried to the door beneath the red glow of a Christmas-light star. Mom was walking toward the back of the gym, moving with a look of purpose as she disappeared behind a line of milling high-school kids at a carnival-style basketball-toss game. A tangle of women at the cakewalk, decked out for Valentine's Day in red sweaters and jackets appliquéd with fabric hearts, blocked my path across the floor. I recognized Blaine's stepmother among them. Unfortunately, she spotted me, too. I didn't have time for a catfight, but I could tell one was headed my way.

"Have you seen my mother or Clay?" I asked, trying to sidestep her as she moved to block my exit. I caught myself looking around the room for Blaine. Where was he, anyway? Marilyn was walking back across the gym now, looking bored and disappointed.

Mrs. Underhill's lips pursed, her perfectly penciled eyebrows arching together in an expression of sympathy and concern that surprised me. She turned a shoulder to the cakewalk activity, her hand coming to rest lightly on my arm. "Heather, I suppose you've heard about this silly plan of theirs."

"Plan?" Did she know about the issues with Proxica?

"This foolishness about taking over Catfish Charley's and Harmony Shores." She batted her free hand in the air, then fanned herself with it. "I mean, really. A bed-and-breakfast in a *funeral home*. Who in their right mind would want to stay there?"

I fidgeted, looking past her, trying to spot my mother. "Mrs. Underhill, I don't know what my family's plans are. I really don't have time to talk right now. Do you know where I can find my mother or my brother?"

A cursory look over her shoulder and a shrug answered my question, and then she homed in on me again. "You know, life in a remote place—a place like Moses Lake—isn't for everyone." Her voice grew louder as a band warmed up on stage. Around the room, the carnival games were being taken down to allow a dance to begin. "Oh, people think it *seems* wonderful. Move to the lake, get away from it all. But things aren't always easy in a small community. It doesn't suit some people."

"I'm sure it doesn't." Where had my mother gone?

"Your father knew that. Goodness, he didn't want to admit it, of course, but he knew this place was wrong for your mother—too quiet, too slow-paced. That's why he never brought her back here to live after they married. He was afraid something would happen like . . . well . . . what happened."

Suddenly she had my full attention. "What do you mean, *what happened*? Mrs. Underhill, if there's something you'd like to tell me, please just spit it out."

She turned her face away slightly, touched manicured nail tips delicately just above her mouth, careful to avoid her lipstick. "I shouldn't say . . . but, well, there were rumors, of course. It was all over town. She wasn't very discreet."

"Discreet about what?"

Her eyes darted from side to side, checking the perimeter. "Well, the man she was carrying on with, of course. Some out-of-towner staying in the rental cabins below the Waterbird. Your mother was seen around town with him back then. Your father found them out. The teller at the bank heard your parents fighting about it. There is an intercom in the drive-through lane, after all."

She patted my arm, and I backed away from her, horrified. I didn't need this right now. I had to focus on the present, to dissuade Clay from his reckless need to save the world single-handedly.

Mrs. Underhill clucked her tongue. "Oh my. I can see that you didn't know *any* of this. I should have kept it to myself. It's ancient history now, isn't it, sugar? I only meant to help you see that this place isn't . . . healthy for your mama. Your uncles are such sweet men, but they don't need to be burdened with . . . hangers-on."

I couldn't listen to any more. Pulling away, I crossed the room to the punch bowl to ask one of the fishermen from the Waterbird if he'd seen my mother.

"She was here a minute ago." He glanced at the game warden, who was standing beside him in uniform. "You see where she went, Mart?"

The game warden nodded toward the folded-up bleachers. "I think she went with Andrea and Dustin to put some carnival games in the storage closet. They're probably back there behind the bleachers."

I thanked them and walked down the sideline of the basketball court, then rounded the wall of folded-up bleachers. My mother was at the other end of the cavernous, shadowy space where exercise pads, stacks of chairs, and gym equipment had been stored. I could see her standing at the end of the long hallway that led to the locker rooms. The hallway was dark, but by the angle of her body, I could tell she was talking to someone on her cell phone.

My feet fell silently as I hurried along the side wall toward her, passing the storage room, where people were moving boxes. Something fell inside the room, and I hitched a step, the toe of my shoe squeaking on the wooden floor. Mom turned around quickly, uncrossed her arms, snapped her phone shut, and dropped it into her pocket, as if she'd been caught at something.

"Heather," she said, smoothing her shirt self-consciously as I drew closer. "Clay said that you'd left for the airport."

Under other circumstances, I might have been hurt by the fact that she was disappointed to find me there, but at that moment I didn't care. In addition to the issues with Proxica and Clay, Claire Underhill's revelation was now whipping my thoughts into a froth. She'd confirmed one of my greatest fears: My mother had been cheating on my father. The man I'd seen her with all those years ago was her lover, and my father had found them out. He'd died knowing that his wife had betrayed him. Maybe he'd even died *because* she'd betrayed him. . . .

"I left for the airport, but I came back. I need to see Clay. Where is he?"

"He and Amy haven't made it here yet." She cast a worried look toward the front door, then tried to cover it up. "They must have decided to go somewhere else for a Valentine's date."

Irritation stiffened every muscle in my body. "You know and I know that's not true. Where are they, and what are they doing?"

She lifted her chin, seeming offended that I had confronted her. "What is it that you're asking about exactly, Heather?"

"Clay's whereabouts. And while we're on the subject, why don't you tell me what he's up to?"

Mom's lips pressed together in a tight, stubborn line, and a retaining wall inside me cracked. Everything I'd been holding back since my father's death burst free. "You know what? Come to think of it, I want the truth. I want you to tell me what happened to Dad.

I want to know why you ended up in police custody that night. I want you to tell me what was going on with you and that man. I saw you with him, you know."

Finally, after so many years, I'd found the courage to just come right out and say it. "You were having an affair, weren't you? You were cheating on Dad. That's why he was so upset. That's why you two were fighting the day he died."

Mom's eyes went wide. "For heaven's sake, Heather. Of course I wasn't having an . . . How could you even say something so reprehensible to me?"

I shifted away, felt the heat rising on my anger, the pot boiling. Of course, this was somehow all about her, all about the ways in which I was causing her pain by trying to get at the truth. "Why the suitcases, then?"

"Suitcases?" Blinking, she cocked her head to one side.

"The suitcases. There were suitcases packed, waiting by the bedroom door upstairs. The day Dad died."

Her hand stretched out and rubbed up and down my arm, bunching the sleeve of my jacket. "Heather, you were so traumatized that day. You don't know what you—"

"Don't tell me what I saw!" My voice rose just as the music stopped. Through the cracks in the bleachers, I saw heads turning our way. Clenching my teeth, I swallowed hard, balled my fists at my sides, and shrugged her hand away. "Don't you *dare* tell me what I saw. I know what I saw. I know what was going on when he died. I saw you with a man. I saw him drive up, and I saw you get in his car. I know Dad was upset about it. Did you realize that the teller at the bank heard you fighting about it? That it was all over town?"

Mom shifted nervously. "Heather, it wasn't what it . . . I wasn't . . ."

"You weren't what? Meeting with your lover? Planning to run

out on us?" I tried to imagine how my father must have felt, but I couldn't fathom it. He loved my mother, worshiped her, supported her art, defended her, chose her over his family. He gave up everything for her, and she had repaid him with betrayal.

Tears pressed my eyes and brimmed on the bottom, giving my vision a watery rim. I swiped them away impatiently. "I *saw* you with him. I saw you sneaking around by the barn with that man."

Her eyes flashed wide. "It wasn't an affair."

Her denial only poured acid in old wounds. Even after all these years, she didn't love me enough to give me the one thing I needed most—the truth. "Was Dad . . . ? After he found out, was he . . . ?" I couldn't bring myself to say the words *depressed* or *suicidal.* "Was it an accident, or was it on purpose? Did he mean to do it? Was that why it took the life insurance company so long to settle the policy? Was that why the police questioned you? Or did they think you and your lover planned it?"

Mom's mouth dropped open. She pulled in air. "Now listen here, Heather . . ." I sensed that I'd crossed some invisible line, stepped into territory from which there would be no graceful retreat. I didn't care.

"I need to know what happened to my father." Tears spilled over, drew trails down my cheeks—hot, then cold. A sob wrenched from me, and I pressed a hand to my lips to stop the trembling. "I have a right to know."

She closed her eyes, sighed, then finally looked at me again. "Heather, I should have told you a long time ago, but it was just so hard, coping with everything . . . after."

"Hard?" I wiped my eyes impatiently, frustrated with myself for breaking down in front of her. "Hard? How do you think it was for Clay, for me? He was our dad."

"And he was my husband," she countered, as if to measure my

grief against hers. "And we may have had our issues. We were two very different people who fell in love when we were practically children and ran away together on a whim, but we were trying to make it all work."

I thought of the countless times, even before my father's death, that she had made our lives difficult, with her flightiness, her need for constant change, her insistence on running off to symposiums, poetry conferences, and music festivals, leaving my dad with the problem of arranging for our care and paying for her antics. "My father gave everything to you. Everything he had. Everything we had," I hissed.

Her jaw formed a hard line, the muscles clenching with determination. This had always been the way with my mother and me. At each other's throats, in each other's sore spots. "That man, the man you saw me with, was not who you think. He was an agent with the Department of Justice. He told me that if I didn't cooperate, they'd send your father to prison. I was terrified, Heather. Where would we have ended up then? I didn't have any way of supporting two children, of paying for lawyers and dealing with a husband in federal prison."

"Federal prison?" My voice rose again, a sardonic laugh following the words. What kind of story was she coming up with now? What kind of nonsense? "My father never did anything that would have gotten him in trouble with the government or anyone else." My father was the most honest, upright man I'd ever known. His faith and his principles ran deep.

"He worked for Proxica." Mom's gaze darted around, checked the storage room door cautiously. "They were investigating Proxica for disposing of chemicals illegally on their farms, and I don't even know what else. The workers on Proxica farms had no idea what they were handling, what they might be living with right around their homes, underneath the yards where their kids were playing. What could be getting into their food and water. The Justice Department thought your father was taking money to keep quiet. He'd gotten a bonus for bringing the Proxica operation in Kentucky on line in record time. The Justice Department wanted me to provide documents—look for things in your father's briefcase.

"I was scared, Heather. I didn't know what to do. I cooperated for a while. I thought I could give them what they needed, and your father would be cleared. I knew he wouldn't willingly participate in something that was hurting people, especially so near Moses Lake. I thought I could clear his name, and then, other than looking for a new job, our lives would go on as normal. What choice did I have? You were about to go to college, but we had Clay to raise. Your father was dealing with losing his parents. I thought I could . . . get us out of this mess. I could do what the Justice Department wanted, and it would all go away."

"But it didn't." My mind tripped and stumbled, dropping over a precipice, ending in a place I'd never anticipated. "It didn't go away, did it?"

Gooseflesh rose on her arms, and she rubbed it away. "No, it didn't. Your father heard rumors in town. He heard that I'd been seen with someone—a man. He confronted me about it. I had to tell him the truth. I begged him to pack up, to take us out of Moses Lake. If he wasn't working for Proxica anymore, he wouldn't be of use to the Justice Department, I thought. But your father wouldn't do it. He wanted to stay here, look into it himself, gather evidence, see if his bosses knew what was going on, see if there really were barrels of chemicals being buried.

"Someone ran your father off the road one night on the way home from work, and he was afraid it wasn't an accident. That's why he got that stupid shotgun out of the closet. That's why I packed the suitcases. That's why we were fighting before he died. I wanted to just get in the car and go, all of us. I told him if he wouldn't leave with us, that I'd take both of you and I'd leave him.

"I didn't mean it. I just wanted him to come with us. I just wanted us to run." She looked away, concealing whatever emotions she felt.

I stood mute, scrambling to assimilate the tidal wave of information, to blend it into what I knew about my life. What I thought I knew. "Why did the police take you away right after he died? Why were you gone overnight? If all this is true, why keep it a secret for so many years? Why didn't you tell me?"

Her shoulders quaked as though a shiver had rattled her, and she hugged herself tighter. "They put me in a room, and they told me that if I said anything about what had happened, if I did anything to hamper the government's case, they'd see that I was prosecuted for murder. I didn't care by then. I didn't care about anything. I just wanted to . . . crawl into the casket with your dad. I didn't know how I was going to survive, how I would take care of you kids. I didn't know if whoever ran your father off the road might come after us. I didn't know where to go or what to do. I was so lost without him. All those months afterward, I couldn't breathe. I couldn't function.

"By the time I started to take in air again, the issue with Proxica had been swept under the rug. I never heard from the agent again, and life went on. Your father's bosses played golf with governors and congressmen. Who knows what happened? Who knows how many payoffs they gave out? I couldn't fight it. I could barely keep my head above water."

I pressed my hand over my eyes. On the dance floor, the song changed to a polka melody that seemed incongruous with the tension between my mother and me. "This is what Clay is into, isn't it? That's why he's here, and that's why you're here. You two are trying to finish what Dad started."

"Yes," she admitted. "A few months ago, when we were initially talking about selling the land, things began coming up. I heard that Ruth had cancer, and that her husband had died of cancer, and that one of her nephews had leukemia. Clay and I started talking to the uncs more about it, and we began putting it all together. All of us wanted to do what we could to see Proxica punished."

"All of us?" I rubbed my fingers over a rush of blood that made my forehead seem to swell painfully. "Everyone? The whole family? The uncs, you, Clay. You were all in on it?"

She nodded. I watched her in narrow slices through my fingertips. She was looking at the bleachers, not at me. Words wedged in my throat, then came out all at once. "And none of you thought you could trust me? None of you had the confidence in me to tell me what was going on and why?"

"You were connected to Proxica, Heather. Richard let something slip during our talks about the real-estate deal—something about the broker having a corporate buyer in a hurry for the farm property that was zoned for a commercial operation, which ours was, because the family had run the dairy there years ago. Between that and things Amy had overheard at work, we could see what was happening. It will be over my dead body that Proxica puts so much as a tire track on any land we own."

I shifted from one foot to the other, vacillating between anger and shock. "You should have told me. You should have *trusted* me. I loved my father. I would have done *anything* for him. It killed me when he died, and now you've put Clay in the same danger. Do you realize that he could have died last night? He was in that truck when it rolled down the hill. He almost ended up in the lake. Where is he? Where is he right now?"

Kneading her hands in front of herself, she looked toward the door. "He and Amy were going to get into the Proxica plant tonight

to see if they could find some old records about the Armidryn
and where it might have been disposed of. Amy said there would
only be a skeleton crew there right now, with it being second shift
and Valentine's Day. She and Clay were planning to take whatever
they found out to your grandparents' farm after that. Clay has
been working out there." Her lips formed a worried line as she
checked her watch.

He's been working out there. Everything made sense now, including Clay's disappearing acts that seemed to have nothing to
do with learning to run a catfish restaurant.

"I'm going out to the farm," I told her, but the idea of revisiting that place, the place where my father had died, sent a wave of
nausea through me, created a foreboding that rooted me where I
stood. I didn't want to go there alone. For some reason, I thought
of Blaine. "He knew, didn't he? Blaine knew what you and Clay
were doing. He was in on it, too."

"Yes," she admitted. "He knew, but . . ."

I'd heard all I needed to hear. Without waiting for anything
more, I turned away and left her there, then headed for the door.
Somehow, I had to get my brother out of this mess. Tonight. Before
tragedy struck our family a second time.

The more silent the surface, the deeper the water.
—*Fisherman's proverb*
(Left by Jim Shivers, an angler watching rain make rivers)

Chapter 19

The tires squealed and the back end fishtailed as I rounded the last few curves on the two-lane road, headed for the farm. I had to get Clay to end this crazy plot before it blew up in his face. If someone connected to Proxica had run my father off the road when he drilled too close to their secrets sixteen years ago, why wouldn't they come after Clay now? Whatever information my brother had discovered should be turned over to the authorities, and the sooner the better.

If, by interfering with the family's plan, I angered them and none of them ever spoke to me again, I'd gladly live with that to know that Clay was safe. Had it never occurred to him that there were state and national agencies—actual branches of law enforcement—charged with regulating companies like Proxica, with protecting the public health? Hadn't he thought about the fact that, by digging into the situation himself, he might actually be contaminating evidence or worse yet, putting Proxica on alert so that they could further conceal their crimes before a government agency could investigate? If Clay had proof of this Armidryn thing, why was he still playing vigilante? Why were the rest of them going along with it? Why were the uncs, my mother, even Blaine willing to let Clay put himself at risk?

Blaine . . .

I couldn't even think about him right now, about what he'd done. Was it his job to distract me, to give the rest of them room to maneuver, to convince me that there might be something special for me in Moses Lake, a chance at everything I'd always wanted but couldn't find—family, a connection, a history . . . love?

I pushed the word away, not even knowing what it meant anymore, what it should mean. Maybe I was too damaged, too messed up to ever find it. Maybe I just wasn't meant for family life. The people you loved, the people who loved you were supposed to be the ones you could trust, the ones who trusted you. Yet everyone here assumed that I knew what Proxica was doing, and I just didn't care. They thought I was the kind of person who had no personal code to live by, who would do anything to come out ahead in business.

My boss saw that person when he looked at me, and so did Richard.

What kind of people assumed the worst of you?

Not people who care about you. As Reverend Hay had put it, *Love sees in you the best possible version of yourself.*

Emotion rose in my throat, and I pushed it away impatiently. I just needed to settle things here and get away, to go home to Seattle and really think. Maybe Seattle wasn't even the place for me, but there had to be someplace where I would fit—somewhere I could combine work and meaning. I had money in the bank. I could take some time off, start looking, send resumes all over the world—perhaps land in an exotic location. Paris or Milan. Istanbul.

There were no ties to bind me. None at all. I could move to the far side of the world, and if Proxica did expand in Moses Lake, I would never even know it.

The idea pinched, bringing a painful little nip as I rounded the final bend in the road and the farm gateway materialized at the edge of the headlight's glow. My father had risked his career, maybe even his life, to stop Proxica sixteen years ago. If they expanded to the family farm, it would be as if the concrete and steel were being laid over his grave. As if his life, his sacrifice didn't matter. Proxica had won once, and if I had come to Moses Lake for no other reason, perhaps that was it: Maybe I'd been brought here for an atonement of sorts. Perhaps I was meant to help finish what my father started. Perhaps the one way I could finally make peace with his death was to protect my family and this place my father loved.

Determination filled me, feeling hot, solid, and righteous as I skidded into the driveway and careened up the lane. If Clay was still here, we were going to have a serious talk, and if not I would figure out exactly what kind of evidence he'd been collecting and storing, how long he'd been doing it, and what kind of laws he was breaking. Hadn't it occurred to him that he could end up in jail for sneaking into Proxica facilities? Was that what he was doing last night before the incident with the Ladybug?

Another possibility struck me, the impact sudden and startling. What if someone had tried to bash his skull in last night and that was why he didn't want the family to know about the accident? Was he afraid Mom or the uncs would blow his cover if they found out? Was he worried that they'd call an end to this thing?

Goose bumps prickled under my sweater. Leaning close to the window, I scouted the growth of trees along the lane, dark and silky in the moonlight, thick enough to hide anything, anyone.

My heart fluttered in my neck as the car rattled over a cattle guard at the low-water crossing, then kicked up gravel in the washed-out ruts on the other side. Could those same people have followed him tonight, could they have caught up with him at the Proxica plant? Was that why he and Amy hadn't shown up at the dance?

A cold feeling settled over my skin as I topped the hill and the trees parted, revealing the farmyard. The two-story house my grandparents had built was silent, the curtains drawn, the windows black, the porch steps littered with pecan shucks and fallen branches now that the renter had moved away. No vehicles were parked out front, but in the small turn-of-the-century stone house next door, a light shone. Would Clay have been doing his work in there? In the house where we'd lived during those months before everything in Moses Lake went terribly wrong? The house where my father died?

I let the car roll to a stop in front of it, sat behind the wheel, the burn of my anger abandoning me when I needed it most. As far as I knew, the stone house had been locked since my father died. How could Clay bring himself to go inside? How could he spend time there? What happened in that place sixteen years ago was the end of everything for us. The end of our family. The end of the laughter and the gaudy Crayola-colored days of childhood. The small, brown door in my nightmares was there.

Even in my dreams, I didn't have the courage to step through that door.

I closed my eyes, tried to imagine it, tried to see myself turning the handle, passing through, finally reaching the other side, finally remembering whatever had happened in the minutes after the gunshot exploded through the little house. All these years, those moments had been blank. I remembered the thunderous sound, the cellar door, and then the memory jumped forward, skipping like film that had been spliced, a broken piece cut out. The next thing I knew, I was bolting through the kitchen, looking for Clay, wanting to save him from seeing . . .

From seeing what?

What had I witnessed that day?

My mother said she had run into the cellar from the subterranean steps on the back of the house, stopped me before I could get down the stairs, before I could view the horrible scene below.

But there was blood on my hands. I remembered it now. I could see it in my mind, see my hands underneath the water at the kitchen sink, rubbing, trembling, a voice—my own voice—keening in my ear.

I'd rushed to wash the blood out of the sink as Clay came up the hill—just a little blond-haired boy, carrying some sort of treasures bundled in the front of his shirt. He stopped to playfully kick a soccer ball and watch it, having no idea that life had gone terribly wrong while he was playing in the woods. I turned off the water, then ran out to stop him, in case he was headed for the cellar door to show his treasures to Dad. I didn't want my little brother to see . . .

Closing my eyes, I pushed the memory away, stuffed it into the quiet, tightly-wrapped place where the other side of the door had stayed all these years. I didn't want to think about whether my father's death was an accident, or whether everything that was happening, his whole life tumbling down at once, was simply more than he could handle. The depth of my fear was too staggering. It drilled to the center of my soul, carved a clean, round path, like the massive metal bits that cut through soil and rock to take core samples, testing the stability of building sites before structures go up.

If my father had left us on purpose, if he'd meant to do it, it would be as much my fault as anyone's. I'd turned on him during those months in Moses Lake, abandoned him when he needed our love and support, as he planned my grandmother's funeral, then watched my grandfather wither away. I'd been so angry with my dad for moving us to Moses Lake that I'd never even considered what he was going through, losing both of his parents in such a short span of time.

The last words I'd said to him were, *I can't wait to get out of this house, and when I do, I'm never coming back.*

If I could have five minutes with him now, I would tell him I didn't mean those words. But there were no more chances to talk to him, to open up and throw my arms around his broad shoulders and have him lift me off my feet in a bear hug.

I didn't want to return to this house, where all those future opportunities had been whisked away. Whatever happened in that basement was stronger than I was. It had been winning the battle for sixteen years. How could I possibly believe that I could defeat it now?

Love is both a sword and a shield, Reverend Hay's sermon whispered in my mind. *It is all the armor we need.*

I did love my family. I loved my father. In some hollow, wounded part of me, I'd been wandering since the day he died and our family fell apart. I'd tried to fill the emptiness with substitutes—work, success, nice clothes, a career that provided the achievement of designing massive structures that would stand for generations to come. I'd tried to pack inanimate things into the gaping hole. But brick and mortar, lines on paper, accolades and achievements, all the things money can buy can't fill the soft, tender place where people should be.

I thought of Ruth and her sister, Naomi, praying on the fire escape, trapped by an evil they couldn't even begin to understand. *God walks with us through the fires of life,* she'd said, her conviction filled with such faith. Deep inside I knew, I'd always known, that there was no way to the other side of this pain but through the fire. There was no way out for me but through that house.

Opening the car door, I stepped out, and started across the yard. On the porch, the swing rocked in the breeze. I remembered sitting there with my father when I was little. I was wrapped in a quilt, curled against him as he talked about growing up on the farm—something about a horse that belonged to a neighbor and my father sneaking out to the barn with the intention of riding it. He had no idea that the horse had just come off a racetrack and didn't know how to stop or turn, only how to run like the dickens. . . .

My lips quivered at the memory, and I was caught between laughter and tears as I crossed the porch and tried to peek in the windows. The curtains were drawn, but the door fell open before I touched it. I wasn't surprised. One of the things that had driven my mother crazy about this house was that, if you slammed the door too hard, it would pop back open. Clay always slammed the door. My mother had scolded him for that over and over. Dad had only laughed at Mom and called her a city girl. *Who do you think's going to break in, a grizzly bear?*

Her eyes had widened. *There aren't really grizzly bears around here . . . are there?*

Just one, he'd said, then lifted his hands like claws and chased her and Clay around the room.

A puff of laughter caused my breath to plume in the night air as I stood on the threshold between past and present. Warmth flowed out of the house, chasing away the vapor and the laughter. Someone had been spending time here. The heat was on. Clearly, Clay was either here now or intended to return yet tonight.

Stepping in, I pushed the door closed behind me, softly, so that the latch clicking into place was almost soundless. If Clay was in the house, I didn't want to provide any advanced warning that would allow him to hide whatever he was doing. I spotted his backpack on the table in the dining room, to the right of the entryway. A floorboard creaked under my feet as I moved closer, the scent of dust and stillness filling my nose. A laptop computer sat beside the backpack, the screen in snooze mode, a laser light show twirling idly on the monitor, sending flickers around the dimly-lit room.

Papers, books, ziplock bags with soil and bits of plants inside littered the table. I flipped on the light, moved closer to look at them, found stacks of pictures of Proxica farms, each photo carefully labeled with the location and corresponding notes that seemed to be written in some sort of code. Beside the pictures sat an official-looking black folder, the results from chemical tests on water samples run at a lab in Houston. Tucked in the side pocket, a similar document appeared to be an analysis of several soil samples. In another file, there were names and case histories of people who'd worked on Proxica farms or in the production plant—their ages, their health problems. Ruth and her husband were listed. Behind the documents about human illnesses were photos and papers detailing unexplained problems with livestock—cancers, birth defects, lack of weight gain, mysterious deaths, pictures of dairy cows with cancerous growths on their skin and protruding from their eye sockets. An autopsy of a dog.

A file that had clearly been stolen from the Proxica offices had been hidden inside Clay's backpack. It appeared to contain some sort of old log sheets for various Proxica farms in Texas, Kentucky, and several other states, many dating back to the seventies. Clay had marked columns of numbers and written other numbers beside them in red.

"Oh, Clay," I whispered. No matter how valid the cause, breaking into the offices of a corporation and stealing property was illegal, not to mention dangerous. With the money and connections Proxica had, Clay could end up in prison. I needed to be careful about how I handled this, who we turned the information over to. We'd have to find someone who would listen, with whom we could bargain for a promise of amnesty for Clay. But whom? I had no idea where to even begin looking.

I couldn't just call the local police department for something like this. Clay would be prosecuted so fast it would make his head spin—and potentially for more than just stealing the documents. With all the terrorism scares these days, there was no telling what the charges might be. Vast stores of ammonium nitrate and anhydrous ammonia were kept at Proxica facilities—fertilizer in the right hands and a powerful bomb-making material if procured by criminals, as well as an ingredient used for the manufacture of methamphetamine in backwoods drug dens of Chinquapin Peaks. Proxica's lawyers could accuse Clay of all kinds of things.

I touched the computer to wake it from sleep mode, leaned close, and scanned the contents—a newspaper article about the class-action lawsuit in Kentucky. There was a jump drive attached to the computer. The article had been saved there. I pulled the jump drive out of the slot, tucked it into my pocket. The computer chimed, the noise seeming inordinately loud in the silent house.

A cabinet door closed in the kitchen. I jerked back. "Clay?" I whispered.

No one answered.

"Clay?"

Something fell and hit the kitchen floor with a smack that reverberated through the house like a gunshot. Closing the computer, I took a step backward, my heart bounding into my throat. The floor creaked just around the corner. Maybe Clay was here, after all.

Maybe someone else was here. . . .

Possibilities raced through my mind as a shadow wavered in the rectangle of light from the kitchen. I heard a rhythmic clicking sound. The shadow lengthened, began to take on a shape.

"Roger," I gasped as a nose and a lolling tongue rounded the corner, followed by the rest of Roger. He trotted happily across the room, and I patted him on the head. "You goofball," I breathed, my heart still hammering. "You stupid dog. Where's Clay? Is he here?"

Roger rolled a look at me, as in, *Beats me*. We crossed the dining room and turned the corner into the kitchen, but there was no sign of Clay. On the opposite end of the room, the doorway to the living area was dark, no lights burning in the rest of the house. Apparently, Roger had been left here for safekeeping while Clay and Amy proceeded with tonight's clandestine visit to the Proxica plant.

Please, God, just let them be all right. Just bring them home safely. The prayer whispered in my mind as I hurried back to the dining room, stuffed everything into Clay's backpack, looped it over my shoulder, and grabbed the laptop. I would take it all for now, put it somewhere safe until I could find Clay to talk some sense into him. If we put our heads together, we could figure out a way to reveal the information about Proxica without putting Clay in legal jeopardy, and then—

A noise pressed through the cracks in the floorboard. A voice . . . no . . . someone coughing? Downstairs. In the cellar.

Time seemed to bend and twist as I set the laptop back on the table and crossed the dining room, then the entryway, moving toward the small, wooden door that lay in shadow at the other end. The vision from my dreams flashed in my mind, the entryway stretching, becoming impossibly long, the door always out of reach.

Fear and need intertwined, an impossible web, pulling me closer, screaming at me to run, to be anywhere but here.

I'm not running. I will not run this time.

I stopped in front of the door, listened. Roger bumped my legs. Laying a hand on his head, I sought comfort, listened for the voice.

I couldn't hear anything. Maybe it was only my imagination, just the joists groaning and settling.

I already had the backpack and the jump drive. I could just leave and . . .

Memories of my last day in this house permeated the door, pressing through cracks, smelling of must and aging wood, blending today into yesterday, yesterday into sixteen years ago. The past, all the moments that had been blank, came rushing back like flames bursting through a firewall. My mother had screamed at me, told me not to come down the stairs, but I'd seen. I'd seen his legs, his feet splayed out behind the desk. He was wearing the boots he liked to wear when it was muddy. His *farmer boots*, we called them.

I'd moved to the bottom of the stairs, touched the banister, felt something warm and wet, a spatter that didn't belong there. I heard him heave a last gush of air, the long rattling sound of it, and then silence, a seep of red running from beneath the desk in a narrow river. I'd rushed toward him, looked down, seen him lying in a pool, his lower torso coated in blood, his legs contorted unnaturally, nerves causing them to jerk before going still.

Mom blocked my path, screamed at me again, told me to find Clay, to keep him out of here. She was grabbing the phone, my father's blood smearing the receiver. . . .

The moments sped after that—running up the stairs, washing off the blood, looking for my brother, the paramedics coming. The awful realization of what had happened.

If I didn't do this now, if I didn't go into that cellar, I never would. I'd be trapped on this side of the door forever.

My fingers trembled on the knob as I turned it. I swallowed the pulsating lump in my throat.

Please make me strong enough. Please.

The scents of must, damp limestone, and soil solidified in my chest as the door creaked open. I clutched Roger's fur, and we started down the steps together. The dog didn't try to bolt ahead, but moved soundlessly with me on the hollow wooden stairs—one step, two, three, and then another.

There was a light at the bottom, a dim glow illuminating boxes, paint cans, gardening tools covered in dust. The workbench where my father liked to create things from scraps of wood was laced with filmy cobwebs. I still had a jewelry box that he'd made for me. *For Heather's treasures,* the inscription read under the lid.

My father had always wanted me to be happy. He would want me to do this, to walk through this fire.

I'm not alone. I'm not.

A circle of light shone around the corner of my father's desk. The dull *clink-clink* of a moth battering itself against the bulb wrinkled the silent air. Descending another step into the darkness, into the past, I slowly squatted down, clutching Roger for support as the desk chair squeaked, testifying to the fact that someone was in it. My gaze traveled slowly over a hand, then the arm of an overcoat, upward until I could make out the form of a man with his back toward me. He'd leaned over the file cabinet on the other side of the desk, his form bisected by the circle of light, so that he was halfway inside it and halfway in the shadow beyond. His short, dark hair, the sunbaked wrinkles on the back of his neck, the way he towered over the chair was familiar.

Past melded with present, and my mind stumbled from one into the other.

"Dad?" I whispered.

But at your rebuke the waters fled,
at the sound of your thunder they took to flight;
they flowed over the mountains, they went down into the valleys,
to the place you assigned for them.

—Psalm 104
(via Jake Moskalak, game warden, north end of the county)

Chapter 20

He swiveled toward me, the chair's squeal splitting the air, the moment seeming to move in slow motion, too bizarre to understand. That couldn't be my father. I knew it in some practical, concrete way, yet an illogical hope floated with the dust, hovered there, then died as the lamplight caught the man's face, illuminating his profile—a long, thin nose, an earlobe that belled outward slightly, a square, chiseled chin with a cleft in the middle. Not my father's face, but I knew him. . . .

I scrambled through memories, trying to place his features, my thoughts sliding on ice, my body suddenly cold. It was *him*. The man I remembered. The man I'd seen with my mother all those years ago—either her partner in an affair, or an agent with the Justice Department, depending on whom you believed. The man who was, in some way, culpable in my father's death.

Without him, everything might have turned out differently. Without him, my father might still be alive.

A firestorm of anger and hatred swirled from that hiding place within me—the place where I'd stuffed all the unanswered questions, all the resentments toward my mother, all the fears and needs and unspoken grief. There wasn't time for it during those terrible months after the funeral. But now I felt the shell cracking, the contents still molten under the surface. How dare he come here! How dare he touch my father's things, sit in my father's chair! Did my mother know? Had she told him he could come here?

"Get out!" I heard myself growl, the sound deep and guttural, animalistic and instinctive in nature. Rushing down three more steps, I grabbed at the antique tools that hung on the stairway wall, and came up with a rusty machete-like potato knife. I raised it like a weapon, the sharp, rusty spike on the end sending an ominous message. Roger barked and tried to squeeze past me. "Roger, no!" I scolded, pinning him against the wall with my knee. "Get back."

The man behind the desk rose slowly, his face moving out of the light, a long, dark overcoat falling around him, making him little more than a shadow.

I should have been afraid, but there was no space inside me for fear. There was only rage, white-hot and molten.

He lifted his hands, his palms raised in a surrender position.

"How dare you come here," I growled. "How dare you touch my father's things. You have no right to be here." I descended another step. Why was he in the cellar? What was he looking for in my father's file cabinets?

His coat caught a sheet of paper on the corner of the desk, sent it floating downward like a falling leaf. My mind rushed back. I remembered a leaf skipping across the floor the day my father died. It was vibrant and red, tumbling along with a smattering of lacy white petals from a late bloom of crape myrtle, snow-like, innocent, beautiful, then trapped in a pool of my father's blood. . . .

I blinked now, trying to banish the past and focus my mind into the present.

"It's best that you leave." The stranger was calm, his voice measured. "Go back up the stairs and get in your car." He shifted in the dim light, glanced over his shoulder, then back at me. "This place isn't safe tonight." The request was authoritative in a way that made it seem almost reasonable, yet I wanted to charge at him with the knife, to bring it slashing down, to let it carry all the anger that had been living inside me, undirected, misdirected, constantly circling in on itself in a confined space.

"I'm calling the police, but first I want to know who you are. Why are you here? What happened between you and my mother before my father was killed? What did you do to him? Did you threaten him?" I couldn't ask the last questions thundering in my head: *Did you push him to the breaking point? Was his death an accident or did he do it on purpose?*

The stranger's long, thin fingers flexed and then straightened, his body language still indicating that he didn't intend to try for the knife. He seemed either unwilling to provoke me or confident that he could overpower me, if I came at him. "I promise you, Heather, that the truth will come out soon enough. But you need to go back to your uncle's house. Lock the doors. Make sure your brother and Amy stay there, and the rest of your family, as well. Our cover may have been breeched. I'm not sure who we can trust."

His words and the mention of Clay and Amy swirled anger into fear. He knew all of us. He knew everything about us. Had he been the one watching us?

At the top of the stairs, the door between the cellar and the house groaned softly and then blew shut. I jerked at the sound, my heart lurching, then settling into place again. "Who are you and how do you know so much about my family?"

"It'll all be out in the open soon enough. Right now I need you to lea . . ."

A floorboard creaked overhead. He lowered his hands, took a step sideways, the bottom half of his face coming into the light again. Placing a finger to his lips, he whispered, "Shhh." He motioned toward Roger, who had turned at the sound of footsteps.

Clay, was my first thought, and I felt comforted. But the sensation quickly evaporated, leaving uncertainty. Roger growled low in his throat. The footfalls upstairs were heavy, the hollow sound of boots on wood. That wasn't Clay.

The stranger motioned for me to come down the stairs, then he doused the light. I hesitated, not knowing which way danger might lie.

Something crashed overhead. Glass shattered.

Roger cowered against my leg in the darkness. I circled my fingers around his collar, held him close, and crept down the stairs, Clay's backpack sliding on my shoulder. The stranger caught my arm when I reached the bottom step, pulled Roger and me into the immeasurable blackness beneath the stairway. I felt the man's body against mine, the backpack pressed between us, his arm encircling me just below my neck. He leaned close to my ear, murmured, "Keep quiet."

"What's happening?" I whispered, terrified.

"Shhh," he hissed. His arm tightened, pulled me farther into the darkness. My body went stiff. As the door opened at the top of the stairway, I fought the urge to pull away, run, scream. A partial sentence drifted downward with a flashlight beam.

" . . . you wanna do with the little whistleblower and her boyfriend? How 'bout we toss them both down here and throw in this can of diesel with 'em? This place'll go up like a tinderbox. We'll get rid of that computer, whatever other proof they think they got, and the two of them all at once. Time the fire department gets way out here, there won't be nothin' left to find. Ain't nobody gonna know nothin'."

"You're as dumb as you look, Frank." The second man's voice was gravelly and rough, chilling in its lack of emotion. "It's gotta look right. Think about it—if her and her boyfriend was out here cookin' a little meth with some anhydrous they stole from the Proxica plant, and it blew up on 'em, they wouldn't be down in the basement, now would they? Dump that diesel can down the cellar stairs and leave the cellar door open. I'll go set things up in the kitchen, then we'll get Hampton and his girlfriend outta the trunk and put 'em in there. Them fumes'll start a flash fire quick enough, and that diesel on the stairs will suck it right down into the basement, too. The whole place'll go, but it'll all just look like an accident—like he got sloppy. Ain't gonna be as excitin' as if that boy's truck had rolled over that gas meter last night. Man, I had that thing set to blow, too. Just a little tap's all woulda took, and we'd have had us some real fireworks. It's cleaner this way, though. Now that we know his girlfriend was in on it, we can do 'em both at once."

Terror raced through me, and I caught a breath. They had Clay and Amy outside? They'd rigged the gas meter at Harmony House? If Clay's truck hadn't veered into the fig tree last night and missed the gas meter, we would have all been dead.

I shifted toward the stairway, but the man behind me held tight as the plans continued overhead.

"Don't let it splash too far from them stairs, but make sure the diesel gets all the way to the bottom. We don't want to do nothin' to make the fire marshal suspicious when he checks this place out, afterwards. It's gotta look like that diesel can just fell over down there and spilt accidental-like."

Frank laughed appreciatively. "Yeah, all right." The top stair

creaked under his weight, dust sifted downward, and the man behind me slid his fingers over mine on the handle of the potato knife.
I let him take it from me.

The second step creaked and the light came on, the bulb swinging
on a single, narrow cord. Diesel splashed in the can as he unscrewed
the lid. Fumes filled the air. A cough convulsed in my throat, and
I pressed a hand to my mouth to stifle it, then pulled my shirt
over my nose, gagging on the smell of diesel as Frank passed just
inches from our heads, then splashed the bottom of the stairs and
began working his way up. Thoughts raced wildly in my head, the
urge to bolt becoming almost too strong to control. I wanted to
run for the door across the room, scramble up the old stone stairs
that had been chiseled from the hillside in back of the house, and
burst into the fresh air. Closing my eyes, I willed myself to be still,
not to move. *He'll leave in a minute. He'll leave in a minute. . . .*

I didn't want to die here in the darkness, in this cellar that had
swallowed the last moments of my father's life.

"Frank, we got comp'ny! Someone's comin' up the driveway!
Turn out that light down there!" Frank stopped, his feet just above
my head.

A string of curses followed him as he climbed the stairs again,
doused the lights, then set the diesel can on the top step. I heard
the click and slide of metal against metal. The cartridge of a gun.

Roger growled low in his throat. I closed my eyes, slid a hand
over his muzzle.

Who was coming now? Another accomplice? Someone else?
Maybe Mom or the uncs, showing up to check on us?

Terror balled in my chest. Anyone arriving now would have no
way of knowing this was a trap. Overhead, Frank kicked over the
diesel can before moving through the door into the house. The
acrid smell of fumes floated on the air.

The stranger let go of me, and I stumbled from under the stairway, still clinging to Roger's collar. "We have to get away from here."

"Go through the outside door." His voice was measured but insistent. "Don't stop anywhere near the house. Hide in the brush, and no matter what happens, stay put." He rushed up the steps, then slipped soundlessly through the door at the top. When it closed behind him, only inky darkness remained. Feeling my way with one hand and clutching Roger's collar with the other, I moved forward, fumes filling my lungs, making me lightheaded and sick. I couldn't get my bearings. Which way was the door that led up the steps to the yard? Which way? The ventilation windows at ground level were tiny and dirt-covered, allowing almost no light.

Overhead, the house had gone silent—no movement, no voices, no footsteps. What was happening?

My head floated and spun. I felt like I was falling. Roger tugged at his collar, pulling me sideways, causing me to stumble against something solid. I pressed against it, coughing, my lungs burning. I couldn't get my breath.

Clutching the desk, I tried again to gain my bearings, to feel my way. Which way? Which way? Something caught my leg, and I lost my balance again, tumbling over Roger. We fell against the desk chair, tipped it and crashed to the floor with it, the sound reverberating through the cellar. I scrambled to my feet again, Roger barking, my heart hammering in my ears.

Beyond the pounding, I heard something, then strained toward the sound.

Someone was calling my name—beckoning me. Not upstairs . . . outside.

Blaine?

A rush of relief came with his voice, and then fear. Where were Frank and his accomplice? Outside? In the house? Were they waiting to see if Blaine would leave, trying to figure out if he was armed? Was a gun pointed his way right now?

Sifting through the darkness with my hands, I found the wall and moved toward a ventilation window on the side of the house, closer to Blaine's voice. Boxes, buckets, and bits of furniture caught my feet and legs. Old tools, rakes, and shovels resting against the wall skittered sideways, each noise sending my heart into my throat. Was anyone upstairs? Could they hear me? Grabbing the handle of a hoe, I held my breath and tapped the glass of the ventilation window. *Please, please let it be Blaine who hears.*

There was no response. Upstairs, someone was moving, the footsteps careful, almost soundless, one floor joist crackling, then another. Someone was still in the house, heading toward the front door, toward the sound of Blaine's voice. I had to do something. Turning the tool over, I swung and hit the glass hard, threw an arm over my face as shards rained down around me.

Blaine's voice pressed through the opening as the sound died. "Heather?" He was outside the window now, his body silhouetted against a blanket of stars. A flashlight beam blinded me momentarily. "Heather?" he asked again.

"Blaine, get away," I whispered, trying to climb onto a box to get closer but quickly sinking through the lid onto the soft contents. "Get away. There's someone in the house. Two men. I think they have guns. They're going to burn the house and—"

Something crashed upstairs. Roger barked behind me, and the explosion of a gunshot split the air, followed by another sound, like the *whoosh* of a campfire bursting into flame after a dousing of lighter fluid. A scream ripped from my throat, and I spun around, tripped over Roger, then climbed to my feet and stumbled across the basement, tripping, falling, scrambling over old bicycles, stacks of buckets, gardening tools, boxes, and crates.

In the darkness, Roger barked, then clawed at something wooden—the outside door, I hoped. I made my way toward the sound until I reached the far wall and the door handle. A tangle of spider webs melted over my fingers, sticky and filmy, as I grabbed on and pulled, but the wood, swollen from so many years of disuse, wouldn't budge.

"Heather, move back," Blaine was on the other side now. "Get out of the way." He threw himself against the door as the fight continued overhead.

A piece of furniture crashed near the cellar stairway, rolling and hitting the door hard, rattling it on its hinges as a series of gunshots exploded. Smoke seeped in from the ceiling, tinging the air with a combination of ashy scents and diesel fumes waiting to burn. Terror raced through me. A bullet splintered the floorboards and struck a joist. Roger clawed at the stones underneath the threshold, trying to dig his way through. Blaine's weight collided with the door again, causing it to give a few inches. Wrapping my fingers around the weathered wood, I pulled. How long before the diesel fumes would catch the flame and draw the fire down here? How long? Another gunshot rang out. Something or someone hit the door at the top of the stairs. Another scream wrenched from me.

"Move back." Blaine's words were ragged and urgent, commanding. "Get out of the way, Heather." Through the gap in the door, I saw him move back a step and prepare to kick his way through. Dragging Roger with me, I pressed close to the wall, Clay's backpack bunching against the stone.

Overhead, the noise stopped suddenly. Blaine kicked the door, and it broke loose from the hinges, tumbling inward and landing on the floor with a thunderous crash. He reached through, grabbed my hand, pulled me against the stone wall of the cellar steps, wrapped me in his arms. "Are you all right? Heather, are you hurt?"

"I'm okay. I'm okay, but it's Clay. They've got Clay and Amy—in their car, I think. There was another man here. He was trying to stop them."

Pushing away, I bolted up the cellar stairs and into the yard. Roger scrambled past me as I coughed, wheezed, and gulped in air. Blaine caught me, grabbed my arm, and we cleared the corner of the house. Across the farmyard, a car barreled from the barn, crashing through the corner of an old wooden fence, then flinging gravel and going airborne as it sped over the earthen terraces, heading for the driveway.

"They've got Clay and Amy!" I screamed. "Blaine, we can't let them go!"

A second engine revved to life in the orchard behind the house. The glow of headlights ping-ponged across the yard, and a dark sedan fishtailed from the orchard lane into the driveway, speeding after the first car. Inside the house, the fire roared, moaning like a giant beast awakening, hungry and powerful. Smoke billowed through the front door, heat flowing outward, causing us to shield ourselves with our arms. Glass buckled and shattered, the panes in the wooden windows exploding, one, then another, and another.

Blaine ran for his truck, and I spun around and rushed after him, Roger on my heels. Moments later, we were racing down the driveway, but both vehicles had disappeared from view. When we reached the county road, darkness lay in either direction, curves and hills cloaking everything, making the cars vanish like props in a magician's trick.

"Which way? What now?" Blaine demanded.

My mind spun in panic. I raked my hair out of my face, then coughed on the sooty cotton in my throat. "Harmony Shores," I gasped out as I shed Clay's backpack into the floorboard. "They did something to the gas meter there. We have to get everyone out of the house." *Please don't let anything happen. I was wrong. I was wrong to act like I didn't care. . . .*

The prayer cycled in my head, blanketing panic with hope, but also with the terrifying realization that the future wasn't a given. At any moment—tonight, tomorrow, five minutes from now—my time with the people I loved could be gone.

Blaine pressed something into my hand. A cell phone. "Start calling 9-1-1. Keep trying until you get reception. Send someone to Harmony Shores and get the fire department to the farm. Give them a description of the cars and tell them we don't know which way they went or where they're headed, for sure."

My hands shook as I dialed the phone, then pressed Send. *No service.* I tried a second time and a third, hoping and praying as Blaine's truck squealed around curves and popped over hills, catching air, then landing again. *No service, no service, no service.* "Hurry, Blaine!" Tears cloaked the words, the phone blurring as I dialed again. "Please hurry."

Blaine's hand caught mine, squeezing for a moment before he reached for the steering wheel again. "We'll get there. Keep dialing. Any minute now, it'll . . ."

"I've got a signal!" I blurted and pressed the Send button. Static hummed, the signal zigzagged from tower to tower, trying to find a connection. The moment seemed impossibly long. I imagined Harmony House in flames. I imagined my family, trapped in that monstrous structure, the uncs moving in their labored shuffle-steps, too slow to get out.

The call dropped, and my stomach plummeted with it. "No!" Frustration threw me back against the seat. "No, no, no!" I dialed again, pushed Send, listened to the tides of static, the endless clicking. . . .

"9-1-1, what's your emergency?" The voice was faint, almost lost, but it was there.

"We need help. We need help at Harmony Shores Funeral Home in Moses Lake. There's a gas leak in the yard . . . the meter. Get everyone out of the house. Please get everyone out. . . ."

"Ma'am, ma'am," the operator interrupted. "I need you to slow down. I can barely hear you. Did you say a gas leak?"

"Yes, please . . . at Harmony Shores Funeral Home. Moses Lake . . ." The call went dead, and the operator was gone.

By the time I was able to connect another call, a sheriff's deputy had already been sent to Harmony Shores. Blaine took the phone to report what had happened at the farm and to describe the cars we'd seen speeding away.

Fists balled in my lap, I collapsed against the seat, tears flowing over my cheeks. "It's okay. It has to be okay." One miracle could lead to two. Clay and Amy could be found, alive and well. I wouldn't allow myself to believe anything else.

"It will be," Blaine whispered, and I felt his hand on my hair, smoothing it away from my face. I leaned into his touch, took comfort from it, tried to let his assurance travel into my body, to become reality as we drove the final few miles, and the lights of Moses Lake appeared ahead.

When we turned into Harmony Shores, my mother and the uncs, still drowsy and confused, were moving onto the lawn with a sheriff's deputy. The deputy checked with dispatch to see if anything had been reported about the cars, but he seemed skeptical, as if my story of what had happened at the farm were too farfetched to be believed. He seemed to be of the opinion that I'd invented the whole thing about the two men breaking into the farmhouse and setting it on fire. The revelation about the strange man in the basement was completely beyond what he was willing to accept, and he forced me to repeat it several times before he could keep it straight.

"Why don't you do your job?" Blaine snapped. "I saw the cars leaving that place, too. I heard the gunfire." He towered over the deputy, and for a minute, I thought he was going to lay the guy out on the lawn. "Get the call out to the highway patrol, the park rangers, and the game wardens. That car could be a long way from here by now. They might try to hide out up in the hills or in the state park."

My mother was frantic, and the uncs were trying to comfort her. "It wasn't supposed to happen like this," she kept muttering. "This wasn't supposed to . . . Oh, Clay. Where's Clay? Why can't they find him?"

A van from the utility company arrived to shut off the flow of gas to the meter. We waited while they went through procedures, then checked the house and reported that there was evidence of tampering around the gas meter. "You breathe too hard on that thing, it'd go sky high," the technician reported, wiping his forehead. "We'll get out here in the mornin' and fix it. Till then, everybody should keep away from the house, even though the gas is off now. All the piping oughta be checked, too. Somebody's been messin' with things—that's for sure."

The deputy looked embarrassed then. He got in his car to make some more calls and ramp up the alert level.

Blaine threw his hands in the air and started toward his truck. "I'll be back. I'm going to do some looking around. One more set of eyes can't hurt."

"That's just what I was thinkin'." Uncle Charley shuffled toward the vehicle, pajama pants fluttering in the breeze as he moved across the gravel in his house shoes and bathrobe. "C'mon, Herb. No sense in us sittin' here doing nothing."

"I'm going with you." I started after Blaine, leaving my mother alone by the cruiser, shivering and staring off into space.

353

Blaine caught my arm gently. "You need to stay with your mom." Even though he didn't say it, I could tell what was in his mind. *You need to stay with your mom in case it's bad news.* He walked back to the cruiser and told the deputy to take us up to the church, where it was warm, then he returned to his truck, where the uncs and Roger were already waiting.

A shiver coursed through me as they drove away, the taillights turning the corner at the end of the driveway and disappearing into the night. Finally, I rejoined my mother, slipped my arm around her shoulders, and guided her into the backseat of the cruiser, the action more muscle memory than anything else. For months after my father's death, I'd moved her around the house as if she were a rag doll, relocating her from the bed to the sofa each day, misguidedly hoping that maintaining some sort of routine would make things normal.

"This wasn't supposed to happen," she whispered as we waited for the officer to secure the scene.

"Clay's going to be all right." I was torn between the urge to comfort and the need to be angry. Finally, I just held her hand. What good would it do to be angry now? What would it accomplish? What had it ever accomplished? "He'll be all right, do you hear me? You know Clay. He always lands on his feet."

"He just . . . He needed to do this. For your dad." Her head dropped forward, her hands wringing in her lap. In the uneven light, her hands looked old, the veins pronounced, her fingers thin. She seemed frail and vulnerable, not entirely prepared for the world outside her poems and her literary analyses of classic novels. In so many ways, she had always been this woman, and I'd always kept myself apart from her, waiting for her to become the mother I wanted her to be, waiting for her to fit my expectations. But I was asking for something she didn't have to give. She hadn't changed,

I realized now. She wouldn't change. She would always be flighty, artistic, introspective in a way that allowed her to shut out the world. I could either love her the way she was or not love her at all.

The second choice was more painful than the first. There were connections in this life, a history that I would never have with anyone but her. "We'll be all right," I said quietly, holding her close for the first time in years. As we drove to the church, she let her head fall sideways until it rested on my shoulder. For a moment, there was just the two of us, clinging to each other as the world spun off-balance.

When we reached the church, Reverend Hay was waiting at the fellowship hall door. There were people with him—two men, several of the church ladies, and Mama B. Even Blaine's stepmother was there. They'd started a prayer chain to bring Clay and Amy home safely.

"Callin' circle's underway," Mama B said, sounding like a mission commander in the throes of a full frontal assault. "We're gonna get our kids back safe. People are up prayin' all over town." Slipping one arm around me and one around my mother, she guided us toward a sagging sofa in the opposite corner of the room. "Y'all just come on in and sit down, now," she urged, looking over her shoulder as we passed the kitchen, where Blaine's stepmother was huddled with another woman, talking in hushed tones while surreptitiously watching our entrance. "Claire Anne," Mama B barked, and Blaine's stepmother stood at attention. "Get some coffee out here. We're gonna need it. And somebody bring me a blanket. These gals are chilled to the bone."

As church members gathered around us, offering comfort and soft, faded quilts, I felt their presence, their kindness, settling over me and seeping deep inside, easing the wild pulse thrumming in my ears. Even Blaine's stepmother seemed to be trying to help, moving around the fringes of the room in a ruffled apron, offering coffee cups and refills. She set one beside my mother without asking, then awkwardly touched my mother's shoulder before whisking away. Mom didn't respond, other than to pull in a tattered breath and clutch the quilt high around her neck.

Leaning close, Mama B forced eye contact. "Hon, now I want you to drink some of this coffee, y'hear? You want cream and sugar in it? Hon, you want cream and sugar?" Somehow, the request brought my mother out of herself. She nodded, her watery eyes fixed on Mama B.

"Claire Anne, get us some cream and sugar." Mama B's voice rattled the ceiling panels, and Blaine's stepmother scurried off to the kitchen, where she received a sympathy eye-roll from one of her friends. "And a piece of that pound cake," Mama B called after her, then returned attention to my mother. "Now, hon, you listen at this here. We're not doing any more of this cryin'. We're gonna have faith and keep praying, and believe on that prayer. That's my little granddaughter out there with your boy, and she may be tiny, but I know for a fact she's tough as a boot. She'll figure a way to come out of this all right, and so will your boy. My family pioneered this land. Some lowbrow, two-bit criminal's not gonna come in here and get the best of us. You hear me?"

Mom nodded.

"You drink some of that coffee now." Mama B pointed at the cup insistently, and my mother released the quilt, letting it slide from her shoulders. Peering around me, Mama B noted that there was no coffee on my end table. "Claire Anne! Bring another cup for Heather. She looks like she's about froze to death." In the kitchen, Blaine's stepmother was gathering things on a tray, her back stiffening every time her mother-in-law called her name.

Watching Mama B comfort my mother now, I couldn't help

wondering if things might have been different all those years ago, when tragedy first touched our family. If we had reached out instead of retreating into ourselves, would these people have received us this way? If I had allowed myself to fall into this community that had so loved my father, would they have caught me? Was my stubbornness, my pride, my resentment, and my guilt more the cause of my suffering than these people were?

Maybe I'd been wrong about Moses Lake. Maybe I'd been wrong about so many things in my life. It shouldn't have taken something like this—the prospect of losing my brother—to make me assess myself, to lift the veil from my eyes. In keeping my defenses high, in striving to maintain a self-sufficient, ordered, controlled life that contained minimal risk, I was missing everything that mattered most. A well-lived life, an authentic life, involved risks—and faith allowed you to take those risks. That was what Ruth had been trying to tell me, the very thing she'd understood as she balanced on that fire escape. The great leaps in life are not made in the absence of fear, but in the presence of faith.

Mama B rested a hand on my knee and patted gently. "Blaine's out there, too. He's out there looking for them, and there's nothing that boy can't do. He was the first one to hold Amy when she was born. Bet you didn't know that. It was a snowy night, and Amy's daddy was out of town, so Blaine stayed over at his auntie's house to watch after her. Lands if she didn't have the baby right there on the kitchen floor with Blaine helping her. He'll find Amy. You watch. Good gravy, where is that coffee?"

Mama B left to check on things in the kitchen. I reached across the space between my mother and me and held her hand. Twenty minutes passed, thirty, then forty-five as the prayer chain grew and took on a life of its own, cell phone calls coming in, information going out. I tried not to imagine where Clay was now.

The clock in the church office chimed once, a solitary note weaving from the quiet shadows of the hallway. One in the morning.

One fifteen.

One twenty.

The old hardwired phone on the wall rang. Reverend Hay snapped upright, sending his folding chair skittering sideways. Every eye in the room followed him as he answered the call, pacing back and forth at the end of the coiled cord. The room grew silent, other than the faint sound of a voice on the other end of the phone, and Reverend Hay's answers. "Mmm-hmm . . . mmm-hmm. That's good news, Mart." Pumping a fist in the air, he gave us the thumbs-up sign. "That's the best news. Praise the Lord!"

A smile split his thin face, causing his eyes to crinkle around the edges as he slapped the receiver into the cradle. "They've been found, praise be! The sheriff's office received an anonymous call to send an ambulance to a car in the ditch on a county road, and when they got there, they found Clay and Amy in the trunk. No sign of the driver or anybody else, and they don't know who made the call. The paramedics think Clay and Amy might've taken in some carbon monoxide. They're in an ambulance, on their way to the hospital in Gnadenfeld."

Love is the mystery of water and a star.

–*Pablo Neruda*
(Left by an anonymous tourist who visited unnoticed)

Chapter 21

Clay's visitors came and went as night faded into morning, while next door Amy's parents, Blaine's family, and Mama B sat vigil around her room. Ruth arrived with the morning light, leaning on the elbow of her favorite nephew. In the doorway, she held Uncle Herb's hand, patted it between hers, smiled at him, and nodded. "We've done it," she said, and then crossed the room to stand over my brother's bed and point the no-no finger at him. "Never, never again, anything like that. To live peacefully is to live well. You remember that from now on."

Clay's grin was tired and lopsided, his lip swollen and bruised on the left, the oxygen tube bumping awkwardly under his nose. He waved at Mom and Uncle Charley, who were exiting the room to make space. "I think I've had . . . enough. . . . adventure . . ." His words grew raspy and trailed off. He swallowed, wincing with the effort, a little mischief twinkling in the eye that wasn't swollen shut. I was almost glad to see that the mischief was still there, even after the beating he'd taken and the carbon monoxide inhalation in the trunk of the car. " . . . for a while," he added, and I wanted to smack him one.

Lips pressing into a line, Ruth turned to me. "You should talk some sense into him."

"We could tie him to the bed," Uncle Herb suggested. "Charley's got an old lariat rope in his truck."

We laughed together, eager to diffuse the tension in the room. For an instant—just an instant—I saw the image of Clay from my dream. We'd come so close to really losing him. We could have lost him. Watching him laugh now, then draw his eyebrows together, wincing, then give in and laugh again, I regretted all the petty thoughts, resentments, and fears that had kept me away from him, from my family for so many years. Our time together as adults almost ended before it began, and if it had, it would have been my fault as much as anyone's.

I'd been so busy focusing on my self-determined parameters of what I felt my family should be, that I'd missed the beauty of what they actually were—fragile, flawed, heroic, imperfect, champions of lost causes. Each with things to learn and things to teach. God had knit us together like plantings in a garden—wild and unique above ground, blooming in different ways at different times, the roots intertwined deep beneath the soil. No matter who else passed through my life, no one would take the place of my brother. He would always be the only one with whom I shared the quiet beginnings of life, the awkwardness of growing up, the secret hiding places of childhood, the early hours of Christmas mornings waiting for Santa Claus, the arguments over space in the backseat of a car, the walk to school on the first day, and the rough times after things didn't go so well.

I looked at him now, his scruffy blond hair in unkempt curls against the pillow, and I saw all of those things. He winked at me and smirked, embarrassed by all the attention as Ruth fawned over him some more, covering him with a knitted afghan she'd brought for him and telling him a story about a stray dog that had wandered into the dairy and wreaked havoc the day before. Mary and Emily were convinced that the dog was Roger.

Clay chuckled wearily and said it was a good thing there weren't two Rogers, and then Ruth ordered him, in no uncertain terms, to rest and get well, before finally hugging him good-bye.

I walked her out, moving slowly to the end of the hall with her as her nephew tagged along behind. "Our Clay is a good boy," she said, adjusting her prayer covering and smiling at me.

"A good man," I corrected.

"There's a strong heritage in him. A heritage of men who are not afraid."

I only nodded, thinking that I wished Clay would knuckle under to fear a little more often. I was already dreading waving him off on his next adventure, whatever it might be. The idea that he wanted to settle down in Moses Lake had never been believable, and now that I knew why he'd come here, I knew he'd be moving on as soon as he was well enough.

"It's in you, too," Ruth pointed out, her fingers circling mine, squeezing and shaking gently. "Don't be afraid to live your life, Heather. It comes and goes more quickly than you'd imagine."

"I've been thinking about that," I admitted. I wasn't sure what was next for me, but I did know that I wouldn't be returning to my old life, to the people with whom I'd surrounded myself. That box seemed too confining now, too limiting. My time in Moses Lake had grown me in ways that wouldn't allow me to fit back into the same container.

We stopped at the elevator door, and Ruth's nephew pushed the button, then stood politely, pretending not to be listening to our conversation. The chime sounded, and the light flickered. We waited while a nurse wheeled a woman with a new baby off the elevator, as the husband followed behind, carrying a suitcase and a balloon bouquet, his face all smiles. I felt the sting of yearning again, but also the vague chill of uncertainty. Did I really have it in me to step from behind the clean glass and steel walls I'd constructed and take a risk on something that couldn't be measured or calculated or planned? Was Blaine *the one*? Was there really something special between us, or was I just trying to see what I wanted to see? Was I as wrong about him as I had been about Richard?

"You'll come visit me in a day or two, and I'll tell you more stories." Ruth's comment tugged at my thoughts, but the deeper questions continued churning, a miniature whirlpool of conflicting emotions.

"If I'm here," I answered. "I mean, I think I will be . . . for a while . . . until Clay's well, at least." Suddenly I felt lost, out of sorts, overwhelmed by the unsettled, unplanned nature of the future. "I quit my job . . . I think."

But now that the Proxica scandal was about to be made public, Mel would be glad we hadn't ended up being officially tied to the company. If I called him, he'd probably act like the whole take-this-job-and-shove-it text message never even happened.

Ruth's fingers released mine as her nephew moved to hold open the elevator door. "Get a good night's sleep before you decide," she advised, shuffling into the elevator. "A tired mind doesn't think well, you know."

"I know."

"And eat something. Whole food, not the processed sort."

I chuckled. "I will." Actually, a trip across the street to the bakery sounded like a good idea about now.

Her brows arched in a way that caused me to see the little girl who had yearned to peek under the circus tent. "You should think about that riddle. The one the tinker wrote at the Waterbird. We German folk are good with riddles. The Irish think they have the market, but they don't. If you have the answer, tell me tomorrow."

I nodded, but in reality, my tired mind was hardly in the mood to contemplate ancient wisdoms. It was just like Ruth, though, to try to use this as a teachable moment.

I rubbed my eyes as I walked back toward Clay's room. In the hallway ahead, my family was exiting the room en masse, stealing nervous looks over their shoulders. I quickened my steps, forgetting about the riddle.

"We're heading to the cafeteria," Uncle Herb offered, shrugging in an indication that I should turn and follow.

"C'mon down there with us," Uncle Charley added as he moved past me. "Your brother needs a little time alone right now." Circling his lips, he flashed a wide-eyed look over his shoulder and sucked in air.

"What's wrong with Clay?" My anxiety ratcheted up. The doctors had said that, while bruised and battered, Clay would be fine.

"Nothin' that ain't his own doin'." Uncle Charley shuffled around and kept walking. "But that could change after she gets ahold of him."

"She . . . who?" I turned to my mother, who was carefully closing the door to Clay's room, leaving it ajar only a few inches before she stepped away and wheeled a hand in a *let's-move-on* sort of way.

"His fiancée," she whispered.

Taking several sideways steps, I peered through the gap and into the room. Someone was standing beside Clay's bed. I could see the back of a pair of faded Levis and a sweatshirt. "Amy?" Surely Amy couldn't be on her feet already. She'd been in worse shape than Clay. Just a couple hours ago, when I'd looked in on her, she was still on oxygen, and they were making plans to take her down to X-ray to discern the best course of action for a separated shoulder.

A little nudge to the door opened it a bit wider, increasing the view of Clay's room. Behind me, Mom grabbed my sweatshirt and tried to pull me away.

Some . . . woman was hugging my brother. She was tall and slim, her medium-length brown hair pulled back in a simple ponytail. She'd curled herself against Clay's chest, sobbing into the sheets as he rested his chin on her head.

I staggered backward, snapping toward my mother's tug like a slinky, stretched too far. *Who's that?* I mouthed, pointing.

Mom's steepled hands touched her lips before carefully measuring her next words. "There are a few things we haven't told you."

I wasn't sure how to answer. Having already felt the world rock off kilter once that day, I didn't know if I wanted to hear the rest of the family secrets. Suddenly my brother's sexy text messages from Fort Worth made sense. There really had been someone else, all along. Was Clay's supposed relationship with Amy all a ruse? An excuse to be hanging around Moses Lake and Proxica? Obviously my mother knew the answers, so I started down the hall with her. Ahead, one of the uncs was holding the elevator for us. "Was Clay stringing Amy along, or was there never anything . . . I mean, did she know it was all an act?"

Mom quickened her pace, jogging the rest of the way to the elevator, forcing me to run-walk or be left behind. Once we were inside, she tried to placate me. "Let's get some coffee, and we'll explain the whole thing."

Frustration, exhaustion, uncertainty, and the remnants of a terrifying night welled up in me, and I smacked the *Stop* button, causing the elevator to jerk to a halt. "You know what? I just want the whole story all at once. I need to know what's true."

Mom and the uncs flicked sideways glances at each other, and Mom laid a hand on my shoulder. "Heather, just calm down. You've had quite a traumatic night, too, and . . ."

"Don't mollify me!" I jerked away from her. "Just tell me all of it. Please! Clay was never involved with Amy, was he? That was all an act, right?" My entire family had been putting on an act, and I'd been left in the audience, with everyone else.

"They needed someone on the inside . . . someone who wouldn't be suspected."

"They, *who*?" I pressed. "Whose idea was this whole thing?" The connections were tangled in my mind. "Who came up with all that malarkey about Clay taking over Catfish Charley's and you opening a bed-and-breakfast in the funeral home?"

"We had to make it look convincing," Mom defended. "To have an excuse to be in town while Clay put his case together."

Uncle Charley nodded enthusiastically but remained as far from me as the elevator would allow. "We had to get the drop on Proxica, see? Bait those slick suckers into the trap and shut the door before they knew what was comin'. Them Proxica folks got powerful friends in the government—state and national. It's a big company. Every time someone's tried to go up against them, a few phone calls get made, and that's the end of it. Meantime, they're makin' money and they got poison leaking into water wells around here, and they know it. They've known it for a long time.

"Your dad figured what was happening years ago—how they were getting rid of that Armidryn. Your brother looked at some of your dad's old papers in the cellar out at the farm. He also did some checking online and read about that lawsuit in Kentucky, and he started to put two and two together—Ruth's husband dying from cancer, and then Ruth getting sick, and others around Gnadenfeld. He started talkin' to folks and lookin' into it some more. You done good getting out of the farmhouse with his backpack, too. They might've burned Clay's computer in that fire, but there's enough evidence in that backpack to prove it all. Everything it'll take to bring them sorry suckers down."

I turned to my mother, feeling as if someone had cut the elevator cable and we were careening downward, headed for a crash. "So it's all true? About Dad . . . about the Justice Department? How could you let Clay get involved in that, after what happened to Dad?"

Mom braced her hands on her hips, her chest rising and falling. "He's your father's son. I couldn't convince him to run away, any more than I could convince your father. All I could do was be here and try to keep him safe. By the time I found out what your brother was doing, he'd already been in touch with the investigator who'd worked on the case sixteen years ago. After what happened to your father, I never wanted to see that man again. I didn't want him to have the chance to ease his conscience, to make things right. He was the one who pushed your father. He was the one who promised to protect your father, and then your dad was gone. One minute I had everything, and the next, everything was gone."

My eyes welled, and I felt the heat of tears on my cheeks. "You had us. You still had us, and we needed you." The little girl in me, the one who'd been locked away during the months following my father's death, broke free, filled with desperation, unanswered questions, and unfulfilled needs.

"I couldn't find my feet," Mom whispered, her face flushed and red, the tendrils of hair on her cheek damp now. She smoothed them away impatiently. "I couldn't find my feet, Heather. I was never strong the way you are, the way your father was. And Clay . . . he's like you in that way. He's like your father. When Clay came here, I didn't know what else to do but come along and help him put this case together."

I swiped tears away impatiently. "What case? What happens now, exactly?"

"They bring the case against Proxica. A class-action suit," Uncle Charley chimed in, as if that much were elementary. "Your brother and that law firm he's with are gonna make Proxica pay for all the people like Ruth, who're sick because of the chemicals. Looks like the Justice Department is gonna get involved, too. Amy and your brother could get a big chunk of money from the whistleblower law. Proxica has a whole lot to answer for and a lot of cleaning up to do around here."

"Clay is with a *law firm*?" Of all the information that had just come my way, that was the only bit I could really grasp.

I heard my mother sniffling, and Uncle Charley offering his hankie. "Yer brother passed the bar three months ago. He didn't want anybody to know it, on account of the case."

Something soft touched my hand, and Uncle Herbert said, "Here, dry your eyes now." He pressed a button on the panel, and the elevator jerked and rattled as it resumed motion.

I was too exhausted for coffee, too exhausted to think anymore. I caught my breath and turned to Uncle Herbert as the elevator settled into position on the bottom floor. "So nobody is moving to Moses Lake, and you and Uncle Charley are actually looking forward to living in the retirement villas in Oklahoma? You're selling everything?" Suddenly my musings about staying for a while in Moses Lake made little sense. The family was leaving, scattering to the wind.

"Well, we got a buyer for the funeral home, and Clay said he'd help us put the restaurant up for sale online," Uncle Charley stated. "No way I'm sellin' it to some broker, after this last mess. That restaurant has history. I want to pick the buyer so I know it goes to somebody that'll take care of it."

Uncle Herb nodded, indicating his complete agreement. "We thought we'd keep the old farm—bring the grandkids down sometimes. And maybe Clay would want to visit, since he's working up in Fort Worth. It'll be a family place, like it's always been—for your brother, and our kids, and for you, if you want it. The little house is gone now, of course, but the two-story is still there.

"And when we asked you about doing the architecture work for the new school, that wasn't a smokescreen, either. We meant it. The fella who bought the house at Harmony Shores might need some work done, too. He took it on as an investment—wants to turn it into a wedding parlor and make the barn and the gardener's cottage into a bed-and-breakfast. Guess that old house has at least one more life in it, yet. Moses Lake isn't that far from Dallas. You could hang out your shingle up there and live down here, drive back and forth when you need to. There's the new fellowship hall at the church to build, too. They're gonna need an architect for that."

Shaking my head, I stepped off the elevator, trying to imagine myself staying here with all of them gone. "Why would I stay in Moses Lake? Everyone else is leaving."

Uncle Charley laid a hand on my shoulder, stopping me before I could turn toward the cafeteria. "Not everybody. Matter of fact, you might know the man who bought the house at Harmony Shores— some fella by the name of Underhill. He's had his man there all week, cataloging things in the house and running the calculations." He motioned toward the chairs outside the reception area in the lobby, where a familiar pair of cowboy boots was sprawled across the green flecked tile, the jeans leading upward to a tall, lanky body crumpled in a vinyl chair, the face hidden beneath a felt cowboy hat that looked like it had seen better days. "It don't appear like he's goin' anyplace."

I stood looking at Blaine, and my heart did that strange, queasy, fluttery flip-flop that was irrational, unpredictable, and completely undeniable. In spite of all the ways we were different and all the complications, the fact was that every time I looked at him, my pulse sped up and I couldn't catch my breath. He made me want to believe in all the dreams I'd been too careful to allow, too afraid to hope for. With him, I wanted to risk myself, to let go, to believe in the romantic notions of fairy tales. He had, after all, done what heroes do. He'd kissed the girl, asleep in her own life, and awakened her to a world she'd never seen before. He stirred, as if sensing we were there, and Uncle Charley leaned close to me, whispering, "We'll leave y'all alone to talk." Then he gave me a nudge in the back, pushing me forward a few steps before he, Uncle Herb, and Mom continued on to the cafeteria.

Blaine yawned, clumsily lifting the hat from his face and blinking against the morning light streaming through the glass doors. For a moment, he seemed surprised to find himself in the hospital lobby.

"Hey," I said, and he turned to look at me, his eyes warming.

"Hey, yourself," he replied, stretching his neck side-to-side and sitting up in the chair. "Everything okay with your brother?"

I nodded, a smile tugging from the inside out. "Everything's fine." For the first time in my adult life, I felt the truth of that. I felt like that little girl, leaping from the fire escape, filled with a faith that strong arms would catch me. "Everything's really . . . good."

I sat down in the chair next to him. "Is Amy doing all right?"

Hanging his cowboy hat on his knee, he rolled his head toward me, still resting against the wall. His dark hair was saluting the new day in several different directions—evidence that he'd been sleeping in the chair awhile. "She's a little better this morning. Mama B finally kicked us all off the third floor so Amy could get some rest. She put up a pretty good fight when those guys hauled her and Clay out of the Proxica plant and put them in the car. She got away for a minute, but the guy caught up to her and knocked her down a flight of stairs. If I'd had any idea she and your brother were planning to sneak into Proxica last night, I would've put a stop to it. I never would have agreed to either of them taking a chance like that, even as bad as I wanted to see Proxica stopped."

Even as bad as I wanted to see Proxica stopped. When he said it, I could see the passion, the burn behind the words. It bothered me that he'd kept that hidden from me, that there had been a wall of secrets between us. What other secrets lay hidden? "I wish you'd told me what was going on."

The soft, earthy brown of his eyes pulled me in. I wanted to fall, to let all the questions fade away, but if the last sixteen years had taught me anything, they'd taught me that the questions you don't resolve are the ones that hold you prisoner. "You made it hard not to," he admitted. His hand lifted from the chair and the backs of his fingers brushed the side of my face. "But it wasn't my secret to tell. I made a promise, and I don't make promises I don't intend to keep. I never wanted to hurt you, Heather. I didn't set out to lie to you, or sidetrack you, or anything else."

"What did you set out to do?" I tried to make it sound like a quip, but I felt myself hanging in air, waiting for the answer. Some small part of me was still afraid, still clinging to the past, still convinced that Blaine Underhill was too perfect to be real. Too good to be meant for me.

His fingers slid over my cheek, into my hair. "Just to spend time with the girl I missed out on in high school."

My mind swirled with a heady mix of emotions. I knew he was going to kiss me, and I wanted him to. "I'm not that girl anymore," I whispered against his lips, and in that instant, I knew it was true. This journey back to Moses Lake had brought me full circle, broken me open in a way that made all things possible.

"You're better than that girl." Blaine's words slid over me, and then his lips met mine. The kiss transported me from the hospital, to a rock ledge by the water, and for a moment we were dancing.

When his lips parted from mine, I laughed softly.

Blaine's eyes narrowed, those thick, dark lashes forming a narrow slot. "What's that look for?"

"I was thinking about the Blue Moon," I admitted. "About the two-step."

"We could do it again sometime." He grinned.

"Okay." A tingle of anticipation lit up my body, chasing the weariness away. "I will if you will."

A movement in the corridor, then a quick flash of darkness against the morning sun pulled at my attention. I looked up and saw a man in a dark coat crossing the hall to the stairway door. Even from this distance, something about him was unmistakable.

I stood up, moved a step closer to gain a better view against the light. My thoughts lost their misty edges, coming quickly into focus. Why was he here? What did he want? What questions could he answer?

"Heather?" Blaine shifted in the vinyl chair.

"I'll be right back." My heart sped up and I hurried down the hall, walking, then running as the stairway entrance slowly closed, the hydraulic cylinder hissing softly. I caught the knob just before the latch could click into place.

"Wait," I called, pulling back the door. "Wait. I want to talk to you."

The man paused at the bottom of the half-flight of stairs, his thumb and fingers resting on the handle that would allow him to exit. For an instant, I had the sensation of being with my father, but I knew it wasn't him. The stranger turned slightly, so that I could see the profile of his face beneath the shadow of his baseball cap.

"Everything's taken care of," his voice echoed against the stairwell. "The men who took your brother and Amy will be prosecuted, and Proxica is finally going to get what has been coming for a long while. It won't matter how many congressmen their CEOs take on island vacations. They're not getting out of this one."

"You caught those men—the two from last night?" I asked, anxious to confirm that the men who had come after my family were locked away somewhere. "Are we safe now? Is my brother safe?"

He nodded, his fingers relaxing on the door handle. "Your brother did a good job. Your father would be pleased. This was what he wanted."

The mention of my dad left me numb. "I saw you the day . . . when my father was killed. You were there with my mom, earlier that day."

His head dropped forward, his cap and the collar of his coat hiding him again. "I shouldn't have let it go as far as it did. I wanted to crack Proxica. I was driven, ambitious. I just needed a little more. He wanted out, you know—your dad. He wanted out that last day. He was a family man. Said his wife and his kids came first. I should've just let him go, but we needed someone on the inside, so I squeezed a little harder. I told him there wasn't any way back to the life he had before—the only way out was through Proxica. Then, of course, we lost him, and we lost Proxica."

The question that had plagued me for sixteen years pressed to the surface. "He didn't . . . Did my father . . . ? It was an accident . . . wasn't it? He didn't mean to . . ." Air seared my throat. I heard each heartbeat inside me, the tempo seeming to slow, bending the seconds into impossible, painful spans of time.

The latch on the street door clicked, and the stranger pulled it open, letting in a gush of winter air. "Like I said, your father was a family man. He wanted to do what was right, but you kids mattered to him more than anything else. He was just trying to keep all of you safe. He wanted to protect you, and that's why he had the shotgun. What happened in that cellar wasn't intentional. Just a tragic accident, but it was my fault it got to that point. It was my case."

He opened the door then and stepped out, his words playing again in my head as he disappeared against the glare.

My body felt light and numb as I turned to walk away, uncertain how to process, after all these years, the answers I'd waited so long to hear. My father had loved us more than anything else. He'd only been trying to protect us. His death was an accident. Neither I, nor my mother, nor his job had pushed him to it. In spite of the ways I'd been difficult, immature, self-centered, and unkind, he'd loved me and was willing to sacrifice anything to protect me. He wouldn't have left us willingly, no matter what.

Looking up, I saw Blaine coming from the lobby, closing the distance between us in confident, even strides. I moved toward him one step, then two, then three, freedom settling over me with each one—as if the burden I'd carried for so many years was being cleared away, like a cache of debris trapped in an inlet along the lake, swept clean when a good rain finally comes along. At last I'd found the answers I needed. God had brought me to them, to Moses Lake, to the only place where He could lead me through the fire into everything that lay beyond.

"Who were you talking to?" Blaine craned to see through the stairwell window as we met.

"Just someone who knew my dad," I answered, waiting as we turned to walk back up the hall. Slipping my hand into Blaine's, I felt myself walking into life, a new life that was like nothing I had ever imagined. Suddenly I knew the answer to the tinker's riddle. I understood it in a way I never had before.

The future is a blank page, but not a mystery.

The truth of that small phrase, of that plain-spoken proverb from the wall of wisdom was so clear to me now. Though we only read the story in due time, the books of our lives have been already written. God has drawn us in shades of charcoal and pastel, known our hours, seen our days, laid down our paths, created each of us as unique and uniquely loved. Our lives come as a blank canvas only because we cannot see as He sees. Before we can conceive our stories, He has watched them in His mind's eye, and not the stroke of a pen happens at random.

Above the book, the Architect watches with a broader eye, a greater plan. He knows what is to be written on every page.

Acknowledgments

In returning to the little town of Moses Lake, I'd like to thank a few people who helped to make this trip possible. Every book is an adventure that begins long before bookshelves and book covers—usually with a writer tapping on the doors of friends and strangers, trolling for research material.

First and foremost, thanks to long-distance friend, BJ Holley, for answering questions and sharing a few funny stories about owning a family funeral home. You helped to bring that big white house at Harmony Shores to life. Thank you to Kathy for letting me pick your brain about real-estate development issues while sharing ice cream in the Free State of Menard. Teresa and I are still laughing over the story about headlights in the pasture. Thanks again to my favorite Wingate fisher-boys for answering fishing questions and lending funny fishing phrases to the wall of wisdom at the Waterbird Bait and Grocery. You're welcome to stop in for a game of dominoes with the Docksiders anytime.

As always, I am grateful for the loving, supportive family God has blessed me with. Thank you to my mother for being a right-hand man . . . errr . . . woman, who can aptly critique a manuscript but will still tell me to eat my vegetables. Thank you to my sweet mother-in-law for helping with address lists and feeding my big boys when I'm away on book trips. Thanks also to relatives and friends far and near for everything you do to make me feel loved and nurtured, and for stopping people in the checkout line and at the doctor's office to talk about books. I'm incredibly grateful to my favorite digital designer Teresa Loman for being such a sweet-spirited soul sister and gal pal, and to Ed Stevens for constant encouragement and help with all things technical. The world needs at least five million more of both of you. Thanks also to my friends and fellow Southern gal bloggers at *www.SouthernBelleView.com*. What a hoot to be sharing a cyber-porch with you and blogging about all things southern. Thanks also to all those who stop by the blog and share your stories. It's amazing these days, how big a front porch can be!

In terms of print and paper, my undying gratitude, cheers, and shout-outs go to the incredible group at Bethany House Publishers. To Dave Long and Sarah Long, thank you for being such talented editors and just plain fun to work with. Julie Klassen, I will miss you as an editor, but I look forward to many more of your wonderful books. To the crew in marketing, publicity, and art, thank you for everything you do. Without your vision and hard work, books would be loose leaf pages in black-and-white, sitting on a desk somewhere. To my agent, Claudia Cross at Sterling Lord Literistic, thanks again for all that you do.

Last, but not least, I'm so very grateful to reader-friends everywhere, who filled the fictional town of Moses Lake with life and laughter last year when *Larkspur Cove* hit the shelves. Without you, the stores would be boarded up and the coffeepot at the Waterbird would go dry, and then who would the Docksiders tell their stories to? Thank you for sharing the books with friends, recommending them to book clubs, and taking time to send little notes of encouragement my way via email and Facebook. I'm incredibly thankful to all of you who read these stories and to the booksellers who sell them with such devotion. You are the fulfillment of a silly little dream my first-grade teacher sparked in me when she wrote on my report card, "Keep that pencil moving with that great imagination. I'll see your name in a magazine one day." God has blessed that dream and stretched it in ways that only He could have conceived, and I am so very thankful.

I hope you have fun on this visit to Moses Lake. The local folk have been asking about you, by the way. They want you to know they love it when you stop by, and you're welcome to stay as long as you like. Sit back, dip a toe in the water, and watch the eagles ride the warming afternoon air. Your presence is a joy and a blessing that no words could aptly describe. Welcome!

Discussion Questions

1. In returning to Moses Lake, Heather is coming home to a place that was special to her as a young child, even though the memory was later marred by tragedy. Do you remember a special childhood place? What makes the places of our childhood live large in our memories?

2. Heather and Clay have vastly different personalities— Heather being more like their father and Clay being more like their mother. Do you think we're always more like one parent than the other? How do our connections or missed connections with our parents shape us?

3. In spending time with her brother again, Heather realizes that there are memories and experiences we only share with our siblings. How are our sibling relationships different from any other relationships? Have you experienced sibling strife in your family at various times? How can we cultivate healthy relationships with our siblings?

4. Heather resents the past efforts of her aunt and the bridge-club ladies to coach and reform her so that she could fit the parameters of Moses Lake. Why do you think they were so intent on this? Did they mean well, or not?

5. Heather recalls her past crush on Blaine shortly after she returns to Moses Lake, but when she meets him again, she learns that he isn't the person she thought he was. Have you ever gotten to know someone you had only observed from a distance, and been surprised at the person inside?

6. When looking into the past, Heather idolizes her father, while her brother finds fault with him and is more understanding of their mother's position. Where do you think reality lies? Is it common for siblings to have different views of family history? Have you ever experienced this in your own family?

7. As she spends time in Moses Lake, Heather begins to recognize that the tragedy in her past has limited her openness to relationships in the present. How does loss in childhood change us and shape us in adulthood? Have you seen evidence of this in people you have known? How can we move beyond past experiences that are painful?

8. When Ruth tells the story of her sisters, Lydia and Naomi, she ends with the dilemma of which one chose the right path—the sister who compromised herself to feed them, or the sister who clung to her faith. What are your thoughts on the paths chosen by the two sisters? How do you think you would react, if faced with such a dire situation?

9. In recounting her family history, Ruth says, "Terrible things had happened to us, after all—death, disease, hunger, our family torn asunder, abuses I cannot even speak of. How could a God who loves us allow such things, you might wonder?" What is your answer to this question?

10. In spite of her cancer and the tragedy in her early life, Ruth is peaceful in her spirit. In what ways, surrounded by a troubled world, can we cultivate a spirit of peace and abundance?

11. Because Ruth's sister, Lydia, was brave enough, she was the only one who saw the circus. Ruth seems to regret that her fear kept her on the hill with the other girls. Has fear ever kept you from doing something that you later wished you'd done? If you had the chance again, would you do it?

12. Heather eventually concludes that she can either love her quirky family the way they are, or not love them at all. Do you think this is true? Should we learn to accept people exactly the way they are, even if we don't agree with some of the things they do? Why or why not?

About the Author

Lisa Wingate is a popular inspirational speaker, magazine columnist, and national bestselling author of several books, including *Tending Roses, Talk of the Town, Good Hope Road, Dandelion Summer,* and *Never Say Never,* winner of the 2011 Carol Award. Her work was recently honored by the Americans for More Civility for promoting greater kindness and civility in American life. Lisa and her family live in Central Texas.

Visit *www.lisawingate.com* to sign up for Lisa's latest contest, read her blog and excerpts from her novels, get writing tips, contact her, and more.